THE WHISTLERS' ROOM

BOOKS BY RICHARD SELZER

THE
WHISTLERS'
ROOM

stories and essays

RICHARD
SELZER

SHOEMAKER  HOARD, *Publishers*

WASHINGTON, DC

"The Spinsters of Eld" appeared in *West Branch* and *Harper's Magazine.* "Atrium" first appeared in *Hotel Amerika.*

The author and publisher wish to thank Yale University Art Gallery for permission to reproduce the following: Juan de Valdes Leal, *Portrait of an Ecclesiastic,* Yale University Art Gallery, Director's Purchase Fund and Gift of Mr. and Mrs. James Fosburgh, B. A. 1933; Thomas Eakins, *The Veteran,* Yale University Art Gallery, Bequest of Stephen Clark, B. A. 1903; William Rimmer, *Dying Centaur,* Yale University Art Gallery, John Hill Morgan, B. A. 1893, LL. B. 1896, Leonard C. Hanna, Jr., B. A. 1913, Stephen Carlton Clark, B. A. 1903, and Mabel Brady Garvan Acquisitions Fund; Jean Baptiste Edouard Detaille, *A Reconnaissance,* Yale University Art Galley, Gift of C. Ruxton Love, Jr. B. A. 1925; Mark Rothko, *No. 3,* Yale University Art Gallery, The Katharine Ordway Collection; Unknown, *Pieta,* Yale University Art Gallery, Maitland F. Griggs, B. A. 1896, Fund; Unknown, *Figure of Christ from a Crucifix,* Yale University Art Gallery, Director's Purchase Fund; and Francisco I de Herrera, *Saint Peter,* Yale University Art Gallery, Lent by Dr. and Mrs. Herbert Schaefer.

LIBRARY OF CONGRESS CATALOGING-IN-PUBLICATION DATA
Selzer, Richard, 1928-
   The whistlers' room : stories and essays / by Richard Selzer.
      p. cm.
   ISBN 1-59376-019-1
   I. Title.
PS3569.E585 W48 2004
813'.54—dc22   2003026683

Text design by Amy Evans McClure

Printed in the United States of America

 SHOEMAKER & HOARD, *Publishers*
A Division of Avalon Publishing Group Inc.
Distributed by Publishers Group West

10 9 8 7 6 5 4 3 2 1

TO ILIANA SEMMLER

Contents

Acknowledgments

I am pleased to thank Jock Reynolds, Director of the Yale Art Gallery, Mary Kordak, Education Curator, Marie Weltzien, Director of Public Relations of the gallery, and Suzanne Warner, rights and permissions officer. Also Patrick McCaughey, former Director of the British Art Collection at Yale. My thanks to Kathryn Rodgers for an early reading of the manuscript, to Wolf Alverdes, owner of the copyright of the original novella *Die Pfeifferstube* by his father Paul Alverdes, for permission to work on that text. Thanks also to Frank Kermode for the chance to dilate further upon his own seminal investigation of that portion of The Gospel of St. Mark in which "the boy in the shirt" is featured. My special gratitude goes to Iliana Semmler for her devoted attention to this work while in progress.

Introduction

Although over fifteen years ago Richard Selzer substituted the pen for the scalpel, the desk for the operating table, his carrel in Yale's Sterling Library for the Operating Room, the consciousness of the physician remains a guiding force in all his work. It is this sensibility that draws us into his writing and that accompanies us along the narrative journey. Whether the mise en scène is a bedside, the Italian countryside, New York's Troy during the Great Depression, or the Garden of Gethsemane, it is the eye and ear of the physician that inform the story we glean from the words on the page. And story is the right word here: Selzer's particular talent is to transform all into narrative, that most natural of human forms, whether it be a painting, a piece about birdwatching, or a playful exegesis of biblical esoterica.

The volume at hand sprang defiantly into existence much as a child leaps into being and embraces an independent life. The parent, in this case, was the author's diary, which I have been editing for several years now. Because writers use their diaries in various ways—to record the events of their daily lives, to explore their own philosophy, to germinate and experiment with ideas for further writing—a diary may grow unwieldy, as happened in this case. The longer pieces, irresistible as they were, came to clog a more chronological presentation, and there seemed no way to achieve a balance. In what has been characterized as an "aha!" experience, we understood suddenly that the diary had been gestating this volume secretly, and that it was time for it to be born. These pieces served as a nucleus, around which some of Richard Selzer's other writings—some previously published, some new—quickly gravitated.

"The Whistlers' Room," the title story, is a free translation and essentially a retelling of a novella by a little-known German writer, Paul Alverdes, published in 1929 and long since out of print both in Germany and in its first English translation. The story forms an ideal stage for the doctor-writer, as it takes place in a German military hospital during World War I. But the center of interest is not the medical condition the men share, but rather the complexity of the relationships the men form with each other, with the English soldier who is eventually placed in the same ward, and with the medical personnel. In a "Postscript" to the story, Selzer comments thus on the empathic doctor: "Dr. Quint was one of those medical men who feel the need to touch their patients, by which he drew from them the nourishment to carry on a task as heartbreaking as it is impossible."

Two other pieces with an overtly medical theme are "A Parable" and "Atrium." In these the focus is on inner reality, not medicine per se, and on the relationships established between the characters, in both cases between a doctor and a patient. "A Parable" describes the interdependence and mutual nourishment that exist between a doctor and his dying patient, a relationship that is seen through the eyes of a narrator who may or may not be a physician himself. In "Atrium," the most recently written piece in the volume, the perceptive doctor-writer meets a boy who is terminally ill with cancer. Although, or perhaps because, the child is not his patient the relationship between the two develops on an even and neutral ground. Their discussion of death glows with beauty as it eschews sentimentality. Selzer has appended an explication to the story, but no reader should be discouraged from arriving at one or more different interpretations.

In his diaries, Richard Selzer turns frequently to his early life. It is this life, lived in Troy, New York, in a house also giving home to his physician-father's office, that shaped him both as a doctor and as a writer and that is so often evoked in his work. "Down from Troy 3" contains three short pieces about those times, giving pictures of family life and the schoolroom. As often in his work, Selzer flavors these sketches with humor both to offset and to make more piquant the nostalgia that underlies it. No one who has read "Rae" could forget the "fan made of Bolognese hawk feathers," which his mother "flirted open" when she performed for the USO and which she bequeathed to Rae, her "best friend as well as her arch-enemy, her confidante, and bitter rival." Nor would anyone forget the Irish spinster schoolteachers, who, "coifed, perfumed, and dressed beautifully," were to the grubby schoolchildren of Troy "an eternal mystery."

The milieu of Selzer's New Haven life also finds place in this volume: "St. Ronan Terrace" tells of his house there, where "In spring we are infested with birds, vulgar with flowers," and of his efforts to discover the legend of St. Ronan. "Birdwatching," a short story, reveals Selzer's unexpected interest and knowledge not only of feathered creatures, but of those who pursue them, following their song with field glasses pressed to their eyes. The birds themselves are described with a scientist's precision, while in the human sphere the arrogance of the fanatical central character is gently countered by his female companion, whose auditory talent far surpasses his.

The two Italian travel pieces, "Piemonte" and "Tuscany," come directly from Selzer's diary entries, separated by nearly twelve years. He visited Piemonte in 1985 as a kind of retreat in which he would make the important decision of whether to give up surgery and become a full-time writer. Less crucial, perhaps, but no less difficult, was his resolve to use that trip to give up smoking. The trip to Tuscany was quite different: He went there to teach a writing seminar. "Tuscany" is notable for its vignette of the old man with emphysema; Selzer often uses his journal as a laboratory in which to create cameo descriptions that he may later use in his published writing.

"The Boy in the Shirt" appears at first glance to be quite different from the other pieces in this volume. It stems as much from Selzer's absorption in the arcana of early religion as it does from his interest in human behavior. Although a self-confessed skeptic whose entire life "has been a search for faith—failed," Selzer's attention has turned, over and over again, to the esoteric matters that underlie both the Jewish and the Christian faiths. The mystery of the boy has perplexed scholars over the centuries, and, as Selzer informs us, countless theories have been advanced as to his identity. Many of these theories have been quite ingenious, but it has taken a writer of fiction to flesh out the boy's story, to give him a past and a future, and, most of all, to supply him with motivation for his actions.

After his retirement from surgery into authorship, Selzer was somewhat surprised to discover that one of the aspects of a writer's life is what he calls "podiocy," something not explicitly in the job description. Expecting to become a "buccaneer" or an "unrepentant libertine," he finds instead that "I have become a Professor of Polite Learning, a strange migratory bird that roosts on podia all over North America." Interestingly, some of these podia have included the Yale Art Gallery and Cooper Union in New York City, where Selzer has established a reputation for giving lectures on individual pieces of art. Two sections of this volume are devoted to those art lectures, one to sculpture, one to painting. Not claiming to be an art critic, his emphasis in these talks has been largely on the clarity of vision the "medical gaze" can lend to understanding art. For instance, he describes the hand of Fray Juan, poised in the air and ready to resume writing, in such a way as to characterize him:

> About that slender right hand, the one held suspended in midair, I would like to dissect it down to the smallest muscles, the lumbricals and the interossei, then expose the tendons of flexion and extension that pass through the carpal tunnel of the wrist on their way to the fingers and to the words on the page.

Hands are important to Selzer and often serve to reveal character, and who but a physician would notice hands with such precision? An artist, true, but it's the physician who understands the underlying structure. De Ribera's portrait of St. Peter shows a man whose life has been quite different, and Selzer focuses on the hands to evoke that difference:

> His hands are big and broad, the fingers gnarled, and with the dirt of Galilee under each of his nails. They have the peasant's physical dignity. What is a hand but an arborization of veins, arteries, bones, nerves, and lymphatics, all covered with pliant skin, whose softness or lack of it reflects the use to which the hand has been put? No two hands share the same pattern of these parts, but each has responded to influences both local and distant. It seems incontrovertible that the arteries and their descendants, the arterioles and capillaries, grow from proximal to distal, greater to smaller. This outward growth depends upon local tissue conditions, the mechanical drag, that persuades the growing tip of the vessel to turn, evade, and deflect itself, so as to attain equilibrium with the other parts. Then, too, there is the lower pressure inside the veins, and the thirst of the fingers for blood

and oxygen. All this to say nothing of the far-off propulsive thrust of the heart, and the slow simmer of hormone and enzyme. At last, after nine months of gestation, what is formed is an exquisitely sensate hand no part of which rebels against any other part.

Rothko's #3 summons a different response, though one equally peculiar to the physician. Telling us that he has always preferred representational art, he divulges to us that "along came Mark Rothko and his #3, which I shall call 'Red' for purposes of this meditation upon it; and with this one painting I have become a convert. Sort of." Gazing at the painting, he begins to lose himself in it:

> Gaze on, and all at once the painting becomes a living organism. There is a controlled seething out of which the painting has emerged. Something like the primitive undifferentiated tissue called mesenchyme, which will develop into all the parts of a human being. It begins to inflate and deflate, like lungs, to throb and pulsate, as though driven by a distant heartbeat. Yes, that's it. The red of blood. Not a dry red, but saturated, drenched. Even your gaze is bloodshot. The upper rectangle is bright red, oxygenated arterial blood that has spurted here. The lower rectangle is venous blood, darker, returning to the lungs for a fresh draught of oxygen. It seeps. . . . The red paint seems to surge up from the artist's unconscious. He is but the conduit.

The art of the physician, like that of the writer and painter, is based on perception and skill. All of these must *know* or, in a sense, *diagnose,* before they can act, whether to cure or to give us a new vision of the world, two things that are more closely related than many think. Richard Selzer, author and physician, combines his talents and his knowledge— and his hard work, because writing is often that—to bring us, in this volume as elsewhere, a view of life that is poetic, without discounting the truths of science, and quintessentially real, without discounting the truths of the imagination.

—Iliana Alexandra Semmler

The Whistlers' Room

I.

It was a bright, spacious room with a wide verandah that stretched for its entire length. From this verandah, one's gaze was lifted over a park and beyond that to fields. Farther still was a tiny slice of the Rhine. Just beyond the verandah was an orchard of old twisted cherry trees, the bark oozing resin. Here the ground was treacherous to the footsteps because of the many turgid, swollen black snails that flourished beneath the trees. In April, the clouds of cherry blossoms induced a kind of languor and reverie in those who dwelt here. Gaze long enough and the boundary between life and dream grows indistinct; what had been real melted into dream; what had been dream took on the solidity of something you can reach out and touch with a finger.

From the verandah the Rhine was a streak of light between the dark branches. What can be said about a room that seems to have been uncoupled and shunted onto a blind siding, while the rest of the train moved on? How large is it? Roughly twenty paces by twenty-four. But in such a room, geometry has no meaning. In such a room, mere size is transcended. There are days when it is tiny, snug, dark, with a low ceiling—a thatched cottage, if you will. On other days, it is high, transparent, buoyant, full of echoes—threatening at any moment to slip its moorings and float away from the rest of the hospital.

Everyone called it the Whistlers' Room, after the soldiers who shared it. Each of them had been shot in the throat and sustained a more or less identical wound, destruction of the larynx. They had been there a long while; some said since the first year of the war, which was now at the end of its third. In the ruined houses and dugouts roofed over with planks and turf to which they had been carried from the battle, with the cannons booming all around, the stretcher-bearers, who were the first to bandage them, had pronounced upon them a speedy death. No one, they surmised, could possibly survive such a wound. But they were wrong. As if in defiance of the prognosis, they had all come through. It is true that the wounds had undergone healing, that is to say, a rich new bed of granulation tissue had grown to cover the damaged mucous membrane of the pharynx and larynx and the upper trachea. Too rich, in fact, as the thick rolls of new flesh grew to such an extent that they closed off the air passage. A new channel had to be made to prevent suffocation. The surgeon had cut a small hole in the neck below the blockage and slipped a curved metal tube into the upper trachea, through which air might pass freely in and out.

The operation is called tracheotomy, and the tube used was of silver, the length and thickness of the little finger. At its outer edge there was a small shield at right angles that prevents the tube from slipping all the way in. To keep it from falling out, a white cloth ribbon was passed through two holes in the shield, one on either side of the tube, and tied at the back of the neck. The tube itself was of two parts closely fitted together, the innermost of which was held in place by a tiny winged screw. Three times a day it was removed for cleaning. Since they could not breathe through their nostrils, these tubes became the whistlers' noses. The boys undertook to clean the tubes themselves, using a small round brush to do so. After it was cleaned, the inner piece was reinserted. To protect the opening from dust and flies, and to prevent mucus from being blown forcefully out when coughing or exhaling deeply, each whistler wore a curtain of white muslin attached to the ribbon. It gave them a priestly look. With their spotless white "collar" they had a ceremonial air. Of this the boys were well aware, and seemed to rise to the occasion of so clerical a vestment. With pride, they each changed their bibs three times a day for a yet cleaner and whiter one. For each of them, the little tube was both beloved and tolerated, comforting and threatening. Their manner toward each other's silver tubes was politeness tinged with mischief.

The room itself was simply furnished. The wooden floor was bare and

gave off an odor of the creosote with which it was swabbed every morning, and something else, like iodine. There were four narrow beds in a
row, each with its nightstand and reading lamp, and a footlocker for personal possessions. From time to time, according to the physical condition
of the patients, a white porcelain chamber pot was placed at one side of a
bed. At the center of the room was a round wooden table with four chairs.
This was where meals were served to those able to leave their beds. In an
alcove, concealed by a thin gauze curtain, stood a washbasin on a stand,
and a toilet. In one corner stood a small pot-bellied stove upon which an
eternal kettle bubbled. Neither mirror nor calendar, no, nor any picture,
broke the plain white plaster surface of the walls. With the whistlers in
it, the whole of this room became greater than the sum of its parts, as
though it were a household watched over by its own lares and penates.

Whenever they breathed quickly or laughed, a soft piping note came
from the mouth of the silver tube, and little thirsty whispers. This is what
gave them the name The Whistlers. After months of being speechless,
the act of talking gave them great trouble at first. They were glad to avoid
it, especially in front of strangers. When they did wish to speak, they had
to close the mouth of the silver pipe with the tip of a finger. Then a
threadlike stream of air would find its way upward through the throat to
play upon the vocal cords, or what remained of them. In answer to this
weak stimulation, there would emerge a painful wheeze, a croaking. It
was not for their cracked notes that the whistlers blushed, but for having
to lift the bib and feel for the secret opening. It seemed, somehow, an
indecent act, which they tried to disguise by turning to one side or making as if to toy with a shirt button that might be concealed under the white
bib. In this way they would occlude the little hole and begin to talk.
Should they succeed in distracting the attention of him who had
addressed them, these affable friendly soldiers, their confidence renewed,
would often become quite cheerfully talkative. It was as if they wished to
show that in the quite everyday event of being hoarse, they were not so
different from other men. Why this furtiveness? They could not say, nor
ever discussed it among themselves. When a fourth man with the same
throat wound was added to the room, from the very first he did the same.

It was just the same, moreover, with the others in the room upstairs,
those who had lost an arm or a leg. They felt no shyness at being seen by
strangers, an empty sleeve or pajama leg dangling. On the contrary, some
of them even displayed their sad blind stumps, instilling a kind of respect

and awe in those who had come off more lightly. It was the scraping and creaking of the clumsy appliances—the wooden legs, with which they had to learn to walk again—that caused them acute embarrassment. Should a stranger happen to catch one of them unawares, the amputee would come to an abrupt halt and pull at his trousers for the lever that enabled him to fix the artificial knee joint in place. Never, never would an unclothed artificial limb go unconcealed, but, once screwed off or other-wise detached, it would be stood in a corner inside the pants and under a coat. These amputees, too, like the whistlers, hated being surprised by outsiders, and would have liked best always to be by themselves. It was the Fellowship of the Wound, a bonding as strong as any brotherhood.

Sometimes well-meaning visitors came bearing gifts to the whistlers. Wine, fruit, cakes, and, not infrequently, scented soaps and colognes, with which they would sprinkle themselves and each other. Not that they themselves could smell, that sense organ having been bypassed, but they were delighted to feel that they carried a pleasant aroma about with them. But such occasions did not long continue. Too often the visitors concluded that those who could not utter a sound, or only in a treble voice, must be stone deaf as well, and they proceeded to shout at the whistlers, some even taking out notebooks to write in enormous letters what they might just as well have spoken. Others, from the very outset, sought to make them-selves intelligible by exaggerated gestures. To the whistlers, this was grossly insulting. Over time, the defect that each of them bore had become no more than a peculiarity that was a badge of honor, deserving of respect, and not a defect at all. But for another loss, that of hearing, say, to be mistakenly laid at their door, was insupportable. Then, in truth, were they wounded anew. As often as not, as soon as a visitor entered by one door, the whistlers would take flight by another. Should one be caught in bed, he would pretend to be asleep, or, putting finger to lips, enjoin silence, whereupon the intruders, like as not, would make a hasty retreat.

Among themselves, the whistlers held lively and intimate talks. They could do so easily in a wordless clucking speech that, lacking the stream of air to make organized language, they fashioned with their lips and tongues and teeth. They called it "barbed wire talk." Their powers of comprehension of these noises had arrived at such a pitch that, even at night with the lights out and when there was no help to be had from meaningful gestures of the hands, the three held long talks from bed to bed. (The low-grade fever from which they were seldom free and the medications they were given kept them awake well into the night.) To anyone listening, it would have sounded like the incessant splashing of heavy drops of water into a wooden bucket or the sputtering of butter in a hot frying pan. From outside the doorway, in the corridor, footsteps; a sister—perhaps on her rounds—would hear them cheeping like a nest of starlings, and she would pause to listen. Immediately the birds would cease their cheeping and fall silent until the footsteps fell away. They never spoke of a future and only seldom of a past before the war. But of their last day at the front and of the exact circumstances in which they had been wounded, they never tired of giving the most vivid and stirring accounts. With the leisure for recollection, it should come as no surprise that each time there was more to add to the recounting. Lying added a certain vitality to life. Sometimes the clucks and whistles grew insistent, contradictory even, but never derisory when an entirely new story evolved. On the contrary, each embellishment was greeted by the rest with perfect credulity. These elaborations were not lies so much as a stepping out of the rigid frame of the event in an effort to be released from the horror of it. Should one or the other of them fall asleep in the midst of a story, he was at once given friendly forgiveness.

2.

Pointner, the eldest of the three, and he only in his late twenties, was the son of a Bavarian peasant. He had been in the whistlers' room for over a year when the next one arrived. His case was by far the worst, in that a poison had infected his blood—septicemia, the doctors called it—and slowly, almost imperceptibly, his condition worsened. He had to stay in bed almost all of the time, ran a high temperature, and had no appetite whatsoever. Soon only an emaciated remnant was all that remained of the hot-blooded, strapping young man who had left home for the army. Still intact, though, was his sense of himself as a man. Nothing enraged him more than when the convalescents from other wards, out of a generosity of spirit, came by and picked him up like a child in their arms and offered to carry him about for a change of scene. Then a dark flush came into his cheeks, and he spat and scratched and hit out in his fury. He was

that ashamed of weighing so little. Nobody would have guessed that once
he had been a butcher by trade, a keeper of all the secrets of the slaugh-
terhouse and a master at making sausages. On the night table by his bed,
he kept a photograph of himself as a reservist, shortly after sustaining his
wound. The frame depicted two gnarled oak trees whose branches were
interwoven at the top, and bore the crown of a princely house. At the base
of the trees, amid the mighty roots, stood an arrangement of swords, flags,
rifles, and cavalry lances. And there, between the oaks, stood Reservist
Pointner, his cap set jauntily over one ear, and two fingers of his right
hand stuck between the buttons of his tunic. In his left, he carried a cane
tied around with a ribbon. His unusually strong jaw gave an aggressive
turn to his short stature and the amiable expression of the upper part of
his face. "Reserve Has Rest" was written on a scroll in bright colors. But
"Reserve" had had no rest; over the months, the aggressive jaw had
slowly melted away, leaving a small, boneless, recessed chin in its place.
This, with the always slightly parted lips and the white gleam of the
upper teeth—which had escaped unscathed—beneath the straw-colored
moustache, gave his face a childlike expression. All the more dangerous
whenever the old hot blood of anger and resentment made him flail at
his would-be benefactors.

Pointner had been wounded in one of the first battles with the English
and had been taken prisoner. After that, he'd lain for a week or two in a
field hospital. One morning, in the midst of a group of lightly wounded
men, he escaped from the field hospital, passing as one of the English
wounded because he was wearing no uniform, but had on a long-skirted
hospital garment of blue- and white-striped wool, with felt slippers on
his feet. On his head he wore a plundered English sniper's cap, which he
had brought with him on the stretcher into the field hospital and had
never surrendered. Somehow he made his way onto an emergency hospital train that took him back to Germany. Speechless as he was then, his
face and neck bandaged up to the eyes, and with no papers throughout
the journey, he was assumed to be an Englishman and treated as such.
The very memory of this, too, threw Pointner into a rage. Surely, it would
have been easiest to throw away the khaki cap, but for some reason, he
could not bring himself to do it. And so he remained a Britisher in spite
of himself, passed over, unwelcomed, unbestrewn with flowers, and left
to one side on his stretcher, shedding tears of rage. It was not until much

later, when he arrived at the hospital where now he lay, that he succeeded in making himself understood.

Even now, so long afterward, and despite severe reprimands for doing so, he kept the English cap safely in a drawer of his nightstand. Now and then, when neither doctor nor nurse was expected to come in, he would take it out and polish the badge and the chinstrap until they shone. Then he would study the cap, turning it this way and that in his delicate fingers where the pink of his nails had turned to blue. Once it happened that a pair of pranksters from another ward raided Pointner's nightstand while he slept, and made off with the cap. Soon enough Pointner discovered that it was missing. By this time, he was bedridden and virtually helpless to look after his basic needs. Still, in the agony of his dispossession, he managed to turn on one side, rise to an elbow, and fling himself from the bed. Unattended, he slumped to the floor, and from his throat there issued a long, high pitched howl that, to the others, was the most eloquent expression of loss and verbal impotence. Whence had it arisen? The sound congealed the blood of his two companions, who raced out of the room on their mission of retrieval. The next morning the cap was back in the nightstand and tranquility was restored. But never would the others be rid of that outcry that was on the threshold of speech.

Benjamin and Kollin, the other two whistlers, had long wondered at the obsessive attachment of Pointner for the English cap, but out of the decorum that governed their lives together, had never mentioned it to him or to each other. They could not have known that, from the very beginning, the cap had been, for Pointner, at once the hieroglyphic fragment that marked the instant of his wounding and the last relic of all the hope and desire of his life before the wound. Unlike the others, he needn't rely on memory or yield to fantasy to reconstruct his wounding; he had only to hold the English cap to have the event spring most vividly before his eyes. Even more, in the act of polishing the chinstrap, his own throat became whole again; the cap had become the replacement for what had been shot away.

3.

Kollin, the second whistler, was a volunteer and a Prussian Pioneer. He had round eyes of a bright blue that were set close together in a thin face.

His hooked nose gave an impression of fearlessness. Kollin had once been ambitious and had set his heart on rising in the military ranks. He often would examine his wound with obvious despair in the small pocket mirror he kept in his nightstand. Many the morning he awoke, having dreamt that he had been cured, his disfigurement corrected. For a moment or two he seemed to breathe normally. At such times he would leap from his bed, his blue eyes shining, to prove it to his comrades. But it didn't last for long. Even before the doctor's morning visit, Kollin had to admit that his breath had begun to fail him. Then he would examine his wound in the pocket mirror and angrily shake his head at the evidence that there had been no change during the night.

Kollin's passion was for numbers and number games. In warm weather, he and Pointner sat all day long outside on the verandah, bent over a chessboard and surrounded by a small clutch of silent spectators. He played an infinitely calculating game, his slightly trembling hands hovering for a long while over the board. While playing one game, he seemed to be cogitating a second game in the recesses of his mind. Now and then he made notes on a scrap of paper. Pointner made his moves quickly, rapping the chess pieces down smartly, then looking out over the park as though bored and indifferent. After Kollin's move, Pointner gave the board barely a glance over his shoulder, but all the same his fever-flushed cheeks grew darker as the threat of checkmate loomed. Still, he continued to move his pieces with a disdainful and superior light touch, which announced that reservist Pointner was not to be caught so easily. At such times, he wanted nothing so much as to whistle a tune just to show that he had every reason not to be concerned, but he was no more able to whistle than the other whistlers. Instead, he would purse his lips, as if whistling, and produce a tiny sound exactly like the warning chip of a finch. Even so, he was already avoiding the eyes of the onlookers, who were expressing their glee over the progress of the game. All at once, when Kollin was just about to tighten the noose and turn his careful preparatory moves into triumph, Pointner erupted. With short round movements from the wrist, like the pats of a cat, he sent the pieces flying in all directions. At the same time, reddening with anger and shame, he stood up, and with a final contemptuous gesture to signify that he would have no more of it, he pulled his cap down over his fair hair and stumped off into the park, without so much as a glance back at Kollin, who sat there smiling and shrugging his shoulders. By then, having relished

Pointner's outburst, the onlookers had lost interest and had left Kollin alone to savor his victory. Pulling out his notebook, he wrote down exactly how he had won. "White," he wrote, and then in brackets "Reservist Pointner gives up." After Kollin's death, there was found among his papers an exact account of every game of chess played in the whistlers' room. In the course of his two-year stay he had played fifteen hundred and eighty-nine games, and of these had won seven hundred and one. The rest had been broken off by his opponent in dire straits. The morning after such an outburst, Pointner would always set out the chess-board before breakfast had been brought in and sit waiting in silence beside it. Kollin, meanwhile, would go on reading an old newspaper, but soon he was unable to endure the pleasures of anticipation and, laying aside the paper, he would take his seat at the board. Sometimes on such mornings Pointner prevailed upon himself to sit out his defeat.

4.

The third whistler, a boy of fifteen, was called Benjamin. He had been christened so in a field hospital close to the front line. One October morning, just as it was growing light, a kind of ambulance, called a *char-a-banc,* arrived. Inside were two long benches opposite each other, the whole enclosed within a gray tent-cloth that came closely down on all sides. It had belonged to a Westphalian battery that had been put out of action the day before. For a long moment after it had come to a halt, nothing stirred. Then, the door at the rear opened, a set of steps was lowered, and a man without a tunic, in mud-caked breeches, climbed down backward. His left arm was bent up to his chest in a large makeshift splint.

"Vice-Quartermaster Joseph," he reported to the doctor who at that moment came out of the doorway of a building with sleeves rolled up and a brown rubber apron over his white overalls. "Vice-Quartermaster Joseph," he repeated, "of the Sixth Regiment with eleven severely wounded men of his battery." These eleven sat dazed and fevered, or hung rather, heads sunken, since there was no room to lie down, along both benches inside the *char-a-banc.* Some clung fast to one another, and no one moved when the covering was thrown back and the bearers came up with stretchers. One after another they were carried out. The last was a boy who was carried in his bloodstained coat in the arms of an immense Army Medical Corps noncommissioned officer. Of them all, this boy alone showed any vivaciousness. He gazed up at the man in whose arms he lay, and tried to say something, meanwhile describing wide circles with his hands across the sky, which now began to show its cloudless blue. He raised his eyebrows and blew out his cheeks, as if in wonderment. He seemed to want to relate a story, but no sound came from his throat.

"Yes, yes," said the doctor in a soft quiet voice, laying a finger gently under the boy's chin, "it is Joseph and his brethren, and you must surely be Benjamin. I'll keep you all together in the best ward we have." From that moment on, the boy was called Benjamin by everyone.

Even so, they were no sooner in their beds than they began to die, one after the other. On the very same day, five of Joseph's brethren were wound in sheets they could no longer warm, and carried out. Next, it seemed that the boy called Benjamin, too, would never get back to Germany. The doctor forbade him food or drink. During the night the house, which had been commandeered for a hospital, was hit by a long-range cannon and set on fire. Benjamin, who lay under a blanket on his pallet, was strapped to a stretcher and taken out naked, the unending stream of wounded men having exhausted the supply of nightshirts. In this manner he came to another house, but owing to the confusion after the shelling, the prohibition on food and drink did not catch up with him even on the next day. Tortured by thirst, he raised his hands and begged a cup of the soup that was being passed around to the others. No sooner had he taken a sip than he felt as though he had been gripped about the throat by powerful hands and throttled. In agony he sprang up from his bed and tore at his mouth as if to tear it open. But try as he might, with his chest convulsively distended, wrenching his head from side to side and striking out with his arms as if swimming, he could not take a single breath. With his comrades shouting for help, he fell back upon the bed, rose once again to his feet, then fell unconscious.

Often, in later days, he told the whistlers how he had stormed death with all his strength and actually reached his goal. At that moment he lost all desire for breath, and, hovering weightless in a void, he felt light and airy. He no longer had a body, and only the spirit remained. He could not feel his lips, his face. At the same time, music rang out in a melody that he could never convey, music that was surely beyond the ability of any earthly musician. "It was not so bad to die," he told the whistlers, "it was a relief of suffering." The whistlers listened with earnest faces and nodded their heads; they did not doubt it. To no one else did Benjamin ever say a word of this, nor of all that he had still to endure in that field hospital.

From his unconscious state, he was awakened by a sudden sharp pain. At once, the celestial music ceased and his agony returned. But just at that moment, as his struggles renewed, he felt cool air streaming into his lungs. He was breathing! And the weight of his body was restored to him, there where he lay in his bed. It was a miracle! Later he was told that, at just that moment, the doctor happened to be on his way to visit other patients nearby, and heard the cries for help. He arrived just in time to catch the toppling boy in his arms. In the absence of his instrument case, he pierced the boy's throat with his pocket knife.

From that time on, Benjamin recovered quickly. But still it seemed that his body hankered yet after the experience that had cost it so dear. One morning, as the doctor was cleaning his wound, the great artery on the left side of the boy's throat burst and shot the blood in a crimson arch from his mouth. The artery had been severed by the bullet, but a piece of sinewy flesh had clapped itself like a plaster over the torn vessel and temporarily sealed it. Benjamin felt the torrent—it had the texture of warm flannel—surging over his hands as he raised them in astonishment to catch it. He looked into the doctor's face, then felt himself bent down backward, and while his head hung over the edge of the table, the knife began to burrow for the artery in his extended neck. With each heartbeat, the blood was pumped up in a pulsatile fountain that fell back upon his face. He was no longer afraid, only light-headed, and even cheerful, as he heard the faint click of the forceps and needle that were stitching him up. It sounded like the clicking of his mother's knitting needles. He felt no pain. When the clicking stopped, so did the flow of blood. A wet sponge was passed over his eyes. He was slowly lifted back onto the table, and saw before him the white face of the doctor, bespattered with blood. In his hand he held a metal instrument and playfully pinched Benjamin's nose with it.

"Well," he said quietly, "here you are again, my son."

It was only later, toward noon, that Benjamin's fear returned. Even with his eyes wide open, he could not read the nameplate on the bed, though it was in large white letters on a black background. He took this as a sign of impending death. Pulling the sheet over his head, he prayed with his hands together and wept for a long while. Toward evening he felt slightly better. He asked for paper and pen, and wrote, asking if he would ever get better, and gave it to the orderly. The orderly made no answer, only put his hand under the boy's back and a cup to his lips. It was a mixture of champagne, red wine, sugar, and a beaten egg.

5.

Five weeks later, the cab carrying Benjamin drove through the park and came to a stop in front of the hospital. He wore a cap without a badge and a tattered tunic that was far too big for him. His pants were brown corduroy with red piping. All of his old clothes had been returned to him for the journey back to Germany. And he stank of the eau de cologne the ladies in the train stations along the way had sponged onto his face for refreshment and which he had not the voice to turn down. This was in place of the cigars pressed upon him, but which he refused with a small movement of his hand.

It was Backhuhn who opened the cab door and helped him to alight. Backhuhn was a Silesian grenadier whose nose had been taken off by a rifle shot. The doctors were in the process of making him a new nose by grafting a tube of flesh—skin, hair, and all—from his forehead to the open wound where his nose had been. This flap of tissue—the doctors referred to it as a pedicle—had "taken" beyond all expectations, but was, at the time of Benjamin's arrival, painful to behold, for it was as large as two fists and towered beyond his forehead. It had the form and color of a chicken about to be put into the oven, and so, of course, the grenadier had been given the name Backhuhn, roasting fowl. He wore the disfigurement as though it were some sort of decoration and was delighted with the name, for it meant that the doctors were taking great pains with him. From time to time he underwent further surgeries, each of which was meant to make the appearance of the new nose more acceptably human. The changes were all but imperceptible. It was as if the new nose were being built by a prankster or someone in a great hurry. Between operations he was allowed to go about as he pleased.

Backhuhn's idea of fun was to slip up behind a servant girl of the clinic and to cover her eyes with his hands. Then he'd disguise his voice and ask her to guess who it was. If she could not, he'd spin her about.

"Do you like me?" he'd cry in a loud voice. "Can you stand looking at me?" All the while grinning and making gurgling noises. When the girl cried out in horror, threw up her hands and ran away, the delighted

Backhuhn sprang after her, making uncouth gestures. In spite of everything, they all became fond of him, for he was big and tall and tried to make his great strength useful to the others. For a long while it was one of his privileges to greet new arrivals and conduct or even carry them to their wards. Nor could he understand why he had been stopped from doing this. As far as he was concerned, his appearance was perfectly acceptable.

"Look at me, comrade," he told Benjamin as he lifted him from the cab. "I had no nose left, not as much as that, my boy (he made a pinch with his thumb and forefinger), but now it's fine again. They give you back whatever you've lost."

His first stop was the bathing room where all newcomers were taken. Two nurses in long washing aprons, with sleeves rolled up, were waiting for him. Benjamin flamed up in embarrassment, for he had never been given over to women for all that needed to be done to his body, which, he realized, was entirely caked with dried blood and dirt. What with the rush and confusion of so many badly wounded and dying men, he had been left to wear the same filthy uniform in which he had first been brought in by the stretcher-bearers. No one had had time to give him more than a hasty cleaning up. He was glad now that he had not refused the copious sprinklings of cologne he'd been subjected to. Still, he looked about, hoping to see a bath orderly come to relieve the nurses. When these two put him on a chair and without ceremony began to undress him, the boy almost died of shame. At the same time, he wanted to prepare them for his filthy condition, and when the younger of the two tried to pull off his pants, he held on to them with both hands, and began to address her in his voiceless way. Neither of the girls could understand him, even when they held an ear to his lips. Far from being discouraged, they jabbered to each other, at length assuring him that they understood, then ran off. When they returned, it was with a chair on wheels with a lid over a boxed seat. Benjamin turned away in tears and shook his head. After that, he let himself be undressed and hoisted into the tub. A chest strap was buckled around him so that he wouldn't fall this way or that. Then the nurses proceeded to soap and wash him from head to toe, cooing over his "poor little arms," counting his vertebrae and his ribs with their fingers. Obedient now, he held out his arms and legs to be scrubbed, giving himself up to them like a small animal. After that, they enveloped him in a warm flannel shirt, put him on a stretcher, and wheeled him down a long corridor to the whistlers' room. Kollin and Pointner were waiting for him at the door. Benjamin saw with delight that they too had tubes in their necks.

6.

Prior to the arrival of Benjamin, Pointner and Kollin had engaged in the rough sexual bantering that is usual among soldiers living without women. On occasion, in a tone of assumed jocularity, one would recount an ancient exploit for the benefit of the other, using all the direct, honest words that are so graphic in the telling. But now, as if they understood that they must not corrupt the boy, without any spoken agreement they stopped. It was simply a shared rejection of the impure. Was it that in each of them there was a hitherto untapped well of fatherhood? Was it the frailty of the newcomer whose appearance was that of an even younger child, a small parcel of life? Was it the memory of some early unhappy sexual awakening of their own? Or was it the room itself that was remodeling the men who occupied it? Whatever the reason, a certain reticence prevailed; they dispensed with all talk that they deemed inappropriate for such young ears.

The whistlers loved one another, not that they would have admitted it, even to themselves, or shown any outward sign of affection. But each time one of them was wheeled away to submit to the knife of the surgeon, the other two could not play games or even hold a conversation. Instead, they busied themselves on the big general ward, each by himself. Again and again, as if for no particular reason, they would go as far as the big swinging doors at the end of the corridor that separated the ward from the operating theatre. At last a stretcher would come trundling through the swinging doors. Upon the stretcher mounded a human figure over which an arc light shone. A closer look revealed that he lay under a wooden frame with lamps inside whose purpose was to keep the patient warm on his return to his ward. His two comrades walked along beside him as at a christening or a funeral. Cautiously one would lift the cloth that protected the man's face from the draft. Then across the stretcher they would nod and wink as though to say: "Only we three know what it is; no one else but us." And the man on the stretcher, aware of their brotherly compassion, would nod back in spite of his pain.

At the same time, the doctor was doing his best to widen by degrees the air channel of each whistler, so that one day they would be able to breathe without pipes. This was done by the insertion every few weeks of larger and larger bore nickel rods, forcing them through the constricted passage of the throat. Great force had to be exerted, as the healing tissues had hardened until they were the consistency of cartilage that resisted all efforts to dilate the canal. Since it had to be carried out without anesthesia, the procedure caused the whistlers the most acute pain. All three of them were subjected to this treatment at the same time. During their martyrdom, with the rods in place, the three of them sat in a row on a long bench, wrapped in white sheets up to the chin, as though they were going to be shaved by the barber. They themselves held the long bent tube that projected from the mouth, held it firmly with one hand lest it be ejected by the wild contractions with which the gullet tried to rid itself of the offending instrument. It could not be held by the teeth alone. With the other hand, they drummed on their knees, at the same time passing the third finger without ceasing over the thumb in a piteous gesture. For they longed to give vent to their pain in one way or another. Sometimes they could be seen stamping their feet violently. But the longer they retained the rod in the gullet, the more acclimated to its presence they became, and the greater the dilatation of the internal tissues. So they were told by the doctor and his nurses. It became a matter of pride to endure the torture without showing the least sign of it. One morning, while the doctor was inserting the rods, one of the nurses said that they were all curious to see which of the whistlers was the bravest and could hold out the longest. From that time on, they sat side by side without a movement, only giving stolen glances at each other to measure their performance. And all the while, with the dreadful rods in place, they listened to the tumult of each other's bodies. And their hands trembled and sweat ran down their foreheads. To the doctor, who observed silently and from a distance the way they denied their hurt even as they hurt terribly, the whistlers were sanctified by the pain he had brought upon them.

"Never mind," he told them. "The bitterer the medicine tastes, the more effective it is." It usually happened that Pointner and Benjamin snatched their tubes out at the same moment, while Kollin sat on a moment longer, though he allowed not a sign of triumph to show on his face. It was Pointner who showed his annoyance, tapping his forehead lightly in disdain, rolling his eyes upward. The very next day, he himself would exert all his strength to win. Perhaps it was the sameness of their dog-eared lives that gave these periodic operations their enormous importance as games of endurance in which each was a competitor. The rest of the time their actions were simple, direct, and uncontaminated by words, which are so often a substitute for the deed. Having dispensed with the need for words, they were, in a sense, the freest of men.

"Talk, talk, talk!" said Pointer, after a visit from several of the amputees. "How stupid it all is. All those words tossed back and forth, and no one listening to anyone else." To which Kollin, the man of numbers, agreed.

"All language is a disguise for real feelings." Of them all, it was easiest for Kollin to bear the muteness. He never trusted the spoken word and so had retreated to the safety and truthfulness of numbers. More than once he had implied that he had good reason for this.

To the whistlers, the operating theatre was a luminous, vaporous place, like Valhalla, where whatever you had lost in the war was given back to you. And Dr. Quint was its Wotan. The whistlers were devoted to him with all their hearts and held him in secret wonder and even veneration, without, however, voicing any more than the kind of tolerance extended to a comrade. Indeed, they never missed a chance to poke fun at his many peculiarities. They referred to him as "the old man," when, in fact, he was only ten years older than Pointner and Kollin. They responded to his cajoling or his praise for their pluck with smiles of pride and downcast eyes. Then, as soon as he was out of the room, they let loose a barrage of witticisms at the doctor's expense. Dr. Quint always showed up in blindingly white medical overalls that gave off a strong odor of disinfectants and vinegar. Beneath it could be seen the sharply creased pants of an English suit, bright silk socks, and shiny patent leather shoes. He liked red ties because he said they were like a red flag to all the priests, to whom he had taken a dislike, probably because their administration of last rites signified a failure in his treatments. Despite the doctor's dislike of the priests and his outspoken godlessness, his treatment of the soldiers was such that he was regarded by everyone as a God-fearing man. How could anyone so selfless and compassionate be anything but deeply religious? Because of his ill-concealed contempt for the military hierarchy, he was usually in ill odor with the officers in charge of the clinic. It was only his exceptional surgical skill and his willingness to spend all of his great energy to the point of exhaustion in the care of the sick and wounded that deflated any number of official reports in his disfavor. He had a small white face, very broad shoulders, and a strapping body that spoke of great virility. All the nurses blushed when he went along the corridors with his quick elastic step, his hands sunk in the pockets of his overalls. His eyes were large and dark and fiery, and slightly crossed, so that he concealed one eye with a concave "spyglass" with a central aperture that concentrated the light. He was seldom seen without this saucer-shaped eyeglass, which was kept in position by a leather band around the forehead. His right eyebrow was permanently raised from accommodating to the glass. It gave him a permanent look of surprise at what he was seeing. When he sat in front of a wounded man, it seemed to the whistlers that, while his one eye was busy examining and diagnosing, the other roved sideways, as if meditating new methods of healing. It was why they never made fun of the doctor's eyes. In fact, each of them longed to take a look through the spyglass with its small aperture. To them, Dr. Quint, with his spyglass, was like a sharpshooter or a sniper peering through a telescope at his target. What they expected to see, should the great moment come, stirred their imaginations to a pitch.

Dr. Quint had the strength of a giant. To keep himself fit, he lifted enormous weights, the heavier the better. He liked to show off his strength to the whistlers just before operating on them. Once, while the nurses were still strapping Kollin to the operating table, the surgeon suddenly grasped the heavy iron surgical chair that stood nearby and held it up in one outstretched hand.

"Do that, if you can, Pioneer," he said to Kollin, who had just been made fast with a knee strap and could only smile with astonishment. After that he submitted to the knife with boundless confidence. Ordinarily Dr. Quint spoke softly, but now and then it amused him to give vent to a loud trumpeting at the operating table. Often, while still sitting over their breakfast in the room, the whistlers heard him from the far end of the corridor shouting at the top of his voice.

"Curved needle!" he would cry out. "Alligator forceps!" To which they listened with delight, nodding knowingly to each other. As like as not, shortly afterward the doctor would pause in the doorway of their room, winking with his exposed eye and holding in his arms the man who had just been operated on, holding him the way one holds a doll, while the nurses wheeled an empty stretcher alongside. He always chose the heaviest and sturdiest patient for this performance, then laid the man carefully in his bed, wrapped in blankets and still in the deep sleep of anesthesia. Nevertheless, he hated shouting by anyone else.

"Please!" he chided his patients, "there is no need to shout or cry out at all. It serves no purpose other than to annoy me." This, before an operation to be performed without anesthetic. "Taken as a whole, it will be utterly painless. Although, I grant you, one bad moment cannot be avoided." Of this, though, he gave warning along with permission for a single roar of pain. After this, as a rule, the patient would sit quietly, until the doctor suddenly threw knife and forceps into a basin, removed the spyglass from his eye, and announced that it was over. To the whistlers, who could make no such sound, the doctor would give permission.

"Shout, Pointner! Shout, Bombardier!" and holding the man around the shoulders in a tight embrace, he would press down the agonizing rod with relentless force past the scars in their throats. And they loved him for it. Still, after each of these dilatations, there came a day of high fever as a shower of bacteria was let loose into the bloodstream.

Even as the whistlers saw the doctor as a father/God who offered them painful love, so did he see the divinity in each of his wounded patients. It was not just the pride he took in his prowess, which is a natural satisfaction that comes to every surgeon, it was that he esteemed them, found each, no matter how unlikely, the repository of beauty. No doubt they were as full of cupidity and cruelty, sadism even, as the next, but by the mere fact of having been wounded, they had been washed clean. Each of them was now flesh that God had breathed upon. That was as far as his own religion went.

7.

From the first, this bone-white room in which the whistlers dwelt had become a tranquil cove into which they had cast the anchors of their lives. No matter the wild sea outside the door, here inside it was always calm. Even more, it was a model of tolerance. The enforced reticence caused by their wounds encouraged it. Instinctively they had learned that the tolerant life cannot be lived entirely in the open. You must be willing to remain uninformed, or pretend to be, about the secret little preferences of others. The civilization inside the whistlers' room was in direct contrast to the barbarism of the war that had engendered it. This had nothing to do with good manners of which the whistlers, like the majority of the soldiers in the hospital, were happily devoid. Rather, it was in the way of a colony of apes, say, that depend upon the existence of each other for survival and companionship. Just so did the whistlers grant each other dominion over their lives. None of them evinced a desire to leave the hospital. For the whistlers, life in their room was not merely bearable; it was the only life any of them could imagine possible. Nor did they take any interest in the war. The reports that trickled in from the front gave them neither satisfaction nor dismay. It might have been a game of soccer. One morning not long after his arrival, Benjamin went for a walk through the wards and corridors of the hospital. At that time he was still quite voiceless. He wished to visit a former schoolmate. On the way he mistook the door and found himself in the ward of the blind. They sat on their beds or on chairs in a green half-light, many with bandages, as though they played blind-man's bluff, and all with faces slightly raised in the attitude of listening.

"Well, comrade, who are you and what have you got?" came a voice from a wheelchair by a window. It was Sergeant Wichtermann who asked. He had received the full force of a bomb burst in the vicinity of Arras. To everyone's surprise, he was not killed. This he attributed to his strong constitution. He was blind. Both legs and one arm had been blown off. His remaining arm had but two fingers. In these he held a long pipe. Benjamin, overcome with embarrassment, looked about. Perhaps there was a man with one eye who might be able to explain to the others why he remained silent. But there was no one.

"Well," growled Wichtermann. "Can't you open your mouth? Are you making fools of us?"

"I'll teach him a lesson, I will," said another, who got down from his bed and angrily showed his fists. All at once, a well-aimed slipper struck the door close to Benjamin's head. With that, the frightened whistler scooted out. Just outside the door he saw Landwehrmann Ferge, a fellow he had met before. Ferge was a good-natured Thuringian with a pasty-colored moustache on his sallow face, but he was shunned by his fellows. A bullet had gone right through his buttocks and torn the bowel. The doctors had fashioned a temporary colostomy on his lower abdomen. This was covered by a large rubber bag applied to his skin. It was this that condemned him to a lonely existence. Ferge had, all his life, a passion for card games. On every ward the soldiers sat at tables in threes and fours playing bridge, poker, and rummy. From anywhere in the hospital you could hear the trump cards being slapped down. Because of the smell, Ferge was not made welcome. "The Asshole," he was called. In shame and loneliness, he wandered by himself. It was this same Ferge who took Benjamin back into the ward of the blind, and explained to them how it came about that he was rendered dumb. Immediately, the young whistler was forgiven. One after another the blind men gathered round him, each in turn feeling for his silver mouthpiece, holding a hand in front of the warm stream of air that issued from it when he exhaled. Sergeant Wichtermann, too, had wheeled up his chair to investigate.

"Ah," he said. "Now I understand. But don't worry, the doctors make everything you need. This one gets a new mouth, that one a new asshole," he nodded at Ferge, who took himself off at the laughter of the blind.

From that day on, the whistlers often visited the blind to play checkers or chess. The chessmen were fitted out with little round tops of lead to give them weight, and they were not simply placed on the board, they were fixed into it with pegs so that groping fingers would not overturn them. Upon their arrival on the ward, Deuster, an army medical corporal, always greeted the whistlers with a quite accurate imitation of their croaking, much to the delight of all, including the whistlers. It is the same pleasure one takes in hearing a foreigner make an attempt to speak one's own language. This Deuster was small and red-haired, with face and hands covered with freckles. He had lost his sight while bringing in one of the enemy, who was lying wounded on the wire in front of the trench. So lamentable were this man's cries that at last, as Deuster said, it was more than anyone could bear. Pointner was particularly fond of him, and each time greeted him as if he were a new discovery, not least because he was the only one among the blind whom he could beat now and then at chess. The sightless chess player saw the whole board in his mind; the opponent had scarcely made his move before a hand flitted over the board to reconnoiter the new battle line, then replied at once with a well-thought-out plan formed out of his darkness and held to with undeviating purpose. Deuster was something of a chatterbox and would now and then make a gross blunder, whereupon Pointner, beside himself with joy, would jump up and skip around the board and hug his opponent affectionately.

"Blind man of Hesse," he'd tease like a loving father, "next time keep your eyes in your fingers."

In the society of the army hospital, deformity was accepted. It was no more a matter for derision than would be a mole. Still, it was the almost universal custom in the hospital for the patients to tease each other about their infirmities. There was no cruelty in it at all, only a certain mutual consolation to be derived. Fusileer Kulka, from what was then a province of Posen, and who for a time occupied the fourth bed in the whistlers' room, rarely spoke to them without pressing his finger to an imaginary tube and rattling in his throat. In his broken German he would tell them in a singsong voice how he came to lose his leg. He had been lying out in the open with his company after they had swarmed out to engage a unit of Siberian infantry, when a bullet ripped his left cheek and passed out through his ear. At that moment, Fusileer Kulka unstrapped his pack, took out a small mirror to see how he looked, for he had a bride back home. While surveying his face for damage, he must have exposed the rest of his body. A machine gunner got his range and shot him twelve times in his left leg. Now he had one made of leather and steel. The whistlers took him between them when he practiced walking with it outside their room, Kollin on his left, Benjamin on his right. Just so did the three totter earnestly up and down the corridor, the whistlers each pretending to have a false leg, even hoisting one shoulder and hip to the fore at every step à la Kulka, and at the same time sinking a little on the other side. The charade caused them much amusement.

One day he told Benjamin that he'd just been to a fine concert in the park. Never in his life, he confessed, had he known anything so beautiful. From that moment on, he had made up his mind to become a musician as soon as he was released from the hospital. This, despite that he could not play an instrument or even read music. He had been a worker in a cloth factory.

"Comrade," he said in an ecstasy, "it comes from within. It is all inside me." Suddenly he fell silent, as though the impossibility of his dream had just become apparent to him. Then he blinked his hollow eyes, and the corners of his mouth twitched. Benjamin, too, knew no more than he what to say, and led him, now dumb, back to the room of the blind.

8.

Fusileer Kulka had been released and sent home, and the year had once more passed into summer when, one morning, the volunteer, Furlein, appeared at the whistlers' room. He had been sent, he told them, by Dr. Quint. He had not been wounded, he explained, but from a mysterious cause, he, too, had suddenly lost his voice and found it difficult to speak above a whisper. It had come on suddenly at dawn, after a night under canvas. He had been sent out of the tent to pass on an order. It was then and there that he discovered that he could not speak out loud. Even breathing had become so difficult that he had to take off the clumsy shooting spectacles from his nose as though this would give him some relief. The whistlers were nothing if not solicitous. They heard him out with nods of consolation and smiles of encouragement. Oh, they knew all about it. His was not an unusual case. Pointner, with infinite delibera-tion, felt Furlein's lean neck, gazing, as he did so, off into the distance. Furlein began to take comfort from their assurance. He glanced shyly at the white bibs that surrounded him, and from beneath which came a soft cheeping and rustling.

"Never mind," Kollin told him. "The Old Man will soon see to it." Furlein was then outfitted with one of the blue- and white-striped linen garments the others wore. This only served to exacerbate the man's symp-toms. Now he had to struggle against attacks of suffocation. Even swal-lowing became difficult. To the impatience of the whistlers, Dr. Quint, having examined Furlein, elected to watch and wait. The whistlers, hav-ing already decided that Furlein was to be one of them, suggested to the operation nurse that he be supplied with his tube right away, a request that the nurse refused. Every evening the three whistlers spoke to the newcomer in kindly, even intimate, tones, implying that he would soon be better if only he would submit to the operation. To all of this, the ter-rified Furlein only shook his head.

In time the whistlers won his trust and persuaded him to look at their tubes, which he did with a blend of curiosity and aversion, but with grad-ually growing impatience to get it over with. "Just look at us!" the three of them coaxed. Weren't they breathing more freely and easily than ever? Nobody who wasn't a whistler could have any idea. . . . Kollin lifted his bib, took a deep breath, and exhaled with emphasis, fanning the blast that came from the little hole with his hand. Benjamin, for his part, could not say enough for the undisturbed sleep he could now enjoy. To demon-strate, he got into bed, covered himself up to the neck, then placed a pil-low over his face until no part of him was visible. Still, through a small gap between bedclothes and pillow, he breathed in and out through his tube. Furlein was convinced. To acclimate himself to the condition, he began to draw out the inner tubes from the whistlers' necks, and clean them. He cut out new bibs and neatly pinned them on. In return, the whistlers did him small favors: He was the first to read the newspaper in the morning; the pastry given to them secretly by the kitchen maids went to Furlein; they poured him a double allowance of the beer or wine that now and then found its way to their room through private munificence.

At last, early one summer morning, Furlein was taken to the operating theater. He was conducted to the great swinging doors by the three whistlers, who rejoiced that soon he would be as well off as they were. Back in their room, they placed the blocks beneath the foot of Furlein's bed. After such neck surgery, one must lie with the head lower than the feet lest blood run into the trachea. But what was this! Not fifteen minutes later, who should appear at the doorway, on his own feet, but Furlein! And there was no bandage on his neck! What had happened? As Furlein related, Dr. Quint had sent a strong electric current through his neck, then suddenly ordered him to shout as loud as he could. "Harness a yoke of oxen to your throat!" was the way the Old Man had put it. Furlein did so, obediently emitting the roar of two bulls. From then on he was able to speak and breathe as freely as before. All this Furlein told the whistlers in his rousing, fine new voice.

"Isn't it wonderful?" he asked, and shook hands all around. With a tiny smile, each whistler offered his congratulations, then they went, all three, outside to the park for their morning airing. Furlein could not have gone without saying good-bye. This the whistlers understood, but they never spoke of Furlein again.

9.

It was in the third autumn of the war that a fourth comrade was added to the whistlers' room that was as clean and white as bone. One morning, Sister Emily, a red-cheeked Valkyrie of uncertain age, came in and laid a heap of fresh linen on the fourth bed that, since Furlein's departure, had gone unmade.

"Early tomorrow," she announced, "there will be a new whistler, a real one, this time. And guess what! It's an English prisoner." The whistlers were shocked. Pointner pushed back his chair and laid down his spoon.

"No, absolutely not!" he clucked at the top of his small voice. Kollin and Benjamin showed their indignation with scowls and whispers.

"It's no use complaining," she told the men. "He's been shot through the throat, same as you all, and there's nowhere else to put him. So just put up with it." She took a piece of chalk out of her pocket and wrote on the nameplate at the head of the bed. As soon as she had left, the whistlers went to read it. "Harry Flint" was his name, and where in every other instance a man's rank was stated, they read "Englishman." The whistlers could not have been more disgusted. Pointner slammed his coffee mug down on the table and went outside into the park, spitting with rage, like a cat.

The next morning, when the whistlers were sitting over their breakfast, the door slowly opened and there stood a round-faced boy of eighteen, with large brown eyes and thick blue-black hair. He was holding a small bundle about the size of a cabbage and wore the blue- and white-striped hospital linen with, over it, a kind of bicycling cape. On his head, a washed-out cap that was too small. He looked for all the world like an immigrant seeking shelter in a beautiful foreign land upon whose shores he had been washed up. This was Harry Flint, or in German, Heine Kieselstein, or simply Kiesel, of the Gloucester regiment. For a long moment he stood blushing in the doorway, then put his hand to his cap in greeting. When there was no response, he made a slight bow at the waist. After that he remained motionless, his hands laid, one over the other, at the waist, on his face a look of shame and fear, but also of pride.

The whistlers appeared not to have seen him, but each seemed deeply immersed in his breakfast. After a while, when Harry saluted again, it was Pointner who, without stopping to stuff his mouth with bread, jerked the handle of his knife in the direction of the vacant bed. Harry Flint sat down gingerly on the very edge of it, as though desiring to show how little room he would need. Almost at once the three whistlers rose and, without so much as a glance at the rifleman, went outside into the park.

When they came back at noon, it was to find Harry sweeping out the room with a broom and dustpan he had found. They could see at once that he was wearing the tube in his neck without any protective covering and secured only by a thin cord. It looked for all the world as if there were a metal button or a screw stuck in the middle of his neck. This would never do! It was Kollin who, shaking his head in disapproval, went up to the Englishman and led him to the nightstand by his own bed. Here he took out a clean piece of muslin and pinned it carefully under Harry's chin. Harry, who had stood without a movement during this ministration, took a small mirror from his pocket and examined himself with delight. Then he rummaged in his bundle and produced a stick of chocolate, which he offered to Kollin, who gave it a passing glance, then shook his head. Harry bit his lip and turned away.

At this time, food was scarce throughout Germany. White bread, cake, meat, and imported fruit had vanished. Harry, on the other hand, had no such lack of these items. Soon after his arrival, a large parcel of otherwise unprocurable food came for him from an English Prisoners of War Committee in Switzerland. Every third or fourth day, along came another parcel of smoked bacon, *wurst* in cans, butter in tin tubes, cakes with almonds, and white bread with a brown and shining crust. All of which Harry offered to the others in the friendliest way. But war is war, and, although the whistlers had long since forgotten their hatred of Great Britain, they obstinately refused to touch even a morsel of the food. This was not always to their detriment, as now and then there came an ominous hissing and an effervescing when Harry stuck in a can opener. Then the meat smelled like bad cheese, and the bread was too hard to cut. Whenever this happened, the whistlers cheered up. They surrounded the table where Harry had spread his treasures, and in the mixture of German and English that had recently become the common tongue, passed the severest criticisms on England and its products. "Stinkfleisch!" they croaked, and held their noses. Poor Harry, out of some benighted notion of patriotism, would then soak the hard bread in his soup, rub salt in the putrid meat, and then swallow it down. Often, shortly thereafter, he turned pale, hurried out, and vomited long and peacefully for the honor of England. Benjamin was the first to yield to the temptation of Harry's treats. When Pointner and Kollin spoke vehemently against acceptance of the largesse, Benjamin expressed doubt.

"Oh, I don't know about that," he said. "I don't know." To which Kollin took umbrage.

"Is that all you have to say, 'I don't know'? Well, if that's so, you don't have to say it again." But Benjamin's "I don't know" was a powerful plea for tolerance within the whistlers' room.

"After all," he said, "Harry can't help being English. Anyway, it's not a crime," he added slyly. "It's just bad luck." Pointner and Kollin laughed, but Harry was insulted.

"Can't you just shut up about it?" he said to Benjamin, but his heart pounded because it had received human kindness.

With the arrival of Harry Flint, Benjamin was no longer the smallest. His physical growth over the past two years had been astonishing to Pointner and Kollin. He had gained six inches in height and was well over six feet tall. His chest had deepened, his arms and legs were sinewy. To the others, he was growing the way a rolling snowball takes on volume. And along with it came vigor and an animal grace. But did he know this himself? He was now far and away the strongest of them, and was often asked by Sister to transport a patient when Herr Mauch could not be found. Sometimes, he did not join the others when they went for a walk in the park, but lay on his bed, thoughts going up his mind like smoke in the chimney of the pot-bellied stove. When Pointner tried to coax him to come with them, Kollin would intervene.

"Let him be, Pointner, can't you see that he is becoming a man?" Alone on the verandah, with the others not present, Benjamin took out a small pocket mirror and studied his face. Was he ugly or handsome? He didn't know. Ugly, he feared, and bemoaned the wide space between his upper front teeth and a certain prominence of his ears. All the while, a tense string vibrated and sang inside him. When he heard the door to the verandah open, he quickly hid the mirror in a pocket, as if caught in a furtive act. At night, the young man's thoughts would take on the echoing grandeur of nightmare. How long the night was! From midnight on, he listened to an owl calling for its mate in the dark outside the windows. Patiently, calmly, it called, until Benjamin, in despair, jumped up and shut the windows. But the silence was just as unbearable. Stepping out upon the verandah, where every cherry tree became a living creature, alert and watchful, he perceived that the owl was already experiencing the dawn that was still in the future for him. He returned to his bed and accepted the plaintive call of the bird as his own.

Benjamin was the originator of the common German-English language they all spoke. Once he had overcome his initial shyness and modesty, he brought forth from his nightstand his English notebook from grammar school days and initiated Harry into the usages and rules of the hospital, and especially of the whistlers' room. He taught him also the art of speaking, or rather croaking, by putting his finger over the tube. He then began to teach him a little German. Harry was a quick pupil and soon transformed himself from the dumb foreigner into a friend who was always ready for a talk. In no time at all, the whistlers got to be very fond of him. One day Harry confided to Benjamin that he had a wife. A war marriage, he called it. He had known her for two weeks; they had only been together for two nights. He was seventeen, his wife a little over sixteen. Often Benjamin came upon Harry seated on his bed, apparently smelling, or even tasting a sheet of paper. When he asked, Harry told him that Mrs. Flint was allowed by the censorship to send no more than four sides of notepaper to her prisoner husband every week. But first she had to learn how to write. In the beginning each letter contained no more than one or two labored sentences, traced in large letters. The rest of the space was covered with neatly drawn x's, each one of them a kiss. Harry loyally responded to each letter, and each time his lips met those of his far-distant wife on the paper. At night Benjamin could hear the rustling folds and the sighs of the prisoner. Once he got up and groped his way across to console his friend with . . . what? A joke? A caress? He didn't know himself. But Harry quickly pulled the bedclothes over his head, in some fear of what might be coming.

10.

As winter drew near, Pointner became bedridden. Under the constant demands of the infection that had never entirely left him, his heart had begun to fail. Far from unhappy, he lay in bed reading until deep into the night. He had long since finished reading all the love and mystery stories in the hospital library, but Benjamin had come to the rescue with a thick volume of the fairy tales of the brothers Grimm. This became Pointner's inseparable companion. Over and over again, with a blissful smile, he read the stories of the Golden Bird, Florinda and Yoringal, Rapunzel, the Blue Light, and the little man with a glow. Soon, he had them all by heart, and still Pointner read them from the book, while Benjamin marveled at his obsession and Kollin shook his head, puzzled at Pointner's apparent reversion to childhood.

"What? Pointner, again you want 'Hänsel und Gretel'? It's all about food, and you are eating only air and sunshine." Sometimes the bedridden man laughed to himself and laid the heavy book for a while in his lap, or beckoned to Benjamin and held his finger to the place where he wanted Benjamin to read aloud. When Benjamin smiled in acquiescence, he sat up and croaked:

"Als hinaus / Nach des Herrn seinem Haus" or

"Sind wir nicht Knaben glatt und fein / Was wollen wir länger Schuster sein?"

Then sank back on the bed, prepared to listen. He had gone from a man of action to a man of nostalgia. It is what happens in a long dying.

From a magazine, Pointner cut out a color reproduction entitled "Antique Torso of Apollo." It showed the headless God with massive thighs, muscular chest, and with his penis missing. This he substituted for the photograph of himself as "Reservist." Beneath the "torso," he scrawled "Franz Pointner—a self-portrait." He had done it to make his friends laugh. When they did not, he behaved as though he had made a gaffe. A few days later, he had removed it in favor of the old picture of himself.

It was now, in the whistlers' room, that each of the four learned the common kindliness that makes life sweet. Often, when Kollin and Benjamin had gone for a walk, Harry Flint sat by his bed for hours and took care of Pointner, cleaning his tube, putting a clean bib under his chin, offering him a sip of water, pulling his bedclothes straight, even bathing him and rubbing his back. Pointner's body seemed made of candle wax that had begun to melt. Whenever Harry massaged the thin shoulders, he had the fear that the pressure of his hands would mold them into a new shape. To all of this Pointner submitted with the contentment of a child who feels protected by the grown-ups. Kollin had taken charge of the cupping glasses that were applied to Pointner's chest and back. He explained how it worked.

"These glasses, applied to the skin when heated, create a suction that draws out the poison from the body."

"Pop! Pop!" Harry would imitate the hollow sound as the cool glasses were pulled off Pointner's skin, then take them to Sister to be reheated. Mostly Benjamin just sat by Pointner's bed and offered something of his own vitality by his mere presence. All three brimmed with tenderness and solicitude. Patriotism notwithstanding, Pointner had long since begun to accept the cakes that arrived from England. Harry soaked them in milk and fed him with a spoon. It had all started with a surprise inspection of the nightstands. In each one, Sister found an opened packet of English butterscotch. She tasted it and exclaimed at how delicious it was.

It seems that at night Harry had gone to each one's bed and given a packet of butterscotch. The whistlers could hold out no longer, and each, thinking he was the only one who nibbled secretly at the honor of the Fatherland, was slowly devouring his treasure bit by bit. From then on, they quite openly helped Harry to devour the white bread and admirable *wurst*.

Kollin had once possessed an attractive baritone singing voice. Now and then Pointner would ask him to sing, usually a military air like "Die Zwei Grenadieren." Closing his silver tube with a finger, Kollin would comply in the croaking monotone that was all he could manage. At such times, his eyes darkening with animation and a lock of hair hanging over his forehead, Kollin became handsome. So said the sisters who came running in to listen.

"That's enough of those war songs," they scolded. "Sing for us a song of love."

One day, when the two were alone, Pointner took out his English cap and put it on Harry's head. For Harry it was a thrilling moment. From that time on, he coveted the cap as he had coveted nothing else. It was a matter of his identity. In peacetime, the hospital had been a State clinic devoted to the civilian sick. Now they, too, wore the same patient's uniform as did the soldiers, except for the military caps, a distinction so punctiliously observed that a soldier was seldom seen without his cap, even in bed. Harry, though a soldier, had no English cap, and since he could not wear a German one, he was compelled to go about bareheaded and to let himself be taken for a civilian. This was particularly embarrassing, as most of the patients his age were in the venereal disease ward, called the Ritterburg. These men were given as wide a berth as possible by the others. In this same Ritterburg were the local prostitutes, the Ritter Fräulein, who were subject to compulsory cure. They were not permitted to leave the ward under any circumstances, although who was to say that at night a lusty patron or two had not been pulled up to the ward by ropes of twisted sheets? No matter the pleasure in such gossip, none of the wounded would have anything to do with the ward or its occupants, let alone be mistaken for one of them.

Pointner could not bring himself to part with his beloved trophy. Still, he allowed Harry to wear it now and then when no one else was about. No sooner was a step heard outside the door than Harry whipped off the cap and returned it to Pointner, who hid it under the bedclothes. He promised Harry that, upon his death, he would bequeath him the cap, and gave Harry his hand on it with a solemn and ceremonial air. It was soon to come true.

11.

One day, Benjamin, to his horror, awoke to the presence of a painful, itching rash over much of his body. Since rash was the predominant early symptom of venereal disease, the boy was overcome with shame and self-loathing. How could this have happened! He had never experienced sexual intercourse of any kind with a woman. In his distress, there was nothing to do but tell Herr Mauch. Perhaps he would be able to do something about it without telling Dr. Quint or the Sister, both of whom Benjamin venerated and would rather die than offend with this news. Herr Mauch, gray-haired and moustached, was the orderly of the department. It was his duty to perform the heavier labors. He stood by when patients needed to be moved from one bed to another, or needed a bath. He washed the dead and brought them to the cellar where an autopsy was sometimes carried out. He went to and fro with the commode when required and had charge of emptying and rinsing out the urinals. The first to appear in the morning, Herr Mauch made a jovial entry into each room, collecting the urinals, making knowing and suggestive remarks about the habits of the soldiers. He wore a peakless cap with a cross on the badge, an old pair of army pants, the regulation tunic, and an apron over all. He laid great stress on being a military personage, although, in truth, he was vastly relieved to have the kind of job that kept him from being called up and sent to the front. For this reason, he made certain to perform his duties on time and according to expectations.

He was full of admiration for his wounded charges, addressing them as "old soldiers" or "corporal." There was nothing he delighted more in than the most bloodthirsty adventures of the battlefield, encouraging the tales with questions about the fierce slaughter. "On! On to battle!" he would cry. The few civilian patients who happened to be in the hospital he treated with scorn.

"To you," he used to say, "to a shirker like you, I am not Mauch. I am Herr Mauch!" His usual haunt was the bathhouse, where he looked after all his utensils, cleaned boots, made lists, and held himself in readiness if needed. Also, he stole like a crow, and could be counted on to produce extra bottles of beer and cigarettes. Even a certificate of leave was to be had through him.

"Oh my God!" he murmured when Benjamin, with trembling hands, had removed his shirt and pants. "Corporal, you have caught the Turkish music. How on earth did you get it?"

"Help me, Herr Mauch," pleaded the boy in a voice that nearly failed him. But Herr Mauch would do nothing of the sort. It must be reported to Dr. Quint, and that was that. Otherwise it would spread to the other fellows.

Benjamin staggered out and hid in a closet until he could compose himself. At the end of an hour, he had decided to die. It could be done easily just by removing the tube from his neck. The little hole would seal up in no time. But he had not counted on the concern of Harry Flint, who had noted Benjamin's mental distress and had observed the absence of the tube in his friend's neck. It was only twenty-four hours later, but the hole had already begun to shrink. The next thing you knew, there was Herr Mauch, crying aloud and hauling him off. Dr. Quint took vigorous hold of the fainting Benjamin and forced a new tube into the opening with whatever force it required. Then with his spyglass he examined the rash. At once his face became serene.

"Scabies," he announced with a touch of amusement in his voice. "Sarcoptes scabiei, the itch mite. It burrows into the skin and lays its eggs in the burrow. There is intense itching and the rash. Just a normal case of it. Go right over to the Ritterburg. In three days, you'll be clean again." Tears of relief came down the boy's cheeks. Dr. Quint turned about on his revolving stool.

"Idiot!" he bellowed at Mauch. "Blockhead! Child murderer! I'll have you court-martialed and shot." But Herr Mauch had already bolted out the door.

At the Ritterburg experienced hands smeared him from head to foot with a green ointment. He was given a long shirt that was also green, and green cotton gloves. Even the beds were green from the ointment and the wallpaper of the room. And so it was called the Hunters' Room, and its half-dozen occupants, the Hunters. No sooner had he taken his place in the room, than the oldest of the scabetics, a white-haired tramp who hated doctors, began.

"They're all liars, these doctors," he gargled, while eating Benjamin's rations. For the boy ate nothing all the while he was in the Ritterburg.

"It's all rubbish they tell us about the little animals burrowing in the skin. It is deep in the blood and it comes out every spring when the trees come out." Benjamin scarcely listened. He looked down through the window into the garden of the Ritterburg, which was strictly shut off from the park. There, in the midst of a bevy of Ritterburg Fräulein, was a yellow-skinned fellow with black hair that gleamed in the sunlight. He was called the Legionary, because he was a deserter from the Foreign Legion who had somehow gotten back to Germany through the lines. He had a wild face, beautiful and adventurous. Benjamin lost himself in fantasies about the amazing experiences he seemed to be telling the girls around him.

12.

There came the day when Dr. Quint performed on Benjamin and Harry what he hoped would be the final and decisive operation. For days afterward they lay in bed in great pain and with high fever. Kollin, the only one left on his feet, wandered in and out among his friends. The rest of his time was spent carving a set of chessmen that he meant to give to Pointner as a present. But Pointner had suddenly begun to sink rapidly. He gazed at Kollin, only waved a hand feebly, then turned away. Kollin, distraught at his friend's deterioration, implored Dr. Quint to operate on him as he had on Benjamin and Harry. But Dr. Quint could not risk it yet in Kollin's case, and he had to console himself with hopes for the future. Thus passed the weeks of winter. The cherry trees, heavy with snow, had woven themselves into a tangle. Now and then a regimental band would form before a window of the whistlers' room and play a few rousing tunes. One of them had the same melody as the hymn in which God is asked to save the "Gracious King" of Great Britain. When this was played, Harry Flint bowed his head and kept time with his finger. News of the war filtered in to the wounded men. It was not going well. Kollin spent some days adding up figures, then shook his head philosophically. Germany was losing the war.

Harry and Benjamin, having been not long out of their beds, were in high hopes of being soon quit of their tubes, when Pointner's end came. For some days he lay unconscious, turning his head this way and that, as though he were wondering about something. His face had become small and peaceful like the face of a child. His eyes, when he opened them, were

always a deeper and deeper blue. But he opened them seldom, and when
he did, the other whistlers collected around his bed and joked with him.
Then he would look at them tenderly, smile faintly, and gaze off into the
distance like a man listening to the rain. With every cell of his body, what
was left of it, he announced, "This is as far as I can go." A great sweetness enveloped him. He asked for nothing; he was beyond wanting
except, now and then, to be turned from lying on his back to his belly,
and to fall asleep in the warmth of his belly, a request that the others hastened to grant. If he felt fear or sorrow, he gave no sign of it. The flesh
allows so few feelings beyond its own suffering. Not once did he call upon
God; he hadn't the habit nor the belief. One evening, having finished his
day's surgery, Dr. Quint paid a visit while Kollin was bathing the dying
man with soap and water. He laid his hand on Kollin's shoulder.

"Pater Seraphicus," he muttered under his breath, then gave a short
barking cough.

"What?" asked Kollin, clearly mystified.

"Never mind," said the doctor and went on his way. The next morning, when they were all still in bed, they heard Pointner getting restless.
He rattled so violently at the drawer of his nightstand that a glass fell to
the floor with a crash. When they turned on a light, there was Pointner
sitting bolt upright in bed and holding out the English cap to Harry. No
toreador, throwing his cap to a friend before a *corrida,* could match it for
courage. All three jumped out of bed to run and prop him up, but
Pointner had already sunk back, his eyes fixed on the ceiling. He never
moved again. Kollin placed his palm on the dying man's chest and felt
his breathless heart stumble and skid. This way he knew the precise
moment when his friend died. Already Pointner's face had taken on the
padlocked look of the dead. For a long moment the room darkened and
went utterly still. Then it passed. The walls breathed again, the table-
cloth was white. Harry, embarrassed by death as the very young often
are, gave a quick glance at the stove, as if he and the stove were exchanging a furtive look. There was no one to notify, only an aunt living in a village somewhere in Bavaria. Pointner's mother had died giving him birth;
there had never been a father in any sense but the ejaculatory, as he himself liked to joke.

Pointner was buried in the small soldiers' cemetery behind the park.
In the first row behind the coffin walked the three whistlers, Harry wearing the English cap openly for the first time. Then came Herr Mauch,

wearing an army helmet and, at his belt, a bayonet. On his arm was the
blind army corporal, Deuster. Behind them walked Backhuhn, the
grenadier, his nose now almost within normal limits. The band played
"The Song of the Comrades," and Herr Mauch sobbed into his helmet,
which he held in front of his moustache. Benjamin and Harry shook with
repressed grief and looked with pale, drawn faces at the ground. Kollin
alone kept a calm face and dry eyes, but when his turn came to step up to
the heap of earth and scatter some of it into the grave, he put aside the
spade and threw on the coffin the chessmen that he had brought with
him in his overcoat pocket.

"You would think," said Herr Mauch when he had controlled himself, "that Herr Dr. Quint would come to pay his last respects."

"No you are mistaken," said Kollin. "A doctor cannot afford to let
himself be emotional. All these funerals would have a weakening effect.
A surgeon especially must be impervious, strong. Would you prefer that
he be a *pißpott* like you, Mauch?" In truth, it had taken the doctor years
to build up the carapace that protected him from the pain of others. Now
the only sign he gave of emotion was a brief, raw cough, like the bark of
a dog. Still, the night before the funeral, unbeknownst to anyone, the doctor had gone to the hospital morgue, lifted the sheet from the heads of
several corpses until he came to Pointner. It was the first time that he ever
looked at a dead man's face and it looked back. A few weeks later Kollin
himself was wheeled into the operating theatre on a stretcher. The final
critical operation was to be put to a test in his case too. Benjamin and Harry
waited in vain for his return. When they saw him again, he lay behind
the white folding screen in Herr Mauch's bathhouse, where the dying
and newly dead were brought to spare the others the emotional strain.

With the death, first of Pointner, then Kollin, Harry and Benjamin
felt an inexplicable vitality. It is sometimes thus, that there is a resurgence
of life in the survivors. For some months the letters from Harry's wife
had grown further and further apart, and finally they ceased coming altogether. Benjamin watched anxiously for some sign of his friend's unhap-
piness, but Harry gave none. Nor did he ever speak of it. The shared
misfortune of their friends' death served to bind Benjamin and Harry
even more strongly together. And then the day came when Dr. Quint
drew out the silver pipes from the neck of each of them. The tiny mouth
above the breastbone closed in a single night, and now they could breathe
quite normally.

"We are no longer whistlers," Harry whispered. But out of deference to their dead comrades, they endeavored to hide their joy. At first they were shy about speaking aloud, as though only without language could they express themselves truly. Now unmuzzled, would they still hold back? Or would a single false word ruin what they had built up together, built up, not with thought, but with instinct and affinity. But soon enough the hesitation passed, and the old camaraderie resumed. For the first time, Benjamin had an inkling of something he needed, although what this was, he could not say, only that it had to do with Harry. For three months, arm in arm, and even hand in hand, they walked along the garden paths, inhaling the fragrance of the pines that had been denied them, stopping every now and then to gaze at each other, breathing deeply, the way a newborn baby takes the first air into his lungs. And it seemed that the cherry orchard breathed in secret harmony with them, all its branches foaming with blossoms, inhaling and exhaling. Hungrily they tasted the vowels that fluttered inside their mouths, the syllables that had lain dormant for so long and that now were swelling and softening. Soon they would flower at their lips and fracture the silence. When they did speak, their new voices were as unpredictable as they had once been at puberty, veering from a hoarse croak to a high-pitched whine. Even so, they continued to live out the rhythm of the night, not speaking, drifting in and out of sleep, existing in a comfortable present, without past or future, that they wished would go on forever. They might have been alone on the earth, enisled. When morning came, they awoke eager for the promiscuous flow of words that the night had interrupted.

One morning, after breakfast, they were both lying fully dressed on their beds. Outside, the weather was cold, the sky smudged with brownish clouds that gave the morning the false flavor of night. All at once Herr Mauch rushed in with a sheaf of papers under his arm.

"Harry Flint!" he called out. "Get ready, and make it snappy! You've been exchanged for one of ours, and you are going home. You must be ready in half an hour. There is only just time to catch the train to Rotterdam. Hurry up!" His words had the electric quality of something shocking that had been overheard. Herr Mauch threw a bundle of clothes on the bed and left the room. Slowly Harry sat up and stared across at Benjamin in consternation.

"No," he said. "No, I am not going away. I will stay here with you." But at the same time, with trembling hands he pulled off his hospital uniform and put on the faded khaki. Then he sat down on his bed with his hands clasped. Again and again he looked at Benjamin, and Benjamin looked at him. They could not speak. They could scarcely breathe. When Herr Mauch once again stood in the doorway, they leaped to their feet and came to stand together between the beds. All that separated the two boys was a few feet of empty space. All at once, with a quick clumsy lurch, they collided into each other's arms. As if in accordance with a will other than their own, the two boys kissed each other, first on either cheek, then on the lips.

A moment later, Harry turned and marched to the doorway. There he turned again to face Benjamin. In one hand he held the same small bundle of his possessions with which he had arrived two years before. Only now, on his head, he wore the English cap. With a swift movement, he brought his other hand up to the cap in a salute, a tight smile fixed upon his face, and then he was gone. Benjamin retreated two steps and sank to his bed, his eyes full of that painful smile, his lips still tingling from what they had touched, his hands raised to his temples in the immemorial gesture of bereavement.

—after *Paul Alverdes*

POSTSCRIPT

What the reader wants to know is what happened next. To the whistlers, as to everyone who came under his care, the doctor was "dedicated," and so he was, but they could not know that this devotion to duty sprang from his own desperate needs. Dr. Quint was fifty years old when he began the Herculean labor of opening the throats of these four whistlers. With his arrival at that age, came change. He who had been supremely confident in his own surgical prowess had begun to feel twinges of doubt. He had presided over the deaths of so many young men. Perhaps he no longer had "the magic touch." Perhaps another surgeon. . . . And he who had placed all his reliance upon science, the unalterable facts of the body, his armamentarium of surgical instruments, and upon the cleverness and ingenuity of his hands, had begun to imagine.

What had begun all but imperceptibly, and grown slowly, had become a fated upheaval. He began to think of the whistlers as four creatures in a larval state, each asleep in his chrysalis, waiting for release. Even as each of them was altered by his encounter with the doctor, so now was the doctor no longer the same as he had been before Pointner, Kollin, Benjamin, and Harry. First came the shock at coming face-to-face with a wound he had never known before, but that he recognized at once was the very wound he had long been seeking. It was upon his treatment of these four that he would measure himself as a surgeon and as a man. You can never know too much, he realized. "It all depends upon me," he thought. "A doctor who has never performed this surgery before." In a strange way, these speechless whistlers would be the oracle that would foretell his own fate. It was no less than his own salvation that he must now work out through the care and treatment of the inhabitants of the whistlers' room. Why these patients, out of so many thousands that he had treated? He did not know. Only that it was so. It was, he thought, like falling in love. Why one woman, out of so many thousands that a man encounters? The whistlers' room was the field upon which would be fought the struggle between the sacred act of Surgery and his own need for love. But it must be done in secret. No one must know. Dr. Quint was one of those medical men who feel the need to touch their patients, by which he drew from them the nourishment to carry on a task as heartbreaking as it is impossible. Just as Antaeus drew strength from touching the Earth that was his mother. They could not know that he needed them quite as much as they needed him. Nor could they know that, standing at the stone table in the morgue where lay the body of Pointner, he had for the first time looked at the face of a dead man, and it had looked back.

When the war ended, Dr. Quint returned to his native village and took up the life of a simple doctor. With his white hair and beard, he might have been Zeus emerging from a cloud. His wife and young son lived upstairs, over the rooms that were his office. He was no longer a surgeon whose interest was in "having" and "doing." Many years ago he had unlearned the natural shame that prolongs innocence and optimism. He had stripped so many bodies and had his way with them. Now he had become a doctor who watches and perceives. He had developed faith in the experience of living, rather than merely holding opinions about it. He knew now that imagining is fatal to a surgeon.

Harry Flint became a lorry driver, resumed his marriage, and in due course became the father of four children, the oldest of whom he named Benjamin.

Benjamin never married. He became an apprentice to a pharmacist in an ancient hillside town that crowded down flight upon flight of granite steps to the alleys that lined the river below. Again, like Troy. Of the time before he was wounded, he remembered only the rumps of the horses illuminated by bursts of distant artillery fire. Again and again he would return to that white room that had been the embodiment of his suffering and that now lived only within himself. And, oh yes, this: At night, in a notebook Benjamin had bought for this purpose, he wrote an account of the life in that room that was the inaccessible past from which he had been exiled, where he had experienced the wonderment of youth and first love. Night after night he rebuilt the room, the way a bird builds its nest, twig by twig, pressing, molding with its own breast. Little by little the room was taking form within him—windows, cots, stove, table, chairs— until he was there. He could step inside it, like a bridegroom, with just that eagerness and ardor. He saw again the scrawny fifteen-year-old boy he had been, suffering the rod to be thrust deep into his throat and fighting to hold back the tears, to be a man among men. He described the silver tracheotomy tubes that to him seemed like fairy pipes. He recalled the noises the room made that were louder than the whispers and whistles of the four soldiers—the way the floor creaked, a sudden snap! a crack! that seemed to come from nowhere, the sigh made by a sudden updraft in the stove chimney. And once, a flapping, as of wings. He described, too, the silence at the moment of Pointner's death, when the others had been full of the sense that something had come and gone from the room.

And the secret harmony of the orchard with Harry Flint and himself. He wrote about that. And he remembered how, in the moments before Harry left, the air between them changed color, and he had thought the life must be leaking out of his body, so that, with every molecule, he had to hold on tight. All this and much, much more, Benjamin recorded. Perhaps in the beginning, by writing it down, he thought to exorcize the room, then pass from his accursed and endless adolescence into manhood. Perhaps through the imagination he meant to free himself from the terrible power of the flesh. But he was wrong; he could not break with the past. To him, confiding in his notebook was the most important act of his life. It was what he was destined to do—to remember and tell. No one had read any of it. The notebook was found in the drawer of a table in Benjamin's room after his death years later.

EPILOGUE

Sometime in October 2000, while browsing in the stacks of the Yale
Sterling Library, my attention was captured by a slender volume entitled
Die Pfeifferstube in German, *The Whistlers' Room* in translation. The
author was Paul Alverdes. For the next hour I stood entranced, as I read
the novella about four soldiers identically wounded during World War
I. To me, the four had the purity and charm of children. The incidents in
their lives were described in language of utmost simplicity. The original
had been published in Germany in 1929; the English translation, in
the United States in 1931. From the library dating slip at the back of
the book, I saw that it had not been borrowed for forty-eight years. That
such should be the fate of so moving a book seemed unfair. Then and
there I decided that I would try to awaken *The Whistlers' Room* from its
long slumber and see it back into print. Even more, to perform an act of
literary ventriloquy in which those who were speechless would be given
voice.

But how to go about it? The author was dead, as was the translator.
The publishing house in New York City, long since defunct. After some
delving, I learned that there is a book in Berlin, Germany, which lists the
names and addresses of the holders of copyright of all books published in
that country. The person I sought was Herr Wolf Alverdes, the son of
the author. His address was given as Burgstrasse 38, Pöring, a place so
small as not to be found on my map of Germany. With little expectation
of receiving an answer, I wrote to Wolf Alverdes, introducing myself as
an American doctor/writer who had come by merest chance upon his
father's book, and who now entertained the hope that this worthy tale
might enjoy another publication. A few weeks later, I received an
answering letter:

Dear Mr. Selzer,
Thank you for your very interesting letter from October 3, 2000.
First of all: it's correct. I hold the rights from my father, Paul
Alverdes. It would be great if you could get a publisher who will
have the translation of the book "Die Pfeifferstube" from you.
I myself would be very happy if you could convince a publisher.
So you should have the rights by myself to your translation and edi-

tion and looking for a publisher. . . . I will help you if it is necessary
every time. I hope I hear from you in time.

Sincerely yours,
Wolf Alverdes

Once again I wrote, asking Herr Alverdes to grant me the copyright
and to tell me about his father. Both of these requests were satisfied in
the next letter.

Dear Mr. Selzer,
Of course you shall have a description of my father's life. I send you
hereby a description in German . . . because my English is not as good
to translate the German text in a correct American English. I send
this immediately, so that you have it in time, hoping you find a publisher in the next time. By the way, I was very pleased to get your very
nice letter in this short time after writing to you.

Sincerely yours,
Wolf Alverdes

From the brief biography of Paul Alverdes, I learned that he was born
in May 1897 in the city of Strasbourg, the son of an Army officer. His
early education took place in Düsseldorf, after which, at the age of sixteen, he was taken into the German army and assigned to a Field
Artillery unit. Almost a year later, and still sixteen, he was severely
wounded in the throat, so that he was unable to speak. His larynx had
been damaged by the bullet. He spent the next two years in an army hospital, where he had a close friendship with an English prisoner of war
and two other German soldiers, each of whom had sustained the same
wound and all of whom underwent multiple surgical operations to correct the injury. *The Whistlers' Room* is autobiography, thinly disguised as
fiction. By the time of his discharge from the hospital, Paul Alverdes had
regained his voice and was discharged as healed, although with permanent hoarseness. He went on to enjoy a career as a writer, mostly of children's literature, literary criticism, and incidental essays. None of his
other work has been translated into English. He was married to a concert singer and they had two sons, Wolf and the younger Jan, who prede-
ceased his father. Paul Alverdes died in Munich in 1979.

A re-reading of *The Whistlers' Room* suggested that certain editorial
changes might improve the story and make it more palatable to the reader

of today. With the encouragement of Wolf Alverdes, and in a spirit of respectful homage, I proceeded to re-translate the book from the German, then to excise everything that was not essential to the telling of the story, in the course of which the text shrank from one hundred and thirty-five to thirty-five pages. It was no longer a novella; it was a short story. Next, I began the task of rewriting, with the intention of sustaining the authorial voice of my predecessor as much as could be. Right from the start it proved impossible to keep my own style from asserting itself. What finally resulted is a book that bears my own signature on every page. This was not done without some misgivings. What right has a living writer to tamper with the prose of one who can no longer dismiss the interloper? I have justified my act of literary surgery by the certainty that, had I not performed it, *The Whistlers' Room* would have slept unnoticed for centuries, if not forever. What I have done, I have done with gratitude and esteem for Paul Alverdes. This work is an act of homage to him.

If it can be said that the word is flesh, it comes naturally to a doctor/writer, this resurrecting of a moribund text. In doing so, I felt rather like the ninth century B.C. prophet Elisha. All prophets are obnoxious. They scold, call down curses, predict the worst, and do not hesitate to flaunt their gift. Elisha was the worst of his tribe. He seems to have spent his time roaming about Canaan, or Judaea, or whatever it was called before it became Palestine, looking for opportunities to perform miracles. Once he was taunted by a group of boys who called him "Baldy." This so enraged the prophet that he called down a curse upon them, whereupon two huge bears appeared and mauled a great many of them. His most famous feat was carried out for the benefit of the Shunammite woman who had extended to him the hospitality of her house whenever he was in the area. She was a well-to-do farmer's wife who had everything except what she wanted most—a child. But now her husband was too old. Not so, said Elisha, and told her that next year she would hold her new baby. And so it happened. But after some years, the boy grew sick and died. The heartbroken mother sent for Elisha, who went alone to the room where the dead boy lay. He lay down on top of the boy, mouth to mouth, hand to hand, and eye to eye. Soon the corpse became warm and turned pink. After a while, the boy sneezed seven times, then sat up, resurrected. In revivifying this story, I am a little bit like Elisha.

In one sense, everything dead is reshaped into something else that is living. The countless dead epithelial cells we shed each day are ingested by microorganisms, which reproduce either by splitting off buds, gemmation, or by dividing down the middle, as in binary fission. The resultant new organisms carry off with them their portion of our stuff. In the case of *The Whistlers' Room,* I have been but the catalyst of such a reaction. I can only hope that a hundred years from now another writer will stumble upon a paragraph of mine, rewrite it however he will, and set it free for his generation to read.

The original novella, *Die Pfeifferstube,* was dedicated to another German writer of the time, Hans Carossa, who was also a physician, and who also experienced life in the army during wartime. It seemed only natural that I next read whatever of Hans Carossa's work I could find. In a memoir entitled *Childhood,* published in 1922, seven years prior to *The Whistlers' Room,* Hans Carossa remembers his early years as the son of a village doctor. The rooms on the first floor were reserved for his father's office; the family lived upstairs, precisely the arrangement of my own boyhood in Troy, New York, in the 1930s. Like Carossa, as a child I would go downstairs to find amusement among the waiting patients. In his memoir Carossa singles out one patient, a young man "with a very small chalk-white face and large blue eyes," who told the boy fabulous stories "in a husky and whispering voice." One of the stories was about King Ludwig in the Corpus Christi procession. It seemed that the King followed the sacred Host, holding a large heavy burning candle at arm's length. It took superhuman endurance to keep the stiffly outstretched arm from sinking even once through two mortal hours: ". . . no other man was capable of it, let somebody only try." The story is echoed in the feats of strength performed by Dr. Quint in *The Whistlers' Room.* The patient in Carossa's memoir suffered from a lingering disease of the larynx, most likely tuberculosis, which "disabled it so that he had to breathe through a silver tube inserted directly into his windpipe and kept firm with a neckband." The boy "listened with wonder to the metallic sound of the air sucking in and out, and gradually came to imagine that the man was lined inside with pure silver." Paul Alverdes' own laryngeal wound, requiring a tracheotomy tube, is yet another instance of life imitating art.

Let the reader imagine my sense of belonging, of homecoming even, as I placed myself in the line of descent from the *Childhood* of the physician Carossa, himself the son of a physician, through *Die Pfeifferstube* of the patient, Alverdes, to my own father, and finally to my retelling of this story. While I cannot, of course, speak for Hans Carossa or Paul Alverdes,

I can imagine that they, too, as I have been, were "beside themselves" in their reinvention of the past. To be "beside oneself" is the proper condition of the memoirist. He is transported out of himself to become another person, identical in name and appearance, but now in possession of a unique perception of the past and the will to express it in words. Just so did Paul Alverdes return in his mind to that whistlers' room to gaze at the scrawny sixteen-year-old boy suffering the terrible rod to be thrust into his throat, and fighting to bear it, to be a man among men. I imagine Alverdes, a decade later, asking himself, "Who is he, that wretched boy, making his superhuman effort not to cry?" In resurrecting this story, I have carried out an act for which I was predestined. Or so it seems. It is as though a fragment of my own ancestral past had been revealed to me, a fragment that I do but hand on to one who will surely come after me.

Down from Troy 3

Two Vignettes and an Appreciation

RAE

Rae was Mother's best friend as well as her archenemy, her confidante, and bitter rival. She was also Mother's piano accompanist. Even when at daggers drawn, they were pulled together with the same force as they were driven apart. As one can only love one's nemesis, they adored and defended each other. At the least hint of derision of her friend, Mother rose up in furious denunciation of the derider—usually Father. Only once did he get away with it, when he diagnosed Rae as a case of "malignant exaltation." Mother didn't know what that was. At any time of the day, Mother and Rae might be heard preparing for their next musicale in the parlor, with the door emphatically shut. Whenever they hit a certain note, high C-sharp I think it was, the crystal bowl on the dining room table started ringing. From behind the door, cries of rapture alternated with passionate remonstrances. It got so that one could tell from the front stoop what the temperature was upstairs. On the rare occasion when the Diva's nose remained out of joint overnight, she would make lofty utterance at the dinner table.

"Poor creature, she's tone-deaf, you know. Can't sing a note. Her vocal apparatus is off kilter. Quite a shame." And she would sigh as if it were her affliction, not Rae's.

Rae was a maiden lady, who nevertheless achieved a measure of maternity through her wardrobe. It had a vaguely intra-uterine motif—

mucosal pink and placental red. Father said she was the apotheosis of gestation, "a regular Belle Geste." Mother cautioned Rae not to wear magenta, as it made her look like an exhausted rhododendron that had reverted from red. Nor was she to wear red when they were entertaining on the wards of St. Mary's Hospital.

"Red stabs a white wall, perhaps fatally." On Sunday only, Rae would appear all in white silk, with white sequins, white feathers in her hat, a white shawl, and pearls. Floating down the street after dusk, sequins aglitter, she might have been a chunk of the Milky Way broken off, or Cassiopeia in her astral chair. I couldn't take my eyes off her. And didn't she know it! Billy was much less enamored and said she looked like a big white mare with the staggers.

Rae always referred to Father as "The Doctor." He, in turn, called her "The Rae," and never lost a chance to comment upon her anatomy. It wasn't fair: She was too easy a mark, as she was a woman of Praxitelean proportions, in some abundance both in front (she called it "the bosoms") and behind.

"If Helen had looked like that," said Father, the Trojan War would never have taken place." But when he died, it was Rae, not Mother, who was inconsolable. (Once I had seen them kissing on the landing of the stairs; the way she broke free as if he had captured her. Was it a game? I wondered.) It turned out that she had counted on his raillery. It gave her the opportunity to "rise above the taunts." Still, the vast bulk of the affections of the two women was reserved for each other. In sashes, scarves, feathers, and with a tiny lace hankie tucked in a sleeve, their wardrobes were interchangeable. They dressed to impersonate each other. Only in the matter of hair did they part preferences. Rae did, Mother didn't, believe in the "permanent wave." I shall try to re-create their dialogue.

"Nothing in life is permanent," Mother argued. "The Doctor says that hair is just an excrescence of the skin, like fingernails. Temporary wave would be more like it."

"The Doctor," retorted Rae, "can be as disgusting as he chooses."

"Besides, Rae darling, you'd look so much more interesting if you let it grow and had a Grecian knot." (Anyone eavesdropping at the parlor door could always tell at what point in the discussion they started talking like the people in Pride and Prejudice.)

"You do not find me 'interesting' enough?" said Rae, with immense punctilio. "That is a relief. I have, now and then, been told in this very house that I am altogether too interesting, that I have 'too much taste.' It is good to know that I am not in such excess after all."

"Aren't we touchy! I spoke only of the arrogance of the term 'permanent,' and the regrettable implication that, once so frizzed, it was one's fate to look like that forever." It would end with one or the other taking the high road back to music.

"I suggest we try 'The Last Rose of Summer' once more, Gertrude, although I suspect it is out of your range."

"My range! You are using rather too much pedal today. It is that time of the month?" And so forth. Whole summer afternoons I would flop in a corner reading, while Mother and Rae sang, played, fought, and made up. It was spirited theatre, and no charge for admission. Like Keats, I sat "among the strife of women's tongues in a hot and parch'd room." When they had run out of retorts, Rae would turn to the piano, single out a certain *solfeggio,* and fish that stream inch by inch until Mother came and made up with her. The next thing you knew, they were in the kitchen eating baked apples in sweet cream.

"Have one more, Rae?"

"I shouldn't."

"Of course you shouldn't."

"No one in Rensselaer County makes baked apples like yours, Gertie. So crisp. The cinnamon!" It was in those moments of reconciliation that their generosity toward each other became truly quixotic. On and on they gurgled and cooed. You'd think the whole history of mankind had marched down the millennia and right up to this moment, and here it would stop and make its stand in the universe.

Rae eked out a "wherewithal" by giving elocution lessons to the daughters of the gentry. As this social class consisted of no more than a dozen families, Rae did not flourish. Even so, because of her there developed a clutch of young women with a penchant for Recitation. *The Rubaiyat of Omar Khayyam* was a favorite, as was Thomas Campbell's epic poem, *Gertrude of Wyoming*. When "Gertrude" died, her namesake was invariably reduced to tears of self-pity:

> Hushed were his Gertrude's lips! But still their bland
> And beautiful expression seemed to melt

> With love that could not die! And still his hand
> She presses to the heart that no more felt.

But Rae's "wherewithal" didn't come entirely from the elocution lessons. Hardly. There was Herman, the elderly, white-bearded, pink lep-
rechaun-cum-dandy who visited her from Albany every Monday
afternoon. (It was the only time when the parlor was silent.) If Rae's
pearls gave off a click of authenticity instead of the dull concussion of
paste, it was entirely due to Herman.

"Oh, that Herman!" muttered Rae to Mother, "with his rummaging."

"Rae, don't!" said Mother. I saw through the keyhole how she held a
shushing finger at her lips and nodded at the parlor door.

"Are you out there? You little sneak!"

"Now Rae, Herman's not so bad. I wonder—what do you object to
most?"

"The way he butters his bread—over and over again, the way a cat
washes its face."

"That is serious."

Both Mother and Rae were in love with Arturo Toscanini and
despised Mussolini. How could Italy have produced two men at such
variance with each other? Both women visited the same fortune teller, a
gypsy named Madame Rosa, who cannily predicted ovations at Music
Hall for mother, and for Rae a romantic liaison: She would fall in love
with a small pink man with a white beard:

"That would be Herman," said Mother.

"Don't!" cried Rae and made retching noises in her throat.

For me, Rae was that extracurricular personage who was indispensable
to the household, the catalyst by which we all flourished. I watched every
move she made—the way her long crimson fingernails clicked on the
piano keys, her knotted necklace of green jade, another of pink coral, the
scent of gardenia, lilac, or mock orange that seemed to emanate from her
mouth. When she was in an elocutionary mood, she rolled her *r*'s, which
sent Billy and me laughing fit to do ourselves damage. Watching the way
she twisted her lips to shape the vowels, Father said she needed to be
wormed. Why hadn't she ever married? I asked Father.

"She's a professional spinster," he said. I wondered how you could earn
a living being that. I asked Rae herself.

"How come you never got married?"

"Married! I should say not! I should never have wanted to behave like such a fool. Spinsterhood is much the more civilized condition. I doubt they have any maiden ladies among the pygmies." I reported this back to Father.

"It's her egotism," he said. "The only husband worthy of her is God Almighty." I reported this back to Rae.

"Like St. Theresa, then," she said brightly.

One April I came down with the mumps. Next thing you know, there was Rae in my bedroom with one of the Hardy Boys books she knew I loved. And she as poor as a bee with only one sting to her name.

"My cheeky beggar," she cooed.

"Don't!" I warned her. "I'm not in the mood."

"What cheek!" said Rae, and made a moue. Rising from my pillows, I pointed to the door. Luckily she set sail before I could think of a name to call her, for which I should have been sorry ever after. Neither Mother nor Rae were to be underestimated in the area of psychology. When properly exasperated by our lollygagging over chores such as tending to the coal stove for the night or shoveling the sidewalk, either one could turn into Lady Macbeth ("Infirm of purpose! Give me the dagger!"), and, snatching the coal scuttle or shovel, do it herself, to our everlasting ignominy.

Then came World War II, and the USO was filled every evening with lonely soldiers and sailors. Such, such was the prevailing mythology. In fact, they were not so much lonely as horny and on the make for the Russell Sage College girls who came to dance with them. Before anyone could protest, Mother had offered herself as a one-woman cabaret, with Rae as accompanist. Night after night, while others of her sex served coffee and cookies and lent sympathetic ears, Mother sang raucous, maudlin songs of Music Hall fame. So that the USO might not be thought louche, she alternated these numbers with songs of a higher tone, such as "I Dreamt I Dwelt in Marble Halls" and "Where My Caravan Has Rested." When she wasn't singing, she danced with the servicemen, flirted, read tea leaves and palms, at which she proved stunningly prophetic, and in general enjoyed World War II to the hilt.

The piano at the USO was no elderly upright like the one in the parlor. From somewhere (Herman again?) Rae had inveigled the use of a rosewood "boudoir grand," into whose concavity a well-upholstered chanteuse might insinuate her form, bosoms and all. A fringed maroon shawl had been negligently thrown upon the top of the instrument. In one number Mother wore it as a babushka and sang a lament that went something like this:

> I didn't raise my boy to be a soldier,
> I brought him up to be my pride and joy.
> Who dares to lay a musket on his shoulder
> To shoot some other mother's darling boy?

Her favorite prop was the fan made of Bolognese hawk feathers, which she flirted open to transform herself from a saucer-eyed orphan into a vamp. No diva enjoyed greater ovations. It wasn't just the voice, which sounded as though a white mouse were ringing a tiny silver bell, it was that blend of gusto and unction with which she rendered innuendo one minute and tragedy the next. More than one youthful eye glistened at the fleeting, crippled smile she let play at her lips at the right moment. Just when the Army and Navy lay in damp tatters at her feet, she'd give Rae the high sign and go bursting into bawdy. I remember only the skeleton of one lyric: there is a young girl who has been betrayed and then abandoned. She is forced to earn a precarious living selling cigars on the street. Was she also selling herself? Her customers were gentlemen in spats and bowlers, real moustache twirlers. The cigars she sold were a nickel apiece. But if she bit off the end, it would cost a penny more. (Each time she sang that last line, there was a tornado of laughter, all the more intense for having followed a sad ballad that would have wet the cheek of Caligula.)

With such a heritage, my musical tastes are a welter of inconsistencies. I don't like rock and roll, acid rock, or jazz. Richard Wagner, Richard Strauss, and Arnold Schönberg—no to all of them, too. Like Tennyson, I prefer "Music that gentlier on the spirit lies / Than tired eyelids over tired eyes." Give me lullabies, ballads, nocturnes, dirges, anything somnifacient. On the other hand, I love fanfares, country western, and every kind of ethnic dance. Mostly I like the songs my mother used to sing. From them I gained an inkling of the divinity that underlies the most vulgar tavern music.

On the occasions that the janitor at the USO defaulted, I was drafted as factotum. Impresario, she called it. When I balked, she called upon my

patriotism and made mention of the "gallant soldiery" who would soon
be off to the battlefields of Europe and Asia, some never to return. There
was nothing to do but go and sweep the floor, set up and then take down
the folding chairs, and help wash cups and saucers. Once I was summoned from the kitchen of the USO, where I was trying to do my Latin
homework. It seemed that La Prima Donna had lost her voice. But the
night was still young! What to do? The next thing I knew, I heard myself
being introduced to the throng with the further announcement that I
would present two "touching ballads that had great relevance to the
times." That these two songs were both of Civil War vintage did not prevent her from making use of them eighty years after the fact. She had
overheard me playing these two mortuary ballads and singing them for
my own private hilarity. I turned her down cold.

"For me?" she whispered.

"Not on your life!"

"For your country, then." I leave unwritten the reluctance with which
I moped to the rosewood "boudoir" piano and began:

> Just before the battle, Mother,
> I am thinking, Dear, of you.
> Lying on the field of battle,
> With the enemy in view.
>
> Comrades all about me lying,
> Filled with thoughts of home and God,
> For they know that on the morrow
> Some will sleep beneath the sod.

All during my performance, Mother and Rae wept shamelessly. Until,
urged toward a high F, my thirteen-year-old larynx gave a croak of defiance and tore the voice to shreds. Mortified, I raced to the end and, vow-
ing matricide, rushed offstage. Hamlet's Gertrude was no more
reprehensible than mine.

"How could you!" I stormed. To which she took no notice, only
remarking on the fun everyone had had. By the next evening, she'd found
her voice and sang her signature number, "Mighty Lak a Rose." At ten
o'clock, having been pelted with *bravi,* she and Rae would close the piano
and stroll home, swollen with patriotism. In the softer color of retrospect,
the two of them were the most "gallant soldiery" at the Troy USO.

Years later I visited Rae at a Retirement Home. Still half carnival, half jubilee, she received me ensconced in a velvet armchair (*fauteuil,* she called it). There, swathed in scarves and with a Persian camel bag as a lap rug, she was waiting pleasantly enough for martyrdom. Her face was a cake of scented soap.

"Cupid!" I implored, "have mercy!" Her smile! A fan made of feathers hung from one wrist. I recognized it at once.

"Your mother bequeathed it to me," said Rae. "The feathers, you know, are those of the extinct Bolognese hawk."

"Yes, I know." It was breakfast time, so naturally Rae was wearing her pearls.

"Have I been missed?" I wanted to know.

"Nobody but me has died of it," she replied. "I've a touch of rheumatism."

"A touch of anything does a person good."

"That what they taught you in medical school? Fresh boy!" Then, flirting open the fan with truly Spanish gravity, she asked if I were in love. I told her no. She sized me up and down.

"A heart ought not to remain unoccupied for too long," she said. "It dries out."

"What about Herman?" I asked.

"Oh, Herman died." She said it with just a hint of archness, I thought, then permitted herself a crafty little smile. It seems that before his demise, Herman had set Rae up in the manner she felt was only her due. I never saw her after that visit. Now I have the Bolognese fan. Once or twice I took it out and tried to flick it open the way she had. But it wouldn't work. For me, opening a fan is a two-handed job.

In addition to Rae, there were often visitors. Grandma Selzer wintered in the bay window, her toothless mouth hemmed in by overlapping creases like the hoofprints of a donkey. Her diet consisted of grapefruit, farmer's cheese, and coffee with cream. All day long she mumbled and crooned to herself, seesawing like an owl and waiting for Father to finish his evening office hours and come upstairs so that she could recite to him the iliad of her aches and pains and her daughter-in-law's iniquities. The martyrdom of the son was the mother's only pleasure.

Every summer, the tempo of life tripled with the arrival of our cousins from Canada. Florence, Esther, and Lily were sent down, sometimes one at a time, sometimes all three at once, to spend their vacation and to acquire a bit of "finish" under Mother's guidance. For Billy, as for me, the presence in the house of three female cousins who were ten to fifteen years older than ourselves was a cause for elation and an opportunity to spy on them unawares. They were not unlike those other Three Sisters, Masha, Olga, and Irina, only theirs was a Moscow of the heart. A good deal of time was spent mooning over the three handsome young men who would appear out of nowhere to kneel at their feet. They were too merry-hearted to sustain the fantasy for very long. Soon would come an ethnic shrug, followed by a harmonizing of "Auf'n Pripachickel" or "Rozhinkes mit Mandeln." Lily was the prettiest and the youngest. At fifteen, she seemed always to be in shy bloom. In addition to every one of the graces, she had a glamorous husk in her voice that made our boy-hearts pound to hear it. Billy was unashamedly in love with her. I explained incest to him.

"Go to Hell with your insects!" he retorted and worshiped on.

It was Florence who came running the morning I woke up blind. There was my body—I could feel it. But I couldn't see! A shriek of ter-ror brought Florence running to my bedside.

"I've gone blind!" I howled.

"Let me see," said Florence. Next thing you know, she'd dipped a cloth and was soaking open my eyelids that had become encrusted from con-junctivitis. When she gently parted them with her fingers, it was as if God had just created the world all over again.

Esther was the first of a number of women to offer me more bliss than it is in my capacity to receive. Passionate, and with all her mighty urges foaming, she was a household menace. Without warning, I'd be scooped onto her lap and subjected to a swarm of wet kisses and hard pinches against which I was helpless, until, having had her fill of me, she'd stand up as if to shake off a cat. How was I to tell her that she had picked up a kitten that didn't want to be stroked? I didn't have the heart. Once, when I complained to mother and showed her my pinch marks, she said to never mind.

"Esther bites with the soft tooth of love." So that was that. Mother adored her three nieces, as they did her. I don't remember a single word spoken in coldness among them. Esther, a gifted *raconteuse,* reenacted her childhood in Montreal among the immigrant poor of St. Urbain Street. This she delivered in a patois that was half English, half Yiddish.

She had a knack of bringing a character to life with a few words. One woman was "meese vee a faird" (ugly as a horse). Furthermore she had a "kalte neshuma" (a cold heart). The landlord of their tenement was a "ballagoolah" (Romanian truck driver). Each story was laced with curses, exhortations, lyric apostrophes, ejaculations, invocations of the dead, and volleys of sobs. Whenever Florence thought Esther was getting too much attention, she punctuated the story with small asides that were to Esther like the wounds of a stiletto.

"She talks too much," Flo muttered to the vacant air. "Pishkopf" (piss-head), she hissed during a spate of Esther's tears, until, thrown off her stride, Esther turned on her in fury.

"Go scold the geese in the attic!"

"You're farbisseneh!" (all bitten up).

"A cholaria!" (a cholera on you).

"A chemna chalaria!" (a black cholera on you).

"Paskootzvah!" (rotten).

"Fakrimpta punim!" (twisted face).

By the time it was over, you'd have to go to Rabelais for something gamier. Before long the insults were being emphasized with small slaps, then hilarious laughter, and next thing you know, they were crooning:

> My sweetheart's the man in the moon.
> I'm going to marry him soon.
> And behind some dark cloud
> Where no one is allowed,
> I'll make love to the man in the moon.

It was a household where women were dominant. Father chose to absent himself from a good deal of the felicity, and Grandpa stayed in his room at the back of downstairs, which he made clear was forbidden to women and children. It was from Mother, Rae, and the Three Sisters that Billy and I formed an idea of the opposite sex. It came as no small shock years later to find we'd been given a skewed vision. After some years the cousins stopped coming to Troy. One by one they journeyed to "their Moscow," only to find that it wasn't much different from St. Urbain Street. They just had to find that out for themselves.

OLIVE

I was seven years old when the house fire put an end to our life on Second Street. Mother said the fire was not without benefit.

"People," she said, looking at Billy and me, "are so much better behaved after a catastrophe, the way the Israelites improved after the Golden Calf affair." A week later we moved to Fifth Avenue, between Jacob and Federal Streets. The year was 1935, and Troy wore the tattered uniform of the Great Depression. Near the south end of the block, railroad tracks crossed the street. The noise and vibration of endless freight trains soon became the background of our lives. The new house was a two-story brick building, vintage early-nineteenth century, and painted a dark brown. As on Second Street, Father's office was on the first floor and the family lived upstairs. Any regrets at having to leave our beloved Second Street vanished at the sight of the crystal chandelier in what was to become the Waiting Room of the office. The wall lamps there wore shields of thin translucent mollusk shell, and were tasseled with pendants of crystal. Such unaccustomed luxury was further manifested in the chastely draped cherubim that sashayed through pinkish clouds on the ceiling of the Waiting Room. Billy and I lay on the floor and watched the pudgy angelets floating among the clouds, wondering if they were the same ones that accompanied the Virgin when she ascended. Father said he had no idea, but he took them as proof positive that the angels had sex in Heaven. For which he received a long historical look from Mother. To my dismay, Father announced that the painted ceiling and the chandelier wouldn't do, not in a town clamped in the jaws of the Depression. They would resurrect the Sumptuary Laws, he said, and throw us all in jail on a charge of Ostentation. Besides, he continued, it couldn't be good for the waiting patients to be confronted with an image of the next world, no matter how sickeningly sweet. Next thing you know, he had dismantled the chandelier and the wall lamps, put all the crystal in boxes and down into the cellar. That was the last we saw of it. Then he stood on a ladder and painted over the clouds and cherubs. It seemed to me an act not only of blasphemy, but of vandalism.

Upstairs? Oh, you can decorate it however you want to. Be sure to include any number of small oriental rugs, all quite worn, a glass-front bookcase, a roll-top desk with lots of cubbyholes, and a number of fat dressers drunk on mothballs. Don't forget the dumbwaiter that connected Father's Examining Room below with a hall closet above. It had long since ceased to be put to the use for which it had been installed and was now a means of forbidden eavesdropping on the sacred rites being conducted downstairs. In the bathroom there was a stained glass window depicting the rescue of Andromeda from the dragon by Perseus. The only objects of any value were a Duncan Phyfe sideboard in the dining room and a grandfather's clock on the landing of the staircase. This was the beating heart of the household. Every hour it cleared its throat and bonged out the hour, basso profundo. "Keep it going, and it will keep us going," said Father, who wound it with immense ceremony every Sunday morning. Both the sideboard and the clock had been willed to Father by old Mrs. Wisemann, a "shut-in," as payment for six years of house calls on which he took care of her and her collie "Brownie," who turned out to be the great love of Father's life. There was also a broncho-spastic mantel clock with maddening Winchester chimes that lied about the time with tuneful insolence. I died to take a hammer to it.

The layout of the house was much the same as the house on Second Street. Down the length of the flat ran a narrow hall that blistered into a large bay window at the front. Here Grandma Selzer stayed during her annual visit. Next to that was the parlor, with two windows overlooking the street and one facing the churchyard next door. Proceeding to the rear, there was the master bedroom, followed by the large marble bathroom where Perseus and Andromeda kept us company at our ablutions. The huge claw-footed tub could have accommodated the whole family. Still farther to the rear was the bedroom Billy and I shared. From Mother I have inherited a firm belief in the influence of décor upon health. Take wallpaper, for instance. After a while, there is no question that you begin to take on its pattern and color. It is the instinct of all creatures to blend in with their environment for purposes of concealment and safety. Until I was ten, our bedroom wore on its walls an endless grove of lemon trees. When Billy and I both turned an unhealthy sallow hue, Mother blamed it on all that green and yellow. The next thing you know, she had stripped off the lemon trees and put up baskets of newly harvested apples.

"That'll put color in your cheeks," she said as the last roll was pasted up. And so it did. That was in March, and come June, we were as ruddy as a couple of McIntoshes. Once or twice in the years since, when all else has failed to restore a wilting patient, I have suggested to the dubious next-of-kin that they redecorate the sickroom. You'd be surprised at how quickly the patient turned the corner.

Behind our bedroom was the dining room, with the kitchen hardly more than a small caboose at the rear. What with the prostitutes and an epidemic of tuberculosis in the city, Mother insisted on washing the dollars collected from the patients. There was a wooden rack in the kitchen where she hung them up to dry. More than once, I was sent to the grocery store and had to pay with a damp dollar. It was given and received between thumb and forefinger. A backstairs led down from the kitchen to the room where Grandpa lived behind the office.

Of all the contents of the house, it was the dumbwaiter that was fated. It happened that, in accordance with the principles of acoustics, the dumbwaiter gathered and augmented the sounds of the Examining Room in such a way that an illicit ear in the closet upstairs might overhear to its heart's content. Little did Father know that even as he listened to the sounds of the internal organs of his patients with his stethoscope, or to the sad litany of their ruined lives, I was listening too. One day, while I was cocking an ear over the shaft, the closet door opened behind me, and I felt myself grasped and hauled. There followed three hard potches on the bottom, the only ones Mother ever gave me. An operatic rage inhabited her face; her earlobes shook with it. And more—a biblical sorrow at the discovery that her child had committed the unthinkable, and was as good as dead. In a moment she would rend her garments, strew ashes upon her head. Minutes later, she had regained her composure. Life would go on as before. But for weeks I searched her face for traces of the hurricane that had swept it. She never mentioned it again, but I couldn't help wondering if what she was protecting was not the privacy of the patients that in my villainy I had invaded, but the very integrity of the household. Was there something I might hear in that eavesdropping that would topple the fragile structure of the family? I never think of that dumbwaiter without a shudder of shame and remorse.

The house was next door to a small Protestant church of uncertain denomination. This hardly mattered, as the church was virtually unattended and had no minister. An old woman lived in a cubicle somewhere inside the church, in return for sweeping and dusting the premises. She had been unfortunate at the baptismal font. Her given name was Olive. Now and then, from the parlor window, she could be spotted standing stock-still in the churchyard for minutes at a time, then scampering out of sight like some wary creature. Naturally, I hastened to make her acquaintance, but it was a year before she stopped perceiving me as a threat and all of four years before Olive and I were on neighborly terms.

One day I caught sight of her trimming a hedge, leaf by leaf, with a pair of tiny manicure scissors. I found the family shears and went outside to help. From where I stood, the old woman seemed grayer, thinner, dryer, more stooped than ever. I could see her shoulder blades working, working beneath her cotton dress. I started trimming. Without turning, Olive spoke.

"It's ready to be seen," she murmured. I didn't have to ask what. It was household knowledge that Olive, in addition to her janitorial duties, was engaged in making "objects of virtue," whatever they were. Over the years I had made polite requests to be shown one of these objects. "Not ready," Olive had always said. And now, at last, it was. There was a momentousness in the way she pocketed her scissors, removed her gardening gloves, and led the way into the church. I followed her to the altar. With each step the old woman took on more and more formality until she might have been a priestess bearing fire into the temple. At the altar, she pointed to what she had created. Spread across the top of the altar was a motto made of red felt. "In Deo Speramus" had been stitched into it with gold thread. On top of that was a white wax cross with a trail of ivy encircling it. The entire work was frosted with what looked like sugar and dots of white paste.

"Now, Olive . . ." I began. But she raised a shushing finger to her lips to indicate that only silence was appropriate. Here was no spidery old woman, I saw, but an artist with a demeanor showing all the pride and responsibility of a genius toward her work. She seemed suddenly to have grown in stature, filled out, taken on a monumental stance. I could almost see the flag she held aloft, whose other end wound about her breasts and thighs.

"It's Latin," said Olive. "Means 'In God Is Our Hope.'" Just then a mouse emerged from behind the altar, skittered across the motto to the wax Cross, and began to feast on a dot of paste. Either Olive hadn't noticed, such being her state of transport, or she had, and chose to rise magnificently above the verminous world. Somehow, the addition of that mouse to the dead composition touched it to urgent and immediate life. A mouse was precisely what had been missing. For the first time I was conscious of standing in the presence of a work of art, one driven by the engine of piety. It was a thrilling moment. I like to think now that the mouse had been dispatched to this church by the Angel Gabriel himself.

On the way back down the center aisle, I noticed three white petals on the dark red carpet. Peony, I diagnosed. It was too early for roses. The hymnals were neatly ensconced in the racks at the front of each pew. The pew gates were closed and latched. A few feeble rays of sun shone through the stained glass. There was a distinctly Protestant smell throughout. At the door of the church Olive turned and, for the first and only time, held out her hand for me to take. It was tiny, the fingers as white and cold as church candles. As though the wax of the "virtue" had once been part of her hand and had run out of those fingers.

THE SPINSTERS OF ELD

The greatest loss to American education was the disappearance from the classroom of the Irish spinster schoolteacher. Pedagogy has yet to recover from the blow. Time was, when in every Irish family there was one daughter who dreamt of rising above the general ignorance and sooty poverty that were the lot of the recently immigrated. With no little fear did she announce that no, she would not go into the mills and factories; she would not enter the convent; she would not place herself in "service" or the department stores. Instead she would go to Normal School, the low-cost system of teacher training that existed throughout the Northeast. To learning, culture, and refinement she took with all the gusto of long deprivation. Soon the map of her mind had fewer and fewer areas marked "terra incognita." It was not without cost, for the learning lifted her above her peers and made her unsuitable as wife to one of the hardworking Irishmen, who were all but illiterate. Were she to marry such a man, one who saw art and culture as objects of derision (never mind that the derision sprang from rage and frustration), bitterness and estrangement would be her lot. And so she remained single and, in all likelihood, virginal. The wealth of her unrealized passion was there to be delivered intact in the classroom and lavished on her pupils. Myself, I lapped it up as if I were a kitten at a dish of cream. Never shall I forget Miss Cleary's happiness at my first bit of writing, a paragraph on *Ivanhoe*. It must have been for her irrefutable evidence that her life was worthwhile. I was her fulfillment.

Upon receiving her certificate from Normal School, the Irish spinster came to reign in the classroom, transforming that stuffy, overheated, malodorous place into very Heaven. Year after year she humanized us with her noble love of learning and her instinct that if you arouse a perception of beauty and truth in a child, you will create a better person. Her presence at the front of the classroom was a rebuke to all that was base and ordinary. It was she, gallant and long-suffering, who magnified America from a land of mere enterprise into a country of great cultural sophistication.

What was she like? Sharp of eye and ear she was, her senses growing more acute with age. From the front of the room she could hear the click of a mouse's tooth against a grain of rice in the coat closet at the rear. Coiffed, perfumed, and dressed beautifully, she was an eternal mystery. We were besotted with her, died to know how old she was, spent hours guessing, all the way from twenty to forty-seven. From where she sat, the sight of her pupils could not have been edifying. Whose spirits could possibly be lifted by a roomful of thin dirty necks and ribbons of snot? Called upon to recite, Reluctance Personified would stand beside his desk, give a hitch to his britches, run the back of his hand under his nose, and begin:

> The shades of night were falling fast,
> As through an Alpine village passed
> A youth who bore through snow and ice
> A banner with the strange device.
> Excelsior!

Here, in a smelly, humid classroom in School 5 in the town of Troy in upstate New York at the height of the Depression, was the reenactment of Longfellow's poem of indomitability, of going ahead against all odds. Years later, as a medical student working in a free clinic, I parted a curtain, stepped inside a cubicle, and watched a man remove his soiled underwear to show me his wound. The curtains never did close behind me, hold them together as I might, so that whatever privacy there was depended on my body to block the view from the corridor. All at once

there came a rush of memory, and I saw again the same painful humiliation as that of the young boy in recitation, his mindless obedience to
authority, his air of hopelessness. No banner with a strange device this
time, but a wound, by which the most pitiable human being is ennobled.

By some intercontinental fluke, the Trojans of the 1930s had picked
up all of the *h*'s that the Cockneys had dropped. Fully half of the second
grade gave each *h* a gust of air—"e, f, g, haitch," went the spoken alpha-
bet. I remember Miss Mahoney's valiant struggle to deflate that "haitch,"
as she insisted over and over that we say "aitch." "Haitch," would come
the refrain, while the powder on her cheeks went on cracking. Miss
Mahoney was a congenital knitter. It had come riding in on her DNA.
Doubtless, she had knitted in the womb. She knitted in the classroom;
she knitted at the library; she knitted on the trolley. She would have knitted at the foot of the Cross. Miss Feerick had a way of looking out the
window while you were reciting, then saying "thank you" in a way to let
you know you'd performed abominably. Miss Vaughan, long after she'd
gone stone-deaf, continued to call out "Silence!" from time to time, out
of sheer habit. Miss McInerney was a large woman of the type called
"handsome," which I have since come to recognize as faint praise for a
plain woman with good posture. Indeed, she carried herself well, and
was gifted with Body English to an astonishing degree. She had a way of
lengthening her nose when she wished to express disapproval, and could
cause her bosom to swell to alarming proportions at the least lapse of
decorum. Miss McInerney's method of teaching was to waft small puffs
of temperament over the class.

"You must all sit up perfectly straight," she admonished. "The com-
pass needle must always point due north." And she would walk up and
down the aisles, tapping each spine into alignment with a yardstick. "It is
scandalous the way children are nowadays permitted to tilt in all directions. I cannot think for the disorder." Father said it was a good thing
none of the children had kyphoscoliosis.

On the last day of school, I muttered the word "Hag." It was amazing
how good it made me feel to say it. But I had been overheard and was
sent to the Principal's Office for a stroke with the ferrule, which I thought
was easily worth it. Only to find out that, come September, Miss
McInerney had been transferred to the next grade higher. I was to pay
for that "Hag" all year long. Ever since, I've learned to keep my tongue
"engaoled; doubly portcullised with lips and teeth." That's how to get

along in grammar school, matrimony, and a hundred other predica-
ments. It is entirely due to Miss McInerney that I have never learned
when to use "which" and when to use "that." Even now I will spend a
whole morning changing all my "that's" back into "which's."

Of all the subjects taught at School 5, Spelling was prime. Frankly,
I'm opposed to any effort toward unanimity in spelling. Surely it takes a
good deal of the charm out of writing always to spell a word in exactly
the same way. Sir Thomas Browne's wife, Dorothy, wrote letters whose
chief appeal lies in her intuitive vision of how a word should look on the
page. She liked her "sheus" to be "eythar pinke or blew." The children of
Troy couldn't spell worth a darn and furthermore we didn't care. Take
the word "chessnut." That's how we said it, and that's how it was spelled.

"What's a chestnut, anyway?" said my brother Billy. "I wouldn't want
to have one of mine up there."

I recall the winter that altogether too much was made of the twenty-
ninth of February by Miss Rogers, she of the volcanic temper. We feared
her as we would have feared one of the Weird Sisters in *Macbeth*. "The
twenty-ninth of February!" she rhapsodized, "'tis rare as the visit of an
angel, and therefore more precious than the other three hundred and
sixty-five." But then, what is insanity? Was Moses crazy when he
smashed the God-given tablets at the foot of Sinai? This same Miss
Rogers rendered "The Lost Chord" in a chesty contralto *au jus* that sent
the very ink in our wells undulating. The harp of Orpheus was not more
riveting. No one alive could be that "weary and ill at ease." Whenever
she sang "Seated one day at the organ. . . ," Billy slew me with a filthy
wink.

Second only to Spelling and Ciphering was the agony of the Palmer
Method of Penmanship. Mastery of it was equivalent to moral purity.
Inability to keep within the lines as you made the endless coil of *O*'s without taking the pen from the paper was evidence of character deficiency.
One would come to no good end. It was only a step from the Palmer
Method to the science of Graphology, which held that a person could be
re-created from his handwriting—complexes, perversions, prejudices,
and all. There was an itinerant penmanship teacher, Miss Kinsella, who
made the rounds of all the grammar schools in Rensselaer County. She
was chock full of pithy sayings and rhymes: "With time and patience, the
mulberry leaf becomes satin" was one of hers. Of her poetry, I have only
two stanzas:

Who would not shun their time and sight to waste
On a vile scrawl, blurred, shapeless, half-defaced?
Not even Love's own patience could essay
To read "I'm thine!" if marr'd in such a way.

Then, Oh! Abuse not the gray-goose quill,
Make it indeed obedient to thy will.
And bid it move in harmony with thought,
Tracing in beauty what the mind has wrought.

The injury that the itinerant Miss Kinsella did to my penmanship has been permanent. Never a fine filigree, in the decade of my retirement my handwriting has let go of all pretense at legibility and collapsed into an invertebrate strew upon the page. The *e*'s and *a*'s are mere dented bulges. The *l*'s, *d*'s, and *b*'s are drunk and teeter every which way. I'd think twice before letting this scrawl be seen by anyone who didn't love me blindly. I'm sure it reveals something darkly personal in my nature, some long-repressed rottenness that *will* come out. This quite agrees with my theory that handwriting itself is more important than what is written in it. Further evidence of such deterioration is seen in a new indecisiveness over when to cross my *x*'s. As in *axle* or *laxative*. Is it better to stop and cross right then and there, or go on to the end of the word and then go back to cross? The same applies to the dotting of *i*'s and the crossing of *t*'s. These are dilemmas that those who process their words don't have to face. They may also be an early sign of senile dementia. Now and then it comes over me that I should stop this infernal scribbling altogether and just nestle among the velvet pillows of achievement. But I can't. I am what I am, and shall doubtless scrawl on to the end.

The school janitor, Mr. Foley—bald, paunchy, and all but toothless—was no Irish spinster's dream of romance. Still, he served as the obsequious, dutiful "husband," whose attention each teacher devised to capture. He was summoned whenever it was suspected that a room was too hot or too cold, or should there be the least danger of running out of colored chalk. I suspect now that Mr. Foley could have had his way with any number of these ladies, but such inclinations were not given to him. Mr. Foley was utterly indifferent to the carnal side of janitation. Mr. Devlin, the Principal, was the only other adult male in the building. He was given to bold, colorful speech, while delivering a stroke or two on the palm with his ferrule, one end of which was flattened into a disk with a central hole, the better to raise a blister with.

"This should shorten your stay in Purgatory by ten minutes," he said to me once, said it with revolting jocularity.

It was with Miss Feerick that I first studied poetry. All the poets taught at School 5 had three names: James Whitcomb Riley, Henry Wadsworth Longfellow, John Greenleaf Whittier, James Russell Lowell, and so on. Trinomality was the basic condition of the poet. How Homer and Dante managed to overcome that handicap, I'm sure I don't know. But then, what did either of them write that could hold a candle to the one lit at both its ends by Edna St. Vincent Millay? It was in the third grade that Miss Feerick gave me a present of a book of poems. She had chosen them, cut them out, and pasted them onto the leaves of a blank notebook. In it were all my old darlings—"The Children's Hour," "The Wreck of the Hesperus," "Snowbound," "The Chambered Nautilus," "Excelsior," "The Village Blacksmith," "The Charge of the Light Brigade," and a dozen others. For years it was my favorite possession. At last, fingered and caressed beyond the durability of mere paper and paste, the book disintegrated in my hands. But not before I had committed all the poems in it to memory. So embedded are they in my brain, that I have only to begin and the whole poem will come marching out. I have received no other gift since that can match it in price.

But now it is more than sixty years later, and I am at the Laurel View Country Club in Hamden, Connecticut. The event is the Spring Luncheon of the New Haven Women's Club. I am the guest speaker. The audience is made up of a hundred or so retired schoolteachers. A hundred Irish spinsters ranging in age from sixty-five to ninety-five. They have dressed for the occasion, mostly in bright-colored silk. From the podium, they are a bed of mixed tulips. A great many are so full of figure as to suggest upholstery. I am the lone male present. Without half these women, no one in New Haven would have learned to read and write; nor would they have known who Joan of Arc was or anything about the French and Indian War. They too scurried into retirement when the girls in the sixth grade had grown bigger than they were, wore great gold hoops in their ears, chewed wads of gum in class, and led active sex lives. It is at the feet of these schoolteachers that I laid my heart; it is they who stir the coals of memory.

Several days before the affair, Miss Peggy Coonan called up.

"You can have baked scrod, baked chicken breast, or pork tenderloin. Which do you want?" I picked the pork tenderloin. "You picked the best

one!" she cried, as if I had called out the right answer in class. I hadn't
been at the Laurel View Country Club more than three minutes when
Miss Ahearn came up and handed me a vodka on the rocks with a twist.

"I read somewhere that's what you like," she said. She further
informed me that she had been my wife's fifth-grade teacher, which
would put her around age ninety.

"What's that you're drinking?" I asked her.

"A kamikaze," she said, and took a demure sip.

"It means 'divine wind' in Japanese," I said. She gave me a look that
said to stop showing off. Immediately, where I had stood, there was only
a little mist of insulted pride.

Either I fall in love with absurd ease, or these hundred were each my
cup of tea. My kamikaze, rather. They are engaged in charitable deeds;
they do good works; they are generous and full of humor; they relish their
retirement. Standing before them after lunch, I strove to acknowledge
my debt, but for once I couldn't find the words. Instead I told them about
the notebook of poems and my essay on *Ivanhoe* and the Palmer Method
of Penmanship. And then I began to recite "The Village Blacksmith."
What was my dismay when in the middle of the second stanza my mind
went blank! I couldn't think of the next line! There followed a long
moment of awkward silence. All at once, from a nearby table, picking up
where I had left off, one of the teachers continued the poem, giving me a
hint, her voice rich with urging and kindliness:

> His brow is wet with honest sweat,
> He earns whate'er he can,
> And looks the whole world in the face.
> For he owes not any man.

When she paused to let me go on, and still I couldn't, there came a voice
from another table:

> Week in, week out, from morn 'til night,
> You can hear his bellows blow;
> You can hear him swing his heavy sledge,
> With measured beat and slow.

And so it went around the room, from table to table, until I heard

He hears his daughter's voice,
Singing in the village choir,
And it makes his heart rejoice.

With that, I took up the poem and finished it to great applause. All at once the decades rolled back, and I was once again standing at my small desk in the classroom at School 5 in Troy, with my beloved teacher prompting. The Irish spinster schoolteacher is no more. We shall never see her like again. Now who will protect us from the vulgarity that has tainted the public taste? As it was foretold, "And the teachers shall shine as the firmament." Just so, has it come to pass. All praise to them, all praise.

The Boy in the Shirt

Of the many strange characters that populate the pages of the Bible, none is more mysterious than the Boy in the Shirt. He is mentioned only in the Gospel of Mark, and there only once, in verse 14:51–52. The scene is the "Agony" in the Garden. Jesus has just been seized by the soldiers and is being taken under arrest:

> A young man who followed him had nothing on but a linen cloth. They caught hold of him, but he left the cloth in their hands and ran away naked.

The loose garment of fine linen was called in the Greek Gospel a *sindon*. It was not a cloak, nor a singlet, nor a shirt, but had something of all three in it. The young man is never seen or heard from again. Who was he? What was he doing in the Garden of Gethsemane on the night of the Agony? How did Mark know of his existence, since he himself was not present before or during the arrest of Jesus in the Garden? The three Disciples who were present, James, Peter, and John the Evangelist, had all fallen asleep while Jesus prayed for the strength and courage to undergo his sacrifice. This, despite the admonishment by Jesus that they remain awake and on guard as he did not want to be seized at that time. They were unaware of the presence of the Boy, who had followed Jesus from the house of the Last Supper to the Mount of Olives. The only other Disciple present was Judas, who arrived later with the arresting soldiers in order to mark Jesus with his fatal kiss. Why was the Boy dressed only in a loose garment of fine linen? Two thousand years of biblical scholarship have failed to shed light on this enigmatic figure.

Among the outlandish theories proposed by otherwise sensible scholars have been these: the Boy is an angel, as evidenced by his characteristically brief visit; the Boy is a somnambulant who rose from his bed and walked to the Garden while asleep, only to awaken in a fright at the moment of arrest; he is the symbol of all those who have abandoned Jesus; he is Mark himself, this despite that Mark was not on the Mount of Olives on the night of the Agony. I believe that he was flesh and blood, not a symbol of anything. I do not believe that he was just a "happen," as Emily Dickinson would say, or that he was popped in to lend an air of reality to the scene, a seemingly unimportant and incidental detail. At the risk of being thought irreverent, I will say that Mark was far from a great writer. His version of the Gospel is clumsy, disjointed. It moves erratically, now forward, now back. The ending is abrupt, truncated, and totally unsatisfying. It simply peters out with the women at the tomb; they find that the stone has been rolled away; inside there is a young man in white who tells them not to be afraid, that Christ has risen and is on the way to Galilee. He tells them to inform Peter and the Disciples, but they leave the scene in a state of great fear and tell no one. And that was to be that, until Matthew and Luke came along with a better ending. Nor was Mark a sophisticated enough artist to use such a "writerly" trick as to insert himself into the narrative to show his close relation to the Passion, the kind of thing Alfred Hitchcock did in his films or the Renaissance painters did with a small self-portrait among a crowd of soldiers or monks. Finally, I reject the attempts by certain scholars to dismiss the Boy in the Shirt as an inconvenience.

A later version of the Gospel of Mark would have us believe that the Boy was one who had been raised from the dead by Jesus and followed him out of "love" for him. From a purely literary aspect, this is not particularly interesting or dramatic. But since when, you ask, is the Bible obligated to be interesting or dramatic? A better story would have the Boy not run away at the time of arrest, but remain to be crucified alongside Jesus, and to be welcomed into the Kingdom of Heaven from the Cross. But that would be pure invention. Even were the events in the Garden of Gethsemane known in the order in which they occurred, the historian is under an obligation to render them vividly. Ordinary "straightforward" telling does not convey the "real real that lies beneath the real," the inmost essence.

This second or "secret" gospel of Mark would place the Boy among those recipients of magic or miraculous acts. I am of the opinion that the power of any religion is inversely proportional to the incidence of the miraculous and the magical in its scripture or torah. Were I to write a new gospel, it would not contain a single incidence of the supernatural. Magic and miracle are the easy, lazy tools of persuasion. When I read in the newspaper that the Virgin Mary has once again been sighted in the branches of a maple tree in Wooster Square, or that Satan yet prowls and slavers in the Men's Room at Union train station, my atheism is bolstered to the same degree as is the devotion of the credulous.

Could it be that the young man had once looked upon Jesus, fallen under his spell, then followed him in hopes of being baptized by him? Could that be why he was wearing only a loose single garment? As for what actually happened, we shall never know. Still, there are those who will cling to King Alfred and the legendary burnt cakes no matter the evidence to the contrary. But "reading" any work of art, sculpture, painting, music, or poetry involves the bent and prejudice of the interpreter. It can't be helped. The finished work, once published and put abroad, is no longer the sole possession of the artist, but has become the blended creation of the one who made it and the one who is "appreciating" it. In such a collaboration, the event depicted becomes something else entirely.

Let me try to reconstruct the event:

It is the night of the Agony. There is a fever in Jerusalem, a current of unrest. For some time the religious authorities have had cause to worry that their hold on the Jewish people will come undone. Jesus "the Magician," with his brilliance, intensity, and the hypnotic effect of his gaze, has won a following. There have been mass baptisms; miracles have been witnessed and word of them has spread. He cannot be allowed to continue. He is an enemy of the state, a revolutionary. He is the self-styled King of the Jews.

Jesus and his Disciples have come together in Jerusalem to celebrate the Passover. But where was the feast to be held?

"Go into the city," Jesus tells the Disciples, "and a man carrying a jar of water will meet you. Follow him. When he enters a house, it will be there, in a room upstairs where we shall celebrate the feast." The spacious room upstairs will ever afterward be called the Coenaculum. O, let me imagine it:

In each corner of the long, low-ceilinged room is an oil lamp atop a tall stand. The play of light upon the wooden walls and stone floor gives the room a vitality as though it, too, were a creature, breathing and throbbing. It is night and the air is chilly. A wood fire has been set in a grate beneath a chimney. A long table with benches on each side occupies the greater part of the room. It has been set with a cloth, upon which rest baskets of unleavened bread and carafes of red wine. The twelve Disciples and Jesus sit, or rather recline, on the benches. Jesus is conducting the meal in Aramaic. He announces to the men that one of them will betray him. They are shocked, and each asks the question "Is it I?" He does not answer, only repeats that one of those at the table will betray him. The meal rises to a mystical crescendo as Jesus bids them eat "my flesh," and drink "my blood," and thereby become one with him.

While Jesus and the Disciples are reclining at the Passover feast, a crowd has gathered in the street below. Among those present is a youth clad only in a loose white garment of fine linen, this despite the chilliness of the night. After all, in the courtyard of the High Priest fires have been lit for warmth. It is no night to be abroad in so flimsy a garment. He watches as each of the twelve Disciples enters the house. The last to arrive is Jesus, who, as he passes the Boy, turns to face him, then raises his walking stick, which is curved like a shepherd's crook, and shakes it in greeting. After a few minutes, the Boy, Gil-od, as if in accordance with a will other than his own, detaches himself from the crowd and slips through the doorway into the house and goes upstairs. In the corridor nearby, Gil-od sees thirteen pairs of well-worn sandals, side by side. For a long moment he stands in the doorway of the room where the feast is being held, listening as Jesus instructs the others to eat his body and drink his blood. The words inflame the youth. The blood rushes to his face, he feels dizzy. He looks up to find that Jesus has seen him. To the dazzled Boy, the face of Jesus gleams, as if with an internal light. It is as if he had reached out and turned the Boy's head with his hands, bringing his face directly into the ardent and intense beam of his gaze. His gaze! That seems to stroke the Boy's body like a hand. At last Jesus turns back to the table, and the cord is severed. The Boy returns to the street where he will wait for the celebrants to reappear.

When the Passover feast is over, Jesus, accompanied by three of the
Disciples, James, John, and Peter, makes his way to the Mount of Olives.
They descend from the city of Jerusalem via a narrow steep street of stone
steps into the Valley of Kidron, cross a narrow stream at the bottom, and
from there make their ascent of the Mount of Olives, whose slope bears
the Garden of Gethsemane. Unbeknownst to them, they are being followed by the Boy in the Shirt.

The Garden of Gethsemane is a large "park" with many ancient olive,
cypress, cedar, and oak trees, as well as a number of tall stately date palms,
fig trees, and lower shrubs, among which is a prickly thorn bush, later
said to be the source of the crown of thorns. The olive trees, some a thousand years old, are well and precisely disposed in equidistant rows. They
reach out to one another, growing closer together each year. From the
base of the Mount there arise a number of paths, each of which leads to a
different part of the slopes. One, the main and most traveled path, is
really a road leading into the olive grove itself. Near the bottom there
is the huge olive press for extracting the oil from the fruit. Donkeys are
the bearers of this oil into the city of Jerusalem. A second path leads to
the tombs of the Jews, where the holy men, rabbis, learned scholars, and
high priests are buried. Funeral processions are conducted along this
path. A third path leads into an area of wilderness, where there are only
rocks and stunted trees. A fourth leads into the Garden of Gethsemane,
and a fifth ascends to the summit of the Mount and there becomes
increasingly uncertain and narrow, until nothing remains of it save the
legend that it turns to a cloud upon which the righteous can be carried to
heaven. It is also the means by which the Messiah, when he returns, will
descend to the earth. There are other paths, too, that close behind you as
you walk them.

At night the Mount is deserted, save for stargazers, the homeless, cut-
throats, bandits, and prostitutes of both sexes. Throughout the park there
are narrow winding paths obscured by dense foliage. By day, the silver of
the olive trees contrasts with the somber dark green of the cypress.
Having been mentioned in Ezekiel as the place where the Messiah will
appear on earth, the Mount of Olives is a retreat perfectly suited as the
setting of an event of great spiritual intensity.

The rustling of the olive leaves in the wind induces a state of trance or
meditation, as when one sinks so deeply into music that one becomes the
music while it lasts. All night the vertiginous aroma of spices—myrrh

and balsam and henna—are intoxicating to the senses and further blur the boundary between what is real and what is imagined. It is a place that expresses itself upon all who venture there, a place destined to become emblematic. It is here that Jesus has come to pray, to ask God that, if at all possible, He might let this cup pass from his lips. He is not ready to be captured and taken by the gendarmes and so has commanded his three Disciples to stand watch and not to fall asleep. But, overcome with weariness, or is it wine? they do fall asleep.

The three wake up just as the soldiers arrive, brandishing cudgels and swords, whereupon they run away. Only remaining with Jesus at the time of his arrest is the Boy in the Shirt. "And with him was a young man wearing a linen cloth over his naked body, and they grabbed him, but he left the cloth and got away naked." He is hardly an innocent bystander who simply happens to be in that place at that time. There is something secretive, not to say furtive, about the presence of the Boy. It could well be that the Boy hopes to be baptized by Jesus, and so is dressed in an appropriate costume for that rite. It was through baptism that the "mysteries of the kingdom" were made known. But nowhere in the Gospels is it written that Jesus performed the rite of baptism. As John the Baptist foretold: "The one who will come after me will not baptize with water." It would have been a unique event were it to be done by him on this night and to this Boy. Why, too, did the Boy run off and leave Jesus to his fate alone? If the Boy truly loved Jesus and desired to be baptized by him, how can one explain his desertion? We know of the timidity of the Disciples. That they have run off does not surprise us. But the Boy, for whom this night was pregnant with the Holy Spirit of which he yearned to partake, why did he too make good his escape? Fear, doubtless.

Clubs, organizations, brotherhoods, and religions traditionally keep secrets that are known only to the Chosen. Take the secret societies at Yale, whose membership is kept secret, as is all of the ceremonial carrying-on that takes place inside the windowless, tomblike buildings. The medical profession has its Hippocratic oath: "I swear by Apollo the Healer . . . that I will teach this art . . . to my sons and to the sons of him who taught me, and to the pupils who have been enrolled by contract and sworn to the physicians' path, and to none other." The ancient Jewish religion was a secret one, perhaps the largest of the "mystery cults" of its time. One of its secrets was the technique of self-hypnosis that was believed to enable the magician or shaman to ascend into the heavens and deal directly with the angels. The Rabbis spoke in parables to disguise their meaning and further deepen the secrets. Early Christianity, too, followed this secret impulse. Clement, an early church Father, in his famous letter to one Theodore, told his correspondent, "Not all true things are to be said to all men."

A distinction was made between the baptized and the nonbaptized among the followers of Jesus. Only to the baptized was the mystery given. Jesus himself was a secretive man. When he cured the demoniacs, he told them not to speak of it. This goes for his other cures as well. He kept from all but his followers the secret of the Communion meal and of baptism as the key to the Kingdom of God.

John the Baptist started Christianity when he baptized Jesus, who then and there had some sort of ecstatic experience. Perhaps he was prone to them, was one of those highly suggestible "sensitives" who can self-hypnotize at will and enter an altered state. Jesus' possession at the instant of his baptism is similar, if not identical, to the possession of tribal shamans by the spirit that enables them to travel to heaven and back to perform "miracles" or magic acts on earth. The modern shaman is one who has been granted the ability to cure others. He does this not only by mastering a technique, but by taking upon himself the suffering of the patient and coming to understand it by intuition. This is called empathy.

Baptism—the Greek word *baptein* means to plunge or immerse in water—was designed to wash away all one's sins and to make one eligible for entry into the Kingdom of Heaven. But The Manual of Discipline, part of the Dead Sea Scrolls created in the early Christian cult of Essenes, goes out of its way to insist that no amount of physical washing can remove sin. Lady Macbeth came to this knowledge the hard way. At first she reassured her husband that "A little water will clear us of this deed." Not much later she smells the blood and laments: "Not all the perfumes of Arabia will sweeten this little hand." Macbeth, too, opines that the blood of Duncan would all Neptune's oceans "incarnadine."

There is a contagious effect of religious ecstasy, as one can observe in certain fundamental Christian churches, especially Black churches in which the congregants make outcry of "Hallelujah!" and "Amen!" and "Praise the Lord!" then stand up and sway and seem to enter a state of ecstasy that spreads to involve the whole congregation.

The Jews of the time were famous as magicians, and proud of it. They often used outlandish cries like Houh! Amoun! E! O! Hu! to work themselves up into trancelike states. From time immemorial, Jews, while praying, have swayed back and forth, rocking on their heels, bowing and straightening, in order to invite an altered state of consciousness. Baptism and Communion were essentially magical acts. Nor were they unknown to many sects. "Eat my body, drink my blood" is quite similar to the cult of Isis and Osiris in which the drink in the chalice, identified as the blood of the deity, is given to the communicant so that the two may be united in love.

John the Baptist told the priests that he was not the Messiah, that one would come whose shoes he was not fit to tie. The one who would come after him would not baptize with water, as he did, but with the Holy Spirit. But from Homeric times on, such a ritual insists upon water. Ezekiel, in the Old Testament, reported the words of the Lord: "I shall sprinkle clear water over you, and you shall be cleansed from all that defiles you. . . . I shall give you a new heart, and put a new spirit within you."

An altogether different conjecture is that the Boy was a male prostitute who was wearing the costume of his trade, perhaps the gift of a satisfied client, an expensive linen piece that could be easily shed for more carnal purposes than baptism. Jerusalem, after all, was a garrison town with many Roman centurions within its precincts. It is not outside the precincts of the imagination, mine anyway, that some of these centurions, as well as a number of the Jewish population of the city, used male prostitutes; and what better place to meet for gay sex than a park at night? *Plus ça change, plus c'est le meme chose.* Might the Boy then have followed Jesus to the Garden to solicit him for sex? In the letter from Clement to Theodore, he saw fit to mention that the Greek words implying that both Master and catechumen were naked were not part of the true gospel. Perhaps not. Perhaps they had been inserted by the Carpocratians, a subsect of early Christians notorious for sexual profligacy who sought to commune with the divine through orgasmic activity. We cannot know for certain which reading of the verse is true. Perhaps neither, perhaps both.

This is not to imply that Jesus engaged in sex with the Boy. But why not? If Jesus was a man during his thirty-three-year stay on earth, then he would have been subject to the ways of mankind. If we know from the Passion that the Redeemer could feel thirst, pain, exhaustion, despair, fear, and shame, we ought also to admit that he could feel lust, and even act upon it. As a man, Jesus would not have enjoyed all the perquisites of omnipotence. Take away his manhood, his human-ness, and you take away God's purpose in dispatching him here for the redemption of the rest of us.

While it would be presumptuous to deny Jesus human desires, we have no idea of his sexuality. In Isaiah 53:2–3 it is written: "For he shall grow up before him as a tender plant, and as a root out of a dry ground; he hath no form nor comeliness; and when we shall see him, there is no beauty that we should desire him. He is despised and rejected of men; a man of sorrows, and acquainted with grief." In Isaiah's pre-vision of Jesus, he would be neither beautiful nor desirable. Ascribing physical beauty to Jesus is part of a later vulgar tradition.

In pondering this mystery, a writer invites the calumny of the faithful. As though in questioning the "historical" Jesus one is questioning the Christian faith itself. To assume that the two are the same would put an extremely narrow perspective on Christianity. One is charged with blasphemy, sacrilege. In another age, one would have been burned at the stake. But, despite appearances, I am a devoted reader of the Scriptures and am in awe of, and envious of, the piety of its followers.

There is an illuminated manuscript of the fifteenth century entitled the *Chichester Missal*. It is situated at the John Rylands University library in Manchester, England. One section of the manuscript is a pictorial representation of the "Agony in the Garden." It purports to show Jesus and the betrayal by Judas at the time of his arrest. In fact, the *Chichester Missal* picture shows Jesus and an androgynous young man wearing a loose but complex garment. They are both fair and beautiful, with delicate facial features. The youth is not fully grown, a teenager, with a small, sparse beard. Jesus is the larger of the two, and enhaloed. His robe is darker, layered. The assailants are dark, swarthy, and hideous, in contrast. They are armed with swords and cudgels. Their brows beetle; their faces are contorted and grimacing: eyes glare wildly, mouths hang open to show their teeth. Theirs are more muzzles than human faces. They are meant to be seen as monstrous and subhuman. Christ and the youth are shown in intimate, not to say erotic, relation to each other. The face of the taller Jesus is bent down toward the upturned face of the youth so that their lips seem to be touching, only side to side, rather than in a full frontal kiss. The left hand of the lissome Boy holds the collar of Jesus' cloak; he appears to be shrinking from the grasp of one of the attackers, shrinking in toward Jesus who bows above him in a gesture of protection. Jesus, too, is in the grip of one of the thugs. Jesus and the youth are barefoot, the heel of Jesus' right foot resting upon the instep of the youth's right foot. The right arm of Jesus appears to be enfolding the Boy to him. The hand emerging from behind the Boy holds a scroll, the words of which I cannot see. It is the mysterious Boy with whom the Chichester artist has identified. His unreflecting brush simply surrendered to his own predilections, creating a rendezvous, not with Judas Iscariot, but with the enigmatic Boy in the Shirt. It was not, by any means, an unfortunate blunder, but the artistic impulse that is always independent of calculation. Such is my interpretation of the *Chichester Missal.*

In an e-mail message dated June 18, 2001, the Curator of Prints and Manuscripts at the John Rylands Library begs to differ with my version of the plate from the *Chichester Missal.* He believes the figure with whom Jesus is shown in intimate relationship is not the Boy in the Shirt, but is, in fact, Judas. They are shown in a stylized kiss, he explains, the mouths side by side rather than in a full frontal apposition, which might have been offensive. He further believes that the expression on the face of "Judas" is not a pleasant one at all, but sly and sinister. Judas, he tells me, is portrayed as being fair-skinned, to indicate that Jesus was betrayed, not by one of the subhuman thugs, but by one of his own. All this having been said, I remain in favor of the figure's identity as the Boy in the Shirt. The eroticism is explicit. The artist was either intentionally or else subconsciously motivated. I present the curator's dissenting opinion out of a wish to be fair.

What is the point of tilting at this particular windmill? The Boy cannot ever be plucked of his mystery. No amount of explanation will draw the truth from this deep well. Interpretation of the Scriptures is not limited to the professional and the devout believer, but is a hobby permissible to the amateur, the skeptic, and others of no particular scholarship or axe to grind. Such a commentator may lack the High and Terrible seriousness with which traditional biblical scholarship is rife. Given that the appearance of the Boy in the Shirt is an enigma and therefore unsolvable, he may also, *mirabile dictu,* be right.

In the pseudohistorical fiction "Three Versions of Judas," Jorge Luis

Borges suggests that God became Judas as a way to save mankind, became the human agent to precipitate the crucifixion and resurrection of Jesus. Thus transmuted into the vile betrayer, He has sacrificed, not his body, but his soul. His sacrifice was not over and done with in a single afternoon on a cross. It is ongoing through eternity. Judas serves God's purpose when he carries out the deed that was his destiny to commit. While Borges is infinitely provocative, and one enjoys his intellectual playfulness, the mystery is not solved by reading him.

I have decided to let the Boy himself tell his story. Why not? Mark, Matthew, Luke, John, and many others have made free with the gospels. It is an ancient tradition.

THE BOY'S STORY

It is fifty years later, and I am an old man. *Perpaucis diebus morituri* (in a few days, I will die). It is time to tell one more part of the story, tell it not in my native Aramaic, but in the Latin I have come to love. Aramaic has little of the dignity of Latin in which the most sublime thoughts can be rendered. *Abstrahit invitum patrii sermonis* (the poverty of my native tongue inhibits me).

Not long after I was brought to Rome, the Disciples Peter and Mark came to spread the Christian faith. A cruel fate was handed to Peter—he was crucified, upside down. Mark, in terror for his life, decided to flee to Alexandria. Rumor of his imminent departure spread through the illegal Christian sect, to which I was now a convert. Some days before his escape, I went to see Mark.

"Who are you?" he asked.

"My name is, or was, Gil-od ben Zvi," I told him. "I was the third son of a stone-cutter in the city of Jericho. My mother died giving birth to me. My two elder brothers followed our father in his trade. In due course, first my father, then the other two began to cough and spit blood. They turned feverish and wasted away. The stone-cutter's disease. At the age of fourteen I was alone and without resources. I decided to leave the city of my unhappy childhood and make my way to Jerusalem in hopes of a new life. And so I set out on foot. After three days of near starvation, I was befriended by a muleteer who gave me what to drink and lifted me to the back of one of his mules. He would take me to within a day's walk of Jerusalem. That night it became known to me what I must do in return. It was my initiation into the mysteries of the flesh. In the ferocity of youth, I cursed the man who had abused me in this manner. But now, from the vantage of old age, I refuse to elevate his acts to the level of the satanic. I know now that I owed him my life. He it was who made me aware of the only thing I had to sell—my youth and beauty. Once in Jerusalem, I learned quickly the streets and marketplaces where I could earn my living. For more than one year, I worked as a rent-boy. I much preferred the centurions to the men of Judaea, who were contemptuous and derisory, even cruel. To the Roman centurions, I was a toy to be played with. They were merry and gentle, taking care not to cause me pain or shame. I was soon well known among them. At last Flavius, the Tribune of the Legionnaires, summoned me to his bed. It was from him that I received the cloth of fine linen that I left in the grasp of the soldiers. And then I met Jesus.

Just outside the house of the Passover Feast I lingered, needing to see him, unwilling to take leave of him. He was not beautiful, not in any feature, but had beauty about him. Thin, fleshless, waxen, almost a skeleton from his fasting, and with a small triangular, earthen face, a straggly beard, and deeply embedded eyes that blazed up. And stooped as if he were carrying a too-heavy weight on his shoulders. When first I passed him in the street, he paused in his step, turned to look at me with, I thought, a certain admiration. He raised his walking stick and shook it in a gesture of familiarity, all the while staring intensely at me. The gesture remained with me for a long time. What I felt was both flattered and strangely threatened. And something else—that another life was waiting for me, until now unknown, a mysterious life that I must find and enter. I seemed then to have set out upon a magical journey in which I had been summoned to take part. Perhaps it was just a childish fantasy.

It was I who was alone with Jesus in the Garden of Gethsemane on the night of his arrest, wearing only the loose garment of fine linen that was not warm enough for a night so chilly that fires had been lit in the courtyard of the High Priest. I stood aside and watched as Jesus knelt and prayed. The three Disciples who had accompanied him, Peter, James, and John, had run for their lives. When the soldiers came, they found us, Jesus and me, alone together. I had followed Jesus from the house of the Passover Feast all the way down into the Valley of Kidron, then up the

Mount of Olives. I did not know why I followed him, only that I was drawn by a powerful attraction that was different from any I had ever experienced. It was an attraction of the spirit. It was love. Precisely what took place between Jesus and myself just prior to his arrest, I cannot say. The part of my mind that governs memory is extinguished for that time. I know only that *hic ibi me rebus quaedam divina voluptas percipit atque horror* (a godlike pleasure and trembling took hold of me). At the same time I had the feeling that I had experienced this moment before, in a previous existence. Perhaps a kiss was given and received, the same kiss given Jesus moments before by Judas, only now purified and chaste for having passed through the Savior.

It is strange. While I cannot remember precisely what transpired between Jesus and myself, I have the image of his face engraved on my eyes, this despite that I beheld him asquint. Even in the darkness of the night, he shone so as to dazzle. Time, which usually dims the memory, has intensified his countenance. No, he was not beautiful. No single feature was what is considered so. I would say, to the contrary, that he was pale, thin to the point of emaciation, and with what seemed a deformity of the spine. I have only to close my eyes to see again his burning gaze, the hollowness at his temples, the black beard, the way he held his head tilted to one side as though listening. Even so, as a hind longs for the running stream, so did I long for him. I remember, too, his brown, rough-textured robe, the well-worn sandals. Of what transpired next, I recall only that there was shouting, footsteps. A great number of men appeared, one of whom stepped forward and greeted Jesus with a kiss. The three Disciples, awakened by the tumult, had already fled for their lives. I alone remained with Jesus at the time of his arrest. He stood and came toward me, holding out his arms as if to enfold me in my terror, to protect me. When he drew me to his breast, I felt saved.

Having seized Jesus, the men now took hold of me, too, by my shirt. Jesus bent toward me, hovering as if to protect me; I shrank against him. I cried out to him in terror. But he drew me close and whispered these words: "Fear not. Before Abraham was, I am." Vertiginous words that came from the depths of the world. For a moment, I was plunged into a vagueness, an emptiness that was being filled up with joy. I did not know it at the time, but when I came back to myself, the prostitute had died and a Christian was born. As they led him away, I wriggled free of the shirt and ran off naked, leaving the garment in the hands of those who had grasped it.

In the darkness of a moonless night, and in my terror, and nakedness, I ran down the paths that I knew so well. The Mount of Olives, you might say, was my kingdom. There was no part of it, no narrow path that I had not walked to and from my assignations. At last, I crossed the Valley of Kidron. Cold and exhausted, I found myself before the iron grille that is the gate of the house of Flavius, Tribune of the legion of Romans encamped in the city of Jerusalem. Flavius had been one of my lovers, and one to whom I had reason to be grateful. He had more than once rescued me from the difficult situations that are the nightly curse of those who earn their living as I did. He it was who had given me the fine linen shirt I wore that night in the Garden of Gethsemane. I do not know how long I lay on the stones calling out to him, until at last I was heard by one of his slaves. Imagine Flavius's surprise at finding me in the courtyard of his house, naked and shivering, at midnight. The dear good man took me in and fed and clothed me and nursed me, for I was feverish. For several months, I remained in hiding, the guest of my benefactor. At last there came the day when he informed me that he was returning to Rome.

"But then I am doomed!" I cried. "The High Priests have been searching for me. I was seen. They will find me. I, too, will be crucified!" Whereupon mercy touched the heart of the Tribune, and he offered to take me with him to Rome, in return for which I would be his slave. I had no choice but to agree. No slave ever had a kinder master. He saw to it that I learned to read and write in Latin. I was attached to his person, saw to his clothing and food, slept in an anteroom nearby. When he fell ill with the quartan fever, I nursed him. But to my sorrow, his body, the body I had loved, and loved to please, melted away before my eyes. When it was clear to him that he was dying, he summoned me to his bed and granted me my freedom. In addition, he said that I would be his heir—I, as well as his daughters and wife—if I gave him my promise that I would not again work as a prostitute. Of course I swore to it, and I have kept that promise. Even more, since his death I have been celibate. I was never to return to Judaea. I was a Roman now, fluent in the language, well read, with a great house and slaves of my own.

All this I related to Mark just prior to his flight to Alexandria. And Mark was amazed. I knew that he believed me. That is how he came to know of the Boy in the Shirt. How else could he have known of my existence? It was I, who was then Gil-od and who am now Marcus Atticus, who told him. I was the Boy in the Shirt.

After Mark's flight to Egypt, I wrote on a scroll of parchment the story of the Boy in the Shirt just as I had related it to the apostle. I placed this scroll in an earthenware jar, which I then sealed.

Why then have I at last revealed the secret of the Boy in the Shirt? Because mine are perhaps the last eyes to have truly seen Jesus; because ever since that night, he has haunted my dreams; and because in the Gospel said to have been written by Mark, there is no further mention of the Boy. Perhaps it was considered blasphemous that a prostitute was alone with Jesus during the Agony in the Garden. Surely it was thought dangerous to the faith of the vulnerable. I was not called to go among people bearing witness, I who had been a prostitute and lain with many men, I who had run away in fear, abandoning Jesus to his crucifixion. But to keep this hidden is to diminish the greatness of the Redeemer. Telling the truth is not meant to detract from his glory. Nor is it meant to shock the faithful. Jesus is greater than his brief history on earth as a man. Let a candle be lighted. Though no man see it, God will see it.

I have decided to visit the Sybil in order that I might know the fate of the scroll I have written. Many Romans consult her; even Christians hold her in esteem for her prophesies about Christ. Just outside the city, in a cave overlooking the Tiber, lives the old woman to whom I appealed for help. She handed me a draught of smoky liquid and bade me drink. She pointed to a pallet. I lay upon it. Almost at once I experienced a strange sensation that was oddly familiar. It was the same feeling I had had those many years ago when I was alone in the Garden with Jesus! In the trance, I heard a voice telling me in Aramaic that the manuscript will be found two thousand years from now, in a place called Qumran in the Judaean desert. It would be found in a cave in the face of a rocky cliff above the Dead Sea. The one who brings it to Qumran must go out upon the Dead Sea in a small boat, for a distance of three hundred strokes of the oars. It must be on the night of a full moon at midnight. From the boat he will observe the path of moonlight on the water. He must follow this aqualune to the shore. It will be at that place on the escarpment, some three hundred spans up from the base, that he will come upon the mouth of a cave, one of many hundreds in these cliffs overlooking the Dead Sea. The opening is hardly more than an irregular crevice that will admit only one man. Once inside, he will discover that there are three chambers, each leading into the next by a narrow crawl space. It is in the deepest chamber of the cave that he must deposit the jar containing the scroll. There it will await the passage of two thousand years before being found and brought into the light.

When I awoke, I asked the old sorceress how the manuscript would get from Rome to this Qumran, but she could not or would not say. She fell into a silence that I understood would not be broken.

On the opposite bank of the Tiber is a vast slum where the poor and the aliens of Rome live. Many are Africans, Palestinians, Syrians, and others. From this place, every day, numerous ships set out for Judaea and other provinces laden with merchandise. It was no easy thing for me to cross the Tiber and go down to the docks from which the ships departed. How I would have preferred to board one and carry the scroll to its destination myself. That would indeed have constituted a well-rounded tale, but I am far too old and decrepit. Instead, I have enlisted the aid of the son of an elderly slave (yes, I too now keep slaves) with the promise of manu-mission—for his father, brothers, and all of their children—and the greater part of my worldly possessions, which are not inconsiderable. Of course, the man is a devout Christian, who gave me his solemn oath that he would carry out my wish. He understood that it was an oath he would break only at grave risk to his immortal soul. My sole instructions were that he transport the sealed clay jar to Qumran where, at midnight and with a full moon in the sky, he is to set out upon the Dead Sea in a small boat. Then, in accordance with my instructions, he is to locate the precise cave. All this I told him again and again, until he had committed the instructions of the Sybil to memory. He is to reveal its location to no one.

Iam moriar paratus sum. Now I am ready to die.

Four Deceptions

A Writing Lesson

I was asked by a student what made me choose a certain subject to shape into a story. Oh, timing, I replied. That has a lot to do with it, whether I've been casting about for a new topic. And chemistry: I have to be ready to receive the event that will become a story; that part is probably physiological. Then, too, there is the simple need to keep the pen exercised. Later I began to ponder this question. Deception, I thought, and irony. Folly, too. And behavior that is at the outer edge of human experience. These are the ingredients I need to transform words into story.

It is moving to watch a hen crouch over her chicks, flap her bony, useless wings and squawk when a hawk circles over the barnyard. It is far more moving to watch her do this when what soars above is not a raptor, but a kite made of paper, wood, and string. The one occurs in the natural scheme of predation and survival. It must be accepted. In the second, the maternal frenzy is infused with irony and black comedy. Now imagine that the chicken can think rationally, that it possesses self-awareness. Moments before the kite will have sailed away, she will look up and see that it wasn't a hawk at all, that her terror was unnecessary, comical, in fact. After the wave of relief, she certainly hopes that no one saw her being afraid of a kite. But we, who watched, feel far more deeply. Her folly is entirely understandable to us. We, too, have been ridiculous in our passions. We, too, have deceived ourselves when love is at stake. Minutes later, the hen is calm again. There are her chicks all around her, for whom she would suffer death, not to mention humiliation. She turns philosophical and quotes Socrates: "With the best will in the world, I succeed only in making myself ridiculous."

What a far cry the hen from that most territorial of birds, the robin, who will fight at the least hint of threat to his dominion. Yesterday, in the park, not more than ten feet away, two robins battled with all their engine, swooping, stabbing, eyes aglitter, wings crackling, and with no thought of my large presence nearby. In the whole forest there were just the two of them, offering each other all their fierce dedication. Only in the spring is the robin so prompt. By fall, his breeding impulse spent, he grows tame, content to travel in flocks for safety and, who knows? For companionship.

I sat one spring day on a glass-enclosed porch and witnessed a battle between a robin and his reflection in the glass. So fierce was his attack upon a presumed rival, that in the final headlong dive, spurting his redness, he smashed into the pane and fell, broken-necked, to the ground. Here, too, were deception and irony, but now leading to a heroic death worthy of Homer. Here is Alcathous just stabbed in the chest by Idomeneus:

> ripped by the spear.
> Down Alcathous crashed and the point stuck in his heart,
> And the heart in its last throes jerked and shook the lance—
> The butt-end quivering in the air till suddenly
> Rugged Ares snuffed its fury out, dead still.

Of the two, hen or robin, the hen's fate is the more tragic: She has to go on living after her shame. The robin did not understand that the world on the other side of the window was not his, but another, a parallel world cunningly made to look like his. (There might well have been, on the other side, a rival robin attacking with the same vigor and recklessness. Now and then, I myself have the sense that the window opens and someone, or something, crosses over. The temperature of the room falls; there is a hush.)

The robin's instinct had failed him. For a bird, that is a fatal lapse. Only a human being can live without instinct. It is a part of us that has atrophied from disuse. What a shock when what was thought to be air turned to glass, and the world snapped shut!

There is a bachelor in his fifties. He is a cellist, but not in the usual sense of the term. He is a lover of the cello, one particular cello. Some time ago he had seen the instrument in the window of a music store. It occurred to him that he had never seen anything so beautiful, voluptuous, even. The distinctly feminine shape, the richness of texture of the wood, and, above all, the dignity with which the cello presented itself in the store window to be sold, like a beautiful slave. Later, if asked, he would not be able to say just why he went into the store and purchased the instrument. Only that the act of doing so had made him happier than he had been in years. Once home, he installed the cello in a corner of his bedroom.

As a young man, he had loved women and had enjoyed a number of close attachments. Once he had come close to marrying. But as the years went on, he had led a more and more solitary life. This, too, he would not be able to explain. It had just happened. His old father worried.

"Aren't you lonely?"

"No," he replied, with a faint smile. "Not at all, I assure you."

"But everyone needs somebody," the old man persuaded.

"I've lost the touch," said the son. "It doesn't matter." The father, far from being assuaged, knew better than to go further. What he did not know about was the cello. He would have been amazed to learn that his son possessed such an instrument, one that he didn't know how to play. He had never shown the least aptitude for making music.

It came to pass that, soon after acquiring the cello, the son began to have disturbing dreams from which he would awaken in a state of almost painful excitement. Although he could not remember a single detail of these dreams, he would awaken with the sound of music just receding out of earshot. Strain as he might, he could not retain the sound, only that it seemed to him both plaintive and seductive. Like the song of the Sirens in Homer, he thought. Before long he began to suffer from the lack of peaceful sleep. His appetite was affected; he grew thin and exhausted like a man in the throes of a debilitating disease. There came the night when, only half awake and moved to do so by a command uttered in his dream, he carried the cello from its corner and took it into his bed. Within minutes he had fallen into a deep sleep, from which he awoke in his usual state of nervous distress, and with the dying strains of music in his ear.

Beside him, against his body, lay the cello. In the crook of his arm the slender neck nestled; beneath his other hand rested one polished haunch. It seemed the most natural thing in the world to reach up and touch the strings. No sooner had he done so than the instrument gave forth a low groan into the darkness that seemed to him, for all the world, a resurgence of the music in his dreams. Again and again he touched the cello into sound, touched it with his fingers the way he had liked to be touched, with long-forgotten caresses that had somehow remained within his fingers, waiting all this time to be performed again. Each time he was rewarded with that infinitely sensuous sound, not a melody, but a slow swelling that hovered at the crest, then relented into silence. It was a music that he would never tire of hearing and that satisfied him completely. When at last he fell asleep, it was the sleep of perfect peacefulness. In the morning he awoke refreshed and hungry.

The boy had just turned thirteen. It was six months since his father's death. He hadn't the courage to visit the grave until one hot July Sunday morning, when, as if in accordance with a will other than his own, he climbed the hill that led to the high graveyard. He pushed open the wrought iron gate of the cemetery. No need to look around for the site. Where, six months ago, his footsteps had retreated, leaving behind the body of his father, the grass, in sympathy, had wilted and died. But what was this! From some twenty feet away he saw, or thought he saw, the gravestone moving, or pulsating. It was the heat, the boy decided, rising in waves. He had seen the same phenomenon when the heat of the sidewalk rose and shook the air. Drawing closer, he saw that where his father's name had been cut into the stone, a swarm of bees had settled. No hive, just the bees, a brassy radiance, bombinating, covering the letters so that he could not read them. Now he was no more than three feet from the swarm. When he reached out an arm as if to wave them away, they paid him no attention. But now, through the seethe, he could make out the letters of his father's name. JUL U S LZ R. As if they could read and had come back to suck the last sweetness from the letters of his name. He himself trembled, as if struck with a tuning fork.

It is another hot morning in July, sixty years later. Breathless and a bit dizzy from the climb, I stand at the same grave, now twin-bedded. I close my eyes and see again the bees swarming on the stone. I am the ghost at their banquet, hoping only to suck up a bit of honey for myself.

From the Diaries 1

MARCH 1985

In today's mail a letter from one of my former Physician Associate students, let's call him Tom, now working on an Indian reservation in South Dakota. Soon he and his wife, also a Physician Associate, will be off to Thailand and the refugee camps. All through school, Tom and his male classmates kept the wolf from the door by selling their sperm to the Fertility Clinic. Twenty-five dollars a shot. Here's the way it worked:

An early morning phone call. Report to Fertility and pick up red-topped test tube. Repair to bathroom and . . . aim carefully (Waste not, want not). Bring tube directly to front desk of Fertility. No dallying. One or more ovulating women somewhere behind those closed doors had been made ready to receive the "donation." Collect twenty-five dollars. Go home and wait for the next telephone call. It was a living.

It occurred to me that since each specimen is used to inseminate more than one woman, and since the same donors are called again and again, there exists in the city of New Haven a chilling possibility: Twenty years later, a boy and a girl will meet. Each of them will see something in the other that intrigues. (Strongly.) This something they will interpret as love. They will marry. A child will be born. Behold! Institutional inbreeding. Can this be good for the city? I wrote a letter to Tom.

"You are all tabooed up," he replied.

"Right. I am, always have been," I said.

I see that the newspapers, magazines, television are full of information about *in vitro* fertilization, contraception, morning-after pills. All the secrets of ovulation and insemination are out there to be seen by children in the third grade. Now that is a mile or two away from my own tender upbringing. Once I asked my mother the difference between an ox and a bull.

"The bull," she explained, "is the father, and the ox is the uncle." And that had to be that for a few years, until I found out for myself.

AUGUST 1986

"Quick! Tony's having a stroke!" It was Larry shouting from the basement. There on the floor lay the family poodle in *status epilepticus,* working as if to shake free of the planet. He had slowed down these past few months, only heaving himself up to follow when we left the room. Most of the time sleeping as if he were saving up his exertions for something important. He was. We tried to hold him, but such a muscular chaos is not to be steadied. An old blue blanket with a fringe was what we carried him in to the car. I sat with him in the back seat, pressing back his frenzy with my hand. He was all foam and excrement and facsimile of running through the park at my heels. Who would have thought the old dog to have so much fierce purpose in him? In the front seat, Janet silent, gathering herself; Larry driving manfully. It would be his first death. I listened with every one of my ears for evidence of his grief. The kindly veterinarian tried, but could not slip the needle into a vein, so fierce the convulsion. Let me try, I said. And while he gripped the leg, I killed my dog. The stillness in the room was as solemn as that which lay upon the earth in the Christmas carol. We got back in the car.

"Lucky you were home this weekend," I told Larry. "You can't say we don't save the good times for you." We laughed and advanced into our loss.

The next morning Janet was at a deep sink full of water, an iridescence of suds. From the chair where I was pretending to write I watched her hold the relic up to the light, examine it for blood and urine and mad saliva. Now she lowered the blue blanket into the sink, bending over it, scrubbing as women have done with deathbed linen from time immemorial. What she could not cleanse it of is hard memory. Still, it was the first step on the path back. I envied her the simple holy task. The light flashing on the suds was a good sign.

From noon on, the day was dark, sunless. We went for a walk.

"This neighborhood of big old houses reminds me of Stonehenge," I told her. "All these great dark lumps standing around."

"Those fits," said Janet, "it would have been too much for Job." By force of will she gave me a faint wintry smile. Just so do we bemoan ourselves upstairs and down, from room to room.

OCTOBER 1986

Janet phoned, said, "Are you sitting down? The man wants $9,000 to paint the house and fix the leaks in the roof." I searched all over my mouth for one of the oaths I keep on hand for a rainy day, found one, and used it. Then I fell into a reflective mood over the descent into worthlessness of the coin of the realm.

In 1935, fifteen cents a week was what you got for keeping the coal stove from going out during the night or for restarting it in the morning if it had. It also covered shoveling the walk in winter, raking leaves in fall, watering grass in summer, and weeding in spring. And all with a civil tongue in your head, or no fifteen cents. Payday was Saturday night and the money had to burn a hole in your pocket until Sunday noon, when the matinee double feature began at Proctor's Theater. In Troy, New York, that cost a dime. The remaining nickel bought a little white bag of cinnamon drops to suck while, for the next four hours, Jeanette MacDonald first took umbrage at, then yielded to, the laryngeal blandishments of Nelson Eddy.

It is a long time since those drunk-with-pleasure days, and much have I traveled in realms of gold, but never have I felt such a thrill of opulence as when I sat in the balcony of Proctor's Theater of a Sunday afternoon. In the last few years alone, I have made my home at the Abbey of San Giorgio in Venice, the Villa Serbelloni on Lake Como, and the mansion of Yaddo in Saratoga, New York, to say nothing of a few dozen caravanseries of the Hilton and Holiday Inn ilk, where each bathroom has its three individually wrapped little bars of soap. Not that I have become blasé about grandeur, not at all. I still like walking into a great hall, a well-appointed lobby, or a burnished refectory, and making them my own. And there are times when a draperied couch has it all over a mere bed.

But the Versailles of my heart is a cozy wooden cottage with a front *and* a back porch, a working chimney wearing a feather of smoke, and, all around, trees of a certain age for shade, birds, and resident deities. Put a meadow of wildflowers back of the fence, and beyond that, a creek for music. And there let me take whatever more of relishment is to be my portion. I don't need much: one easy chair, a kosher salami, my share of vodka, a tin of smoked oysters, a fresh clean notebook, pencils to last, a volume of Shakespeare, and a cat. It is the only place I would ever dream of having a cat, and then it would be as a hired domestic, subject to instant dismissal. The real use of a cat lies not in its appetite for mice, but as a foot pillow in winter, a purpose for which it is ideally constructed.

APRIL 1987

Ophthalmos—the eye. It is the word the ancient Greeks used for the most important place in the city. In Athens, I suppose, that would be the Acropolis; in Florence, the Piazza della Signoria; in Paris, the Champs Élysées, and so forth. In New Haven, Connecticut, for me, it is the Yale Sterling Library. And what a serene eye it is, next to the wild and bloodshot city all around it, where murder, rape, and robbery are an every Monday, Wednesday, and Friday affair. At Sterling Library, where I come to read and write most days, there is no crime to speak of, unless it be the crime of sloth. Although I can't swear to that. Perhaps, if the books could bear witness, they would tell of murder in the archives, rape in the stacks. I doubt it; all the passion here is in print. The only murder I know of committed on these premises is by a paranoid professor of Slavic languages, who periodically removes all of his rival's books from the card catalogue, effectively assassinating him each time.

If the library is the eye of the city, its inner courtyard is the retina. This is a square space enclosed on four sides by the internal walls of the building. No more than fifty paces per side, it is the perfect size for contemplation. Stone walkways border the grass and radiate from the four corners to a central fountain. Against the walls are masses of white azalea and pink rhododendron. Some days the air is coppery with bees. There are two large trees—a beech and an elm—and several lesser dogwood. Numerous birds live in this courtyard. Purple finches and sparrows are in the majority, but I have also seen robins, iridescent grackles, mourning doves, and, once, a Maryland yellowthroat. This year a pair of cardinals are raising their brood in the elm. It is ravishing to watch the male fly from tree to fountain and back again. If I were a bird, I would not live anywhere else.

The fountain in the center bears the date 1769, the year of its creation, I suppose. What it lacks of the lavish, it makes up for in simple charm. In fact, it looks rather like an old-fashioned kitchen sink. The square cistern is of greenish lead, each side showing four gods, only two of which are still recognizable by what they are holding: Ceres, a sheaf of wheat; Bacchus, a bunch of grapes. So much for immortality. This basin is supported at the corners by four sandstone creatures about three feet tall that might once have been Chinese carp, but that have long since melted "like wax before the fire," so that only the rare fin and one bulging eyeball can still be made out. At the upper rim, the cistern is adorned by leaden *putti* with wreaths in their hair, each bestriding a stone fish. From the mouths of three of these fish, pathetic twines of water limp. The pipe of the fourth fish is broken, so that only now and then is there a sad hiccough or hollow bubbling that bears no relation to the florid *cascatelli* of its distant cousins in Rome, Trevi, and the rest. Corroded and rusting, patched here and there with screws, bolts, cement, and wire, this fountain has located beauty in a kind of orthopedic decrepitude. Yet it wears with immense dignity its heritage as the sole survivor of that race of lead fountains that were all, long ago, melted down for bullets in some forgotten war. And just see how considerately leaky this fountain is. Only moments ago, a bosomy dove stepped up to a puddle, looking for all the world like Rachel at the well.

Seven massive benches of pale weathered oak are placed at the periphery of the courtyard, each one with the name of the donor carved in the backrest. Smoothed and desplintered by generations of Yale buttocks, they stand as mute and glorious evidence of the gluteal continuity of scholarship across the ages.

Yesterday I was startled by the sudden appearance of two youthful gods (I had not seen them descend). In a moment they had stripped down to one bra and two fig leaves and were sprawled on the grass just short of flagrant delight. You can bet I wrote no more that day.

But, you say, why go on about a courtyard? Especially this one, which has no history. No queen was beheaded here, no duel fought at dawn, no emperor crowned. Everything you say is true. But this courtyard is what I should like my mind to be—orderly, cultivated, policed of all banality, inhabited by winged ideas, and visited by beautiful distractions.

JULY 1988

Fresh new buildings charm me not, charm they never so freshly. Just as a gourmet loves his cheese, the older and moldier the better, my taste runs to ruins—a half-tumbled abbey, the fallen columns of a once-great temple whose roof is whatever cloud is passing overhead. It should come as no surprise that my favorite artist is Piranesi, with his hundreds of vast ruined vaults and that aura of ill-fatedness.

But here in Connecticut there are no ruins before which one might meditate upon ancient glories, the fleeting nature of life. The closest we come to ruins are the thousands of stone walls of the simple pile-one-on-top-of-the-other variety built by the early settlers to demarcate their property. But each of these walls seems to me more a harsh sermon in stone than a bona fide ruin. You could hardly imagine Pan sitting cross-legged on one of them and playing his pipes. It is regrettable that this absence of ruins is unlikely to be corrected in the near future. The minute an old building shows the least sign of falling into wrack, it is razed and paved over for a parking lot.

Frankly, I think the architects are missing the boat. Were I to practice architecture in this new-fangled state, I'd specialize in ruins-to-order: a pagan altar slab to suggest human sacrifice, a dark frown of a tower with a hollow dismal echo that the susceptible might think to be the resident spirit giving voice. Right in the center of New Haven I'd put a stone labyrinth with drawings of bulls on the walls, a mazy sprawl of corridors into which only the more daring would venture. And on the outskirts of Hartford, something barbaric, like Stonehenge. Every ruin, by definition, would have its own hermit living nearby, someone emaciated who looks good in goatskin. Think what it would do for tourism!

From public ruination, I would branch out into the private sector. For every homeowner there would be a garden enclosed on three sides by tall hedges and on the fourth side by an equally high stone wall to be used specifically for wailing. It is what every family needs. I can think of nothing in the therapeutic armamentarium so beneficial as to press your forehead against a cool stone and just let go. These wailing walls must be built by the head of each household so as to foster an intimacy between stone and flesh. To that end, I offer a few instructions on how to build a wailing wall.

1. At the outset, having prepared the mortar, stand beside your pile of stones. Pick up each of your tools one at a time—trowel, chisel, mallet—and invoke blessings upon them.

2. Be at ease. Remember that even before the first stone has been placed, the whole wall exists within you, waiting to grow out of

your hands. Bricks, by the way, are impermissible. There is no element of fatal selection in the making of a brick wall. With bricks,
it is just one after the other.

3. Dwell upon the source of your stones. From where have they been
gathered, these gray sadnesses that you intend shall lie with one
another for a thousand years?

4. Now begin. Pile stone upon stone and apply the mortar until what
there is is a wall with naked hollows of sorrow, and here and there
a pocket of commiseration, where in time moss and small ferns
might cushion a penitent brow or soak up the tears of widow and
exile. Each stone will have felt your animating breath and the grip
of your hand.

5. Notice that the higher the wall rises, the lighter the stones become,
as if the wall itself, eager for completion, welcomes each stone and
shares in the labor. Lighter and lighter they will grow until the top-
most are as feathers that at any moment may group themselves into
wings and fly up in celebration of what you have made.

6. Is it finished, the last stone set? Now stand close, lean your forehead against the wall. Wail and be consoled.

People of Connecticut, let us build ruins and stone walls, so that a
thousand years from now (unless the gift of prophecy has deserted me)
Connecticut will be known as the State of Ruins and the Land of the
Wailing Wall, where any stranger who wanders within our borders will
say with gloomy delight, "Connecticut *was*."

MAY 1989

Boston, for Commencement at Boston University School of Medicine.

But first, birdwatching with Doon and Rossi in Mount Auburn cemetery, one of the premier warbler spots in New England. Every tree drip-
ping with them. And all the azaleas, lilac, dogwood, and chestnut trees
in bloom among the gleaming marble statuary. I shouldn't have been surprised to see a man and woman in fig leaves peeping from behind a mau-
soleum.

At nine-thirty, had to leave for Commencement. Marched to the stage to the tune of "Pomp and Circumstance" (I have collectively marched three and a half miles to that tune). Read the Program slowly so as to have something to do other than listen to the Presidential Welcome, Invocation, Expressions of Gratitude, and Congratulations that are the meat and potatoes of the American Graduation Ceremony. The Class, and therefore the audience, preponderantly Asian—Japanese, Chinese, Korean, Vietnamese, Indian, Pakistani. The rest, Jews. Throughout the ceremony, the audience gypsied about, creeping up like paparazzi, eating sandwiches and French fries, drinking cola. Now and then a faction at one end of the great arena would break out in cheers and applause for no apparent reason. This outburst would die out and be replaced by another from somewhere else. Doubtless there was a reasoned pattern to it, but, imprisoned on the platform, I could make neither head nor tail of it. Gave the Commencement Address—my twelve-minute job. Then led the new doctors in the Hippocratic Oath. Cried, as usual.

That night, supper at Fancuil Hall. Then strolled on Commonwealth Avenue, the air balmy; petals of dogwood, pollen, winged seedlings falling all around. Sat on a marble bench, fell sound asleep. Awoke with a start, looked about to see—had I been mugged? I had not. Went back to the Ritz Hotel. The park bench was better.

AUGUST 1990

Jon and Regine visiting. I hear from out back what sounds like a parrot calling. But of course it could be no such thing. Not in New Haven, Connecticut. Again it squawks and at last, setting aside the expectation of scorn, I say:

"There's a parrot out back."

"Don't be silly." Another squawk, and we look at each other with wild surmise. What else could make such a noise? Out we troop with the family field glasses, and there, high in the oak tree, clinging with its talons and beak, is a green and scarlet bird that strongly resembles a parrot.

"It's a parrot," says Jon.

"Isn't it!" I reply. Actually I have been hearing it for two weeks—that raucous chatter—but think: Oh, must be a squirrel defending his nuttery. No, Doon says, it's a nestful of young flickers. Then the other morning: Rawrk! Rawrk! from the yard: a green parrot with a red face high in the oak. Janet calls the radio station. Yes, they know whose parrot it is. Enter Happy and Yvette.

In mid-afternoon, Happy appears in the driveway holding a large cage in one hand and a bag of sunflower seeds in the other. Happy is one of those melancholy, blue-lipped, emphysematous, cadaveric, basset-faced men who are given the sobriquet "Happy" out of the same peasant irony that identifies a man who has lost three fingers as "Fingers." There is nothing cruel about such proletarian humor; rather, it is gentle and welcoming. For the next four hours, we will bushwhack through the underbrush, our heads turned treeward, hoping to catch sight of Koko.

"He's lonesome for me," says Happy. "He misses me. Every morning he sits on my shoulder while I make his breakfast."

"What does he eat for breakfast?"

"A plate of hash browns. He loves 'em." And shielding his heavy-lidded eyes with one hand, he scans the treetops calling out "Koko! Koko! Good boy!" banging on the cage to attract the homesick bird's attention.

"There he is!" I cry, pointing. At the sight of his beloved, Happy's features decompose further into a smile of ecstasy.

"Koko! Good boy!" we call out in unison. But Koko Good Boy isn't having any, only looks down at his master from on high, now and then giving back a Rwark! of defiance.

"Take a handful of seeds," instructs Happy. "Let him see that you're eating them. When he sees that, he'll come down in a hurry." By the end of the afternoon I have eaten enough sunflower seeds to impact the colon of a hippopotamus. And Happy's color has deepened from a bluish cast to a deep livid cyanosis.

"Let's quit for today," I say. On the way to his car, Happy speaks of his love for Koko, the fun they have.

There is a happy ending to this story: a week later, a telephone call from Yvette. Koko was home. He'd just turned up outside the kitchen window. He was, even then, eating a plate of hash browns.

SEPTEMBER 1990

Throughout my life as a doctor and a writer, I have held Anton Chekhov next to my heart. Sometimes, in the prime of my senility, I entertain a fantasy. Dare I confess it?

In a reading room of the Sterling Library there is a gigantic globe of the world. One day I gave it a spin, then braked it with my palm when the Crimea came into direct view. I located the city of Taganrog on the Sea of Azov, where Chekhov was born and raised. I found, too, the city of Odessa on the Black Sea, where my ancestors lived for generations and where my father was born. The distance? Some 300 miles. An overnight boat ride would bring a traveler from Odessa to Taganrog. Next I looked for Yalta, where Chekhov spent so much of his adult life. It is but half that distance, a mere 150 miles. O let me imagine it!

A man and a woman, unknown to each other, stand side by side on the deck of a steamer. He is a Chekhov; she, a Selzer (or whatever we were called over there). Before long a certain look would have been exchanged, words spoken. He would have petted the small white dog she held on her lap. She would have gazed down at the strong, well-groomed hand that stroked the dog, perhaps she would have flushed and smiled, ostensibly out of love for her pet. All at once it is announced by the deck steward that there will be a four-hour stopover at Balaclava to take on a cargo of caviar and vodka. At Balaclava, the two disembark, arm in arm. In her other arm she holds the small dog. At the waterfront hotel the woman waits on the verandah while he arranges for the room. Later, between passionate kisses, she whispers, "What name did you use?"

"Gomov. Dmitri Dmitrich Gomov. Do you like it?"

"For me," she replies, "it is the hero in a romantic novel." The man called Gomov shakes his head and smiles sadly.

"No," he tells her, "not a novel, only a short story."

And then what? you want to know. Four hours later they get back on board the steamer. At Yalta he watches her descend the ramp, carrying the little dog. On the wharf a man in a top hat and carrying a gold-headed cane is waiting for her. . . .

Nine months later, in Odessa, she is delivered of a child, a boy with chestnut-colored hair, gray eyes, and high cheekbones.

"A little Russian!" exclaims the delighted father. "We'll call him Sergei." From the time he was five years old, his parents argued over the boy's future. If you asked the father, he would become a doctor, a surgeon, like himself.

"He has the hands for it, strong and gentle."

"A surgeon! Never. He's a poet. His eyes, already they have that yonderly look, as though he has departed for another world. Besides, just because kittens are born in an oven does not make them loaves of bread."

"Half a century later, in his consultation room, a doctor reaches for his notebook and opens to a blank page. Taking up his pen, he writes: *Goldie,* a novel by Julius Louis Selzer.

And now another fifty years have gone by. Sometimes in my own consultation room or in the room of my house I call the scriptorium, I close my eyes and imagine my ancestor Chekhov there with me. I kiss his hands, his eyes, stroke the cough out of his thin wracked body, as though I were smoothing out a wrinkle in cloth.

AUGUST 1991

Did my Ovid.

On Olympus there was unrequited love. Hermes, the messenger god, loved Aphrodite; but his passion was not returned. In desperation he stole one of Aphrodite's sandals and wouldn't give it back until she granted him her favors. Of that single union a son was born, who was raised by the nereids on Mt. Ida. At age fifteen, and now the most beautiful boy in all the world, he left his nurses and went to explore the land. But he had been given no sex education up to that time. One day, while walking through a forest, he was noticed by a nymph, who lived in a crystal-clear pool of water. Enamored of the youth, she tried to entice him into her pool, but he wouldn't go and made as if to run away. The nymph, fearing to scare him off, came out of the pool and hid behind some bushes where she could spy on him. The day was hot and the boy, standing at the edge of the pool, suddenly threw off all his clothes and dove in. When the nymph saw that, she could no longer restrain herself and followed him into the water, wrapping herself around the struggling youth. (Imagine the poor boy, with that aggressive nymph committing frottage on his beautiful, innocent body!) When his struggle to free himself seemed to become successful, the nymph cried out to the gods, imploring that she and the youth never be separated. Such being the perversity of the gods, the request was granted, and in an instant nymph and boy were fused into a single creature with breasts and both male and female sex organs. And so was created Hermaphroditus, the product of two gods.

May Ovid forgive me for the thousand translating liberties taken.

JUNE 1992

Despite appearances, I have little of the literary temperament that would keep me impaled upon a writing desk. I am not steeped in ink, as once I was in blood. Truth to tell, I much prefer birdwatching, botanizing, gardening, cooking, gossiping. I should like the time to perfect all of my idiosyncrasies. In short, I'd rather be a man than a writer. Day after day, I poke at the carcass of this notebook, hoping to prod it to its feet, but the bloated thing *will* wallow where it lies. I feel like the scribe aboard Noah's ark.

Imagine a vast skull-shaped vessel with culs-de-sac and fossae and bony ledges reached by a plexus of rope ladders. Here and there in the walls, there is an opening into a crawl-space. In the great hold below the deck, the candles are never entirely snuffed. The shadows they cast give to the ark the pulsatile movement of living flesh. Echoes rise from the wooden floor; there is the creaking of boards, the plonk of hoof upon plank, lowing. One creature barks, another coughs. In addition to keeping a precise daily log and census, it is my job to help the three sons gather the manure and throw it overboard. The others dole out food, spread new straw, and watch for land, if ever there is to be land.

It is humid in the ark. The least exertion causes my glasses to fog up. Heat radiates from the great throbbing, blood-filled bodies all around. Horses and cattle are tethered, sheep and goats given free rein; chickens and geese step among the hooves. The savage beasts are caged separately in another part of the vessel. At night I listen to their roaring, their trumpeting. Overhead, the air is sliced by birds flying from ledge to ledge. Engulfed in reek, I sleep soundly, too soundly, as though the miasma itself were narcotic. Waking, I pull myself up, hand over hand, to one of the orbital sockets, those "deep dark cabins of the head" that open out on whatever of the world is left. Once there, I open my eyes, not so much to see—there is nothing to see—but to feel the cool air on my eyeballs. In a world that is utterly vacant, one yearns for contact, collision even, to strike, to tilt, the sound of boards ripping, grinding, any evidence that one is not all alone on this water.

On this ship, dreaming is continuous. Awake and asleep, I dream. So thick and hot come these visions that sometimes they will organize into ropes of mist. One might reach out to grasp them. Noah's wife, who had to be forcibly dragged on board, seems now to be reconciled. She and the daughters-in-law have strewn hay thickly in a roped-off part of the deck. She refers to it as The Manger. Already, several of the animals have lain there to give birth. The old woman told me that to give birth in a manger is appropriate for a beast and worthy of a god. I wonder what she meant by that.

Noah calculates that we have been en-arked for thirty days and thirty nights. Will it never end? I am never hungry anymore. Not only am I seasick, the richness of the air is suppressant to the appetite. It is the same for the other humans. Not so the animals, who must be fed and watered. And we have almost run out of fodder. Already, one of the cows has stopped lowing and settled to the floor. The sheep have gathered in a circle, nose to nose, as if awaiting the passage of a storm. Either let there be food for these beasts, or let them die now! I could not endure a slow famine, with them dropping one by one. Better a massacre than that.

Outside it continues dark, utterly dark although . . . Yes . . . I do believe the rocking has diminished. Japheth insists that the water is receding, but how can one know? The horses have grown thin and frenzied with hunger. Only a short while ago I let them nuzzle my neck, but now I am afraid of them. No longer gentle, they have the look of stray vicious dogs. Just beneath my desk is a trapdoor leading down a long flight of steps that curve forward and back in a gentle S. These steps end in a nubbin that resembles an arrowhead. I've named it Coccyx. Sometimes, when the claustrophobia becomes acute, I open the trapdoor at the head of the staircase and imagine going down all the way to the Coccyx. Then an easy rappel, a last exultant leap . . . to the earth! If ever there should be earth again.

Again and again I ask myself why I haven't thrown myself from the deck into the sea, have an end to it at last. Why? Because something tells me that I have not yet completed the task for which I was brought aboard almost forty days ago. Besides, if I leave, who will set down the record of this voyage? Ah well. Where is that notebook? The quills of damnation? Come on! Spin, you Jade, spin!

Only in a diary is one allowed to go mad.

DECEMBER 1992

It has all boiled down to a belief in magic. Even the persistent skeptic is not free of the need to attribute supernatural powers to inanimate objects.

For twelve years I have carried with me a green malachite stone the size and shape of a robin's egg. I go no place without it. Just to reach into my pocket and let the warm stone drop into my palm is reassuring. To worry it is to free me from worry. Everything will be all right; I will not be struck by a stray bullet, I will not miss my plane; I will not have one of those sudden fits of mental vagueness at the podium. The malachite egg was given to me by a woman who loved me, who loves me still.

"This will keep you safe," she had whispered. It is a stone that is dearer to me than his turquoise ring was to Shylock. Six years ago it was joined in the other pocket by a little silver ball that contains an internal spring and hammer. When the tiny "works" are agitated, you hear a chiming so sweet as to make me think of my mother's voice that sounded as if a white mouse were ringing a tiny silver bell. Walking down Prospect Street each morning, there is a cascade of celestial notes. I am Oberon wearing a codpiece hung with just such bells that jangle as he strides through the forest. Such a pretty clinking as he must leave behind. In New Haven, too, heads turn to see who it is that scatters sweet music from his pants. Could it be Oberon, King of the Fairies? On especially threatening days, I will put the malachite egg and the silver ball in the same pocket, as I have found that doubles the protection.

JULY 1993

I have always told lies, as much for the sheer pleasure that lying gives as to invent delectable circumstances for myself and others. Lying gives a certain vitality to life. Besides, there's no "Thou shalt not" about it in the Ten Commandments. That part about not bearing false witness is something else entirely. While my father is not remembered for his veracity, Mother was continually on the *qui vive* for such lapses. Once, having caught me in yet another lie, she warned:

"If you think for one moment that I'm going to supply you with a fresh halo each time you break the one you're wearing . . ." She had a way of not finishing these remarks, generously allowing the guilty to imagine the worst for himself. A few years before she died, Mother read one of my books.

"I had always hoped that one day you'd grow out of it, the lying," she mourned, "but I see that you . . ." And here she let go of her voice, let it drift away from her lips in a way to let me know more, much more, than mere words could, the bottomless depth of her sorrow.

But now it is years later. I am aboard the 7:45 A.M. train to New York
City, which always makes me more ill-haired than I usually am. The heat
and humidity are suggestive of Dante's *Inferno*. The train is full of
Wallstreeters dressed in the uniform of their regiment: dark pinstriped
suit, rep tie, suspenders, and oxblood wing-tip shoes with tassels. They
have a sharp-eyed, metallic look, as though within the hour they will be
riding the thermal currents over lower Manhattan.

I was glad to be meeting for the first time the publishers of *Raising the
Dead*. Feeling reckless, I took the shuttle from Grand Central to Times
Square, transferred to the #1 downtown train, and got off at Houston
Street. This feat, performed for the first time, gave me a surge of pride.
At Viking I met the editor of the book; then to the director of publicity
and the marketing manager, all of whom professed to be overjoyed to
meet me. It's always thus before publication. I was told there is to be a
British sale and an excerpt in *Discover* magazine. The dust jacket looked
like coma itself. We had lunch, without which no book has been published in North America for fifty years.

Now I am racing across Varick Street to get the uptown train, repeat-
ing in reverse order my great deed of the morning. All at once I hear a
woman's voice calling out urgently.

"Wait! Oh wait! Please wait a moment, sir!" At the curb I turn to see
a dark-haired woman of about thirty, with Latin coloring. She gives her
name as Diaz.

"Excuse me," she pants. "Are you an author?"

"Yes."

"Are you Richard Selzer?" I admit it.

"I heard you speak last winter at the New York Academy of Medicine.
It was the night of the hurricane, remember?" She turns then to say to
her companion, another young woman:

"I *told* you it was him!" Then goes on telling of how that night she had
braved the storm because she had read one of my books, how at the
Academy she had stood alone in the lobby, feeling out of place, wondering if she should leave, when I came up to her, thanked her for coming,
and "chatted warmly." (Did I do that? Probably, as there was no one else
there.) All of that on a street corner in New York!

All at once . . . it was not New York, filthy, steaming, and thick with
exhaust fumes. It was . . . Warsaw . . . No . . . St. Petersburg in the winter

of '98. I could hear the jingling of horse-drawn sleighs, the crunch of hoof upon snow, the clip-clop where the snow had been pounded from the cobblestones. The woman was young, fair-skinned, with high cheek-bones and slanted eyes. She was wearing a charming hat of dark brown Persian lamb, and she carried a large muff of the same material. I could not help but notice how the steam of our breaths melded, while all around us gaslights flickered. Her voice was high, Slavic. When she laughed, the notes froze and hung in my ears like tiny icicles. Looking down, she saw that I was barehanded, then removed one tiny hand and slid the muff over the fingers of my right hand. Inside it was warm, mysterious. A carriage approached, the driver sitting immobile, his whip standing in the crook of an arm. I hailed him, held open the door, and helped her to step up and in.

"Where are we going?" called the coachman.

"To Paradise!" I replied. Those tiny icicles!

But now it is the 5:07 P.M. train back to New Haven. Slick and eager as was the morning train, just so spent and chugging is the evening one. As we chuntered eastward, one after another ties are loosened, jackets shed, briefcases shelved. The faces of the Wallstreeters soften. At each station a contingent rises and gathers toward the door. A young man bends to peer out at the parking lot, where a young woman carrying a child is waiting. The man smiles. Within sight of the nest, a hawk is not a killer; he is a husband and father.

So much for the day's prevarication.

DECEMBER 1993

So! After everything I've done to preserve the English language in all its lovely variety—rescuing the odd marooned expression, reconstituting a comatose subjunctive; after the invention of both *lunaqua* and *aqualune* for "path of moonlight on the water" and the resurrection of *vaccimul-gence,* the art of milking a cow, one would think I deserve to be left in my tent of dalliance. But no, once again there comes the blare of silver trumpets calling the old warrior forth to take up vellum and quill and go roving with a hungry heart. This time, it is in service to the word *irpe,* a word so rare as to have been used by only one writer, Ben Jonson, and by him only twice. Once, in a play called *Cynthia's Revels,* and again in *Palinode.*

I should say at the outset that Ben Jonson left no instructions as to the pronunciation of the word. Was the terminal *e* to be silent so as to rhyme with burp or chirp? Or was it to be given its full *e*-ness, as in Burpee or chirpy? We do not know, and so must make a harmonious choice: irpe, I think. As in Iolanthe.

In *Cynthia's Revels,* a character named Amorphus is instructing Asotus on how to capture the attention of the woman he loves:

> Maintain your station, brisk and irpe, shew the supple motion of
> your pliant body, but, in chief, of your knee and hand, which cannot
> but arride her proud humor exceedingly.

(Note: *arride* is synonymous with *delight,* but of course you knew that.) As can be seen, we are given a clue to the meaning of *irpe* by its placement in the midst of a set of specific bodily attitudes to be assumed for a definite purpose, that of winning over the affections of a woman. The use of the word in *Palinode* is equally suggestive:

> From Spanish shrugs, French faces, smirks, irpes and all affected
> humors, Good Mercury defend us.

Here *irpe* is included in a list of facial arrangements and gesticulations deemed affected, and given a negative, xenophobic slant. And now to the task with all my engine:

It is clear that the noun *irpe* indicates a posture at once debonair and cavalier, a blend of guile and bravado. It is not so premeditated as a smirk or so involuntary as a sneeze, but something in between. An *irpe* can be partial or full. The partial *irpe* is limited to a toss (but a quality toss) of the head in conjunction with a grimace. It is quite similar to the act of perking or holding oneself in a smart, brisk manner. While pursing the lips is optional, contraction of either right or left corrugator supercilius muscle so as to raise one eyebrow is essential. This *irpist* is blasé. In full *irpe,* the head is held wry, and the entire frontalis muscle is contracted so as to furrow the brow. The orbicularis oris draws the mouth into a pout or a moue of skepticism. This *irpist* is bored. The full *irpe* is a handsome cringe. One leg bears all the weight, the other being flexed at the knee. An elegant bow will surely follow. Already the torso begins to fold, while the head, loath to participate yet, remains erect. One hand is aloft in mid-flourish, the other let fall behind the body. (Just such a bow was made to the throne by the Prince of Wales on February 13, 1788, and was universally admired.) As for arriding the heart of a lady, a bow like that would kick up the heels of Chastity herself.

Still, as an instrument of flirtation, an *irpe* is devoid of passion. An *irpe* is ambiguous; you never know quite how you stand with an accomplished *irpist*. As in . . .

He bent to kiss her lips only to find her hand had been interposed at the last moment.

"Not here," she murmured.

"Tell me," he pleaded, "do I have any chance at all?"

Irping with great flair, she reached behind and turned the key in the latch. With the other hand, she gathered her flounces. What did she mean? Was he to follow her inside? Or had he been dismissed? Just then she irped again with even greater brilliance. Should he stay or go? What torment of indecision! He dared not risk offending her. In the end, he tore himself from the doorway and ran off without a backward glance. Damned irpette! he thought. Already he regretted his precipitous flight, and smote his breast at what he saw, too late, was a failure of nerve. But how was he to know, with her irping like that? In the dry and bitter years that followed, he would sometimes imagine her—*sola, perduta, abandon-nata*—having come to regret the cruel irpery with which she had cast aside his love. He certainly hoped so.

Podiocy

It is more than ten years since I walked away from my beloved work-bench in the operating room. Once freed from the privilege and the burden of caring for the sick, I would, I knew, spring up straight like a sapling that had been weighted down all winter by heavy snow. I dreamt of a life more romantic and adventurous than surgery. Surgeons don't get to commit but a fraction of the sins to which the rest of mankind is entitled. They don't have the time. Now I would make up for that life of constraint. I would become a buccaneer. Or an unrepentant libertine. But such were not given me. Instead I have become a Professor of Polite Learning, a strange migratory bird that roosts on podia all over North America. I never thought I'd sink so low. But then, there was a living to be made, a readership to be confronted, new readers to be gathered. I would have colleagues, friends. Besides, wasn't Homer a troubadour? What, I asked myself, could possibly happen? And replied: disgrace. To be an actor, to ruin oneself before a room full of strangers—it is scandalous. It was worth a try.

In the privacy of my tiny nutshell of a scriptorium I lit a candle to Duffy, the previous Bard of Troy and immortal habitué of the Central Tavern, its sainted raconteur; to Duffy, whose kind regard for an unhappy boy served as an antidote to despair and to the indifference of "cold planetary hearts." It was from Duffy that I learned the art of Body English—how to utter the equivalent of an exclamation mark without

making a sound, how to insinuate with a simple tilt of the chin. While it
was from Duffy that I learned the thousand implications of a silent shrug
and just when to lay a finger alongside my nose, it was from Mother that
I acquired coquetry—how to waft puffs of temperament out across an
audience to telling effect. From both I learned the strength of the spoken
word, how it can raise you up high, higher than you deserve, so that others will come under your spell.

Behind a locked door I began to rehearse as for a play with only one
character, interspersing my recitation with dollops of wit and ebullience.
I chatted to myself, waxed and waned, grew tragic, hilarious, turned
aside wrath with a soft word, and, in the face of the worst hectoring,
remained in the very pink of politeness. Debonair, that's what I was. The
way I bounded onto the stage, offered the first row a mischievous twin-
kle, and began. And all in the privacy of my study. Before long I had mas-
tered the long pregnant pause and all that forgotten eloquence of Duffy's
shrug. Let me say right at the outset that I was not to the podium born.
Surgeons, you know, are as mute as grass. We are men and women whose
nature is to have and to do, not to seduce with oiled tongue. I was not,
after all, a Mark Twain who with a phrase could snatch the veil of care
from an auditorium of mourners; or a Charles Dickens who could cause
a thousand hearts to beat as one. The path from operating room to lecture hall was strewn with boulders, rutted, and overgrown with poison
ivy. Imagine a short, scrawny old man with a vertebral column that over
the years has taken on the shape of a seahorse, and with a cap of aluminum hair. His voice is a thin, reedy tenor, further afflicted with a lisp.
(How often in the years since have I yearned for the larynx of Stentor!
Such, such is the man who would embark upon a career of Podiocy?)

It wasn't two weeks after my retirement from surgery when, to my
astonishment, there came an invitation to speak at a small college in
Vermont. Having made the mistake of arriving on campus several hours
early, I proceeded to grow more and more nervous. Why was I here?
How could I have let this happen? Podiocy, I thought; it is a torment
overlooked by Dante. At last the hour of the lecture was at hand. Down
the center aisle between row upon row of perfect strangers, I was led like
a garlanded bull. Now the dreaded Introducer had delivered what
amounted to my eulogy. Nothing to do but rise and throw myself at the
podium. Did I lift a finger to an ear? Two hundred pairs of eyes followed

it there and back. Did I pass a hand through my hair, dare to scratch the back of my head? Did I draw a finger from cheek to chin as if I were taking inventory of my features? Two hundred pairs of eyes were nailed to the sight. I shrank under the weight of their gaze. Just before I might have swooned or died, some glandular resource, hitherto unknown, sent me into the altered state of consciousness that is the only condition in which Podiocy can be safely practiced. It is the same state into which Milton placed Adam during the birth of Eve, anesthetized, but with the "cell of Fancy" kept open so that Adam could describe exactly what happened during the rib resection. Spellbound, the Speaker's voice now seems to him not thin and reedy, but a rich meaty baritone that, once having left his lips, rumbles across the floor, causing the furniture to vibrate. The silence in the hall is not that of sleep or boredom; it is the silence of rapture. It was my own mumbled "Thank you" that awakened me that afternoon in Vermont. There was applause. I was fêted at a reception, signed copies of my books, received an honorarium. Hallelujah! I was earning a living!

Now that I have served more than ten years at the podium, I hope I may be permitted to reveal a few of the secrets of the profession. Of all the kinds of public utterance I have given—jeremiads, exhortations, expostulations, ejaculations—I have eschewed only orations. It matters little what an orator says, only how he says it, with what "presence," the brilliance of his eye, the distention of his nostrils, the contraction of his supercilius muscles. The orator in command of his facial strategy is like the Pied Piper of Hamelin or like Orpheus, who beguiled the beasts, the trees even, to draw near. It is said that oratory is dangerous in that it might inflame its listeners to wickedness of thought or deed. Oratory is just as dangerous to the orator himself, who is apt to fall in love with his own tics and hemiquavers and come to actually believe what he is saying. No matter with what modesty he may begin, there will come that moment, mid-speech, when he, too, must succumb to himself. The bedazzled orator loses all proportion and with his plummy tones, each sonorous revelation underlined by an impressive rhetorical pause, can send a susceptible electorate into the streets. There are no lisping castrati in Congress. They know better than to run for public office. To become a successful orator, you need a booming voice whose mere echo can bring an audience to its feet and have it run off madly in all directions. The orator knows that the tonsil is mightier than the sword. Personally, I detest orations. Having had to translate a number of Cicero's in high school, I don't mourn the burning of the library in Alexandria where, it is said, a great many more of his *Orationes* were kept. I thank God they lie beyond the reach of archeology.

As for the ritual of the American Commencement Address, it is way too long, made even longer by consisting of platitudes delivered in a voice that has been sterilized in an autoclave and that has never uttered anything but the Ten Commandments. Since word has gotten around that my limit for a Commencement Address is twelve minutes, I am much sought after upon those occasions. Within that brief span, there is not a word of instruction on how to live beyond reproach in an otherwise imperfect world. At medical schools I take pains to ladle out large dollops of grotesque medical school humor. "Good writing is everywhere," I tell the graduates, and quote from my version of a textbook of parasitology: "Tapeworms may be harbored for years and, except for the inconvenience of the gravid segments crawling out of the anus, the host continues in robust health, enjoying both food and drink." (Show me the writer who wouldn't die to have written that!) For a time it seemed that no one in North America could become a doctor without my yammering away at the rites. Say what I will, I always cry when the doctor/parents come onstage to "hood" their doctor/children. It is what I have missed.

As I said before, I have marched three and a half miles to the tune of "Pomp and Circumstance" alone. I have only to hear the first three bars of that number and the blood freezes in my veins. Most Commencements are held in May or June, when the climate is apt to be torrid. In full regalia, one swelters toward dehydration until what makes its bedraggled way from the platform at the Recessional is nothing but a soggy cap and gown with no one inside, and only the little gold tassel to put up a brave show. There was one Commencement in San Diego that, for my sins, was held al fresco on a lovely grassy knoll. There we all sat in the noonday sun like mad dogs and Englishmen, while a hot wind called a Santa Ana blew in from the desert. The vowels wilted as they came out of my mouth, and the consonants never even made it past my teeth, but were portcullised there. Such a Commencement is likely to result in its antonym—a Termination. It is not to be done again without a tank of oxygen on the dais and an ambulance parked alongside.

Later, at the suggestion of the Dean, I drove down into Mexico, in hopes of escaping the heat. Upon getting out of the car in Encinada, I discovered that Mexico, too, had come under the curse of Santa Ana. Which brings me to the nameless saloon into which I followed a white chicken to get out of the broil. The doorway to the saloon was curious in that it was incompletely divided by a plywood partition. One side of the partition was labeled Entrada, the other Partida. The separation having been done, I imagined, to avoid collisions among the tequila-sodden. Inside, torpor: The metabolic rate of the premises had slowed to hibernation. Yet I knew full well that it is just such a saloon that springs to sudden violence. Knives are drawn; blood spreads across the floor. I have read my Borges. Sawdust had been cast upon the floor. Chickens stepped about freely. Now and then one of them would lower its head and beak the sawdust. Along one wall were several unoccupied tables. I took a seat at one of these. Running the length of the opposite wall was a bar decorated with blue and white tiles. In front of the bar, a row of high stools upon each of which a motionless man perched. Only the infusion of new smoke into the haze gave evidence that any of them breathed.

A man slipped quietly from his stool, walked to a corner of the room, lowered himself to the floor, tilted his hat forward, and pulled sleep over himself like a blanket. Then all was still again. Soon it would be time to leave. Now, it happened that one of the bar stools, the one nearest the doorway marked Partida, was tilted at an extravagant angle such that its legs completely blocked the passageway. Perched on the very rim of this stool, with only the barest overhang of his buttocks resting on the edge, was an emaciated man, his head collapsed upon his forearms so that it seemed deflated. The loose shirt of the sleeping Mexican was unbuttoned and hung outside his pants. From where I sat I could see that his chest did not expand symmetrically, but that the inflation of the left lung lagged behind the right. The tail of the shirt idled over a funnel-shaped scar on the posterior left chest. Where an abscess had been drained? Or an ancient knife wound? I thought about the fragility of the human body, how it can be slain by the single pass of a pick, how from the smallest puncture the whole of the blood can run. I ordered another Bohemia. No knife so furious, I thought, but would relent at such a bared grief as this chest.

But now, standing in the center of the saloon, resting one boot on a shoeshine box, stood another man, squat and powerful. His shirt and pants upholstered his body tightly. He was slightly drunk, singing to himself from beneath a great awning of hat. In contrast with the man at the bar, he exuded gracefulness and good health. An old man with a pale, exhausted look was shining his shoes. His dry, fleshless hands moved above the sawdust in which he knelt. At last the old man gave a final flick with his cloth and backed off. The big man delivered the remainder of his song aloud, emptied his glass, and tossed a coin. Here was a man whose appetites became him.

Now he was ready to leave. He approached the Partida, only to find it blocked by the stool of the sleeping man. It is always so, I thought. There is the cripple, the wounded, preventing passage. He awakens our folded, sleeping souls and harries us until we do not know which way to go. The big man paused. It did not occur to him to leave through the Entrada. Or if it did, he would insist on his right of way. He threw one leg over, straddling the legs of the stool, then tried to bring his other leg across. But there was no room to do so. For a long moment he stood in his awkwardness, then hopped and shifted his hips over the barricade until he stood on the other side. All at once a look of cruelty crossed his handsome face. With a quick movement, he kicked the stool out from under the sleeper, then spun and swaggered into the sunshine.

Miraculously, the unseated man did not fall, but remained clinging to the bar like an insect. His knees, locked in extension, did not buckle. It seemed a defiance of gravity. In a moment he would fall. He must fall. Just then, the old shoe-shiner stood up and walked to Partida. I was surprised by his height. He was by far the tallest man in the saloon. I watched him pick up the fallen stool and, with infinite care, insert the edge of the seat beneath the buttocks of the man, shifting it slightly to get the steadiest set. The knees of the man on the stool flexed passively as his body accepted the gift of the bar stool. The old man withdrew and lowered himself to the floor, where the chickens welcomed him back into their midst with clucks and flutters. One of the birds bent to peck at the foot of another, where there was an open red sore. The wounded bird cackled and gave a graceless flapping jump. It was time to leave this bar. I did so through the Entrada, for in this saloon in Mexico I had learned how to avoid the loss of grace.

Lectures on Art: Sculpture

THE IVORY CRUCIFIXION

From time immemorial, ivory has been used for carving. Extremely smooth and without the granular character of marble, ivory has the paradoxical property of being both sensuous and pure. The tusk of an elephant is a highly developed upper incisor tooth, mostly dentine with a thin cap of enamel. In the Middle Ages, the chief market for ivory carvings consisted of the Church and the royal households. There was always a shortage of the raw material until Marco Polo opened up the trade routes that passed through Baghdad and Damascus. When banditry made these roads impassable, the ivory trade dwindled until the early sixteenth century, when the Portuguese Empire included Goa (an enclave on the western coast of India), parts of China, and Macao.

In 1541 no less a personage than St. Francis Xavier went to Goa to convert the heathen, with mixed results, although by 1570 three-fourths of the city was said to be Christian. This might have been due as much to ethnic cleansing as to missionary success. Today the city of Goa is in great disrepair. The only buildings of note are the churches, one of which houses the skeletal remains of St. Francis Xavier. With the comparative availability of ivory in the sixteenth and seventeenth centuries, carvings became largely secular—combs, pommels, dice, buckles, buttons, and chessmen.

The *Ivory Crucifixion* was acquired by the Yale Art Gallery in 1967 from a dealer in Dublin. It is thirteen inches long and weighs three and a half pounds. It happens invariably that when I have left the presence of the figure, it seems so much larger than it really is. Out of sight, it is in the mind's eye many times its real size, evidence that suffering magnifies the sufferer. The tusk in its original state is calculated to have been one yard long. It was carved in the late sixteenth or early seventeenth century in Goa. In all probability the sculptor was a native convert or someone in the employ of the missionaries. The bulk of Goan ivory carving has been deemed of little artistic merit. I don't know about that. The usual subject was Jesus as the Good Shepherd sitting among his lambs and ewes, with the repentant Mary Magdalene lying about. In another Goan carving, the Virgin Mary is shown wearing a sari. She has distinctly Asian features, including long black hair in a simplified style. The Yale Christ is, beyond doubt, the masterpiece of the genre.

Figure of Christ from a Crucifix, Unknown

Gazing at this ivory Christ, one cannot help but think of its anonymous sculptor, think of him applying his knife, chisel, and mallet to the raw tusk; think of the months and even years spent in creating the statue; think of the way he must have held the tusk with one hand, cut and scraped with the other, pausing to blow away the ivory dust, realizing the essential crucifixion that lay hidden in the mass of dentine; think of him smoothing and polishing the surface. Had he pumice with which to rub it? Or did he use a paste of crushed seashells, ashes of bone, coarse fish skin? Had he tiny drills? Spoonbits? Did he soak the tusk in wine or vinegar or a solution of phosphoric acid to soften it for the knife and chisel? All these tools and techniques were used: matters of craft and handiwork that would appeal to the curiosity of a surgeon.

Now see him, our unknown artist, crouching at his workbench, darkening the tusk with the shadow of his own body, letting his breath play on it. These things are important—how else infuse the inert mass with his own aura? How else incorporate his personality and temperament? I like to think that piety was the engine that drove him in this enterprise, that his was a worshipful knife, but we know very well that it is not always good heart that makes good art. Cézanne did not attend his mother's funeral because he didn't want to lose two hours of good light. And Giotto, shortly after he painted St. Francis of Assisi taking Lady Poverty for his mistress, rented looms to the impoverished women of Florence at a return of one hundred and twenty percent. So far as I know, no one has ever claimed that Robert Frost was a man of generous heart toward his fellow artists.

Gazing further, one thinks of the great lumbering beast that had dumbly, and unbeknownst to its handlers, carried glory in one of its tusks. The Yale Christ is of a soft shade of brown, with highlights suggestive of the candlelight in which it was doubtless most often seen. The ivory is seamed, cracked, pitted, and weathered. This is a tusk that has labored and endured, perhaps suffered its own form of crucifixion. An altogether fitting undifferentiated substance, a mesenchyme, for the depiction of an event that has enthralled much of Western Civilization for two thousand years.

This statue is an ideal convergence of beauty and pain. He is closer to the lissome, androgynous Christ of the Italian Renaissance than He is to the sixteenth century Isenheim altarpiece by Matthias Grunewald, in which there is no trace of transfiguration—no Savior, only a martyr. There, the wounds are detailed. Broken bits of wood still stick in the flesh. Blood drips. The hands are convulsively cramped, the feet deformed. The parched yellow skin is turning grayish green. It is festering and bruised. There is exhaustion in the drooping face, with its scraggly beard and open bluish lips. The tortured brow is rent by thorns. All in all, the Grunewald altarpiece exudes a dreadful splendor. But this Yale Christ shows none of the fleshly torment. In the accepted style of the period, Christ's suffering is placed at an aesthetic distance, so that it becomes less human than universal.

The arms are not present. Surely the girth of the tusk would not permit them. They would have to have been carved separately and then fixed into sockets at the shoulders. One imagines arms outstretched upon a crosspiece. The legs, too, are absent, brutally amputated, truncated, and fractured at mid-thigh. The deformity gives a mute eloquence to the figure. Why, one wonders, had the artist not begun to carve a few inches higher up on the tusk? There would have been room for the legs. Because, the sculptor is likely to reply, *here* was the Christ, only here and nowhere else. That is the way artists talk.

It is noteworthy that the position of the body makes use of the natural curve of the tusk, not unlike the prehistoric cave paintings, whose artists made use of the mounding and declivities of the cavern walls to suggest movement and to give perspective. The knees, had they been present, would have been drawn forward and upward as if to ward off a blow to the midsection. Precisely because of the absence of arms and lower legs, the figure is all the more expressive. It is often so; an absence makes a declaration that a presence cannot, much as a silence can be more evocative than a shout.

John Keats instructed us that "heard melodies are sweet, but those unheard are sweeter." Similarly, the German poet Rainer Maria Rilke gazed at a headless torso of Apollo and found that the vision of the God had transferred itself from the absent eyes to the torso, which "glowed like a chandelier, his gaze, only turned down, not dead, persists and burns." Rilke offers proof of this: If not, how could the surge of the breast blind the viewer? And what of the "smile that passes and returns in the thighs"? In the end, Rilke's "Antique Torso of Apollo" is looking at the viewer. The roles are reversed. "There is no part that does not see you." And then comes the command from the poet through the torso: "You must change your life." A meditation that might apply equally to this Yale Ivory Christ.

No less than Rilke's "Antique Torso of Apollo," this figure is imbued by the artist with the property of unearthly persuasion. Apollo's is a proud and godly sermon that evokes remorse and self-examination, while Christ uses His wounded body to arouse compassion and pity. The face is not the only doorway to the spirit. I have seen sorrow more fully realized in a buttocks eaten away by bedsores, vulnerability in a kyphoscoliotic spine, supplication in an arthritic hand, fear in the arching of a child's neck, despair in the blind numb placement of a diabetic foot on the ground. Not long ago I was informed by a man's kneecaps that he was going to die. Turning blue, they notified me that he was running out of oxygen. As soon as I got their cyanotic message, I summoned the family for a last visit.

Before some works of art, we are humbled, stunned. They seem to exist apart from and beyond the human; they speak, if only "murmuringly heard." Such mysteries are not meant to be solved; they are meant to be deepened. This Christ is not supernatural or magical. It is our imagination that makes it seem so. Some objects realize their full potential only in our vision of them, and whether one is Christian or not, this derelict Yale Christ, without arms or legs, speaks powerfully to the emotions.

Where the ivory figure triumphs is in the uncanny achievement of both serenity and anguish in Christ's face. Viewed from the left and below, the expression is one of suffering, pain; viewed from the right and below, there is the countenance of everlasting peace. What we have, then, is a Christ suspended between two worlds, the world of the body (not yet entirely abandoned) and the world of the spirit (not yet entirely attained). It is the moment of transition, the interface between the human and the divine. While the pain is almost over, the sculptor has held back the repose of death that would have extinguished all character from the face, that would have caused it to descend into bland insensibility. Even at rest, there must be character. Here, repose and agony—call it Passion, if you will—are locked in mutual opposition. The contrast is dramatic, the expression unstable. Nor is there any sign of what is called the Hippocratic facies, the classic mask of the dying described by the Father of Medicine, and characterized by pinched nostrils, pointed nose, sunken eyes, hollow cheeks, and leaden skin.

The anonymous sculptor shows an instinctive knowledge of facial anatomy. See how he has shut the eyes gently, as if in sleep. He understands that it is only the upper eyelid that moves in closing. The lower lid has no muscle that would help it to meet halfway. He has placed the whole burden of the agony on one or two skin folds, making precise use of that portion of the frontalis muscle called the corrugator supercilii—the knitter of the brow. This muscle is composed of transverse fibers that are attached at one end to the frontal bone at the inner end of the orbital socket, where nose and eye meet. The other end is attached, not to the bone as is usual, but to the dermis, the deepest layer of the skin itself. Even without benefit of gazing into the eyes, we are entirely absorbed in His condition, which is one of utter self-absorption. He is alone, isolated in his Passion and aglow with His suffering.

As for the expression of the body of Christ, it is exerted entirely by the tension of the torso, which both writhes and sags limply. The exaggerated rib cage and the engorged neck veins serve to convey the straining of the body as it strives to exhale against the inertia of the diaphragm. Each rib ends in a bony knob that is riveted to the sternum as to a battleship. The posture of the body combines with the dramatic fall of the head to the right shoulder. There is the wealth of His hair, grown past the shoulders and spreading like a dark star from the crown of His head. Missing, too, is the crown of thorns, although a faint trace of red at the hairline may be evidence that it had once been there. There is also a bit of red at the mouth and at the side wound. The head fallen thus is reminiscent of the passage of the *Aeneid* in which Virgil describes the death of one of his heroes, Euryalus:

> ... And on the shoulder
> the neck droops over, as a bright-colored flower
> Droops when the ploughshare bends it, or as poppies
> Sink under the weight of heavy summer rainfall.

The idealized posture of Virgil's dead hero, who was also one of the good guys, is typical of heroic death, such as that of Leander or St. Sebastian. It is characteristic of the death of a hero or a righteous man. Notice that there is not the natural equipoise of the sleeper, whose muscles and joints are relaxed. Nor does it have the heaviness of a corpse. There is tension in every part of His body.

The drapery that conceals Christ's nakedness is tied to the body by rope that weaves in and out. The folds are dramatically accentuated by being sharply incised and by a rather sophisticated use of light and dark. If there is anything in Christian art more hypocritical than Christ's loincloth, I don't know what it could be. The blame is not the artist's; he is, after all, a child of his time. It was thought pious to protect the modesty of Christ, and he made no distinction between nakedness and nudity. The nude in art is most often an erotic figure designed to arouse carnal thoughts. The naked human form, on the other hand, is far from erotic. It is piteous, vulnerable, supplicant, and ashamed. The nude is not ashamed, but joyous and proud of the fact. To be naked is to be devoid of physical pride, defenseless. It should come as no surprise that, to a doctor, the human body, whether naked or nude, is the greatest subject for art.

Covering up Christ with a loincloth at all, even a plain diaper, is a trivialization of the Incarnation. In the same way, it is far more diagnostic for a doctor to watch a man remove his soiled underwear to show his wounded body than it is to read a yard of data from the computer. And here on this Ivory Christ we have the Imperial Diaper itself, an obi right out of kabuki theatre. Festooned and draped, it produces the ironic effect of riveting the imagination on the genitalia cowering way beneath. If one is asked to believe that what existed at the very beginning entered the atmosphere of His creation in human form, then one must accept that, while in human form, He engaged in human activities and that he had the complete anatomy of a man. It is not only hypocritical to carve or paint for Christ a loincloth, it is artistically dishonest. It is a far cry from the phallic religions and fertility cults that antedated or were coeval with Christianity, and that celebrated the sexual and the procreative. In stripping off the loincloth in his rendition of the Crucifixion, Michelangelo was not trying to *épater le bourgeoisie;* he was restoring dignity to the Incarnation.

The artist who would prettify or soften the Crucifixion is missing the point. The aim was to kill horribly and to subject the victim to the utmost humiliation. It involved a preliminary whipping with the dreaded Roman *flagrum*—a leather whip with three tails. At the tip of each tail there was a small dumbbell-shaped weight of iron or bone or wood. With each lash of the whip, the three bits dug into the flesh. The victim was tied or chained to a post, and two centurions stood on either side. The wounds extended around to the chest and abdomen. Profuse bleeding ensued. Then the man was beaten on the head with reeds so that his face was bruised, his nose broken. In the case of Jesus, in order to further deride him and to mock his appellation as King of the Jews, a crown of thorns was placed on his brow and temples.

At one point a Roman soldier hurled the spear that opened the wound in His side. Jesus, weakened by a night of fasting and prayer, as by the flogging and blood loss, was not able to carry his own cross to the place of execution as the punishment required. Simon of Cyrene did it for Him. Then His hands were nailed to the crosspiece, and the whole apparatus was raised and set into a groove on the upright part. The height was approximately seven and a half feet. To add to the suffering, Jesus was assailed by extreme thirst, as is usual in instances of severe blood loss and dehydration. On one occasion, a disciple was able to reach up and give Him a drink through a hollow straw. To ensure maximum humiliation, the cross was set up in a public place, along a main highway or at a cross-roads or on an elevation of land such as the hill of Calvary. Death resulted from shock, both traumatic and hypovolemic, and from respiratory failure due to the difficulty of expelling air from the lungs in the upright and suspended position, in which the diaphragm does not rise easily. It is altogether understandable that Jesus, the night before, said to God: "If at all possible, let this cup pass from my lips."

Crucifixion was practiced not only by the Romans, but by all of the peoples of that time, including—rarely—the Jews. After the slave uprisings led by Spartacus in Rome in 71 B.C., six thousand insurrectionists were crucified at one time. In A.D. 70, in Judaea, five hundred Jews were similarly executed each day. In the late 1970s, a burial mound outside the city of Jerusalem was excavated and the skeleton of a young man unearthed. A spike had been driven through both heel bones and was still in place. Ordinarily the iron spikes were withdrawn after death and reused many times. In this instance, the spike had become bent during the driving and could not be retrieved.

A sculpture such as the *Ivory Crucifixion* exists all by itself; it has no companions, no background or surroundings to describe or to reflect upon. The entire artistic burden is carried by the figure affixed to a plain brown piece of cloth and hung inside a glass case. Alone, it retains its purity. Christ is portrayed apart from all *situation,* unmolested by any intrusion. And yet, full of the vitality and the allure produced by the coalescence of body and spirit. I mean no disparagement, but at the Yale museum this beautiful Christ hangs on the wall immediately adjacent to a sacrilegious elevator. It is rather like giving a little girl a doll, then nailing it up on a wall out of her reach. Out of harm's way, you tell her, but she is not consoled. She had wanted to take care of it, to hug and kiss it. But that is a shortcoming of The Museum, and no, Art is not Life, we are told. Surely a more congenial place might be found? A niche, say, lit by candles to encourage the possibility that, at any moment, He might relent into the uncarved tusk from which he had been wrested. In much the same way,

hanging a Titian in an apse makes the dark shadows of a church work
for him.

I deplore the practice of covering paintings with glass. The reflection
is always wrong, so that you can't see for the glare. And if the painting is
dark, a Murillo say, or a Zurbaran, all you can see is yourself. Not long
ago, at the Cleveland Art Museum, I watched a woman putting on lip-
stick in front of a *Temptation of St. Anthony*!

Confronted by the Yale Christ, with its missing parts, the cracks and
darkening of the ivory, it is only natural that one's thoughts turn to ruins.
In the matter of ruination, I am all on the side of the ravages of time. It is
not destruction but gentle evidence that everything created and those
who created it will one day return to that state of shapeless quiescence
from which might spring a new art or even a new species. Could this have
been on the mind of John Keats when he addressed the sky children?
"For on our heels a fresh perfection treads." I'm opposed to the restora-
tion of old paintings. Such cleaning, scraping, and touching up are futile
attempts to deny the finitude of things, rather like embalming a corpse.
In the end, it is all the same. The restored painting has little resemblance
to the lovely "ruin" it had become. The new product is apt to be garish
and vulgar as well as counterfeit. Surely it has been robbed of its dignity,
and looks for all the world like someone elderly who has been got at by a
swarm of plastic surgeons. When will art historians learn that Time adds
its own slow strokes to every work of art? A scab of lint, soot, dead bugs,
and cobwebs gives a kind of fourth dimension to a painting, just the right
hallucinative touch to an *Annunciation*. A *Deposition From the Cross*, seen
through a film of mildew and flyspeck, is suitably darkened, the sorrow
of the Virgin magnified. As in the ruin and decline of the living human
body, Time is the gentle nurse that eases a work of art into the irretriev-
able past. As far as I'm concerned, she can have her way with me, too.

I'm not at all sure that a museum is the best place to encounter this figure. You aren't allowed to touch it, to palpate it, as a doctor would examine a patient—arguably no less sacred a personage. You can't brandish it
en militaire and then go off on a Crusade to the Holy Land to rescue
Jerusalem from the likes of me. Nor can you pick the statue up and march
in procession behind braziers of incense to the angelic blare of trumpets.
It is not, after all, a trophy, something won on the field of battle or in a
contest. No, all you can do is peer at it through glass, which is all right
for an icon that carries with it the implication of being on high and at a

respectful distance. Icons are meant to be prayed to, knelt before. They're nowhere near as useful as amulets, charms, or the welter of *bondieuserie*—scapulars, rosaries, medallions—that are on sale outside shrines. An amulet can be palmed, worn about the neck, kept in a pocket or, if no one is looking, kissed. An amulet gets you safely through the day. An amulet asks of you no worship, piety, or confession. It simply offers all the ancient power of superstition, and in the absence of faith, I have found that superstition does very nicely.

Still, the Yale *Ivory Crucifixion* teaches the essential holiness of the body. Just as every elephant contains within its tusk such a possibility, so is every body pregnant with the sacred, the unspeakable, the beautiful. The clearest evidence of this is in the body wounded, of which the crucified Christ is the literary, religious, and artistic exemplar.

There is a book called *The Bestiary* that was hand-copied by monks in the twelfth century. In one chapter, we learn that an elephant, having fallen down, cannot get up again. Therefore, when an elephant wants to sleep, it leans against a tree in order to do so. A hunter, wishing to kill the beast and harvest its tusks, saws partially through the tree so that, when the elephant leans, the tree and, with it, the elephant will tumble. The fallen elephant cries out for help. The largest elephant in the herd comes running, but is unable to raise him up. Together they trumpet for help, and the other twelve elephants arrive, but they cannot raise their fallen comrade either. All fourteen elephants call out together, whereupon a runt of an elephant, the smallest and most insignificant in the tribe, appears. He pushes his proboscis and his tusks under the fallen one and lifts him easily to his feet. According to *The Bestiary,* the runt is Jesus Christ who, although He was the greatest, was made insignificant and obedient even unto death in order that He might raise up men. To the readers of the twelfth century, this was a wonderful story. It gave them real pleasure to think of Christ as an insignificant elephant. Just as eight hundred years later, it gives us pleasure to know that one elephant, the Yale elephant, carried within its tusk a powerful image of that same Jesus Christ. It is a dramatic closure that is utterly satisfying.

THE SIXTEENTH CENTURY
BAVARIAN PIETÀ, ANONYMOUS

If there is a certain advantage to ignorance, why then I am well suited to
dwell upon this five-hundred-year-old, anonymous *Bavarian Pietà*. I
know nothing about art history or the philosophy of art. I know only that
the word *pietà* means pity or compassion. So much the better, I tell myself.
Erudition dilutes the visceral impact of a work; knowing corrupts seeing; all of that. Nor am I an esthete who boasts an especially refined sen-
sitivity toward beauty. I'm at least as enamored of craft as I am of art. I
like the process of making, be it practiced in woodcarving or surgery. My
strongest qualification for examining a work of "religious" art is that I'm
an infidel, and as such unlikely to imbue this figure with any morality
simply because its subject is sacred to others. I come to it neither as pilgrim nor as idolater disposed to elevate a piece of wood to the status of
icon. My chief drawback is that I'm sentimental, prone to tears at the sight
of a mother mourning over the corpse of her son. "Look and see," she

Pieta (16th century
Bavarian), Unknown

seems to say, "you who pass by, and ask whether there is any sorrow like mine." The anonymous sculptor avoided the mawkish that infects so much religious statuary. I shall simply let his integrity be the antidote to my softheartedness. I have called this lecture a Fantasia. No other genre seemed to permit me the latitude. Let us begin.

Be it understood right off that the subject of the Pietà—the Virgin Mother holding the dead Christ on her lap—has no historic basis. Such an occurrence is not mentioned anywhere in the Gospels. It was the invention of the mystics who flourished in southern Germany in the thirteenth and fourteenth centuries, one of whom, the Dominican friar Heinrich Suso, wrote *The Little Book of Holy Wisdom* in which he caused the Virgin to say: "I took *mein zartes Kind,* my tender child, upon my lap and gazed at him, but he was dead." That was all it took for the notion to be seized upon as a subject for devotional art. Within a few years it vied for popularity with such old favorites as the Annunciation and the Gifts of the Magi. The earliest carvings were called *Vesperbilden,* evening statues, because of the time of day when Christ was supposed to have died. With the appearance of Michelangelo's masterpieces of this group, the term *pietà* had replaced it. The mass appeal of such a *sitzgruppe* (sitting group) is understandable. The Black Death, bubonic plague, having just swept across Europe and decimated the population, there was a hunger for Compassion to accompany the Passion of the crucifixion. Christ's suffering seemed to be at some emotional remove, something unique and not easily palpable. Mary was someone with whom all of the people could identify. Her tragic loss had been reenacted in every village where a youth had died and a mother was plunged into sorrow. It was the Franciscan order that developed the cult of the mourning mother in an effort to bring Christianity to the lower classes, and to give it a vernacular flavor.

The earliest Pietàs, those of the thirteenth century, were quite obsessed with the physical effects of the crucifixion—the lacerations, protruding ribs, blood, Christ's dried open mouth. The Savior was shrunken, preternaturally small, and was placed entirely on the Virgin's lap. The German mystics held that Mary in her grief imagined that she was back in Bethlehem holding her baby son, her *zartes Kind,* on her lap. Much of the emotional force was derived from this implicit contrast between Christ as infant and as man crucified. Gradually, over the next two hundred years, the Christ of the Pietà grew to full size, as seen in the depictions by Michelangelo. Over the years, Christ moved down from the lap of the Virgin to lie more horizontally across her knees, and finally to lie upon the ground with his upper body leaning against her knee. The position of this Christ dates the statue in the late sixteenth century. It is interesting that Michelangelo put Christ back on his mother's lap.

At age eighty-nine, a few days before he died, Michelangelo took up a Pietà he'd begun ten years before, and then abandoned. In an early version, Mary stood holding a slender Christ in her arms, lifting him toward us. In a last burst of activity, the sculptor cut away Christ's head and shoulders, and began a rough new head out of the Virgin's own shoulder and bosom. Next, he cut into the new heads, drawing them even closer. The two figures are not sinking; she holds him effortlessly from the rear. Christ, too, is upright. One sees the chisel marks seeking to resolve the final riddle of the mother/son relationship, the way they merge into a single figure. Such is the Rondanini *Pietà*. All by itself, it is worth a trip to Milan.

Nicodemus, a great teacher among the Jews, sought out Jesus.

"How can a man return to his mother's womb and be born again?" he asked. "It is not possible." Jesus explained that one was born again from on high. It was different. There is some doubt that Nicodemus ever became a follower of Christ. Still, he was present at the crucifixion. Of the Disciples, only John the Evangelist attended the execution. The others stayed away out of fear for their lives. In Michelangelo's beautiful *Florentine Pietà,* we see Nicodemus lowering the body of Christ from the cross to his mother's lap. Each rendition of the Pietà by Michelangelo seems a titanic effort to connect with the mother he had lost when he was six years old, his way of establishing a mystical communion with the beloved. In the *Florentine Pietà,* the sculptor participates in the person of Nicodemus, which is a self-portrait. In the Rondanini, the two bodies, mother and son, are actually fused as they had been before they were separated in childbirth.

If it is only since the thirteenth century that the Pietà appeared in the West, such a figure did exist in the cult of Isis and Osiris in the sixth century A.D. There is in the British Museum a statue of Isis holding the body of Osiris on her lap. And five thousand years ago in Sumeria, during periods of drought, the priests chanted the prayers of Dumuzi the shepherd

and of Inanna who was his mother, his bride, and also the Queen of
Heaven. Now it seems that Dumuzi the shepherd had been sacrificed to
the underworld, where he had been tortured and afflicted by demons,
much as Christ would later suffer His Passion. Inanna, the goddess,
weeps for him:

> Into his face she stares, seeing what she has lost—
> his mother who has lost him to death's kingdom.
> O the agony she bears, shuddering in the wilderness.
> She is the mother suffering so much.

Inanna is seen historically as the precursor of Ishtar who preceded Isis.
And here now is Mary, the latest in a long line of Great Mothers.

Yale's *Bavarian Pietà* measures sixteen inches from the top of the Virgin's
head to the base. It is some fourteen inches at its widest, and some ten
inches deep. It resides in a vitrine atop a chest-high pedestal. The wood
from which it is carved is linden, a tree lofty and airswept, bearing heart-
shaped leaves and scented yellow flowers. Linden is a fairly soft wood,
light in weight and easily carved. In England the tree is known as
the lime and has inspired a good deal of poetry. My boyhood favorite
is the line: "Ere the bees had ceased to murmur through the umbrage of
the lime." This by the Scottish balladeer, Aytoun. Such things are important, like the knowledge of one's ancestry.

The back of this piece was hollowed out with a chisel, the marks of
which can still be seen. After the carving, pieces of linen were glued over
splits and knots in the wood, then it was covered with a "ground" substance, and painted. Over the years it has been painted and repainted.
Much damage and patching has taken place, and many layers of paint
peeled off. Splits in the Virgin's head and in Christ's elbow have opened
up. The toes on both of his feet have been damaged, as has the left breast
of the Virgin. A species of Christian termite has at one time made a pilgrimage, as is manifested by a number of tiny holes here and there. The
conservators of the museum have expressed concern about the "insecurity" of the paint, the way it lifts and flakes. Insecurity? Let it go, I say,
like that poor Tower in Pisa that wants so much to fall, only we won't let
it. Let that go too. With all of that, one might say that the Yale *Pietà* has
suffered its way into art. It is clear that we are not seeing this statue as it
looked at its creation in the sixteenth century, nor in the seventeenth cen-

tury, when, in all likelihood, freshly bathed students, young men of impeccable morals (or at least dressed in white for the occasion), carried it through the streets of Augsburg on a litter of rosewood and hay. Solid and thick though she is, yet once (it was witnessed and sworn to by many) a sparrow flew right through her. Never mind all that. (Besides, I may have made that up.) It is enough to say that, only now, rid of its layers of paint, its gilt, the bits of cloth and wax, and reduced to the very wood that yielded itself up to the hands of the sculptor, only now has this *Pietà* taken on the patina of holiness:

> The soul's dark cottage battered and decayed
> Lets in new light through chinks that time has made.
>
> *(anonymous)*

It is the impermanence of the statue that is endearing. By virtue of its perishability, wood is preferable to marble or bronze, which are depressingly indestructible. All efforts to restore paintings and sculptures to their original condition are misguided. Insects, worms, damp, smoke, soot, grime—these are the agents of decline of every creation. This *Pietà* is the ultimate flower of the linden. From its girth, it is close to the root, with the rich damp earth clinging to its rhizomes. One can almost smell it. Such cannot be said for metal or ivory or any other material from which sculpture is made. To the absence of ornamentation of any kind, add a lack of fine detail, which might have distracted from the central purpose, the sorrow of the Virgin. When a sculptor concentrates on detail, there is always the risk that his intention will be lost or diluted. Here there is no suggestion of the vanity of the artist. He has kept himself out of the work. It is almost not art, in its rudeness.

With the central axis and pyramidal outlines, it is Christ that first attracts the eye. Here is God whittled down to a strew of bones athwart the Mother's knee. He is very far from beautiful, but rather, dwarfish—a child, really, except for the beard—and pallid, a sailor drowned and washed up from the sea. For so long have I looked at this statue that I sometimes forget what I'm looking at—the looking is all. And each time I see something I hadn't seen before. I'm like that character Bergotte in Proust, who thought he knew Vermeer's *View of Delft* by heart; he had studied the painting for years. On his last visit, before his death, he saw for the first time a small patch of yellow wall. Not long ago, I discovered the Virgin's shoe protruding from beneath her mantle. So! This Mary is not barefoot, nor does she wear sandals, as one might expect to be worn in first century Palestine. She is wearing shoes! And it is such a quiet statue. In the hushed wood there is none of the trapped frenzy of *The Dying Centaur,* where every vein and muscle is in full play. But for all its stillness, there is the hint of something having happened, as if Christ had just tumbled from her lap like a ball of yarn she had been knitting, leaving the chair of her knees empty. And every now and then there is the ghost of movement in the folds of her cowl.

Physiognomy was not the concern of this sculptor. Mary's face is almost hidden beneath the cowl. What we can see of it shows no expression. With rare exceptions, sculpture is not the best medium for portraiture. The fine imperfections that distinguish a face lie outside its precincts. Gouged or chiseled into marble, the small crow's-feet lateral to the eyes, or a scar on the cheek, would take on an impact far exceeding its importance in the living subject. The balance of the features is thereby upset, and the result is apt to be caricature. Should the sculptor gloss over such corporeal architecture, the result will be bland and lacking expression. I would leave portraiture to the painter and the photographer. Let sculpture's subject be the flesh as the spirit thickened. The face of Christ is fixed and vacant in death. His forehead is narrow, the eyes deeply recessed. His beard separates into two whorls at the tip. It is the only part of the statue that invites touch. See how he lies against her knee like a garden the birds have suddenly deserted, or a song broken off in the middle. Already the rigidity of death has fixed his extremities. He is broken, hips and shoulders dislocated, arms and legs strewn every which way, as though he had fallen from a great height. And of course, he had. There is no greater height from which to fall than the Cross. Again, there is the regrettable loincloth. Were I a sculptor, I'd sculpt only nudes. Clothing is a caricature of the body. Only in nudity is the whole truth of the body revealed.

If it is the dwarfish collapsed body of Christ that first captures our gaze, soon enough the balance shifts, and the Virgin begins to assert Herself. Our attention moves from the dead Son to the grieving Mother. After all, to Him death has already done all it can do. The Virgin's misery is hidden beneath her cowl, and even there it is internalized. Her face is not contorted; there are no tears. Her sorrow is transferred to the voluminous uterine mantle into which she would take her child again, if she could. I would guess her age at forty-nine. If Jesus was thirty-three when he died, and she, sixteen, when she bore him. You can tell she's not Italian, Spanish, Greek, nor of any Mediterranean extraction, from the way she grieves—without the least flamboyance. No sobbing, acrobatics, tearing of the flesh, no demonstration whatever. She mourns like the stolid *Hausfrau* that she is, all her grief drawn down into a tiny silver bead that she keeps beneath her breastbone. Just as the body of Jesus is disproportionately small, the face of the Virgin is anachronistically youthful, in order to recall with tragic irony the young mother who once held her baby in her arms. Suddenly, the once-deplored loincloth becomes the swaddling clothes of the infant Jesus.

See how she bends as if to listen. Perhaps there is one word left hiding in his mouth that might come forth, borne upon a final sigh? Or is she thinking how she might retain the last bit of warmth from his body, where his back rests upon her right leg, to keep it there for all time? Such, such is the madness of grief. Now bend down to peer beneath the cowl, and see that she looks at him as one looks after a ship that is sailing away. You and I know what she cannot, that in three days he will have risen. Meanwhile she will clasp the mantle tight about her and grow old, with rags of hair on her shoulders. Ah! You cry. Let her be! Why disturb her grieving with the vulgarity of language? For God's sake, let her be! And it's true that even as I invite you to look, my heart cries out "Don't look! O don't look at the place where life has departed."

This Mary is about as far from being the Queen of Heaven as you can get. What with her firmly knit knees apart, stretching and defining the skirt, she suggests the ample rooted ancestor, the tree from which she has come down to us. Surely she is too heavy to undergo anything as airy and light as an Assumption. It's hard to imagine her being muscled up to heaven by masses of air. She's more apt to feel the way Emily Dickinson did:

> I never felt at Home—Below
> And in the Handsome Skies
> I shall not feel at Home—I know—
> I don't like Paradise.

Alone, she sits, unaccompanied by weeping angels or saints in ecstasy. And so we must reinvent the hullabaloo of Calvary. She would have been watched, don't you think? By a cluster of other Jews—Old Nicodemus, Mary Magdalene, Joseph, John the Evangelist, by children, pigs, dogs, old women, a donkey. The centurions would not have left yet. Two of them would be throwing dice to see who would win Christ's clothing. The last of the thieves would by now have died. Another soldier would be hammering out the spike that had affixed his feet to the cross; it could be used again. The mallet strikes the big nail with a harsh ring that we don't quite hear. Nor do we hear the mule-drivers shouting to one another, the clatter of a cart laden with dates and pomegranates. A woman carries a pitcher of water on her shoulder; another takes her turn at the well, bending to haul a bucket. It is evening. Smoke from cooking fires drifts through the olive grove that descends the hill of Calvary. The shadow of the Cross has lengthened; a moment more, and it will have blended into the twilight. Torches would be lit, I'm sure, for it is dark when the small band wends its way to the tomb. No moon composes the roofs of Jerusalem where, presumably, storks are nesting.

Imagine the woodcarver. With his eyes closed, just by running his hand over a piece of finished wood, he can tell whether it is oak or chestnut or linden. At first, he nibbles the wood with his gouge like a mouse making a hole, taps the handle of his chisel lightly, then with increasing boldness, as he is taken over by the need to release the figures slumbering within the wood. Imagine the creases that roam his forehead as he reacts to each new challenge to that chisel. Note the way his hands enter and absorb the wood—its grain, texture, the knots and curves—just as the wood welcomes his hands in a kind of corporeal transaction. The hand and eyes of the sculptor never leave his work. After all, it is here, from this point on earth, that his soul has taken flight. Still, you have the feeling that he could have carved this statue blindfolded. And it is true that he is guided as much by instinct as he is by faith. Oh, he makes mistakes! When the tiny tresses that one side of the Virgin's waist were carved, the sculptor inadvertently made a hole in the thin wall of wood. Does this matter? In surgery, yes. But not here. A writer, too, in his absorption and excitement, will press the pen too hard so that it gashes the paper, but the words will not be wounded. Now see how, when not engaged, his hands settle at his sides, keeping their ingenuity until he summons them once again to their task. By the time this *Pietà* is half carved, the sculptor can touch sorrow with one finger.

The light in the Yale Art Gallery is cause for despair. It is like the noon-day sun in August, stamping itself upon an open courtyard. One day, I swear it, I shall bring a slingshot and a little bag of pebbles and put out

the cruel eye that molests the *Pietà*. There are works of art best seen by
other than incandescent lighting. A Crucifixion, say, ought to be revealed
by lightning, a single arrow of it that would nail the event in place forever. Perhaps it would be seen only once in a lifetime, but that would be
enough. The Taj Mahal is at its most bloodless solitude in moonlight.
And doubtless there is somewhere a work of art that can only be fully
appreciated in the gleam of the aurora borealis. For this *Pietà* I should
have preferred a more lambent play of light, one that trembles as it gilds.
An oil lamp that draws insects and gives forth dreams and memories; a
lamp for which a match must be struck, the wick trimmed each time, and
that must be blown out, leaving behind a brief fragrance of smoke. Best
of all would be the light of a candle. Set the candle in its holder and touch
the wick with a match. Almost at once the wax at the base of the exposed
wick will melt, for that is where the heat is greatest. At the outer rim of
the candle it is cooler, the melt there slower, so that the rim all around is
raised and there is formed a cup at the top of the candle. From this cup
the liquid wax is drawn up into the wick much as sap is drawn up the
trunk of a tree, by capillary action. Once above the surface of the pool,
the wax mingles with air, vaporizes, and turns to flame. Now it is a thing
alive that answers to the least gust, your breath even. And it is fragile, as
life is fragile. The candle, purified in the fire, sacrifices itself in order
to give light. It is the transubstantiation of wax into the sacred. Surely,
this *Pietà* deserves to be seen by such a light. In such a light, our brave
museum sentries would stand a proper vigil. In such a light, viewer and
artist would be united across the centuries.

It is not just the lighting that gives one pause; it is the Virgin's neigh-
bors. Really, a curator ought to pay more attention to the compatibility
of those depicted in the same room. If she could speak, and perhaps one
day she will, this Virgin might well complain about the company she is
forced to keep at Yale. Who could blame her? What with, on her immediate right, the cold fanatic Isabela of Spain, called *la católica,* the very
same Isabela who sponsored the voyages of Columbus and instituted
the Spanish Inquisition, installing the brutal monk Torquemada as its
president. Just see how she keeps a sharp eye out for infractions, among
which she might number the revelry of Hieronymus Bosch and the
Temptation of St. Anthony just opposite. And what must our Virgin make
of Botticelli's gossamer, fey Madonna just around the corner? Only to the
left and overhead, like an image of thought in a comic strip balloon, is

there a powerful rendering of the scene that never leaves her, the crucifixion of her son. It is strange that, amidst all the chaos of the fabulous, it is the simple *Pietà* that dominates the room, keeping itself to itself, a Jew among the goyim.

The tragedy of King Lear was first performed in 1606, about a hundred years after this statue was carved. Ever since, it has not been possible to gaze upon a Pietà without the tide of Shakespeare circulating in our veins. In Act V of the play we have the emblematic Pietà of all literature. Edmund has just confessed that he has given orders for Cordelia to be killed. The Duke of Albany cries out to the gods to defend her. And, as if in reply, there is the ritual entrance of King Lear carrying in his arms the corpse of Cordelia. The old man sinks to the ground, still holding his daughter, and from his mouth there issues that thrice-repeated onomatopoetic cry of pain:

> Howl, Howl, Howl! O! You are men of stones;
> Had I your tongues and eyes, I'd use them so
> That Heaven's vault should crack.

But Lear, the pagan, dismisses any belief in divine justice or glory in an afterlife:

> She's gone for ever,
> I know when one is dead, and when one lives;
> She's dead as earth.

That is the moment of clarity for the stern, truth-seeking king. There can be no regeneration. But now despair is followed by illusion:

> This feather stirs. She lives! If it be so,
> It is a chance which does redeem all sorrows
> That I have felt.

But, of course, it isn't so, and nothing is redeemed. Reality returns:

> O! See, see!
> And my poor fool is hang'd [Lear means Cordelia]
> No, no, no life
> Thou'lt come no more.
> Why should a dog, a horse, a rat have life,

> And thou no breath at all?
> Thou'lt come no more,
> Never, never, never, never, never!

Once again, the old man slips into madness in which he believes Cordelia still lives:

> Pray you, undo this button: thank you, Sir
> Do you see this? Look on her, look, her lips
> Look there, look there.

He sees something, points, and becomes silent. Words are no longer necessary, nor even possible. When Lear dies, we mustn't think there has been any sort of transfiguration by which Cordelia perdures. Lear may be deceived, but we are not. It is madness, not heaven-sent mercy that gives Lear the illusion that Cordelia lives. The old man, kneeling in heartbreak, has become the emblem of just how much one can lose.

Two Pietàs, then. The one encrusted with the jeweled speech of genius; the other ungarnished, mute, all its expression extraverbal—a matter of form, shape, texture, posture, yet all the same, bearing within that silence the whole weight of the Christian epic. We do not hear her lamentation; there is no heavenly choir, no pride in having given birth to a god. There is only sorrow for her dead child. Alone in her chaste gravity, she sits, holding out for us the terrible evidence of human cruelty. In the hush, we seem to hear the mother's reproach, her question:

"Look and see, you who pass by! Do you see what they have done to him? To my son? Is there any sorrow like mine?" Immediately we think of Lear's question.

"Why should a dog, a horse, a rat have life and thou no breath at all?" In each case, the question itself is the answer to the death of Cordelia and of Christ. Lear dies believing that Cordelia lives. Could it be that the Virgin, driven mad with grief, imagines that once again she holds upon her lap her *zartes Kind,* her tender child?

For so long have I looked at this statue that sometimes, while standing before it, I too have gone quietly mad. Once, I was quite sure I heard the Virgin speak! She was telling her story. Listen!

"Five hundred years ago, two woodcutters entered a thick dark forest

in Bavaria. Deep inside these woods, they came upon a linden tree of considerable age and loftiness. Each took up his axe. You can imagine how
their blows rang through the woods, the sounds following each other in
pairs—*thunk-thunk, thunk-thunk*—frightening the birds and other small
creatures. For a long time they hewed until, all at once, there was a hush.
Then the two woodcutters knew that with the last pair of blows a critical
point had been reached. A moment later, the stricken linden cleared its
throat, the way a grandfather's clock does just before it strikes the hour,
and with a harsh scream and a thump and a cloud of dust, it lay still after
the fall."

All this I heard the Virgin say. Now, five hundred years later, I think
to hear that far-off crash, only coming from within the glass case in which
the *Pietà* is ensconced, as though the sculptor had captured the sound and
tucked it into a hollow behind her eyes. Just so was a mighty linden tree
reborn as a tiny twig of desolation. Listen! There she goes again:

"In the thirty-eight years I've been at Yale, I've watched countless visitors swim near, just outside my vitrine. They could be ornamental carp
in a pool, the way they open and close their mouths. I used to listen to
what they were saying, but I don't anymore. In all that time, only one
nice thing has happened. It was just before closing time. A cricket that
had found its way into the Yale Art Gallery, and then up to the third floor,
began to chirp. How did it get here? You can't imagine how happy it
made me to hear that lovely sound. I'm not the only one who heard it.
The small elderly man with horn-rimmed glasses and hair the color of
aluminum, the one who comes here and stares at me all the time, he heard
the cricket too. I saw him pause and look off into the distance, cocking
his ear as if he were a blind man listening for the stars to come out. For
three days and three nights the cricket sang, and then no more. What
could that mean?"

Works of art are never finished. Like electrons, they are unstable, res-
onating back and forth with the gaze of each viewer. Works of art are
always in a state of becoming. It may not be what the artist intended them
to be. In the act of gazing, sculptor and viewer fuse into a single person.
Just so have I carved this *Pietà* to fit the outermost reaches of my imagination. The 16th-century Bavarian woodcarver is no longer anonymous.
It is I. I am he.

THE DYING CENTAUR

There is no deformity but in monstrosity; wherein, notwithstanding,
there is a kind of beauty, Nature so ingeniously contriving the irregular
parts as they become more remarkable than the principal fabric.
                                                    —Thomas Browne

Centaur, from the Greek *kentron* meaning "goad" or "stimulation"

Initially, the centaur was merely decorative; later he had the power to
ward off evil; and then, in the seventh century B.C., the legends as we
know them began. It goes without saying that the centaur was imagined
sometime after the appearance of the horse in Europe. The horse was not
known in the ancient Middle East before 2000 B.C. It came down into the
valley of the Euphrates from "Upper Asia" (the Caucasus, or the land of
the Tatars). In Babylonia the horse was called "ass of the mountains,"
indicating that it was a foreign importation. The horse came to Greece
by way of the Hittites, although another theory would have it that the
horse originated in Africa, then spread northward and to the east, from
Libya to Crete. There is an early seal depicting a horse being transported
by sailboat. An ancient writer named Berosus wrote that before human
beings, the earth was inhabited by monsters. Among these, he mentioned
manlike creatures with the hindquarters of a horse.

But that is all supposition. Here is how it all really began: A mortal
named Ixion was unwise enough to lust after Hera, Queen of the Gods.
Having managed somehow to enter the bed of the goddess, Ixion proceeded to have his way with her, only to be noticed by an outraged Zeus.
At the last moment, Hera was whisked away and a cloud was put in her
place. From the union of Ixion and this cloud a son, Centaurus, was born.
He was sent off to the mountains of Thessaly to grow up however he
could. As a man, he amused himself by copulating with the wild mares
of the mountains and so sired the entire race of centaurs. These proved
to be a lascivious, lawless lot, bent on drinking wine, rapine, and pillage,
as has been immortalized in the friezes of the Parthenon. All the centaurs, that is, all but one—Chiron, who was fathered, not by Ixion on a
cloud, but by a Titan, and, therefore, could not die; he was immortal.
Chiron, beloved by Zeus, was wise and kind. He was expert in music,

Dying Centaur, by William Rimmer

archery, and sculpture. Many of the greatest Greeks as youths were sent to Chiron for their education. Among them, Jason and his Argonauts, Achilles, Actaeon, and Asklepius, to whom he imparted the secrets of medicine as given him by Apollo. Chiron, it may be said, was the first physician. So kind was he that, upon the death of his pupil Actaeon, Chiron sculpted a lifelike statue of him in order to console the young man's dogs. It came to pass that Chiron, caught in a battle, sustained a wound from an arrow. The wound probably occurred in the transitional area where the man became the horse. It is just here that such monsters are most vulnerable. That is their weak spot, their *locus minoris resistentiae.* So painful was this incurable wound that Chiron crawled into a cave and implored Zeus to take away his immortality so that he might die. In doing so, Zeus committed what may be the first act of Assisted Suicide. But out of love for Chiron, Zeus raised him up to the stars, where he remains to this day as part of the constellation Sagittarius, evidence, if any were needed, that there is a world above and beyond that we can look up to and make use of.

The centaur had a normal human upper body with the addition of a horse's back, hind legs, and tail. He combined the beauty, power, and speed of a horse (minus its humiliating need to graze all day) with the brain of a man. He was of varying degrees of shagginess and possessed either human or horse genitalia. He was a hypermasculine creature whose existence permitted speculation about the boundaries between species. In him, the violence and sexuality of the horse were superimposed upon the virility of man. Among the ancients, monstrosity—deviation from the normal physique—was not a misfortune, but a tribute to Nature's abundance and creativity, her infinite combinatorial powers. In the Middle Ages stone carvers rendered the centaur on the doorways of churches and on the capitals of cloisters. They were usually shown as archers shooting birds and animals. Even under the authority of the Christian church the centaur has flourished, mostly as the embodiment of wickedness. Animal imagery made evil concrete. Great writers strove to explain the nature of man as he contrasts with other species. Here is King Lear describing his wicked daughters Regan and Goneril, both of whom have contracted a lust for the same man, one other than their husbands:

> Down from the waist they are Centaurs
> Although women above;
> Beneath is all the fiend's.
> There's hell, there's darkness.
> There's the sulphurous pit—burning, scalding
> Stench, consumption, fie, fie! Pah, pah!"

By the sixteenth century, monstrosities such as birth defects were considered a punishment by God. Or so said Ambroise Paré, the Father of Surgery, and an otherwise sensible physician. Even now, among certain Christian sects and in pagan cults, monsters, like AIDS, are examples of justice carried out, of divine displeasure. It has long been known that vestiges of organs of other animals have appeared in the human body, all the way from microscopic nests of cells to sizable sections of differentiated abnormal tissue. These are called embryonic rests. While I do not suggest that functioning remnants of a horse are to be found inside us, such an embryological occurrence does open the mind to the myth of the centaur.

Although it was generally agreed that centaurs could engage in sexual intercourse with human females, I have seen no representation of *amplexus,* or clasping, as it is called in reproductive biology. The offspring of such a match would be hybrids possessing both human and equine genes. Such hybridization between newts and salamanders has produced progeny with anatomical features of both species. Just so has science tried to desacralize monstrosities. The cast of those occurring unintentionally —hermaphrodites, siamese twins, and such—is being replaced by others made in a laboratory. The disappearance of the centaur from art and myth would suggest that the hybrid species became sterile down through the centuries. It could be that certain psychopathic personalities who disregard all the rules of civilized society and give free rein to their hot-tempered, lustful, and unmodified urges might be heirs, however distant. I know one or two such creatures myself. What with the transplantation into man of genetically altered organs of other species, the heart valve of the pig, say, and animal cartilage, or the invention of patented mice with one or more human genes, we are creating a whole tribe of "monstrosities" in the literal sense of that term. The notion of a creature with the physical properties of more than one species seems much less fanciful. All you'd have to do is make one, not in a cloud, perhaps, but in a laboratory, then clone it and Presto! A race of centaurs. I am possessed by an imaginary *tableau vivant* in which a nurse hands a newborn centaur to its human mother. I can't help but wonder what society's response would be to the appearance of such a neonate. Had its existence been discovered by amniocentesis and ultrasound examination, doubtless a "therapeutic" abortion would be performed in the interests of modern eugenics. Should the centaur come to full term and be born, all life support would be removed from the "nonviable teratoma," a reenactment of the ritual murder of "freaks" in times past.

The centaurs had few, if any, female companions of their kind, nor was there any rumor of domestic life and reproduction among them. This explains their rapacious treatment of the Lapiths and the Sabines and other tribes with whose women they mated in violence. With his fornicating, drinking, hunting, and fighting, the centaur was the embodiment of the masculine id. He was a creature who slipped from one species to the other and back again, now man, now horse. Such a state of instability

would further promote fits of rage and cruelty. In painting after painting, the centaur is shown with tossing arms, wild hair, grimace, and agitation. His contempt for man is obvious: Man is but half himself, short
and slow of step—a lesser creature unseated by the gods and condemned
to creep upon the earth. The centaur was a transgression of anatomy and
so must live sinfully.

Search as I may, with the exception of *A Family of Hippocentaurs,*
painted around five hundred B.C. by the great artist Zeuxis, I have found
no centauresses. The painting itself was lost at sea, but not before the
satirist Lucian had seen and described it. What follows is my own imagi-
native version of Lucian's description: The female is lying on fresh young
grass, one foreleg flexed with the hoof drawn under as if to kneel; the
other leg is braced to spring up. In one arm she cradles a baby centaur,
giving it suck at her human breast; another, its twin, she feeds at one of
her horse teats. The human and horse part of her flow seamlessly, the one
into the other. Above her looms the male. He is huge and muscular, with
a black mane that falls from his head to cover his back. His chest, too, is
swathed in it. Laughing, he holds up a lion cub that he has captured, holds
it close above their heads to frighten the babies who press themselves into
their mother, never ceasing to suck or to take their terrified sidewise gaze
from the cub. Even in the bosom of his family, the male is all wildness
and cruel play.

The Dying Centaur by William Rimmer was acquired by the Yale Art
Gallery in 1968. The statue, made of plaster and then painted, had been
created in 1869, but was not cast in bronze until twenty-five years after
Rimmer's death. Of the sculptor, we know that he was born in 1816 in
Liverpool, England, and was taken to Nova Scotia at the age of three.
Later the family moved to Boston. Rimmer's mother was a servant girl
of whom little mention has been made. The father was another case
entirely. He seems to have been a Figaro, someone who could make or
fix anything. He supported his family as a shoemaker, but he was also
adept in music, foreign languages, science, art, and literature. Our sculptor was his father's child in that he taught his seven children music and
made each one a flute, then conducted *Hausmusik* on frequent occasions.
Like his father, William gave his children lessons in anatomy, art, and
languages. If he wasn't Chiron, who was he? Both father and son labored
under the certainty that they were the illegitimate descendants of the
Dauphin and the rightful heirs to the throne of France. Both men's lives

were tainted by the bitterness of having been deprived of their royal birthright. Without meaning to suggest a diagnosis, I must say that the delusion of nobility of birth was a not uncommon symptom of insanity in the nineteenth century.

William, too, earned a precarious living as a cobbler. He also raised silkworms at home, and both these pursuits ended in failure. Like his father, the sculptor was a mercurial, unpredictable man of many talents, an isolate. At age fifteen he made his first sculpture, a nude representation of his father entitled *Depression*. It showed a remarkable native talent. Unable to make a living as a cobbler, Rimmer (naturally) decided to become a doctor, as that term was used then. He never attended a medical college nor had he any bedside teaching, but apprenticed himself to a practicing doctor to the extent of reciting to him once or twice a month for two years. His only other medical training took place in an anatomy dissecting room, which he visited a number of times. At the end of two years, Rimmer declared himself a doctor and began to practice medicine among the granite quarriers of northern Massachusetts. At this, too, he was unpopular and ineffectual. He was described then as "conceited, overbearing, stubborn and thin-skinned." In short—a surgeon! What with his manual gift and sense of anatomy, one would like to think of him as a good surgeon, but he had only the surgical personality.

We must not think too harshly of Doctor Rimmer. The doctor of 1850 was largely ineffectual. The best thing he could do for the sick was to let them alone, to get better or not. The predominant therapeutic measures were cupping, bleeding, purging, emetics, blistering, sweating, opium, and toters. Baths, douches, and poultices of turpentine, called stoups, were the procedures of choice. And enemas. The enema remained in the household armamentarium well into the 1930s, to be inflicted upon a child at the first sign of lassitude, moping, or nightmare. I remember several enemas administered by my mother from which the Devil himself would have arisen purified. And in the mid-1950s, I worked under a surgeon who firmly believed that a turpentine stoup applied to a silent, distended, postoperative abdomen would stimulate the sleeping intestine to produce what the nursing staff called "good results." Far from any contempt for Rimmer as a doctor, I feel a consanguinity. My own age of medicine has passed. Many of the operations I performed are no longer used. New treatments and techniques have rendered them obsolete. Given another few years, I shall join Dr. Rimmer in his obsolescence.

After ten years of failure, Rimmer gave up medicine in order to realize his potential in art. Of his sculptural output, only six pieces are extant, of which *The Dying Centaur* and another, entitled *The Falling Gladiator,* testify to his great skill. Both were crafted in the cellar beneath his doctor's office. He made no preliminary sketches, had no models but his own body. Lacking any contact with other artists, never having studied under one of the masters of European art, Rimmer was a *naif* whose art was "self-begotten," in Yeats's term. Still, on the basis of what remains, Rimmer has been called "the American Michelangelo." Surely, he was the most gifted American sculptor of his day. In his lifetime he received little or no recognition. Even now, he remains virtually unknown and unsituated in the context of American art.

You cannot look at this statue and say: "So what?" There is nothing "so what" about it. Painting and sculpture, unlike writing, are voiceless, silent. They converse by another pathway. The message and response are swift and powerful. Language must be read and digested. That takes time. In trying to do justice to *The Dying Centaur,* the temptation is to sculpt language with the same lack of restraint, the same undiluted passion with which the artist made the statue. There would be rendered on the page all of the fanatic, the grotesque, the frenzy and brutishness, the sensuality. But I'd better not. I should be led out of the Yale Art Gallery and made to sit on the Stool of Repentance, or worse. On second thought, I'll do it anyway.

There is nothing of the androgynous, the frail, or the translucent. Only a great lump, muscled and bursting. Rage and pain steam from the body. Here is a flank that would quiver if you touched it. The blood and breath are yet lodged within the dying body. He is pure energy and supremely graceful, the incarnation of the gallop of a sculptor's hand over the plaster, which has taken on an explosive property as if it were not plaster but TNT, a statue about to go off. Through this centaur, William Rimmer is hurling his volatile personality directly at us. He has tapped the rumbling subaqueous stream of his unconscious. Gaze on, and soon the carver begins to emerge from his carving. It is his own arm upthrust, his own neck wrenched back. The centaur mirrors the artist's fantasies of beauty and power. The statue is a projection in plaster of Rimmer's psyche, a self-portrait. Rimmer and the centaur are one and the same.

Using his knowledge of anatomy, Rimmer has wrapped the chest and haunches with great accuracy. The external oblique muscle of the abdominal wall interdigitates with the serratus anterior and latissimus dorsi of the thorax, both front and back. In the bulging neck, the great sternoclei-domastoid muscle tilts the head toward the ipsilateral shoulder, turning the face to the opposite side as in an upward and sideways glance. At the base of the neck, you can discern the suprasternal notch between the two clavicles, and above, in the midline, the prominence of the masculine lar-ynx. Now move laterally and encounter the deep cleft of the axilla between the pectoralis major in front and the latissimus dorsi behind. The arm is pulled upward by the deltoid muscle in complex collabora-tion with the trapezius and other muscles. From the sprawl of the equine parts, the human stretches his arm upward. We do not miss the lost hand; is it clenched in anger? Or open as if to implore aid? We do not know, nor do we need to. There is only a herd of muscles and organs bent on grasping the meaning of defeat and death. The hair is human though suggestive of a tossing mane. The tail is noble, stylized. Notice that it is to the human that the navel is given.

The figure flows from the horse to the man with the sinuosity of water, only with the tautness of a coiled spring. More apt, perhaps, since the cen-taurs fought with bow and arrow, would be to see the equine part as a great drawn bow in the act of shooting the human arrow to the skies. There is some exaggeration of the vertical/horizontal relationship of the two torsi, which are at more than a right angle to each other. Exaggera-tion, too, in the hyperextension of the engorged neck. It is anatomy brought to the edge of distortion. Rimmer has pursued to the point of vertigo the rupture with accepted form and has infused it with dynamic turbulence. You sense a centrifugal energy inside the creature that causes his muscles to bulge, to strain at the confining skin. See how the human is all but thrown from the horse; only the bridge of flesh keeps him astride. The centaur does not fall, but hovers at the instant of falling. This is no creature reaching up out of death for transcendence. He is gallant and undefeated. The mouth is open, but no sound emerges. There are events that cannot be put into words; they are beyond language—pain, orgasm, the moment of spiritual enlightenment, the spark of inspiration, and the experience of death. The unheard cry is a halo about the crea-ture, a trumpeting torn from every part—shoulder, neck, haunch, hooves. Here, indeed, is the body as language. Still, there is, as well, some-thing of the stricken seabird afloat upon barbarous and abrupt waves, who raises one wing in a last attempt to fly.

With each visit to *The Dying Centaur,* I find the statue has made a new inroad into my imagination. Now he seems to me a figure of dance, a *pas de deux,* the horse playing *porteur,* who lifts, supports, and displays his human partner in an equipoise achieved only by the greatest dancers. Unlike the *pas de deux* of *Les Sylphides* or *Swan Lake,* this duet veers dangerously toward the acrobatic, as seen in the hyperextension of the neck and the dramatic *epaulement* of the upthrust arm. In every *pas de deux,* it seems to me, the union of the two bodies is the goal, one that is never achieved. The striving is all. The two dancers become one only in the imagination of the audience. *The Dying Centaur* is that fusion, captured. The sculptor has tempered the boisterous leap of a Baryshnikov, say, with the vulnerability of that folded foreleg. Energy radiates upward from the pit of the stomach to pour through the chest and into the neck. Energy descends through the small of the back and from there downward along the thighs, where it is dissipated. The face of the centaur is the only part that is erased, blank. As in ballet, the body has all the expressiveness that the face lacks. Even the space around the statue is called into play; it eddies and swirls, lending to the mirage of movement. In the paradox of sculpture, he is movement immobilized.

A psychoanalyst might interpret this statue as a creature in conflict with itself, the human working himself loose from the animal base—a vision of the unresolved war between Dionysus and Apollo, the bestial and the sublime. A theologian might see it in Christian terms, the human half reaching for salvation even as the animal half sinks back to earth. There are those rationalists who would dwell upon the scientific: The wildness of the centaur may well have come from eating too many of the hallucinatory mushrooms that grow in the mountain forests of Thessaly. The biped, remarks the scientist, is not as firm of foot as the quadriped. Nor does the human possess a tail for balance, or to shoo flies. He might ponder the centaur's diet. Did the man part eat meat and vegetables, and then by some gastric alchemy turn it into oats for the horse part? The grafting of a branch of one species of tree upon the trunk of another produces the horticultural equivalent of the centaur. The writer may liken the centaur to the making of a metaphor in which two disparate and seemingly unrelated images or objects are blended or juxtaposed to produce something other and greater than either part. But all of that is what unweaves the rainbow. What the centaur offers is a prescientific, pagan image of life. Besides, give me the teeming sable corners of the imagination.

I read somewhere, in Borges I think, that to the Incas and Aztecs, a man on horseback was a single creature. When a soldier fell from his saddle, the Indians saw what they thought was a single animal divide into two parts. They were terrified and fled or gave themselves up to be slaughtered. Had it not been for this, perhaps the Indians would have killed all the Spaniards instead of the other way around. The living equivalent of such "centaurs" are the gauchos of Argentina and the Tartars of Mongolia, who spend half their lives on horseback, even sleeping in the saddle. Once, while driving on a mountain road near Troy (New York, not Asia Minor), I caught sight of a shirtless youth riding bareback in the woods. So dense were the trees that I had only a glimpse. He appeared in profile, with the horse's head hidden in the undergrowth. Only the boy's head and the horse's body were visible. Be still, my heart! I put on the brake, but he had already gone. Still, I had seen the centaur, and I shall take that to the grave, and beyond.

The centaur is in our blood; he both darkens and illuminates our minds. He is the antidote to excessive reason and logic. He is the uncensored id that remains feral and free, no matter the constraints of what is called civilization. Barbaric is the centaur, and without mercy or conscience. But honest, too, and without hypocrisy. *The Dying Centaur* by William Rimmer reaches back to childhood. But childhood has long passed, and with it the echo of hooves. Only now and then the mist parts. Then slowly the walls and partitions of the museum turn into trees, thicken into woods; the floor is thrown up into ridges; it sinks into ravines. The drinking fountains and all of the internal plumbing of the building become a mountain stream. We are no longer in the Yale Art Gallery in New Haven, Connecticut, but in the mountains of Thessaly. All at once there is the unmistakable sound of hoof beats. Who is the horseman? It is the horse/man. There he gallops, wild and solitary, wearing oak leaves in his hair. He bends to drink from the cold mountain stream. His musky smell penetrates the forest. Sweat glistens on his neck. His breath is that of a deer who has been feeding on violets. But what is this! The centaur's haunch is red with blood. He is fresh from battle. Wounded, he sinks to the forest floor, throws back his head to smell the rich earth, the ferns and mosses, the wild mushrooms that have given him such delight. He raises one arm in the gallantry, the bravado, the extravaganza of death.

A Parable

The scene is a room at the hospital. I am standing in the open doorway. It is early morning. A man is lying in the bed. He is emaciated, his skin covered with purple blotches where the blood has leaked into the tissues and congealed. He is motionless, inert. Only his breathing gives evidence of life. It comes in short rapid bursts interrupted by long stretches of apnea, as though a creature sat astride and rode him till he could not take a breath. Then it would start in again. It is called Cheyne-Stokes respiration. When a patient starts that, you know it won't be long. There is suppuration around his eyes, blocking his vision. He makes no effort to clear the phlegm rattling in his throat, only coughs mechanically now and then. It is clear that he is dying.

A doctor, at least I presume he is a doctor, comes into the room. I step aside to let him pass. He is wearing a blue scrub-suit such as is worn in the Operating Theatre. He is elderly, with hair the color of pewter, and blue eyes. His arms are thin and hairless and white. They end in hands that seem too large and heavy for the arms. They are red and shiny from years of scrubbing with stiff brushes. He takes a tissue, moistens it, and wipes the purulence from the sick man's eyes. Now I can see that his eyes are dark, the color of wet stones. They move to bring the doctor into focus. From the doorway of the room where I am standing, I see the lips of the doctor move, but I cannot hear what he is saying. He bends closer, placing his mouth almost to the man's ear, and raises his voice. Now what

I hear is a soft humming. During the night the patient has slid down in the bed and has become knotted among the sheets. The doctor slides one hand beneath the patient's hips and the other beneath his shoulders and lifts him up, embracing him, enclosing him as if his arms were a cloak or a hiding place where the man, in his misery, might rest safe and secure.

The man in the bed tries now to speak, but his voice is broken, fissured, bleeding, and he cannot. All that emerges from his mouth are syllables in their larval state, mangled, and coagulated in a viscous, unintelligible soup. From where I stand, I imagine that the sick body is hot, so hot that it gives forth warmth, like a stone that has lain out in the sun. A steam seems to rise from the bed. The old doctor holds his hands over the body of the man as if to warm them. The man makes another effort to speak. When the doctor turns his head to bend an ear to the lips of his patient, I can see the deep furrow that divides his brow, extending from the bridge of the nose up almost to the hairline. It gives his face a pained expression. It is a line of pain. Had he been born with it? I wonder. No, I think he had not. Rather it had appeared on the day that he treated his first patient. At first it was merely a shadow on his forehead, then a slight indentation that, over the years, has deepened into this dark cleft that is the mark of all the suffering he has witnessed over a lifetime as a doctor. It resembles a wound that might have been made with an axe.

Now the doctor lowers his hands into the heat and the steam and places them on the naked abdomen. Gently he presses, palpating, all the while speaking.

"Am I hurting you?" he asks, or is it the hands themselves that ask the question? The man in the bed shakes his head. The doctor bends forward a little, bringing his cloven brow within reach. Could he have meant to do so? The sick man finds the furrow with his finger, touches, then strokes it from one end to the other, a look of wonder upon his face, as though he were just waking from a deep sleep. As he does so, a spicule of light appears to emanate from the doctor's forehead. It is a warm light that grows to engulf the two men and the bed. The doctor does not withdraw from this touching, but smiles down at the patient with his sapphiric gaze.

The doctor covers the man's abdomen and lifts the sheet to expose his feet. They are blue and, I think, cold, despite the fever. The doctor takes one foot in his hand and begins to massage it gently, the way you rub the blood into a frozen part of the body. The man closes his eyes as if to concentrate the comfort he feels. His breathing slows and eases. Within minutes he is asleep.

From the doorway the two men and the bed appear luminous. They exist in a miraculous light. Miraculous? Why not? There are certain moments of harmony and revelation when miracles might be expected. They seem right and proper, like the luminous glow that has appeared to envelop the sick man and his doctor so that they themselves seem to be composed of light. On the contrary, if there were no miraculous light about them, it would be astonishing.

It is as if I am witnessing a feast. As if a table has been set with linen and plates and silverware. Candles have been lit. Ah, so that is the source of the light! There is bread in a small basket and wine in the goblets. The two men are dining together, each the nourishment of the other.

The doctor covers the man's feet, turns, and walks toward the doorway. Once again I stand back to let him pass. I see that he is bent, his fingers gnarled, arthritic. He does not move his arms, but lets them hang at his side. His gait is shuffling, hesitant. What is it that he is whispering to himself?

It is the next morning. I am once again standing in the doorway of that room. The doctor, dressed in the same blue raiment that matches the color of his eyes, is making his rounds. He walks up to the bed, where the man is lying perfectly still. His fingers reach for the man's wrist. He draws down the covers and observes the chest and the face, places his palm over the man's heart. Now he reaches up and closes the patient's eyes. With this small gesture, he sends the dead man on his way. As he leaves the room, it seems to me that the furrow is not quite so deep and dark as on the day before.

St. Ronan Terrace

Let me tell you where I live now. St. Ronan Terrace in New Haven is a dead-end street or, more politely, a *cul-de-sac*. We have occupied Number 6 for thirty-six years. To move out would be unthinkable. The next occupants would find bits of my flesh stuck to the banisters and doorknobs. It's an old wooden colonial, circa 1910, with black shutters and any number of architectural deformities. There has never been a time when the paint was not peeling. The décor is "world federalist," as no two objects appear to have originated in the same country. I am, I hope inoffensively, proud of it. Once it was filled with children and pets. In their place we have creaks, slippered footfalls, and the whisper of pages being turned. It's a house that doesn't always give the way a good many in the neighborhood do.

For thirty years Janet and I have looked after the house. Now it has turned itself into a Bed & Breakfast and looks after us. Scientists from all over the world have slept at 6 St. Ronan Terrace. I am the Assistant Hotel Manager and bellhop. I carry luggage up and down stairs and do valet parking, which has caused any number of Dents of Contention among the guests and hilarity among my ungrateful relatives, who insist that I have never learned how to park and am a terrible driver. I also make coffee for breakfast and, since the visiting scientists are from all over the world, I carry on conversation in French, Italian, German, Japanese, and Korean, the last two at a distinctly "pigeon" level. My Korean consists mostly of medical phrases learned, out of necessity, during my Medical

Corps years in the Far East. There is a certain shock value in saying at breakfast *"Ore appumnikka?"* (Where does it hurt?) and *"Yom yoh masayoh"* (You'll feel better soon). The guests, however, behave as though I am fluent enough to qualify for the job of Interpreter at Babel.

There is a shortcut to the Science buildings. At the bottom of the garden a wooden gate leads through a dense forest of bamboo, planted twenty years ago by my son Jon. You emerge from the bamboo and cross a vacant lot strewn with Queen Anne's lace and blue chicory. It resembles an old-fashioned bedspread. Soon you come to a park with a weeping beech, cryptomeria, cedar, and linden trees, all of great age. And then there is Yale. All the beauty of the house lies in the garden, which blooms from March through November, seducing twenty species of birds, butterflies, bees, and any number of small mammals. At night the squabbling of the raccoons lends a wild, jungly note to the yard.

St. Ronan Terrace is no more than five hundred yards long. It ascends steeply in a voluptuous curve to bury its head in the flank of the Yale Divinity School. From the window of my scriptorium, it looks for all the world like a pretty green snake lying on a hill. Seven houses comprise the neighborhood. Of these, one has been made into a residence for autistic children. Sometimes on summer nights we can hear the melancholy sounds they make. Over the years, eminent men and women have lived in the other houses: Eero Saarinen, Richard Ellmann, Robert Brustein, Ronald Dworkin, Robert Yerkes, and Brand Blanshard. They have all come and gone. Only we, whether out of steadfastness or failure of the imagination, have stayed on.

For a long time all any of us knew about the name St. Ronan was that Sir Walter Scott had written a satirical novel entitled *St. Ronan's Well,* his purpose being, he said, to "celebrate homely things." Scott set his novel at a mythical mineral spring in Scotland, noted for its ability to redeem health and drive away care; and he peopled the spa with a clutch of eccentrics and other odd outscourings of the human race, each with his own share of folly, vice, and imprudence. It would not be a gross falsehood to murmur that we present-day St. Ronanites might each, at one time or another, have stood as the model for a character in the book. Since it is the well itself that is the central focus of Sir Walter Scott's story, we are further entitled to our literary name by the existence of an underground stream or rill that flows down the Terrace, unseen until it surfaces in the garden of one of the houses at the bottom. There, by a clever combination of damming and excavation, it has been caught in the form of a pond with an intermittent overflow to the gutter of the parent street. As far as I know, it is the only such rill-cum-pond in the city of New Haven. With time, the pond has grown lush, having become surfaced over with lily pads and punctuated by tall reeds and grasses. Willows trail their tendrils over its banks and the water teems with wildlife. Goldfish, waterbugs, and frogs are the predominant fauna, although cardinals and blue jays are daily bathers. Once I saw a small green heron feasting on the goldfish. The kingfisher, too, has his occasional way with them. Sharing the kindly fruits of the Terrace with the humans is a tribe of raccoons, one of which has learned to unscrew the lid of a mayonnaise jar to get at a chunk of apple placed there to give a lesson in humility to any arrogant child who might suppose unscrewing to be an exclusively human talent.

All seven houses were built in the first or second decade of the century, and each has its own distinguishing mark. Ours, as I have said, is a white frame barnish structure of the pseudocolonial genre. The Saarinen house is English Tudor on the outside and, as you might expect, clear and bright and pristine within. Number 12, at the top of the hill, it is a bashful structure with a dense mantle of trees that keeps it hidden for months at a time.

In the spring we are infested with birds, vulgar with flowers. In the winter we are the last street in the city to get plowed out, an inconvenience that has produced some Olympic-class sledders and saucerers from among our midst. Twenty years ago there were on the Terrace six giant oak trees, each over two centuries old, between and among which the houses had been carefully inserted. Two of these have since toppled politely, without harming anyone. A third is in extremis. The rest flourish on.

It had been heaven to live on this street except for one mystery, which nagged at the back of our minds and which, from time to time, surfaced like the asp in a basket of fig leaves. It had to do with our name. Who, we died to know, was St. Ronan? Where and when did he live? None of us could accept that our heritage was something concocted by a mere novelist. Not even Walter Scott. There must be more to it, we said to each other. One day, while browsing in the stacks of the Yale Sterling Library in accordance with a will other than my own, I came across a book enti-tled *Ancient Celtic Tales*. With a shiver of discovery I saw that the open-ing chapter was called "The Story of St. Ronan." Imagine my excitement as I read those fated words. I seized and clutched the book to my breast. My hands trembled. My heart pounded. "Be still," I told it. At last, the mystery of St. Ronan was to be revealed.

It seems that somewhere in rural Druidic Gaul there once lived an old man named Ronan who was a Christian, the only one in that part of the world. It is not told how he came to this faith. For whatever reasons, Ronan had chosen the severest kind of hermit's life, living alone in a mountain cave that was too small to accommodate his entire body, so that his feet protruded from the entrance while he slept. Like most hermits, he ate only nuts and berries; his single garment was the skin of an ani-mal. One day the chieftain of a nearby pagan village, while hunting, caught sight of the old man's feet and dragged him forth to see whose they were. Ronan and the chieftain then embarked upon what was to become a long series of conversations, which resulted in the secret con-version of the chieftain to Christianity. This was done at no small cost to the new convert, who was ridiculed by his colleagues and castigated by his wife for neglecting his duties and spending altogether too much time sitting in front of a cave with an old man.

Now it came to pass that one day, while the chieftain was up on the mountain visiting Ronan, a huge fierce wolf raided the village, laying it waste and killing the little son of the chieftain. When the grief-stricken father learned of this, he went back to the cave to seek solace from the old man. Whereupon Ronan rose and went down to the village with the chieftain. He asked to see the body of the boy. It was brought to him in a coffin, which Ronan then opened. As the villagers watched, Ronan prayed and, bending over the coffin, he breathed upon the face of the child. All at once the color returned to the dead boy's cheeks; he stirred, took a breath, then another, and sat up. Jumping out of the coffin, he ran to his happy father's side. It should come as no surprise that on that very day the entire village was converted to Christianity. When, in time, the old saint died, his body was placed in a cart drawn by six oxen and taken to the spot where he was to be buried. But before this could be accom-plished, the whole cortège—cart, oxen, and saint—had been turned to stone, which rock formation can be seen to this day somewhere in what used to be Gaul.

All this I read, then replaced the book on its shelf at the library, wild to return to St. Ronan Terrace and spread the news of our origin among the inhabitants. There was general rejoicing. A grand party was held that very night. For the first time we felt ourselves bound together as a clan whose lost birthright had been returned. But the old order changeth. The original celebrants have long since departed St. Ronan Terrace. New skeptical people have moved in. Many times in the years that followed I have tried to find again that volume of *Ancient Celtic Tales,* if for no other reason than to squelch the legions of disbelievers who accuse me of having made the whole thing up. But the book was never at the library. Never again. Search how I would for a misfiling, there was no sign of it. Had it been borrowed and not returned? It had not. Nor was it to be found listed in the card catalogue! But I read it. I swear I did. And will go to my grave in the unshakable certainty of having done so. Let those who will, doubt on and build for themselves whatever golden calf. I know what really happened and I take comfort in the conviction that St. Ronan would agree with me. It is no easy job to convert the heathen.

From the Diaries 2

Thinking about the Old Testament—all those crabby old prophets beating the ecclesiastic drum for all it's worth. Can all that nagging be good for anyone's soul? Of them all, only Isaiah is supportable. In the midst of his conversations with Jehovah, he would stop to complain about his stomach cramps: "My bowels vibrate like a harp," he bemoaned himself. And on another occasion, "My cramps are like those of a woman in labor." You just can't help liking a prophet with spastic colitis. Then, too, there are those devious kings. Saul, who forbade the solicitation of witches; then when curiosity got the best of him, he stole out to visit Her of Endor to raise the seer. Then there is David giving to Uriah to carry to Joab that letter suggesting that the bearer be placed in the thick of battle so as to be slain. Abraham turned Hagar and her little son out into the desert without food or water the minute Isaac was born. Jacob tricked Esau out of his birthright. And on and on. Out of this they made a religion? After these men their sons are named? To say nothing of Jehovah Himself insisting on ten plagues long after Pharoah had surrendered. "I said ten and you're going to get ten." That sort of thing. It's no wonder I have lapsed.

Thinking about the soul and its manifestations. In sculpture, as in surgery, it seems to have two components: first, a sense of masterly ease, a spontaneity, a tossed-off flavor that doesn't show the long, hard work behind it. This is called, in Italian, *sprezzatura*. The second is even more vague. Seen in the repose of an athlete, it is an utterly unconscious grace that pervades the whole personality. This is called *disinvoltura*.

All this sparked by looking at a photograph of *The Dying Gaul* as shot from above. He is naked save for the leather necklace; one hand grips his thigh as though to hold on to himself, lest he drift away. The noble head is bowed; he cannot raise it. All the beauty lies in strength become frailty. I don't know the immediate cause of his dying, as the torque lies loosely about his neck. He seems to me to be short of breath; he has lost much blood. The chest heaves, the fixed shoulder sustaining his sinking body. All the musculature working now to hold him aloft. See the way he pushes himself up with his arm as though he knows that once he goes down he will not rise again. Yet he sinks, he dies. No, he has not been strangled.

For a description of a man murdered by strangulation, we go to Shakespeare's *King Henry IV,* Part II:

> But see, his face is black, and full of blood,
> His eyeballs further out than when he lived,
> Staring full ghastly . . .
> His hands abroad displayed, as one that grasped
> And tugged for life, and was by strength subdued.

Immense physical beauty in another has the power to draw the soul into the observer's eyes. Soul greeting soul, as it were.

JANUARY 1995

Letter from my host at the Society for Art, Religion, and Contemporary Culture, where I had performed. At the podium, my pages having mutinied *comme il faut,* I had apologized for scratting through them to find the ones I needed to close the lecture. All this while delivering a monologue about scratting at the podium, how shameful it was. In the midst of which a man called out from the audience, "Don't worry about scratting in public. We're all enjoying it." Followed by loud applause! By then I could have taken a Q-tip to my ear without fear of reproach.

JULY 1995

Letter from a woman who has had a lifelong interest in "striped equids." Zebras! She informs me that no two zebras are exactly alike. Like fingerprints.

A man from *Yale Alumni Magazine* came to interview me. But I turned the tables on him when he mentioned owls. It seems he knows all about them. Here's what I learned: Barn owls are the best hunters. It is done by hearing, not sight. In full flight, the owl listens to the squeak of the mouse and gauges the time/distance ratio. It is a form of sonar, such as is used by bats. The night vision of owls is excellent as well. The female owl, like the female redtail hawk, is much larger than the male, although no one knows quite why. Perhaps the female doesn't like to leave her eggs any longer than necessary and so has to hunt for larger prey—rabbits rather than mice. The male doesn't brood for her while she is hunting, so her eggs are at risk while she is away from the nest. The talons of an owl are fearsome; the prey cannot know what hit—a merciful death. Owls mate and lay their eggs earlier than any other bird. I've heard them hooting for a mate in December. Usually they mate in February, feed on skunks, who are emerging from hibernation then. The interviewer lives up in northeast Connecticut, sees owls and deer and coyote in his backyard. The great predator of the white-tailed deer is . . . the domesticated dog! The interviewer, too, is plagued with a surfeit of raccoons. Just so did I avoid being interviewed, for once. And just see what I learned! Only he could not tell me why owls hoot in minor thirds.

OCTOBER 1995

It was only last week that I went up to Troy to give a benefit reading for the library. It was raining when I entered the city limits, a gray mortuary rain that left a death mask in each puddle. I decided to go down to St. Joseph's church to see again the Tiffany stained-glass windows I hadn't seen in many years. All the way from New Haven to Troy I had looked forward to it. Once inside the nave, I saw depicted in glass all the familiar scenes. There were the Apostles, the Holy Family, the Rabbis marveling at young Jesus as he preached in the temple. There, too, the Roman centurions, Mary Magdalene, and all the rest. In the rain, the windows, while of that green-gold so revered by the alchemists, were static, inert, not at all as I had remembered them. I sat in a pew and fell to pondering the cruel tricks of memory, my place in the universe, and other grand *peut-êtres,* when all at once the clouds over Troy parted and the sun struck the stained glass, turning it molten, pulsatile. A river that had been gray turned golden and began to flow. There came the seraphim with burning hair, Adam and Eve ex-Paradised. The faces of the saints took on the tints of human flesh; their eyes glowed with a martyr's fire. Here was an art that required sunshine to fulfill its promise. I reached up to make sure I was wearing my glasses, that it wasn't just the old myopia and astigmatism that had given Troy an aura of "glory" half a century ago.

But an hour spent in a glass furnace is enough to make you short of breath. An excess of foreplay is tiresome. It was both painful and a relief to leave that church, about the way you might feel on leaving Heaven, I suppose. Outside, the fiery maples and yellow sycamores seemed calm by comparison. They were also more to my taste. There is the same central aloofness in stained glass as there is in a jungle. Still, those glass rabbis and saints at St. Joseph's are no less metamorphosed and exalted than the heroic figures of mythology—Castor and Pollux, Orion and Cassiopeia— who were pitched to the stars. It's just a different celestial body that touches them to life. Come to think of it, I'd far rather be vitrified at St. Joseph's than be some anonymous comet set in Cassiopeia's chair

There was a time, can you believe it? when the very mention of the name Troy brought forth hoots of derision. Comparison with Nineveh or Gomorrah was not in our favor. There were even those who assigned to Troy a certain low-ranking anatomical location on the body of North America. Bad cess to those who cast such stones! To this day it continues. Not long ago, I met a woman who used to live in Albany. I told her that I was going to visit Troy that week.

"Not deliberately!" she exclaimed. It all had to do with the prostitution that flourished in Troy in the first half of the century. A false respectability insists that we not refer to the fact that throughout the Great Depression the economy of the town was quite propped up by that particular traffic. But from Plattsburgh to New Haven, Connecticut, it was common knowledge that Troy was the place to go for sex. The going rate in the thirties was two dollars a screw, which is what my father charged for a house call. Nick, my garageman in New Haven, and I are of the same antique vintage. Each time I go to have the oil changed, tires rotated, a tune-up, he makes salty reference to the Troy of yesteryear, when he and his buddies would travel there for a weekend among the fleshpots. These objectionable reminiscences invariably end with a nudge in my ribs and the suggestion to whoever might be hanging around the garage that "Doc's goin' up to get his ashes hauled." Nick's wife, Carmella, is not amused. She thanks God that she has brought up her five daughters in New Haven and not in a whorehouse like Troy. I stare at her in disbelief. New Haven? My God! Did He who made Troy make this? But we must pray for those who do not understand us. The great calamity of Nick's life is not so much that he is the father of five girls, but that he is not the father of a single boy. Once the tires have been rotated and the oil changed, I can speak freely.

"You're just like Job in the Old Testament, Nick."

"How so?"

"He, too, was rich in valuable she-asses."

It's hard to imagine that once Troy, like Mahagonny, was a city of sensuality, that men and women thronged the streets, bent on buying and selling forbidden pleasures. To look at the city now—drooping, moribund, breathing only six times a minute, like a hibernating bear—it takes a leap of the imagination to see it as it was, ardent, passionate, and tense with the expectation of delight and profit. For "those" women of Troy, sex was a commodity no less than the collars and cuffs manufactured a few blocks away. Like all goods for sale, they had to look attractive to a customer. They had also to be vivacious, cheerful, and brave. They earned every penny they got.

Among my Trojan readership, there are those models of deportment who deplore that I mention our heyday of prostitution. It happens that not infrequently I am in Troy earning my living at the podium, most recently before a gathering of the literati called the Ilium Club. I had no sooner finished the reading, when the first hand shot up.

"Why must you bring all that up every chance you get?"

"Bring up all what?" I feign innocence.

"That stuff about streetwalkers and houses of ill-repute."

But whoring, I insist, is no more degrading than earning a living at the podium. I do but give back to prostitution its ancient innocence. Furthermore, what with the pollution of the Hudson River and the rise of homelessness hereabouts, Troy itself has become a poor old whore soaking her sore feet in a poisoned stream. I offered a bit of doggerel to the Ilium Club:

> O, do not disparage lascivious carriage,
> 'Twas a way of paying the rent.
> When times were much harder,
> Who kept bread in the larder
> But the ladies who came and went?

APRIL 1996

I should have wept more. All those tears I had the bravery not to shed in youth have backed up into the blood and made old age bitter. Whenever the back-pressure from repressed weeping grows urgent, I make horse-radish according to the following recipe:

Ingredients:

> 6 oz. firm fresh horseradish root, peeled
> 1 medium beet, peeled
> 2 T. fresh lemon juice
> ? t. sugar
> ? t. salt
> 2 t. white vinegar
> 3 oz. freshly shed tears

Directions:

The grating is crucial, rather like the kneading when bread is the goal. It must be done by hand, making quick, smooth strokes, using an old-fashioned grater laid across an ample bowl. Eschew all kitchen appliances that are sure to grate too finely or too coarsely. Instinct and intuition are the best guides for getting the consistency just right. In the making of horseradish, one must, as in any art, be receptacular. Concentrate the mind upon the higher motives and avoid any lewd fantasies. Such are the poetics of horseradish.

Using a long wooden spoon, toss the grated horseradish and beet so as to blend the red and the white into a deep rose. Too pale, and the result will be punitive; too scarlet, and it will be anemic to the taste. During the grating and the tossing, lean well over the bowl so that your tears will fall directly into it. The fresher the horseradish, the greater will be its lachrymagogic effect. In certain parts of the Caucasus, and especially in the Crimea, an assistant (sous-chef) stands opposite the Chef and catches his tears in twin lachrymatories held against his cheeks. These are then poured into the mixture. But this is not the Crimea, and such an intermediate step is both wasteful and unnecessary. The flow of tears should be encouraged until the contents of the bowl are damp but not soggy. Add salt and sugar while continuing to agitate with the wooden spoon. Now add the white vinegar until the particles adhere and can be tamped down. Discontinue lachrymation at this point. Upon tasting, the horseradish should administer the equivalent of a sharp slap in the face followed by an impression of the rataplan of snare drums on a parade ground. Some have also described a burst of Pleiades in a midnight sky.

Spoon the horseradish into jars, cover and keep in a dark cool place.

AUGUST 1996

*The computer as witch, bringing about the marvelous with
a wave of her mouse.*

It happens that now and then I'm inveigled into leading a writer's workshop or giving what is falsely put forth as a Master Class. These are strangely like those Home Economics courses that used to be taught to girls in High School, where they made a few dozen cupcakes, then ate them all up. We make a few dozen metaphors and eat them up, too. Emily Dickinson was right: "We play with Paste—'Til Qualified for Pearl." Here follows a list of dubious notions I expressed during the last of these imposturages:

In writing, clichés are to be avoided; they are contemptible. Not so in life. People speak in clichés, communicate through them, transmit events by them. It is one more way that Life differs from Art.

In writing, it is fine to be romantic, the way Chekhov and Balzac were. It is not fine to be sentimental, which is to soften the truth in order to produce a happy or sad feeling.

Writing is not painful. That is the false lamentation of those who write books called "How to Write Well." Writing is a delightful and judicious contrivance. Never once have I writhed on the floor groaning after *le mot juste*. Writing, to me, is what purring is to a cat.

Be he who he may (I've been looking for a chance to use those five monosyllables. It is English, yes, but with a Hawaiian lilt, something that should be sung while doing the hula), be he who he may, a writer would do well to hone his pen on the stones of the past, the Old Testament, for one. There is no more gorgeous prose anywhere.

There is the matter of tone, which can be high, as in *Wuthering Heights,* low, as in *Huckleberry Finn,* or middling, as in the works of all those who can't sustain a high or low tone throughout the course of a book. Tone establishes the relationship between reader and writer. If Eve had been tempted by a turnip instead of an apple, the book of Genesis would have a lower tone. It would then deserve the term "Vulgate." It is perfectly legal to apply high tone to a low character; as Lady Margaret Beaumont said to Henry Adams, "I don't think I care for foreigners."

It is twenty-five years since first I wet a pen, and nobody can say that I've been a *lazzarone.* (It is enriching to your prose to look up the meaning of every word you don't know.) You might as well know that writing has kept me from the *va-et-vien* of society. It has also diminished somewhat my experience of what is commonly called Life.

The method I use in the workshop is devoid of order or system. It is, rather, slipshod, slapdash, fancy-free, doggone, and any other composite barbarism you can think of. In my classroom there are many mansions and no Commandments. In the greatness of my fond heart, I try only to make the English language more interesting and colorful and to ensure that every word is used precisely. Because of my former profession, and because every physician in North America is writing a novel, I have sometimes been called upon to "teach" doctors how to write. This is no cinch, as there is no group of college graduates more ignorant of reading or writing than doctors. Apparently these pursuits are incompatible. Training in medicine ill prepares one for the rigors of writing.

Not long ago I was asked by former colleagues at Yale School of

Medicine to give a seminar to a group of would-be doctor/writers. For thirteen weeks, every Monday night for three hours, we gathered to write our hearts out. Here, in full, is what these doctors learned: The difference between prostate and prostrate. It is no easy thing, I told them, to lie prostate upon the ground, even for those of us who have one. You cannot write "'No!' he hissed" because there is no "s" in it. To hiss you have to have an "s." The word disembosom has nothing to do with breast surgery; it is to be used figuratively, as in "Permit me to disembosom myself of a secret." This is entirely unlike the word disembowel, which has every right to be taken literally. They learned, too, the difference between prone and supine, a knottier distinction, I admit. Even so eminent a doctor/writer as Robin Cook in one of his immortal novels has a woman placed in the prone position so that a pelvic examination might be performed on her. I would suggest that any woman so positioned put her clothes back on and get a second opinion. And, finally, they learned the importance of punctuation, how it can change the meaning of a sentence, as in "'Good Heavens!' Mr. Sandhill ejaculated" and "'Good Heavens! Mr. Sandhill ejaculated!'" That is what they learned. I learned never to do it again. All this having been said, there is something innately civilized about a group of like-minded people gathering together to labor in the same vineyard. It offers, if nothing else, a mutual spirit in which triumphs can be shared and disappointments consoled.

MAY 1997

Third visit to the Blake exhibit at the British Art Collection. Struck by the balletic movement of the figures in the *Jerusalem* series. The idea occurs to write a fourth lecture on just this subject to include in "The Body as Sacred Space." Must educate myself in the subject of dance, about which I know nothing at all. Blake prefigures Martha Graham by two hundred years. I wonder if she or other choreographers have mined this lode. Phoned the curator of the Blake exhibit, who referred me to Robert Essick, author of *The Visionary Hand*. This seems a project worth immersing myself in. We'll see. But to begin from ignorance in both dance and Blake! That is arrogant, if not rash.

There is a profound difference between Blake and Michelangelo, in that Michelangelo fondled even as he carved. The lust of the artist was the engine that drove his chisel. Not so with Blake, in whom whatever sensuality there is has been damped and replaced by the sanctification of the flesh. He has floated free of the carnal. Michelangelo's figures, though divinized, are nothing but erotic objects.

Blake gave his dancers voice, thereby breaking the taboo against the vocal expression of dancers. They weren't supposed to speak or sing, no more than they are allowed to show the strain and sweat of each pose and gesture, but must achieve *sprezzatura* at all times.

Against the stone wall of Saybrook College on High Street there stands the solitary trunk of an ancient wisteria vine. Straight up it rises to thirty feet above a depressed yard separated from the street by a chest-high stone wall. So riven and decayed is this trunk as to be entirely eaten away on its anterior surface. For its middle third the only continuity is a thin shell of the posterior bark, and even this bears a large hole. The upper end of the vine divides into two gnarled, arthritic branches that spread like the arms of one crucified. Yet each of these branches is heavy with large fragrant racemes of wisteria that are all the more beautiful for the surprise they evoke. How can it be that so much life flows across this all-but-nonexistent portion of the trunk? Could this be the final surge of a superannuated plant that will not be alive next spring? The way some trees are said to burst into fiercest bloom before dying out. Surely this is a monumental display of endurance and style in a living thing that insists upon carrying out its duty to bloom. For that is its destiny. Gaze long enough at this transcendent vine, with its violet crown of flowers, that has the shape, as it has the ambience, of the Crucifixion, evoking from the awestruck the same blend of ecstasy and horror, and one is tempted to kneel.

Ran back to the library and phoned the campus photographer to come at once. Surely, I implored, here is a sight as worthy as any in the Yale Art Gallery. To the urgency in my voice that good man responded at once. Within minutes, there he was! Taking picture after picture, and plotting with me their future. No sooner had he begun, than, one by one, people stopped to gaze and marvel. It is true that the wisteria had been there all this time, with hundreds, including myself, passing by as if blind, until I had been made ready to receive. Such is the way with all miracles. If I have accomplished nothing all year, I shall have conducted the attention of a few pedestrians to this phenomenon of nature.

DECEMBER 1997

(About myself)

Invited to give an onstage commentary after a performance of the play
Wit at the Long Wharf Theatre. The leading role is that of a Professor of
English who is dying of far-advanced ovarian cancer. Her special interest has been the poetry of John Donne. In the course of preparing the talk,
I have been reading his "Holy Sonnets" and wondering at the terror of
death that inspired them. I trust it isn't the bravado of a seventy-year-old
that insists I do not share that same fear. Whatever else have been my
nemeses, fear of death hasn't been one of them. Federico Lorca, too, could
not take his gaze from his own death. He alluded to it at least five times a
day, and couldn't get to sleep unless friends came to tuck him in. Even
then, he would protract their visit by any pretext. On occasion, Lorca
would preenact his last moment, complete with twitching, strangulation,
and grimaces. This is not to say that I welcome the terminal event. Not
at all. *Lente, lente currite noctis equi.*

I had two old friends, both distinguished professors at Yale. They are
newly dead. From them I have learned that a lifetime of scholarship ill
prepares one for death. Both of them wasted their few reserves in mourning the passage of youth, ashamed of old age and infirmity, and fear of
dying. As though it were a singular fate to which only they were condemned. After all that reading and writing about literature, there was
left only a childish vanity. "Come, come, I consoled them both. No man
is alone, not Laocoön, not Tobit—he had the angel Raphael with him;
either the serpent or the angel has you by the hand." But they had already
stopped listening.

Why I'm not plagued by the same demon, I cannot say. My morbid
inclination is as strong as anyone's, as witness the unlovely details of the
morgue and autopsy room in my early writings. Only the horror seems
to be restricted to the general; I haven't taken it personally. Now, if given
the choice (one never is), I would choose for my subjects the beautiful,
lofty, and noble rather than the deformed and deviant. I would much
prefer to think of Walt Whitman as a handsome poet with a beard full of
butterflies than a smelly old man infested with lice.

The noble obligation to tell lies occurs most often in situations of love
and sickness. I have so obliged many times in each category. In the words

of John Donne, such benevolence "mellows me for heaven, and so fer-
ments me . . . as I shall need no long concoction in the grave but hasten
up to the resurrection."

Watched a video made by Angelo Volandes, a third-year medical student.
It's entitled "Experiencing Illness." The subject of the film is a seventy-
year-old man with the most extensive neurofibromatosis, such that his
appearance is grotesque and repulsive to most people. There is no inch of
him—face, hands, neck, scalp, chest, back, all—that is not covered with
the soft buttery tumors, many that are scabbed over from scratching. In
the film, he tells of his life of rejection by society, family, everyone. Out
of the depths of his loneliness, he points a finger at the world and says,
"*j'accuse.*" We see him at the supermarket, where the cashier won't touch
his money for fear of contamination. He must open every encounter by
saying, "Don't worry, it's not catching." He dare not go to church for fear
of disturbing the other congregants, although he very much wants to go
there. God, it seems, has escaped blame. He cannot go to the beach to
swim, as he doesn't want to take off his shirt. As a child, he relates, he
was forbidden to go to gym class at school, although he loved sports. Nor
was he permitted to graduate. Once, long ago, there had been a girl, but
she had left him with a broken heart.

   In another clip, he turns the soil of his tiny garden with a hoe. He'll
grow vegetables there. It is the act of a human being, not an animal. From
out of the horror of his face, his eyes, deep-set within the bulging tumors,
glitter with a fierce rage. He is depressed; there is moisture on the tumors
just below his eyes. But he is not comforted. He wants to live! "I hope I'll be
here next year," he says, while making his bed.

   In the film there is an interview of the professor of dermatology, whom
I know and who has been his doctor for decades. He expresses profound
sadness that nothing can be done for this patient, not a single thing.
No medicine, no surgery. He laments that the experience of illness is
neglected in favor of the teaching of the disease itself. Partly, he says, this
is due to the burgeoning of technology ("which is good," he is quick to
defend) while the spirit of medicine has been left to languish. Watching
this film, I would have to agree. But I know too that there are limits to
empathy. One cannot feel the pain of another. It isn't transferable. So it is
with the Hell of neurofibromatosis. "There but for the grace of God," we
say and retire into our smooth, comfortable skins. Perhaps, I don't know,

I cannot entirely condemn the man's brother and sister for avoiding him; the sight of him must wound them anew each time. It would take a saint to kiss these wounds. My hat is off to Angelo for following the man with his camera so that the rest of us can behold the limits of hopelessness.

Hours after watching the film, I have the sudden realization that I met this man many years ago, that he had been my patient, that I had removed one of the tumors that had partially obstructed his nostril. I want to find someone to laugh with, to eat and drink with, to make love to.

JANUARY 1998

Day in, day out, fair weather or foul, I leave home at eight o'clock in the morning and walk to Sterling Library. There, from eight-thirty on, it is me you can find sitting at a table in Cross Campus, or in the Great Reading Room, or dozing in an easy chair in L&B (Linonia and Brothers), another room in the library. I am alone, except when a pilgrim or supplicant intrudes. Everyone knows where to find me. Out of the corner of my eye I see the miscreant sidling up, but I pretend ignorance in the hope that he will think better of interrupting my train of thought. He hesitates for a moment, then tiptoes nearer until, with a soft flannel cough or a sibilant "excuse me, professor," he announces his presence. (When they call me "professor," I know that the jig is up). Now I am he who looks up as if startled, stares for a moment, raises one eyebrow in what might be a show of annoyance, and says: "Oh?" or "Yes?"

Truth to tell, I have been extracted from a welter of dreams, images, and words, tumbling one over the other without sense or purpose. Nevertheless, some irritation is called for. No harm in a bit of it, I say. It's the least coming to me for what follows. And who might it be that dares so to intrude? A student, perhaps, assigned to write an essay on my work and wanting to clarify a cloudy image or two; or a fellow writer wondering if she might deposit her manuscript of five hundred pages for my perusal and opinion; or a member of the library staff or of the faculty asking me to feel a lump somewhere, or have a look at a rash. It is only to be expected in my unofficial role as Resident Physician at the Yale library, in which facility I conduct a flourishing medical practice, one that is untainted by any passage of money from patient to doctor. No, this is Medicine as it should be, pure, incorrupt—a rarity, some say, in these

times. I have been seen reading an X-ray instead of a journal in the
Periodical Room, and examining a hernia or, famously, trimming hyper-
trophic toenails in the Men's Room. A breast lump involves a bit of sub-
terfuge. Patient, followed minutes later by doctor, repairs to the small
office of the Security Guard just inside the Main Entrance, with the
Guard, whose name is Mezzanotte, to sound the alarm by calling out
the code word "Midnight!" Is it any wonder, I ask you, that I get almost
nothing written, save for a few prescriptions? Like the lilies of Solomon,
I toil not, neither do I spin. Such is my activity from half past eight until
noon. For which I have assumed that my name shall be written by that
angel in the Book of Gold right after Abou ben Adhem's (may his tribe
increase).

At noon I leave the library and go to one of a half-dozen eateries
in the area. At Naples a slice of pizza and a cup of exculpatory coffee
gets you two or three hours at a small table in the corner where you can
read and write, or just pretend to *la vie de Bohème,* never mind that
the bearded Bohemian alone and scribbling at a nearby table is the win-
ner of a MacArthur Fellowship and sends his children to private school.
At Educated Burgher the niceties of nourishment may be devoutly
eschewed, but on Friday their New England clam chowder is ambrosial.
Then, too, there is the Yankee Doodle, a counter where a hamburger
deluxe is slid within arm's reach no more than three minutes after the
order is placed. Mostly I lunch alone, but it happens sometimes that I am
sat down next to by a real professor and am treated to the galloping
tongue of academic gossip, than which there is nothing more delightfully
venomous.

Every Monday I lunch at Mory's with the seven other members of the
Boys Friendly, an ancient and fabled eating "club." The others are all
English professors of gray or balding eminence. Three are octo-, one is
hepto-, two of us are sexa-, and two are a pediatric quinta-genarian. It is
the only place I ever go where I am not the oldest person alive. The membership of the Boys Friendly is limited to eight by the size of the tables
down at Mory's. A new member is taken in only when an old one dies. I
am presently the newest addition, having replaced John Pope, a renowned
medievalist, who died at age ninety-five. I serve for the others as a curiosity, answering questions about medicine in which they are keenly inter-
ested. In return for teaching them anatomy and physiology, I am taught

literature. A quid pro quo that I greatly enjoy. One day the subject was Gray's "Elegy in a Country Churchyard" followed by his *Anatomy*. That sort of thing.

Upon returning to the library, I must sink deeply into one of the great, broken, disemboweled chairs in L&B for a nap. I take it as a personal affront when MY chair is being used by one of the pilgrims for the same purpose. More than once it has been necessary for me to evict the cowbird from the song sparrow's nest, if you know what I mean. So far, no one has presumed to awaken me from my siesta, although there is often a villain sitting nearby, patiently waiting for me to regain consciousness. To think that Jesus Christ died for the likes of him!

From one-thirty to three in the afternoon, I renew my flights and epiphanies until it is time to go to the Yale Gym, where I pretend to exercise. Here I am indeed the oldest person alive. The oiled undergraduates, farting like gods, lower their gaze as I lower my gnarled carcass to a mat and begin a pathetic pantomime that consists of sitting up, then down a few dozen times; pushing up and letting fall, until only fall is left; stretching; breathing deeply; and, at last, going to the Fitness Center to ply an oar in the "hulks." Best is the sauna, where I am quite the *salonier,* if I may say so.

At four o'clock, I may be seen turning the key in the door of an old white frame house called the Elizabethan Club at Yale, or, more fondly, the "Lizzie." Here, every afternoon at four, tea is served along with small sandwiches and cookies. The sandwich schedule is absolutely unvarying. On Monday, tomato; Tuesday, cucumber; Wednesday, chicken salad; Thursday, cinnamon toast; Friday, tuna fish; Saturday, cheddar cheese; Sunday, cream cheese on date and nut bread. That is how the membership knows what day it is. Otherwise we are quite at sea. Every Friday at four, the vault containing the priceless old books is opened for members and their guests. I am one of six who know the combination and take turns displaying the treasures. Hack the flesh from my bones and I shall not reveal it. Whenever someone from Harvard is present, we speak only in Latin—e.g., *Hic liber editio princeps est.*

At five o'clock, I take the Yale shuttle bus home, where I pour myself a nipperkin of vodka, or two. Or three. Then exchange pleasantries or otherwise with Janet. The hour of six finds me sitting deeply by the blazing ingle, Mozart and Meatloaf drifting from the kitchen, where Janet is listening to the radio, and the "Blessed Assurance" that in half an hour I will hear the cry "Dinner's ready!" In accordance with the principle of Equality in the Workplace, cleaning up the kitchen falls to me. At eight o'clock I'm in my scriptorium, writing letters, reading, or dozing in preparation for the night's sleep. Such, such is my Daily Round, *il mio piccolo mondo.*

FEBRUARY 1998

How do I feel? Februarian, that's how: sullen, gray, cold. As for the writing, I have all but hung my harp on the willow tree. Only the diary still breathes. Therein I pour out whatever comes first—sermon, story, idlings—and who cares what others may say?

Remembering the brave smile on Father's face, his pale hand raised in greeting, as Billy and I were led into the room at St. Mary's Hospital. A father on his deathbed, taking leave of his small sons. Only now do I feel his woe. Until now, it had been mine, unabated through the years. But his! How much greater, in the knowledge that we would be left defenseless and poor, to grow up however we could (given his all-too-accurate evaluation of Mother as a responsible parent). Who will rid me of this turbulent dream?

MARCH 1998

Mia virtuta stanca, wrote Dante in Canto II (lines 127–130), and I know what he meant. If I could, I'd offer up "my wilted strength" and strive to go on. Try to be like the tree that goes bare and slow-sappy in autumn but keeps inside its bark a new generation of buds waiting to open. But no, Fancy is reduced. I'll not be riding Eohippus, the little penhorse, back and forth across a page, not for a while, if ever again. It is the time of impotence and idleness. And with it has come self-doubt. The entire shelf of books I am accused of writing seems little more than a flamboyant gesture, not so much of egotism, as it is with some, but done to draw attention away from a disfigurement, to conceal a wound. Might as well not have written any of it. Too late to retrieve it now. To think that once I had the notion that I might just climb the ladder to Parnassus! But its rungs are way too far apart for me to manage. Me wings is furled. Best to know that. But now comes another voice from somewhere inside. Never mind, it says. It happens every Spring. While the rest of Nature gets set to bloom, you turn crepuscular, go all posthumous. It's just the seasonal turning over of the plasm. Takes a while to come to a simmer again.

In a strange way, there was a price paid for leaving surgery. It was my manhood. Where before, I had been guide and ally for the sick, a Knight Templar, so to speak, I am now a species of fauna that lives on paper and ink, whose leavings provide no nourishment to the land, a small creature at the bottom of the food chain. A bookworm.

MAY 1998

Arrived at Sterling Library at eight-thirty, determined to work. No sooner had I picked up the pen than the March of the Pilgrims began. Would I sign this book for a nephew who is graduating from Medical School? Could I recommend a good orthopedist? Would I read these poems and make suggestions? Would I feel this lump? What do I think it is? (Give it to me straight, Doc. I can take it!) No use to protest that, like Cézanne, I was *"sur le motif,"* in which inviolable state of rapture he would not even attend his mother's funeral. Gave up and went to the Yale Art Gallery.

Visited Eakins' *Veteran*. Once again it is the hands that take hold of my imagination. The way they make their appearance in a dark lower corner of the painting, as though amputated and thrown there out of the way, or rather, like a pair of gloves discarded. Yes, they are more gloves than hands. I cannot imagine those fingers in a gesture of animation, flexing, fanning in a spray, apposed in prayer, holding a brush, caressing. They are lumpish, fused, anything but gracile. Precisely because he was a great painter, we ask ourselves what Eakins intended by such rudiments. The discrepancy between the exactitude with which the face of the Veteran is portrayed and the merest suggestion of fingers prompts us to the question. Had George Reynolds discontinued posing before Eakins painted his hands? Had some time elapsed between the rendering of face and hands during which Eakins lost interest in this work and added the hands as an afterthought? Is it possible that Thomas Eakins simply could not draw hands? Now we search the face of the Veteran for some clue to his hands. Had Eakins meant to suggest the countless amputations of arms and legs during the Civil War? Perhaps, then, the answer lies in what these hands withhold from us—the history of their actions, caressing no less than killing. But there is no answer other than the very act of having painted them. The hands are left to explain their own decomposition.

Still mystified, I withdraw to another room where hangs Rothko's #3, which I call "Great Red." Here there are no forms, only the vibrating transition of one red into another. Migrant bits of color pass back and forth across the darker border between, like electrons traversing a membrane. All the life is there at the borderland between red and red. In Van Gogh, the forms themselves vibrate. Rothko, having dispensed with form, has only the vibration itself.

Born and raised when form, depiction, representation were the goals of Art, for a long time I could not see this painting, and then, one day, I had the right eyes for it, and saw two reds bleeding into one another, the exfoliation, the shedding of red. Sometimes it is necessary to live with a work of art for a long time before its secrets are revealed to you. Reform your ideas, and your judgment will follow suit.

The painting smoulders. In a moment it will burst into flame. Stand back! If ever a canvas radiated fire and heat, this is the one. You must screw up your eyes to bear looking at it. It is an oven painted from inside. Here is the artist as Prometheus, having filched fire from the Gods and hung it within a picture frame. Such an egotistical red, asserting itself, unaware of anything but its own redness. You hate it, but at the same time you must admire such vanity. It is a red that makes your mouth water in a Pavlovian response. After a while you thirst for a cool soothing green. What can it mean? Never mind, later the meaning will come clear. How difficult, false even, is the application of words to this painting, but they are all I have, and so I shall try.

What time of the day did he paint it? Noon? Midnight? Those twin images of the day when the hands of the clock are upraised in supplication. No, it was at sunset. Only then could there be such a hot crimson smear. There are no vistas, no planes, no perspective. The eye need not adjust to location. No sky, no sea, no earth. Only a red silence before which we must stand in praise. All at once the canvas begins to pulsate; it flows, runs, bleeds. Oh, I know the color of that upper red—bright arterial blood, spurting. Below it is darker, venous, seeping. A hemorrhage upon the canvas, bringing news of death. From what? A burst organ, the heart perhaps, that pumps its contents out through a rent that is the size and shape of the painting. There is a bloodspray! You are incarnadined.

The childishness with which he painted—headlong, impetuous,

smearing. But it is only when we behave as children that the gate to the senses swings open. In "Red," Rothko has deconstructed the world and put it back together in accordance with his secret instructions. All at once I think of Keats, dying in Rome. There is only the other youth, Severn, to tend him:

> Keats: "Did you ever see anyone die?"
> Severn: "No."
> Keats: "Well then I pity you, poor Severn. What trouble and danger you have got into for me. Now you must be firm, for it will not last long. I shall soon be laid in the quiet grave. Thank God for the quiet grave."
> And at the end: "Severn, lift me up, for I am dying. I shall die easy, don't be frightened! Thank God it has come."

What hurts is not any unfulfilled promise as a poet. Surely his glory is of the ages. It is the long foreknowledge of his death, from the moment, years before, when he first spat arterial blood and knew that he must die. Then he wrote: "When I have fears that I may cease to be/ Before my pen has gleaned my teeming brain." Painful, too, is his having lived and died a virgin, although burning with passion for the girl he loved and would never possess. There was a Paradise Lost I can weep over. Only for Death was Keats no virgin. That One he had possessed a hundred times at Guy's Hospital. All this I see as I gaze into Rothko's "Red."

It seems to me that what the viewer must do is discover the speck of truth contained within each painting or sculpture. This is best done by waiting, standing in silence, and gazing. It has nothing to do with the intellect or with taste or the possession of lore. Most often the discovery is made by chance. It just happens. It is a bursting through into that other world where the imagination roves freely. Perhaps it is not unlike the recapturing of the past by Proust that was triggered by eating a madeleine? Let it be the angel Gabriel come to hover above the inert object made of canvas and paint, marble, or wood, announcing it to the viewer who awakens to find himself "all dewy wet," in the words of James Joyce. To achieve this awakening, you must stay afloat and ungrounded on the river of instinct. For it is not upon the bank but upon the stream, not by riparian intellect but by quick fluvial feeling, that the mystery of art will be solved.

Sometimes I imagine that *St. Peter, The Veteran,* the *Ivory Christ,* the *Bavarian Pietà* and the rest are themselves waiting to be set free by the gaze of the viewer, so that they might live again in us. Should I fail to discover these works of art, how desolate and disappointed they will be. Just so does the obsessive gaze become an act of liberation of what had been imprisoned, an act comprising instinct, magic, mercy, daring, and remembering that is tantamount to a resuscitation by which the dead are raised.

JUNE 1998

Sunday noon. Janet and I walked downtown for lunch, then to the movies.

Nice long silence; then, "Shall I break the silence, or are you in your Trappist mode? I shouldn't have let that nice long silence become pregnant. It makes what's said next so important."

"Say you're not going to confide in me."

"Heavens, no! I do not put my trust in things of this world." An even nicer, longer silence, after which the following:

Janet: "You say you're not afraid to die?"

Me: "No, I'm not. Let death come when it will."

Janet: "I find that bizarre. Are you depressed?"

Me: "Not a bit. Fact is, I'm rather cheerful these days. Only, I'm
    ready."

Janet: "It's not normal."

Me: "I'm not normal. Dense of you not to have noticed all these years.
    Besides, I've gone the full limits of whatever small talent I have.
    I can't do any more. What's left will be compromise, repetition,
    settlement—a refusal of life."

Janet: "You mean us, don't you?"

Me: "Watch out or I'll run off and leave you with nothing but a fine-
    tooth comb. You can have the family darning egg, too."

Third and last silence broken by me humming.

Janet: "I must pretend not to hear you. What's that you're hum-
    ming?"

Me (singing): "Pale Hands I Loved Beside the Shalimar / Where are
    you now? Who lies beneath your spell? / I would have rather felt

them round my throat / Crushing out life, than waving me
farewell."

Janet: "Are you threatening me?"

Me: "*Honi soit qui mal y pense.*"

Janet: "What a lovely time. These Sunday afternoons are our best
times, don't you think?"

Me: "I surely do."

SEPTEMBER 1998

I am very far from being a collector of books. You wouldn't know it from
the shelves of them that line three rooms of my house. Most of these came
to me by a will other than my own. Be it said at the outset that I have
never purchased a book because of its future monetary value. I can say
with pride that my library is worthless. Any number of the volumes were
sent by those who sincerely wanted me to have a certain book. It would
do me good in many ways; it would prove fascinating; there is a character in it that is reminiscent of me. Such a book is invariably inscribed by
the donor so that I would be less likely to discard it, or, basely, to sell it to
a used-book dealer. Another aliquot of books were sent by the very
authors who wrote them. Some, out of a sense of collegiality. After all,
we are both writers, aren't we? Others, in hopes of receiving a few words
of praise to be printed on the second edition or used for advertising. A
few are sent by kindred spirits calling out into the void. Presenting you
with a book is a way of laying claim to a portion of your thought, whether
you like it or not. Even if the book, given ages ago when its pages were
not yet cut, goes unread, you are aware of its presence on the shelf, bid-
ing its time, lying in wait for that moment when you will reach up idly,
take down the volume, blow off the accumulation of dust, and open to
page one. But what is this? I say. The pages are uncut! For a brief moment
you are torn between pique and curiosity. Curiosity wins. Now you sit
down to read the first page. But first you rummage in the desk drawer
for one of your old scalpels. It is not long before you discover that the
book is a romantic novel that will plow the narrow but ever-fascinating
furrow of domesticity. The heroine is a woman, no longer young; neither
is she old. She has ash-blond hair (the author has put it in French: *blonde-
cendre*) that is set in waves. She is seated at a tiny desk (*bonheur de jour*) in

her boudoir. Now and then she dips her pen into an inkwell and writes. It is clear from the speed at which she jots that she is in a state of high anxiety. Now you have reached the bottom of the page.

In order to find out the cause of her agitation and to whom she is writing, you must slit the page. To be perfectly frank, you could as easily leave this distressed heroine to her own devices and close the book. But then, there are those pages to be slit. If there is anything more satisfying to a surgeon than to insert the tip, then the belly of his blade between the pages of a book and make an incision, I don't know of it. There is the soft susurration as blade splits paper, the fine new erose edge of the pages, and the exquisite knowledge that you are the very first person to read this book. It is as much a bride as a book. Then, too, there is the element of destiny. You and the book were created perhaps two thousand miles and two hundred years apart, but only now has Fate revealed that you were made for each other. The slice once having been made, neither of you will be the same as you were. But let us leave the surgeon, who is soon as besotted with his heroine (her name is Charlotte de Sevigné) as he was with his knife. To remain with them any longer would be in the grossest ill taste.

Another shelf of my library is occupied by books that I have written myself. Is it immodest of me to suggest that these nine are my favorites? Of course, it is immodest, but that's the way it is. Between braggartry and hypocrisy, I prefer the sin of pride. It's more honest.

Here and there, while browsing in my library, I come across a volume that I borrowed some years ago and failed to return. If it is a good book, why then I enjoy a frisson of pleasure at having gotten away with a small theft. If it is a bad book, I experience an equally brief feeling of shame and self-loathing.

Time was, when, as a child and youth, I spent a good part of my allowance or meager earnings in the acquisition of books. Even during internship and residency, I purchased books, though these tended to be less literary than pertinent. One I recall was *Diseases of the Rectum: Diagnosis and Treatment*. Now that I have retired from medicine, I no longer buy books. I borrow them from the Yale library, where I spend the better part of each day. Lately, what was once a strong interest in books has become an eccentricity. Now and then, at the library, I patrol the Great Reading Room, where of an afternoon there sleeps the Yale student body, and unbeknownst I pick up a book that has been left lying on a table, just to see what the sleeper was reading. I should not like this penchant of mine to become common knowledge about the campus.

DECEMBER 1998

A day *tout seul chez moi.* Listened to *The Magic Flute.* Two great voices— Sarastro and Papageno. Wrote ten letters, one to a psychologist who is investigating the phenomenon of visual hallucinations in the blind. What he calls "phantom vision," to relate it to phantom limb. Apparently these are quite common, varied, and interesting, both to the one who experiences them and to the psychologist. They are multicolored, consist of many different moving images. Some are dramatic, religious, or archetypal. Others are of mundane objects. One subject experienced the feeling that the chair in which he was sitting rose into the air and became enveloped with green foliage. There is a tendency to fail to report or to deny these hallucinations, so as not to be considered peculiar or even crazy. In phantom limb, the missing limb is experienced. It occupies a position in space and can generate sensations such as pain and heat. Auditory hallucinations have been reported in people with hearing loss. It seems likely that a similar "neuropsychological" mechanism accounts for all of these and provides a sensory-perceptual "fill." Is there some neural network for the "body self" that generates these hallucinations?

Some of these hallucinations are threatening, even dangerous, but some are enjoyable. They can be quite companionable, and can give the feeling that one can actually see. This is a fascinating subject, and one that tempts me to write a short story about phantom sensation. About a blind man who experiences phantom vision to a high degree. The premise will be that there is another life of the body that is being lived at the same time as the one we know and are aware of. Only this second body-life is hidden, subtle, and able to be called forth only by the impaired, who can tap into it. Phantom vision would only occur in someone who had gone blind after years of seeing, not in one who was born blind. Must think of the phenomenon and its ramifications. Could this be at the bottom of all the "visitations" of Mary and Jesus? Could Francis of Assisi and Theresa of Avila and Catherine of Siena have been severely neurotic people who could call upon this second, underlying body-life? Catherine, who was an anorexic, would be a likely candidate for it.

JANUARY 1999

Koju Fujieda is a professor who teaches English to medical students in Japan. For a year he has taught my book *Letters to a Young Doctor*. Each week we exchange an e-mail message, his asking the precise meaning of a word or phrase, mine giving him that information. Over the course of a year, Fujieda-san and I have become friends. He sends me his haiku; I send him a paragraph of new writing. At the end of the course, each of his students was asked to write a comment in English on the book and on its value to future doctors. What follows is my own response to the professor's request for an authorial statement, all to be bound together in a small book.

1998 was the year that Japan was returned to me. Here's what happened: Forty-three years earlier, in 1955, I was in the first year of Surgical Training at Yale University in New Haven, Connecticut. Without warning, I received the news that I had been drafted into the United States Army. Within days, I was undergoing Basic Army Training in Texas. Within weeks, I was en route to the Far East. I remember being transported from Washington State to Vancouver, Canada. Then on to a dreary frigid place called Cold Bay, Alaska, and thence to Tokyo. Before this I had not traveled more than one hundred miles from my native town. No sooner had that first morning dawned, than the sadness at having been snatched out of my surgical training melted away, and I did what countless other Americans have done—I fell in love with Japan, its people, culture, art.

Mine was a two-year adventure in the Far East. For the first year I worked as a doctor in Korea, then still a third-world country. My patients were mostly Korean refugees. I had to learn not only some Korean but the much easier Japanese, which, no matter their suffering, the Koreans were reluctant to speak, as the hated language had been forced upon them during the long, cruel occupation of their country by Japan. It was in Korea that I first tried my hand at writing. The result was an unpublished novel, *The Bronze Gong*. I was to do no further writing for two decades.

The year spent in Japan was not so rigorous, but extremely rewarding culturally. I was like a kitten at a dish of cream. *Oishii desu* (delicious). Everything, kabuki, NOH, ukiyo-e, the ceremony of tea, the cuisine, and the translated literature, both classical and modern. Bashō as well as Tanizaki. It is forty-four years later, and I have not returned to Japan. Perhaps not physically, but oftentimes in my mind. During this time I taught and practiced Surgery at Yale University until 1986, when I retired in order to try to realize my potential as a writer. Somewhere along the way, nine books of essays, memoirs, and short stories were published.

Fortune was smiling at me on the day in 1998 when I received a letter from Professor Koju Fujieda, who was about to teach one of my books, *Letters to a Young Doctor,* to a class of medical students at Fukui Medical College. He would teach it in English. Would I, he wondered, correspond with him by fax or by e-mail each week to make sure his interpretation of the work was correct? I would, indeed, although first I had to acquire e-mail and learn how to use it. And so, for the duration of the course, Fujieda-san and I have written to each other, mostly on matters pertaining to the book itself. He had a number of triumphs when he found mistakes that I or my publisher had not seen before. Now and then he found a word that wasn't in any dictionary. Of course not! I had made it up. I marveled at the ease with which he read and taught my admittedly difficult and ornate prose. Even here at Yale, it is considered *taiheng muzukashii* (too hard). As time went on, he would send me lovely haiku of his own making, and we exchanged many words of friendship.

If there is one last suggestion that I might make to the future doctors of Japan, that would be to refrain from becoming so enamored of medical technology that you lose sight of the "beating heart" of the profession, which is the patient. In one chapter of *Letters to a Young Doctor,* an elderly woman announces to the doctor that she is going to take her terminally ill husband home from the hospital. The doctor protests that it might prove to be too hard for her, that she herself is old and frail, that there would be too much mess to clean up. To which the old woman replies: "How much mess can one man make?" And with that powerful question, she becomes ennobled and raised to a level to which the doctor could only hope to aspire. Listen to the patients. They are trying to tell you something that is both beautiful and true.

MAY 1999

On Indolence: A letter to a first-year medical student

In every letter you complain that you must memorize so many facts. Be advised that a lover gladly commits to memory the smallest details of the body of his beloved. "They are working us too hard," you cry, and forget that when the weather precludes gardening, a clever abbess will see to it that the gardener is otherwise employed about the convent. "I forget half of everything I study," you say. But that is all to the good. For you are now entering a higher state of knowledge than that of a year ago. To have learned so much and to have forgotten half of it is a kind of graduation, and therefore deserving of congratulations. If all goes well, you will learn even more next year and forget three-quarters of it. By the time of your internship, you will have learned and forgotten everything. Sanc sieve hood is the proper condition of a doctor. Then, if called upon to recite the blood supply of the large intestine, you will be unable to utter a word. But confronted with a patient suffering from ulcerative colitis, you will know at once the etiology, pathogenesis, natural course, differential diagnosis, and therapy of his disease, as well as the blood supply to the large intestine. The facts will come zinging down about your ears like a hailstorm. Where were they when you perspired to remember them? Far below and out of sight of your sieve, there is a fine-meshed net in which they all hang, awaiting retrieval.

I have some personal knowledge of indolence. Once, some sixty years ago, I explained to my teacher that I hadn't done my French homework because in the middle of the night it occurred to me that God had forbidden it. You see, I instructed Mademoiselle Douton, after the Flood the descendants of Noah undertook to build a tower that would reach unto Heaven. So arrogant did God consider this act that he caused the raisers thereof to speak different languages so that they could no longer communicate with each other. The people scattered and the Tower of Babel remained incomplete. Would it not, I reasoned, be wicked to study French in defiance of the Divine Will? I have always thought it heretical of Mademoiselle to give me a failing grade.

No, indolence is only to be permitted in clever women. There is something infinitely sensuous about a whopping clever woman who lolls about on cushions all afternoon eating chocolate-covered bonbons. But indolence in a dull woman is not to be borne, whether by the men who must lug her out of the sun should she threaten to spoil, or by the peppy members of her own gender who tumble about ceaselessly, doing the work of the world. In men, indolence is called sloth. While despising it with all the venom of an overworked drudge, I confess to a grudging admiration for the silken art. "Ah, to fleet the time carelessly as they did in the golden world." My favorites at the zoo are the lions; when they are not eating, they sleep. This doesn't seem compatible with the spurt and slash of a surgeon, but then, life is made up of such paradoxes.

There are certain marriages, the two parts of which are so perfectly conjoined as to seem foretold by the prophets. One simply knows that energetic and prodigious heroes will clink from their loins like coins of great value. Such conjugations are said by some to be the hope and wellspring of the human race. Their progeny read the *New York Times* at the age of two. At three, those same toddlers will play one of the early Haydn sonatas.

The parents of these children are given to ill-founded boasting at cocktail parties. All too often, the braggarts are hoist by their own petard. The little pianist will have stabbed the family cat in the bathroom. No, prodigiousness in a child is not to be prized.

In any case, I know of no child prodigy who can hold a candle to St. Macedonius of Syria, whose birth was the direct result of his own prayers.

We other parents who have not been joined in such perfect union, the "for worse" having proved equipotent to the "for better," quickly come to understand that our children are but fragile specimens of the clay, holding each his portion of indolence or sloth, and with every possibility for an undistinguished life. For it is our own defects they are most likely to adopt. The lesson here: forget genius; so few have it. And just do the best you can.

I used to have two aunts. Elaine was fat and Sally was thin. Elaine sat and Sally darted. For many years they lived together in perfect harmony. Early on, Fat Elaine had bestirred herself long enough to capture the affections of Rich Herman, with whom she had omnivorousness in common. Their slow oleaginous bliss was short-lived, as Rich Herman died of acute necrotizing pancreatitis after a week of Olympian feasting. The Death Certificate blamed Natural Causes, which is a euphemism, not a diagnosis. Now it happened that Elaine was Herman's sole heir, and so was able to continue her peristaltic existence to the end of her days. Aunt Sally, on the other hand, was a mere pit of a woman, whatever fruit there was having long since shriveled away. So desiccated was she that one had to restrain the impulse to fling her into a tub of water like a Chinese mushroom until she reconstituted. Round and round she raced, up and down, rummaging, sweeping, traveling every inch of the house that was not directly beneath Her Corpulence.

I loved to visit them. The three of us would be in the parlor, Elaine lolling on the divan like a huge breast that had slipped its moorings, and Sally squirming on the edge of the ladderback chair.

"I don't for the life of me see how a person can lie around all day and do nothing," said Sally of Elaine. "I have to keep my hands busy." She had just tatted twelve miles of lace.

"With me, it's the jaws," said Elaine, and reached one huge apron of arm for another bonbon.

And so it went, Elaine cheerfully paying the bills, and Sally cheerfully tending both the house and Elaine. Years later, when it began to be time for them to die, I prayed that Elaine would go first, but only by ten seconds. Elaine could not have survived without Sally to turn her over. She'd have gotten bedsores and other settling disorders. Sally could have survived, but it would have been a technicality without her great golden egg to brood over. Happily, they both lived to great age and died within the same week. I visited them a month before. To my astonishment, they were exactly the same size! Elaine had lost a hundred pounds, and Sally had gained a hundred pounds.

Then and there, I formulated my Theory of Family Fat. It goes like this: Every family is allotted by heredity and other factors a certain fixed tonnage. Should weight be lost by one member of the family, the same poundage must be gained by the other members of the household. Family fat, like all other matter, can be neither created nor destroyed. Unlike most scientific theories, mine is useful, for it allows members of a family to swap fat as the occasion arises. Say that a mother has an unmarried daughter who is fat and getting dangerously long in the tooth. This mother can simply gorge herself with food, eagerly gaining pounds even as her daughter grows svelter and svelter. At the end of six months, a husband having been achieved, the loving mother can either give the fat back to her daughter, keep it herself, or dump it onto her son-in-law.

In light of this theory, Sally and Elaine take on a certain poignancy. Elaine had merely kept unto herself the bulk of the family fat in order that Sally could the more easily fix and putter. Sally had divested herself of fat so that she could better nurture Elaine, the precious fat pool of the household. When they were ready to die and this lopsided dispersion of fat was no longer necessary, each of my aunts sensibly, and with perfect amicability, split it right down the middle.

So much for indolence. Next comes venery, then guilt.

Yours, *ex pulpito*

JANUARY 2000

New Year's Eve, I went outside at eight o'clock to smell the moon, then went to bed. Some people have no sense of occasion.

Already 1999 seems quaint, altogether in the distant past. The written number is an untranslatable hieroglyph. Went to visit Maynard Mack. He is getting stronger—can stand holding the bar with his good hand, and supported by someone on the other side. In this manner, he takes twelve steps. He remains obsessed with going home. Paranoid about the nursing home, unfairly I think. He is doted on by the staff. I wonder if a visitor's health abashes. It seems rude to be up and walking when he is immobile and confined and utterly miserable. Could it be that one's efforts to be diverting, the cajolery, grate on his nerves? Does he think me egotistical and unconcerned? Now it is I who am paranoid. It's contagious. The other patient in the room is a hundred years old. A flitch of bones laid out between undisturbed and spotless sheets. Motionless, expressionless, he has a kind of vegetable dignity. From a tumbler on the shelf, his teeth look down accusingly. Teeth can give much dirtier looks than eyes. It is ridiculous, I told them, for a set of submerged dentures to take offense at a seventy-one-year-old just because of his comparative youth and mobility. But the teeth glared on. "You!" they said.

Changed the subject to *The Merchant of Venice* and the Bible. The part where the King of Morocco, wooing Portia, asks her to forgive his dark skin. It is due to the closeness of the sun in his country. She turns him down, and "all of your complexion." In the Song of Songs, too, the opening lines: *Nigra sum sed formosa* ("I am black but I am beautiful"). The racism goes way back.

Maynard said he's lost all interest in anything Roman, including Virgil, because of their cruelty in punishing by crucifixion. We agreed that Abraham, Jacob, David, and many of the Patriarchs were no damn good either. Excepting Noah and Isaiah. Made Maynard laugh out loud over Noah's tippling and Isaiah's spastic colitis. Did my heart good.

"Machine City" is on the lower level of the Sterling Library. It is so-called for its many food and drink machines. Plastic tables and booths are numerous, each with a suspended light bulb under a red lampshade. The soul of "Machine City" is not readily visible. Its ugliness is absolute. Here employees and graduate students eat lunch; here, too, Teaching Assistants and Instructors meet with their students. Every Thursday, and on days when the weather is bad, I go there to eat lunch. Today is one of those days.

I am sitting at one of the tables, pretending to read. Oh, all right, I am spying on them again. At the nearest table are three beautiful young Puerto Rican women who work in the library. The fourth seat is vacant. They are eating a communal lunch, to which each has brought something. There are bowls and cutlery. They eat with gusto, using their black hair, black eyes, even their bosoms in the act. Sofia is well-upholstered, Liliana and Isabela are fashionably slim (you see that I have named them). They are dressed in citrus colors—lemon, orange, tangerine, and lime. As much skin is showing as is consistent with working in a library. It is the color of honey, or the flesh of a mango. From every wrist, neck, and earlobe there is the flash of gold. The mood at the table is oxymoronic— animated languor. They could be reclining on Cleopatra's barge.

Alone, enchanted, I watch as if from a promontory. I am close enough to eavesdrop. For weeks, I have died to know what they are saying. The flow of language—Spanish and English—it is the passionate cry of birds. At any given moment one, two, or all three are speaking. Or humming against their teeth. Or singing *sotto voce*. It has the effect of blurring the sound so that I can make out almost nothing. Isabela has one of those mouths that whisper something even when they are silent. Even her hands are loquacious. The air around them is tremulous. They speak of music and dancing. I can tell by the way they move their shoulders and snap their fingers, causing breasts to swing independently. They speak of clothes. I can tell from the way they pass their hands over themselves, making blouse-shapes, designing skirts with their fingers. They speak of men and of sex. This I can tell from the muffling of a voice by a hand held in front of a mouth, by the intense stillness of the others, the laughter that follows. I imagine the pupils of their black eyes dilating. If they are aware of my presence, they give no sign. Surely, there will come the moment when one of them, Liliana I think, will feel upon her cheek the warm breath of my attention. She will look up to see me smiling, signal to the others with her eyes. Then all three heads will turn, the way deer in the forest turn at the sound of a distant footstep. But they do not. They are intent upon their own iridescent lives.

What's this! Sofia has made a remark taken personally by Isabela. The teasing continues. Daggers of fury; the clatter of bracelets, churning of beads; the drumming *agitato* of red fingernails on the table. A loud "No!" rises from the swollen throat of the victim. In it I recognize the groan of a soldier whose wound is being probed. In a moment, she will give her persecutor bloody teeth. Then comes a ripe Spanish curse that makes all three laugh until my own chest aches with it. The way they sway together, cling, then fall apart. From outside the circle of light, heat, and moisture in which they flourish, I luxuriate in their presence. In another moment, I will throw discretion to the winds, take four fated steps and sit in the fourth, the vacant chair.

"*Madman! Have you lost all sense of propriety? Stay where you belong, Gray-head.*"

"*If a man is not given a bit of latitude now and then, where will he find his recreation?*"

"*Be reasonable.*"

"*Since when has reason stood up to human behavior?*"

All at once, as if a bell had rung, they rise from the table that is littered with their secrets, gather the remains of lunch, and fly about in several directions. Crumbs are brushed from bosoms, hair is clutched and patted, cheeks are felt for any damage. On the way out, they saunter past my table. I make my eyes small, perhaps I close them, and inhale deeply. Their scent! When I open my eyes, they have gone. Their table is enclosed in a silence that is like a beatitude. I try to stare them back into existence but it doesn't work.

All at once, I have a vision of an old gray man rocking back and forth on a plastic chair in "Machine City." His head is a skull with a candle guttering inside. It is not a pretty sight.

JANUARY 2001

Reminded by a scene in "Envy," by Yuri Olesha, of a raised round black birthmark I used to have on the left anterior axilary fold. It was identical to one that my father had in exactly the same place. I was perhaps four or five, watching my father lathering on shaving cream, an act he infused with great sensuality. It was then that I saw the mole, thought how ugly it was, so black against the whiteness of his skin. At puberty I, too, grew a mole that was the twin of his. When I remarked upon its ugliness, my mother (Father was already dead) said that had I been kidnapped, she would have recognized me years later by the mole. Ten years later, as an intern in Surgery, and undressing in the locker room of the OR, my mole was noticed by one of the senior residents, who suggested that I have it removed. He offered to excise it. I agreed, without thinking. No sooner was it removed than I felt a wave of regret and guilt that a vital connection between my father and myself had been severed. Now, where the nevus had been, there was a faint scar, like the buried stump of a tree that had been hewn flush with the ground. It was from this experience that sprang the stories "The Birthmark," "Minor Surgery," and "Fur Baby."

This is not the only recognition of my father in me. I have the sense that we shared more than a pigmented nevus. He, too, was a sensualist, but one who acted out his dark urges. I have the faintest recollection of scandal, having to do with his women patients. It was said to be the reason why his practice did not flourish. We were poor; he had to take on jobs such as Jail Doctor, and Physician at various institutions for the retarded, the insane, and unmarried pregnant girls. From what long-forgotten corner of the swamp of childhood has this heaved itself up? Childhood casts the heaviest shadow on a life. Writing compensates one for the childhood that was not to be savored.

MARCH 2001

In Troy with the film crew to make a segment of Bill Moyers' documentary on the Hudson River Valley. The first location is the Oakwood Cemetery.

The Crematorium looks for all the world like a huge saurian that was turned to stone in some ancient cataclysm and now is the god of this sacred ridge overlooking the Hudson River Valley; the way its copper roofs glint in the sunlight; the canopy of stars at night.

Accompanied by old friend and master architect Patrick Quinn, I climb the narrow spiral staircase, which ends three-quarters of the way up the tower. From there on it's hand-over-hand up an iron ladder to the belfry, which is the eye-socket of the beast. It is windowless; a fierce wind is blowing; the temperature up there, below zero. We gaze out over the Hudson River, with the Catskill Mountains to the south and the Adirondacks to the north. We see the Cohoes Falls, the confluence of the Hudson and the Mohawk. From there we descend to the Chapel and Reception Room of the Crematorium, with its elegance of onyx and marble and malachite, the oak fixtures and beams, the Tiffany windows. Everywhere we are followed by the crew of cameramen, sound and lighting men, and the producers. There isn't a drop of spontaneity in it. The crew is extraordinarily friendly. I am made to feel accepted. From the cemetery we go to the South End Tavern for lunch. It is Thursday; there is corned beef and cabbage. And Genessee beer. In the afternoon we traipse in Washington Park, where Patrick dilates on the variety of the architecture. We are let into the limestone mansion, where Billy and I played as small children. It is now a fraternity house of Rensselaer Polytechnic Institute.

Next day, we go to Music Hall, where I sing several songs that my mother sang in the same spot sixty-five years ago, "Mighty Lak a Rose" and "Mexicali Rose." It is an impersonation. Then down to the river itself. Last stop is the Troy Public Library, where I read excerpts from *Down from Troy* and *The Exact Location of the Soul*.

The others head for home immediately. Exhausted, I sleep another night at the hotel, drive home in the morning.

Already the events in Troy have slipped out of focus. A certain Richard Selzer went to Troy to impersonate another Richard Selzer, whom no one alive can remember having seen or spoken with. The imposturage cannot be refuted. Only I know how false it is. Again and again I ask myself why I did it. I was not being paid. Is it to boost my beloved homeland? To bring the tattered old town into view? Perhaps it is just the chance to play the ham, which only the pathologically bashful are able to renounce.

JULY 2001

In re the supernatural: We owe allegiance to two selves—one in the visible, the other in the invisible realm—which must somehow be brought into view or touch or into an audible range. And so we are ancipitous—two-headed, like Janus. It is our fate to be amphibious. When we think we have all of this world, we get a glimpse of some other, and the minute you let yourself fly into that empyrean, you forget the limitations of what's solid and real. Best is to be a wise doubter.

SEPTEMBER 2001

The Anatomy Lesson

If this were 1632 in Amsterdam instead of 2001 in New Haven, I would dissect a fresh corpse before a paying crowd drawn from the upper classes. In all likelihood, the corpse would be that of a just-hanged criminal, the further to punish the miscreant. I would not be shabby in a scrub suit, but resplendent in corduroy, and wearing a hat with a brim, and a broad collar trimmed with lace. Afterward, there would be a banquet. But it is 2001, and we have dispensed with elegance, and are entirely utilitarian. While Dr. Tulp began with the hand and the forearm, I shall begin with the face, especially the muscles of expression. By the way, Dr. Tulp got it all wrong. In a grotesque transposition, he put the right arm on the left side of the body. The dissected tendons are not those of the left palm but of the dorsum of the right hand! What could Dr. Tulp have been thinking of!

We dissect, and are struck by the logic, the orderliness, the good sense of the body, all in accordance with the laws of nature and evolution. But reduce it to shreds and still we cannot grasp its innermost essence—the soul.

We are fascinated, too, by the freakishness of the body, its abnormal mutations.

There is something about the dissection of a body that makes one think of a funeral rite. But here no coin in the mouth for the Elysian ferryman. As Chekhov remarked in the throes of a dissection, "Where is the soul in all of this?"

The face in the act of expression is an undulating surface of skin beneath which the bones are distinguishable. Between the skin and the bones lie the muscles that pad, mold, and carve the face into hillocks and declivities, the better to frown or to smile.

In the act of retching, the muscles around the eye undergo energetic contraction such that tears are squeezed from the lacrimal ducts.

FEBRUARY 2002

On the dining room table there stands a tall cut-glass vase of red and white lilies. They were given to Janet by a guest at the Bed & Breakfast. Their odor stirs the imagination. It is not the odor of sanctity, in which flesh laid in the ground would not putrefy. It has the same odor as Troy, where, in the thirties and forties with tuberculosis rampant in the town, Death was ubiquitous. On every block, His presence was announced by a large bouquet of white lilies pinned to the doorpost of a house. No city block but was so festooned. The streets of Troy were full of their smell.

The lilies on the dining room table are about as far as you can get from the funerary lilies of Troy. They are the hot, pagan *Speciosum lilium rubrum,* with heavy pendulous buds and blossoms with pinkish-white petals spattered with a violence of bloody red. The petals are deeply recurved, the better to thrust erect the genital apparatus, which vibrates in lascivious carriage at every errant breeze. Six St. Ronan Terrace is a-reel with the scent. All the pictures on the walls have tilted. Smoke issues from the chimneys even though there are no fires in the grates.

MARCH 2002

Yesterday, ate my lunch in the atrium of the hospital. At a nearby table a young mother and her child in a wheelchair. The child, bald and with a tube in one nostril leading somewhere under the bathrobe. The mother massaged the child's legs, which were in splints to prevent foot-drop or spasms, I gathered. From time to time, she offered her child a sip of coke through a straw, then held a basin for the child to spit it out. I could not tell the gender of the child, whose pretty face with its delicate features and the glistening bald head seemed the quintessence of childhood. It was as though I were seeing a reenactment of "Atrium." I was deeply affected. Driven and cornered, I now wear only the thin flannel shirt of vincibility. Either I am becoming "emotionally labile," as the clinicians say, or I am looking at life with my heart rather than with my eyes. No wonder, as my vision is no better, and the discomfort increases.

APRIL 2002

What with the blurring of my vision, to say nothing of the constant slow vermification of my muscae volitantes (floating concretions in the vitreous humor), the world has become out-of-focus, in fact as well as in fancy. Everything is suffused with indistinction and peopled by phantoms. It is rather like swimming beneath the surface of a stagnant pond teeming with schistosomes, snails, *Dracunculus medinensis,* and what ever other parasites. Now, whereas before this gave me cause to shudder at the prospect of blindness and at the "uncertainty" of the real world, I have lately embraced my affliction, the way a martyr seizes for himself the Kingdom of Heaven. In the shifting haze, I find numerous pregnant possibilities. It is an adaptation that a writer can make and that a surgeon, say, cannot. For instance, in such a "spiritual" state, it is easier to commune with the dead. Why, only this morning I had a long chat with my paternal grandmother Sophie—in Yiddish! In which she admitted to me that Julius had not been fathered by the same man as his two older siblings. I allowed as how I had figured this out while she was still alive. In such a discarnate, "flow-y" state, bottles tilt and my toothbrush floats in the air, moving to and fro in a ghostly parody of its earthly raison d'etre. In short, it is the ideal milieu for the artist.

Birdwatching

"Oh my goodness! A yellow warbler!" She was breathless with the discovery.

He turned his field glasses to where she was pointing and diagnosed the "bird" as a leaf waggling at the end of a branch. Oh well, she sighed, and gave herself up to the sibilance of the great waterfall on the Mill River. It spoke to her of peace, of love.

She'd taken it up to be near him. It was something they could do together. In more candid moments, she admitted to herself that she had no interest in birds. Furthermore, it made her feel like an intruder peering up into the trees, spying like that. To say nothing of a lack of hand/eye coordination (she was sure it was genetic) that verged on disablement for a birdwatcher. Especially during the spring migration. She didn't mind hawks, turkey vultures, or great blue herons. You could see them with the naked eye. But the warblers were tiny; they made her feel even fatter and clumsier than she was. But what could she do? She adored him. And she vowed never, never to give the least hint that she might rather be somewhere else. And the pains he took to make sure she saw a bird!

"There," and he'd point, "just to the left of the trunk of that cottonwood. Two-thirds of the way up, then out along the middle curved branch, the one with a bend in it. Oops! Just hopped out. Now! Right out in the open. A classic view. See the orange breast? That's a blackburnian warbler. Did you get him?"

"Oh, yes!" she'd lie. "Gorgeous!"

They had been birdwatching in the park all morning. She had endured the usual complaints that the damn leaves had come out too early this year, that you couldn't see the birds for the foliage. She'd heard all she wanted to about the decline in numbers of warblers each year and the tales of birdwatching derring-do, how on this very date a year ago, right here they had seen a prothonotary and a Kentucky warbler! Worst of all was the habit common to all birdwatchers to attribute human emotions to the birds.

"Spiteful pecker, hiding behind the trunk," or "The show-off! Been preening here for hours." That sort of thing. It was a form of anthropo-morphism she found particularly irksome. In spite of herself, she developed a certain competency. The secret was to pretend she wasn't there. Then the bird wouldn't dart off to bring news of her intrusion. Bird psychology, she called it. For another thing, she had an ear. Hear it once, a birdsong would belong to her from then on. The others complained that each year they had to learn them all again.

Arnie had come by the passion genetically. His father had delivered it unto him at the intracellular level. And his father to him, and doubtless all the way back to *Pithecanthropus erectus*. Such people must feel the wings of the birds beating in their blood. It was the greatest calamity of the old man's life when, at the age of sixty, he had quickly gone quite deaf, couldn't even hear the trip-hammer of a pileated woodpecker. For a while he had continued to go along with them.

"You can always use your eyes," Arnie said, said it with the voice of an adult consoling a crestfallen child.

"It's nothing to be ashamed of," she had chimed in. But of course it was. She could understand that, not being able to do any listening, having to hear with your eyes. She had seen how he waited to see where Arnie aimed his glasses, then followed suit. He, who all by himself had been the Early Warning System of the New Haven Bird Club. Soon enough, the shame of being earless in the woods grew too painful, and the old man stopped birdwatching. Without the testimony of half the essential birdwatching senses, he had simply left the field.

She and Arnie had been birding all morning without any good sightings. She had long since let her field glasses just hang and lost herself in contemplation of his perfect back. It always surprised her a little to find on closer inspection that he did not have wings. Even his hair looked muscular. While, in her pink and white sunhat, she felt like a trampled peony. Idly she sparred for a moment with a spike of her hair, then gave up. She remembered the first time they had gone birdwatching together. It was a morning rather like this one—as soft and warm as milk straight from the udder. He was an expert, of course, and it was her first time.

"Look!" he pointed to a brown basket hanging from a branch. "An oriole's nest. The male gathers the nesting material, brings it here and she shapes it round and round with her breast. They hang it out there to keep the eggs safe from the damn jays and crows. A marvel of architecture, isn't it?"

"It's more of a marvel for your having seen it," she said. "I mean snugger. Nature untrodden is wonderful, I'm sure, but how would we know that?" she explained, and promised to put his smile in her safe deposit box at the bank. That was the day he'd told her how as a small boy he had taken apart the grandfather clock in the front hall. I was looking for Time, he had explained just before the strop was applied.

She remembered how, on that enameled morning in May—the very Ides, in fact—he had turned and bent toward her, held out his hands to help her cross a stream on stepping-stones. She had let herself be taken and drawn across from stone to stone until she was safely on dry land. When, in fact, the stones weren't that far apart, and she could have hopped over on her own just as well.

"Oh," she breathed, "many, many thanks." That double "many" was a fine excess, she thought. But it was his gesture that made her fall in love with him once and for all. She remembered, too, how just then a wood thrush began to sing nearby, the loveliest fluting sound in all the bird kingdom. Right then he had gazed off in the direction of the sound, his eyes gone muzzy with the beauty of it. Ever since, the wood thrush had been her favorite bird. She loved its shyness and coquetry. The way it sat still and sang for a long time, then the minute you thought you'd seen it, away flew beauty, and that was that.

Another time, they were crossing an open field that was once used for archery practice in the days when archery, like croquet, was one of the reigning sports at Female Academies of Polite Learning. When it became respectable for girls to work up a sweat, the Archery Field was allowed to ripen into a prairie of poison ivy, tall grasses, and wild roses. The day was hot and sunny. High overhead a red-tailed hawk, dipping to a chipmunk, screamed. She could taste that scream on her tongue, like brass, and imagined the collision of feathers and fur, the way stiff sleek wings brushed the earth, the terror ruffling the fur of the tiny beast. The spring migration was at full throttle and the warblers were popping out of the bushes like corks out of bottles of champagne. Looking down, she saw their shadows where they walked, his tall and majestic, she thought; hers, a shapeless mound that might have been something he had on a leash.

"I'm too fat," she announced. "Don't you think I'm too fat?"

"There's a good reason why you upholster a sofa," he had answered.

"Well, then," she said, and felt her fat sweeten all the way deep to her bones. This was the man with whom she would happily birdwatch until death and thereafter.

Then there was the time they had stopped to eat lunch under a copper beech tree. They hadn't been there more than a minute when he whispered something she had to cock her ear to catch.

"Will you look at that!"

"Will I look at what?"

"Those two mourning doves on the ground." She looked and saw one bird sitting on top of the other. "What are they doing?"

"They're doing it right out in front of Gawd and everyone." His voice was rich with mischief. All at once the climate turned tropical. Lianas hung from the beech tree; a cockatoo screamed; monkeys chattered. She told herself, very firmly, to behave.

Sometimes she followed him all morning without exchanging a word. She knew from the permafrost at the back of his eyes that he had constructed one of his long silences, but even that was interesting about him. After a while, she couldn't stand it anymore and spoke up.

"What time is it getting to be?" He pointed at the sun.

"Oh, almost noon, right?" But she knew he wasn't in the mood to talk.

"Heads up!" Arnie had stopped dead in his tracks and cocked an ear. Dutifully, she too halted and, with all deliberate speed, raised her glasses halfway, so as to be on the qui vive, as he put it. (His mother had been born and raised in Montreal.)

"What?" she whispered.

"Red-eyed vireo." In the big oak, two-thirds of the way up to the left of the main trunk in a space between the two curved branches. "Damn leaves! Just a second and I'll find it." Again and again the bird sang, the same monotonous, distinctly unmusical notes. Like a robin, she thought, with a sore throat.

"That's a scarlet tanager, I think," she ventured timidly. And regretted it at once. To so far forget herself as to contradict . . . !

When he lowered his glasses to look at her, his dark brown eyes were almost black. The way they spurted male brightness right at her! A hush fell from the trees, kept falling all around her. She felt bested by obscure forces.

"You're mistaken," he said. She could detect the annoyance in his voice at having been challenged. And by her! "It's the red-eyed vireo, beyond peradventure of doubt." She knew he was angry by his having said "peradventure" instead of "a shadow." On and on sang the bird, whatever it was, while he resumed scanning the oak tree. All at once, despite the frantic gesticulation of a weeping willow, she heard herself mutter under her breath the two most dreadful words in the English language.

"Scarlet tanager." Could have bitten her tongue off the next moment. Too late, he'd heard her. Now he, too, dropped his field glasses and turned to face her, arguing. Like all Frenchmen, he talked with gestures. His cupped hands suggested breasts of air just inches from her own.

"I tell you, it's not," he said with quiet hydrochloric scorn. "I ought to know the song of the red-eyed vireo. Heard it a thousand times. And that's him."

"That's he," she wanted to say but didn't. Instead she raised her glasses in order to put an end to what might become a silly argument. All at once she saw it, red all over and with black wings, even saw it raise its head, open its beak and sing, like a robin with a sore throat. Now she watched it flitting as though a ruby were being tossed branch to branch.

"That's him," she said to herself, and pointed her glasses in another direction entirely to suggest a sighting, praying that he wouldn't see the scarlet tanager, which was now directly overhead in one of the lower branches. Just sitting there spitefully, right out in the open. She held her breath, then saw the telltale pursing of his lips, the clenching of his perfect jaw that told her he had, and knew.

"Different bird," he said. "The vireo took off."

"Yes," she said with all the regret she could muster, "I saw something fly out of the oak. Must have been the vireo." The end.

A Tale of Two Cities Revisited

As a doctor, I have witnessed my share of sad endings. Having spent the greater part of my life trying to prolong the lives of my patients, I am now temperamentally unable to kill off the characters in my stories. It is why so few of them get finished. In a review of one of my books, I read that, among my other sins, I am "terminally sentimental." That's me, all right. I come from a family of weepers in whom lachrymation can be brought on merely by saying "Once upon a time . . ." in a lugubrious tone of voice. We know what's coming.

I have even rewritten the endings of other people's stories to give a doomed character another chance. Take *A Tale of Two Cities* by Charles Dickens. As you may remember, Charles Darnay is the handsome young husband of Lucie, the lovely daughter of Doctor Manette. He is also an aristocrat and therefore an enemy of the Revolution. Having been seized and thrown into the Bastille, he is awaiting the guillotine. On the eve of the execution, in an act of excruciating gallantry, Sydney Carton, an English look-alike of Charles, worms his way into the Bastille, and exchanges places with him. For the reason that he does this, I refer you to the original text. Oh well, I'll tell you. For some years, Sydney Carton has been in love with Lucie. Upon being rejected by her, he embarked upon a life of drunkenness, dissipation, and wanton pursuit. Now it is his only wish to secure Lucie's happiness, even at the cost of his own life.

It is the morning of the execution. An axe-colored dawn has broken over Paris. Sydney Carton, posing as Charles Darnay, stands at the foot of the guillotine. He has just delivered his immortal last speech: "It is a far, far better thing that I do than I have ever done. It is a far, far better rest that I go to than I have ever known." Now he kneels to place his neck in the path of the dreadful blade. A hush falls over the crowd. . . . All at once there is a commotion on the scaffold. Shouts and curses are heard.

"*Zut, alors!*"

"*Fout le camp!*"

"*Merde!*"

"*Sale cochons!*" and many other disagreeable accusations are exchanged by the executioners and the revolutionary guards. It seems that the guillotine has broken down. The blade is stuck and cannot be released to fall. It is as though the instrument could not bring itself to kill so heroic a man. Now blows are being exchanged, muskets fired. Sydney Carton, lost in a vision of his own glory, is unaware of the *mêlée.* The crowd, being French, is overcome with emotion at this apparent sympathy of the guillotine for its intended victim. Singing *La Marseillaise,* they swarm over the barricades and onto the scaffold. Sydney Carton feels himself being lifted and carried into the throng. A cloth soaked in chloroform is placed over his face. He inhales deeply—once, twice, three times—and loses consciousness.

When he awakens, he is on board a ship. A beautiful young woman kneels beside him, cradling him in her arms.

"How long have I been here?" he asks.

"Two days," she replies.

"Who are you?"

"Ma foi! You do not know me? I am Lucie, the daughter of Doctor Manette and the wife of Charles Darnay, the man whose life you saved." Recognition slowly dawns upon the face of Sydney Carton.

"Lucie! It is you!" he whispers. "But where are you taking me?"

"To England. You will come to live *avec Charles et moi.* We shall have a ménage à trois."

"*Vive la France!*" cries Sydney Carton as his head falls back upon the soft, soft bosom of Madame Darnay.

And that is how *A Tale of Two Cities* ought to have ended.

I learned later that chloroform hadn't been discovered until 1834, some decades after the French Revolution. Oh well. . . .

From an Italian Diary

PIEMONTE

OCTOBER 1, 1985

In Piemonte, where the foothills of the Italian Alps begin their ascent, there is a village called Vaglio. I have come here to decide whether or not to retire from surgery. But after thirty years of rummaging in the "rag and bone shop," it is no easy thing to lay down the tools of the trade. Surgery, I tell myself, is a young man's game. Stamina, daring, the thrill of playing the star role in a heroic drama—have they begun to wane? I have no wish to be an old lion whose claws have long since gone blunt, but not the desire to use them. And where is it graven in stone that, once having been ordained a surgeon, you must stand at the operating table until the scalpel slips from your lifeless fingers? All this I tell myself. But you do not walk away from the beloved workbench of your life with a cheery wave of the hand. So it is that after two years of backing and filling, I have sent myself off to Italy, determined not to return until the decision will have been made. Then, too, there is my smoking, which no amount of self-loathing or guilt has induced me to give up for more than a few months at a time. And I a surgeon! A friend in New Haven had offered me the use of his ancestral house in which to mope and palely loiter. For weeks I have been studying spoken Italian, which, at age fifty-six, is no cinch; I haven't suffered so much since I teethed. Trailing my sorrows behind me, I have come to these mountains to divorce myself from my two passions—surgery and cigarettes.

OCTOBER 8, 1985

Here one week, and already I am feeling the symptoms of withdrawal
from each. I miss the patients, who have never ceased to inspire, entertain, and instruct me. I miss the murmuring tactile pedagogy of the operating room, where the secrets of the craft are passed from one generation
to the next. Teaching surgery is like teaching nothing else, for *there,* just
beneath the surgeon's hands, "lurks the culprit—life." To say nothing of
the *handsomeness* of this work, the collegiality of the men and women who
labor herein. As for smoking, I have always had the same lack of abstinence as Eve for apples. But unlike Eve, who was expelled for indulging,
I smoke and am imparadised. All in all, the week has been an endless
dark night of the soul.

Vaglio is an L-shaped village of twenty houses, each with its balcony
dressed with potted geraniums and a caged canary. No window but is
festooned with polychromatic laundry. The nearest city is Biella, a
provincial town some twenty kilometers away. I had no sooner stepped
off the bus than Guglielmina appeared. She is my friend's cousin, who
had been alerted to my coming. At eighty-five, Guglielmina is a tiny neat
parcel of hospitality. Four and a half feet tall, with white hair and a lyri-
cal smile, she is one of those women whose soul is visible. Her voice is a
thin piping that comes from a piccolo inside her chest. She is dressed
entirely in black. Minutes later, I am in her kitchen eating a bowl of lentil
soup. Her body, she informs me, is untarnished, and of her virginity
Guglielmina is fiercely proud. The black she wears is in mourning for
her brother, whom she nursed for the last eight years of his life. Although
I beg her to call me Riccardo, it is *professore* this and *professore* that. For
the duration of my stay, Guglielmina will dote on me. Each morning my
shirt, socks, underwear, and handkerchief are spirited away, only to be
returned that evening, hand-laundered. Each day a free-range egg is
brought in a basket along with fresh bread, a few mushrooms, or a jar of
her prune jam.

OCTOBER 14, 1985

I may as well admit it: Guglielmina and I have taken quite a tumble for
each other. We go mushrooming together; we pick apples and pears; we
smile and wave to each other from our balconies on opposite sides of the

street. This morning she dropped off yet another jar of prune jam, which I must spoon down, no matter the intestinal consequences. (The term *disembowelment* has taken on meaning altogether different from that denoting a surgical procedure or *hara-kiri*.) I am not permitted to make my bed, wash my dishes, or attend to any of the domesticities. At the least sign that I may have rinsed a saucer, her eyes go from blue to black.

OCTOBER 17, 1985

It is a fine thing to live among beasts. I am thinking here not of dogs (certainly not dogs!) or cats or canaries, but of animals used for sustenance— cows, goats, donkeys, chickens, geese. I love to see chickens let to walk wherever they will, so that an egg is a pleasant surprise. In the evening, the cattle are herded down the street by Giorgio, another cousin, and his self-important little dog. Now and then Giorgio gives forth a sudden throaty yell directed at the cows. I have translated it as "Sweep on, you fat and greasy citizens!" This does not appear to affect the speed of migration at all, but I don't doubt that his shrieks and bellows serve some useful purpose other than to make me jump in my chair. Giorgio is a scowly, heavy-set bale of rags with a straw hat and a droopy moustache, the kind of burly man who rarely laughs and even then does not take the pipe out of his mouth to do so. Once, having lost my way in the upper pasture, I followed the sound of cowbells until I came upon Giorgio and his small herd.

"*Son io perduto,*" I told him. "I am lost." Immediately his fierce scowl vanished and, leaving his beasts in the capable paws of his dog, he led me to the path that descends to the village. The next time I met him, we greeted each other as best friends.

OCTOBER 22, 1985

Vaglio! I thought happily, and settled in for what was to be the remaking of me. And so it would have been, had it not been for the dogs. If there are twenty houses in Vaglio, there are forty dogs, each carrying a peck of teeth in its mouth. It is the literal truth that, in the three weeks I have been here, I have not listened and failed to hear the barking of a dog. Barking by day, barking by night. A visit to the market begets a sound howling, as I am passed on from house to house by the testy creatures.

First one dog will bark, then another, until all the dogs of Vaglio are in full cry. Turn over in bed, and I invite an hour of yippery. Are the Vaglioli deaf? Or has the noise become as inaudible to them as the clatter of a freight train to one who lives beside the tracks? Not for me the sweetness of Sir Walter Scott, who, writing under tremendous pressure and desperate for sleep, was kept awake all one night by a howling dog. In the morning he wrote in his journal, "Poor cur! I daresay he has his distresses, as I have mine." No! About these dogs I have become as neurasthenic as Kafka, for whom the chirping of a cricket on the hearth would bring on a crisis of nerves. This is hardly the best sanatorium for the curing of a tobacco addict.

OCTOBER 25, 1985

Over the passionate protestations of Guglielmina, I have decided to leave Vaglio. O! but she was dashed at the news and, truth to tell, I have never been sorrier to part with anyone of so brief an acquaintance. But go I must, for I have turned murderous, would surely run amok with the kitchen knife and spill all the canine guts of this village. The farewell to Guglielmina lasted as long as the Tomb scene from *Aida*. It was only terminated by my promise to go no farther than the Sanctuary of Oropo, a day's journey up the mountain. From there I am to return to Vaglio. Would I deny her the joy of another visit? Could I be so cruel? I keep mum. With all the ferocity of the about-to-be-abandoned woman, Guglielmina washed, ironed, and mended every raglet in my repertoire. How she clung to each piece I tried to put in the dufflebag! Defeated at last, she placed two jars of prune jam in amongst my shirts. From the bus, at the sight of her standing alone on the edge of Vaglio wiping her eyes with a handkerchief, I all but relented. But just then all forty of the dogs of Vaglio opened their throats. And that was that.

OCTOBER 26, 1985

A superannuated bus climbs a narrow mountain road that has no outer railing. Each new curve presents a dizzy vista, with here and there a village glinting like a speck of mica. Sitting on the abyss side of the bus, with an arm resting on the ledge of the open window, there is nothing between elbow and earth but a few thousand feet of space. At every stop there is a roadside shrine composed of a statue of the Virgin and a spray of artificial flowers, before which the newly alit might kneel and give thanks. Half of these Virgins are black, so as to coordinate color with the Black Madonna to whom the shrine of Oropo is dedicated. Beneath one of them there is printed the inscription *nigra sum sed sum formosa,* "black I am, but I am beautiful," as it is written in that verse of the Canticles.

Several hours on the bus and you arrive at the Santuario, a complex of gray stone buildings set within a shell of mountains called the Conch of Oropo. The Black Madonna resides in a chapel inside a glass case with a backdrop of dark blue starry sky. Said to have been carved by St. Luke himself and brought here from "the East," she nevertheless has the features of ten thousand other Madonnas carved and painted during and since the Renaissance. Only that her face and hands are black—as black as can be. The Infant, too, as one might expect. Countless are the miracles attributed to *la Madonna Nera,* most having to do with runaway horses, house fires, and last-minute rescues from the butchery of Italian surgeons. The walls of the guest-house corridors are covered with primitive murals depicting such divine intercessions. The premises are teeming with nuns, priests, and pilgrims, the latter put up in a vast *foresteria* or pilgrim hostel, whose appointments are, to say the least, primitive. The nuns in charge are a race of plump elderly women, no one of whom, like Guglielmina, is over four and a half feet tall. They wear shoe-length dark habits cinched at the waist, from which hangs a clackety wooden rosary. The wimple is a pleated bonnet of the American pioneer woman style, white and starched, whose sides extend some inches in front of the face like the blinders of a milk horse. The wearer can look neither to right nor left, only dead ahead, and so must rotate the entire body in order to bring something into the field of vision. This, I suppose, is meant to lessen the chance for idle distraction, but it also transforms these tiny nuns into rabbits with their ears folded forward.

The room to which I am led holds two beds, a writing table, a chair, and an armoire. Just below the window a wild stream races down a gorge of tumultuous boulders, all bleached white. The roar of the water is unceasing, but, unlike the dogs of Vaglio, it is oddly soothing. Within hours I am not aware of it, save as a reassuring *cordon sanitaire* between the outside world and me. For another ten thousand lire (five dollars) I have a private bathroom with a toilet of the civilized sit-down genre, as opposed to the democratic-socialist *gabinetto.* If there be any flaw in the

Italian national character, it is a sheeplike acceptance of the *gabinetto*—a floor-level hole above which one is expected to hunker, and which is death on every joint of the body except the temporo-mandibular. Only the native American bedpan is more to be feared. Within hours I am as settled in as bricks and mortar. The Yale School of Medicine—does it still stand? Does surgery continue to be practiced in our land? Or has the millennium come and gone behind my back? Seen from the height of Oropo, surgery seems rather a barbaric act, the superimposition of an artificial illness—the operation—upon a previously existing one, in the hope that the combination will redound to the patient's benefit. How often I have presided at the operating table when it has not. Well! I *am* making progress. No cigarettes for three weeks and a healthy scorn for my profession. I am right where I belong. World, I am no more of ye!

NOVEMBER 2, 1985

It is the seventh day of my pilgrimage. This morning I made a long climb to an Alpine lake. Far below, the sanctuary looked less Christian than pagan. From the lake a vivid stream collapsed, thrashing its tail all the way down. On the way up I was surprised by a small herd of cows and goats. That close to me and I had not heard their bells! Just so loud is *il canto di torrento*. I stepped aside to let the animals move in single file across a wooden footbridge. Animals have the right of way here. As they passed, there was that blend of cud, manure, and milk that is the fragrance of cow. The cowherd was about my age, his jacket worn jauntily over one shoulder, the sleeves swinging free, and with a blue and white knitted cap above a deeply tanned face. By far the most graceful cowherd of my life. All at once he reached for a pouch, rolled a cigarette, fished for a match, struck it, and lit up. Looking up, he saw my eyes in ransom to his tobacco pouch, tossed it to me with a gesture of invitation, and I was undone. Among his herd were four black and white calves, each with the map of Europe stamped on its hide, and the usual pipsqueak dog. The goats, especially the nanny-goats, stepped in and out of the woods like nymphs. One daredevil leaned over the edge of a precipice, then made a little hop into *nothing* to tear a last mouthful of leaves. One male, twisted and off-balance, looked for all the world like the ram in the thicket. Farther on I met an old woman beating at the underbrush with a stick and shaking her head. Now and then she gave a sharp-eyed, foraging look, squatted to peer, then muttered under her breath.

"What do you see?" I asked.

"*Niente,*" she said. "*Niente di funghi, niente dis castagna.*" No mushrooms, no chestnuts.

"*Che peccata,*" I sympathized. Too bad. My reward was a smile I shall put in the safety deposit box at the bank as soon as I get back to New Haven.

NOVEMBER 5, 1985

There is something altogether too precise about the church bells of Oropo, each peal in perfect harmony with every other. I am always aware of the sullenness of metal. How very far from the little cowbells, whose soft disorderly noise floods the slopes with warmth and light. Rung by the random movements of the animals, these cowbells are altogether unselfconscious. For cattle there are no holy offices, no schedule of hours, only the giving and taking of nourishment. I should far rather be a cowherd than a priest. It is the cowherd who walks the holy and maternal earth.

NOVEMBER 7, 1985

What a revival these Alps have wrought! I am three inches taller and up to the edge of corpulence. A little paunch has come to sit on my lap and loves me to rest my hand on him. Just so long as he don't go and get important—ask for a gold watch and a fob. No cigarettes for four days A.C. (After Cowherd).

But now it is the next day and the craving has returned, aggravated by the delicious smell of woodsmoke. Why should a chimney, a dragon, a cannon, have smoke and I no puff at all? A long walk will help, I decide. In the company of Fulvio, a young pilgrim with whom I have struck up, I climbed a steep path called the Via Crucis, as it is lined with the Stations of the Cross. Halfway up, just beyond Jesus Comforts the Women of Jerusalem, we found Achille, who was looking without success for the Marriage at Cana. The three of us agreed to suspend our pilgrimage and go to a wayside trattoria instead. Achille is in his late seventies, a tiny man with wisps of white hair, blue eyes, and four teeth, two upper and two lower. He is far more spirited than spiritual.

"I no longer have the lovely innocence to believe in angels," he announced. He had come to Oropo to deal with his doubts about the existence of God Himself. Once we were seated around a bottle of grappa, Achille put forth the news that he is a virgin and proud of it. Shades of Guglielmina!

"But why?" Fulvio wanted to know.

"It is my condition," the old man explained.

"Have you never wished to marry?" I asked him.

"I should never wish to behave like such an ass." With that, he turned to the young man and raised his glass.

"Ah, Fulvio," he toasted, "a beautiful name of ancient Rome." There followed several hours of wine, song, jokes, and theology. Thanks, doubtless, to the Black Madonna, my Italian, though hectic and brawling, enabled me to take part. Achille said it sounded as though a herd of sheep were inside my mouth, crowding to get through a narrow gate. The restaurateur brought out a platter of sliced wild boar, pasta, more wine. It is no wonder that all the other gods loved Bacchus.

A crisis. I returned from breakfast to find my duffelbag, briefcase, and typewriter neatly stacked in the corridor outside my room, and the door padlocked. What could this mean? Had my imposturage been discovered? Was I to be expelled? Out of a fusillade of Italian from a passing priest, I extracted the word *madre* and, pocket dictionary in hand, rushed off to find the Mother Superior. With a patience that is not of this world, the tiny nun explained that I could not stay in that room any longer. It had been promised to five women pilgrims from Yugoslavia. They were to arrive, she told me sweetly, in one hour.

"*Una hora!*" I cried. "*Ma impossibile! Aspett' un momento, io t'imploro!*" (the cry of the stuck pig). She went on: I would have to move to the great dormitory with the other *pellegrini*. The other pilgrims? Every artery ran cold at the thought.

"*Santissima,*" I began quietly, but she had already turned ten degrees to the left, so that I was hidden from view by the blinders of her bonnet. Perhaps she had not understood? Madly I riffled the pages of the dictionary.

"*Cara sorella,*" I began again. "I need privacy; I need my writing table. Most of all, I need my toiletto. In the great dormitory there is only the *gabinetto diabolico.*" All this I said. She turned another ten degrees to the left.

"*Son io Americano,*" I shouted. And explained that Americans are unable to... Riffle... Riffle... what is the word for squat?... *accoccolarsi.*

"Non posse accoccolars'," I yelled around her blinders. Silence. What was the matter with that nun? Didn't she understand Italian? I ran around to face her directly, whereupon, with a serenity that passeth all human nature, she blinked. It was the blink of doom. I had all I could do to keep from picking the rabbit up by its ears.

I went to remove my belongings from the corridor of the guest-house. From behind the door to my erstwhile room came the lovely song of the torrent. I made my way to the cavernous dormitory where hundreds of Italians, mostly Sicilians and Neapolitans, milled about or stood in line at one of the *gabinetti*. The cell that I must share with two other pilgrims was marked by the absence of hot water and the presence of a single bare lightbulb hung from the ceiling. For the three of us, there was one large bed! All of which, I swear it, I could have borne with resignation. But the *gabinetto*? Never! Once again I was a goy among the Jews.

Of my martyrdom I shrink to speak. Only to say that no amount of calling upon the Black Madonna induced her to intercede in my behalf. In despair I turned to the prophet Isaiah, who complained to God about his bowels—that they vibrated like a harp. His belly cramps, he lamented, were like those of a woman in the throes of childbirth. Yes, I thought, Isaiah is my man. Who couldn't feel warmly toward a prophet with spastic colitis? But prophets just hand out bad news, dire warnings. By the waters of Oropo I sat and wept over the passing of a better day.

TUSCANY

JUNE 30, 1997

It is a false premise that writing can be taught. The secrets of art are best learned in secret. That having been said, I am in Tuscany, where for three weeks I have led a workshop in Creative Writing. For the past week, I've had a backache. Here's what happened: From the window of my room on the second-floor room of the farmhouse where we are installed, I looked down upon a huge bale of hay rolled up into a kind of mat, and tied. Sitting cross-legged on this bale was Isabel, one of the students. Below, making run after run at the hay mound in an effort to join her, the beauteous Jessica. Seven, eight, nine times she threw herself at the bale only to fall back in ignominy. From on high came the cruel laughter of Isabel. All at once I saw my destiny. Down the stairs I raced, out of the house, and crouched on all fours at the base of that bale of hay.

"Use me as a step," I said. When Jessica hesitated, I cried out again like a man in the studio of his dominatrix. "Use me!" And Botticelli's Venus heard my note of urgency. Next moment, I felt the momentary pressure of her bare foot in the middle of my back and looked up to behold Venus Aloft! And smiling down at me from that glory of hay. That was a week ago, and I still hold myself bent and rigid so as not to provoke my vertebrae. Was it worth it? Can you ask?

JULY 1997

I have taken to visiting the nearby village of Montalcino in the afternoon for a glass of grappa at the tavern in the piazza. There is always the same cast of characters. This man is Luigi. He is seventy-nine years old. For seventy of those years he had smoked cigarettes with the greatest satisfaction. I can relate to that. Three years before, he had been given the choice: death or abstinence. He had chosen to quit. Each day at precisely five o'clock he appears on the piazza. It is a moment the rest of us have been waiting for. Ah, there he is now:

The rest of his body has adjusted to the wreckage of his lungs. It has accepted every wheeze and whistle, the dry sticks rubbing together in his chest. The intake of his breath is the tearing of cloth. His clothing conspires to hide the evidence. Hidden beneath the loose cotton, long-sleeved shirt is the stiffness of his rib cage that is fixed at greatest expansion from the air it cannot exhale, and the belly that billows in and out in the effort to raise his diaphragm. What it cannot hide is the flaring of his nostrils to take in the last bit of air, the veins at his temples, engorged to bursting, the working in and out of his neck.

Still, he sleeps, bathes, dresses himself with infinite care each day, combs his aluminum-colored hair just so. (He has placed all his faith in a haircut.) And every afternoon he walks down the streets of the village of Montalcino toward the central piazza. The only evidence of accommodation to his condition is the cane he flicks rather jauntily every third or fourth step to show he doesn't really need it. At seventy-nine he is a man for whom appearances have always counted. On the streets of Montalcino, he calls out *"Giorno!"* or *"'Sera!"* as if announcing the time of day rather than making a greeting. Among his more sluggish, heavy-footed cronies outside the coffeehouse, he alone is spruce. A slender man, tiny, although made larger by his stride, with sapphiric eyes embedded in a deeply tanned face. He is clearly the favorite.

"Simpatico," says a woman, and points with her head. Laughter bubbles in his wake. In addition to the cane, he wears a white straw hat with a wide brim that undulates about his head. His shoes, hardly more than slippers of light brown leather, are scrupulously polished. His trousers too are white, of patterned silk. The shirt is worn open at the neck and loose over a belt. A single gold chain winks at his neck.

"You want to take my picture? *Prego!* What are you waiting for?" And opens his arms wide in invitation. The audacity! It makes everyone laugh. On down the street he ambles, flourishing the cane, his struggle less apparent. I send my mind to follow him to the doorway to his house, then up three penitent flights of stairs to the landing. Only when he has closed the door behind him does he permit himself the gasps, the panting, the wild stare of air hunger. But it is his face that is exhausted. From smiling.

Lectures on Art: Painting

THE PICTURE FRAME

First, the Picture Frame, that enclosure that holds the painting in, lest it expand and occupy the whole world. For it is the frame that is sane while its contents are mad, lawless, irrepressible, without restraint. And it is the existence of the frame that protects us from assault by the painting, the way a cage protects the visitors to a zoo from being mauled by wild beasts. The frame is protector of the artist as well, who would be obliged or hounded by his vision to cover more and more canvas. It is the frame that establishes safe and sound limits for the artist within which he can roam free. Imagine the Sistine ceiling a thousand times larger than it is: to

Portrait of an Ecclesiastic, by Juan de Valdés Leal

stand beneath such a painting would surely prove fatal. The frame is the work of carpenter or craftsman, the disciplinarian who sets limits upon the behavior of the naughty artist. And the frame is both beginning and ending. You look at a painting, and it is the frame that says "Once upon a time. . . ." As you turn to leave, it is the frame that gives you permission to do so, which, in a sense, passes you on to the next picture.

"How do you know when a painting is done?" a child asks.

"When there is no more room," says the painter.

ON SEEING FRAY JUAN

For some months, every day, I have been going to the Yale Art Gallery to see just one painting. It is entitled *Portrait of an Ecclesiastic* and is by Juan de Valdés Leal, a Spanish painter of the seventeenth century. The corpse-like figure in the portrait, seated at his writing table with pen poised in air, was for a long time believed to represent the dead St. Bonaventura, who, according to legend, was supernaturally granted three days between his death and his burial in which to finish writing the life of St. Francis of Assisi. Fascinating as this identification may be, there is good evidence against it. This priest is wearing the black habit of a Franciscan; he also wears the biretta of a Doctor of Laws and the shoulder cape worn by canons, bishops, and cardinals, manifestly inappropriate for St. Bonaventura. He also wears the Cross of La Orden de los Dominicos, the mark of an official of the Inquisition at the time of Charles II. Moreover, evidence of the sitter's identity is provided by the partly damaged inscription on the long scroll at the left, which states that the portrait represents Fray Juan de San Bernardo, an ecclesiastic of high rank, who held office in the Inquisition and whose books and sermons still exist. Fray is the title of respect given to certain Spanish priests.

The painting is dated at 1680.

The medium is oil on canvas.

The dimensions are: 185.1 x 112.4 cm (72 7/8 x 44 in).

I am a surgeon or, rather, was a surgeon in the city of New Haven for thirty-three years until my retirement sixteen years ago at the age of fifty-

eight. Wisely or not, I elected to continue living in the city where I had
laid open the bodies of half the population. Almost every week I am
accosted on the street by someone who announces: "You took out my gall-
bladder," or something of the sort. Now it is a fact that, once having left
the operating theatre for good, I deliberately repressed all that went on
in that place, purged my consciousness of it until it seemed that I had died
and been reborn into another incarnation, only with the singular knowledge of what I had been in that previous life—a surgeon. Each time I am
reminded of my doctoring, either by a former patient or colleague, it is as
though a prehistoric animal, long since thought extinct, has appeared
again upon the earth. Ever since my retirement from medicine, I have
engaged in the act of writing, to what avail I know not. For some months
now, I have been afflicted with writer's block and have been unable to
write at all. Often, in my enforced idleness, I go to the various museums
and art galleries in the city to pass the time of day. I am not at all a con-
noisseur of art, nor a student of art history. It is for me just a destination.
The Yale Art Gallery is a mere three blocks south of the Yale Library,
where I do my reading and writing. A brisk five-minute walk brings me
from my carrel in the library to the cubicle where *Portrait of an Ecclesiastic*
is hung. It is hardly an arduous pilgrimage.

I do not know why this particular painting, out of so many that I have
seen, has captured my imagination to the extent of becoming (I may as
well say it) an obsession. What struck me at first was the languid elegance
of this priest, his time-worn melancholy that seemed quintessentially
Spanish. But as one visit followed another, the feeling of cohesion
between the priest on the canvas and myself has grown stronger. It is as
if there were a magnetic attraction between us, a force that I cannot resist.
I suppose I have always been drawn to the priestly esthetic. It comes from
having been born and raised in an Irish Catholic town where any number of my childhood friends at one time or another entertained the possibility of the priesthood. What I should like to achieve in setting down
this encounter is a measure of cool and objective clarity, what the Italians call *limpidezza*. It is what I would expect of him, if our roles were
reversed. But I know full well that mine is not an intellectual frame of
reference, but a product of the emotions and the glands.

In my more rational moments, I remind myself of the differences
between us. He is a priest; I, a surgeon, or what is left of one. He is a painting; I still have some small claim to a real existence. He has great beauty;

I have none. He has sworn to repress his darker urges; I have been more than willing to give in to mine. He has a legalistic mind and a religious habit that give him a certainty of what is right and wrong and the appearance of authority; I have no religious beliefs, and mine is the wrong-shaped head for law. What we do have in common is this baleful incommodious alcove at the Yale Art Gallery, with its family of martyrs. Just to the left of my priest is St. Bartholomew in the process of being flayed alive. Strips of skin, any one of which would be suitable for use in skin-grafting, hang from his body. Standing free in the middle of the alcove is an anonymous *Christ, Man of Sorrows.* It is of polychromed wood and dated in the twelfth century. Blood pours from the Savior's brow to cover his shoulders and neck. Somewhat out of keeping is an allegorical painting called *Love of Virtue.* It consists of a winged youth, clothed in drapery and crowned with leaves. What is he doing here? Ah yes, he is the guardian angel of the place, its *genius loci.* This alcove is more like the apse of a cathedral than a museum space. The air in it is different from that in the rest of the gallery. Is it really air? I have but to walk past the partition, then turn left in order to feel the difference. It is at least ten degrees cooler, and thinner, purer, harder to breathe, as though the alcove itself were at an elevation of ten thousand feet above sea level. Each time, upon entering, I give an involuntary shudder and feel my nostrils dilate, the better to breathe. On such an Alp even a chamois would lose the path. Still, in the heady coolness and the silence of the alcove, I am more alive than anywhere else.

Fray Juan sits at a writing table in a room that is not dark so much as under the influence of darkness. Fully half the painting is black. He is dressed in a full-length black cassock, from beneath which emerges the tip of one cloth shod foot. He wears a black biretta trimmed with silver plumes, and a short black and silver satin cloak trimmed with gold braid. On his breast he wears a Dominican cross. A knotted silken rope tumbles from his waist to the floor. It is a kind of rosary, I suppose. I want to ask him about it, say "What about that cord? What's it for?" There is an unearthly neatness about him; nothing out of place. Would a speck of red be sacrilege? On the table, there stands a small statue of Christ on the Cross, and several books one atop the other. There is also an inkpot holding two feathered pens. All the light in the painting is concentrated on the face and hands of the priest and on the notebook or tablet in which he is writing. He is clean-shaven and thin to the point of emaciation. The facial bones are visible beneath his skin. Only the mouth is full and sensual. He is captured in a moment of reverie in which he has ceased writing. He has the appearance of one who is conscious, in contact with reality, but also apart and solitary. Just so have I, too, time and again lost myself in the infinity of reverie. Just so have I retired to that tiny hidden place in my mind in search of the immensity of, say, Brazil. Or is he listening to the ocean of his childhood? The pen he holds in his right hand is aloft in the air, his wrist hyperextended as if to restrain the pen from the page. His gaze is to the right and downward, or rather off into the distance, as is customary with a writer in the throes of composition.

Day after day, week after week, I have come to the second floor of the gallery. Each time I step off the elevator, the uniformed guard greets me like an old friend. Why not? I am a pebble dropped into the glassy pool of his tedium. Mostly, I am alone in my contemplation of the priest. It is not a painting that draws crowds. Once a young couple walked by hand in hand, looking more at each other than at the paintings. On another occasion, a middle-aged woman with blond curls like wood shavings peered from around the partition that separates the alcove from the main exhibition space. She looked us both up and down, turning her gaze from him to me, then back again in shameless curiosity, before moving on. When she had left, I could detect a hint of disdain on his face. Through the window came the mournful cooing of the pigeons on the ledge.

It is true that in the early weeks I saw only a sterile priest, remote from dirt and blood, one given to philosophy and legal argument, one who had renounced all sensual pleasures and devoted himself to enlarging and purifying the power of the Church even at the cost of the lives of thousands of Jews and Muslims, one whose devotion to his cause has blinded him to the cruelty of his actions. There was nothing exalted about him. More humbug than holiness, if you asked me, back then. And with fanaticism visible in the pinched nostrils and the cartilage in the pinna of his ear.

I imagine the room in which he sits—the white tiled stone floor, the recessed window of leaded glass, and the huge beams of the high convent ceiling, made of dark and gleaming wood, fitted precisely by master builders and made to last until the Resurrection. I cast about in my mind for something that would touch his cold barren convent cell to life, perhaps the light wise hand of a woman arranging peonies in a vase. Oh, take away that Crucifixion on the table and those volumes. In their place, let there be a lamp to give a brave glow. Let there be a moth fluttering in it. Yes, a single moth, a life-desiring creature, would do to animate that cell. Give me a garden over a convent any day, a garden with butterflies by day and fireflies by night, a garden that is both womb and sanctuary. What better place to frisk and fructify—but that is just what this priest has no interest in doing.

About that slender right hand, the one held suspended in midair, I would like to dissect it down to the smallest muscles, the lumbricals and the interossei, then expose the tendons of flexion and extension that pass through the carpal tunnel of the wrist on their way to the fingers and to the words on the page. Only then would I be able to decipher what he is writing. Last night I had a dream that I was the one holding the writing tablet, not he. And that I could read with ease every word written in it. The handwriting was oddly familiar. But, as it is with dreams, the text did not make it over the boundary into waking life. Perhaps, as I have dreams, he has visions. They're made of the same spun glass, aren't they? One mustn't take his visions too seriously; they may be due entirely to excessive fasting. Hypoglycemia. As for my dreams, well . . .

Since I am giving a picture in words of the painted man, it is only fair that I give an equally graphic portrait of myself in the same medium. I too am slight and give the initial impression of fleshlessness. There are those who have termed me hardly more than skin and bones. This is not something achieved by abstinence from food, but is a result of genetic influence and a high rate of metabolism. I suspect that we are about the same height—five feet and eight inches. Standing erect, he would doubt-less give the appearance of being the taller, as I have slowly shrunk in height with the years, what with one vertebra collapsing into another. It would appear that we are within a few years of each other, although he has worn himself out with his dreadful privations, flagellations, what-ever, and so looks somewhat older. As for the color of our eyes, it is the same ambiguous gray. Our hair is pewter color, although his is neatly trimmed, and mine is invariably a wild tangle. I am disheveled and shabby in my dress, an old man tossed up and left. There is no congenial-ity among the articles of my apparel; they are at war with one another, while he is all of a perfect piece. In each of us there is the suggestion of androgyny. It is something about the hands, the tilt of the head—a flair, though inexact. Speaking of hands, there is in each of my palms a hard nubbin of scar tissue just proximal to the metacarpophalangeal joint of the fourth finger. That finger is drawn down into partial flexion and cannot be fully extended. No matter, the fourth is the weakest, a mere Siamese twin of the middle finger. This is called Dupuytren's Contracture, after the French surgeon who first described it. Nothing mysterious about it—doubtless a congenital aberration. There is no precipitating event. The scars resemble nothing so much as the stigmata of the Crucifixion. And this: At the midpoint of my forehead, extending from the bridge of the nose up for an inch, there is a deep groove that I call my Line of Pain. In early times it would appear and disappear in accordance with my state of mind, but now it is always there.

If I have not written about the painter Juan de Valdés Leal, it is because he is a barrier between the priest and myself, a reminder that the object of my attention is a thing fabricated by man, rather than a sentient creature such as I. It is precisely that notion of him as a work of art that I hope to overcome. The painter is also my rival; he too had once delivered his obsessive gaze at the priest in search of transcendence. It maddens me to think of that. It isn't that I hate Valdés Leal, not at all. He was a painter, doing his work, I tell myself. But such jealousy is impervious to reason. Still, now and then, I cannot deny it, I see the artist's devoted hand, outstretched and trembling under the force of creativity, as he splashes black over the canvas that eagerly receives it, then bends closer to paint the folds of the cassock, or capture that look of absence, of vagrancy, upon the countenance of the priest. I am of the opinion that this portrait was among the last pictures painted by Valdés Leal. Why do I think so? Because, after painting this priest, why would an artist paint anything else? Valdés Leal had painted a living man who went on living for a while thereafter, then ended by dying. Who, looking at this painting, could fail to think of the real man who was the model? Infidel that I am, I know that it was the painter who gave him immortality, who rescued him from the anonymity of death. It was the artist who consecrated him, not God. But for the distance of the centuries, my name would surely have been on his list of heretics and destined for auto-da-fé. It has always struck me that this "act of faith" better described the victim of conflagration than the superstitious bumbling of the Church, so sure in its barbaric pruning of Medieval thought.

Today is the eighteenth time I have come here. The Security Guard—his name is Moises—has lately been eyeing me with something more than curiosity. At my appearance his face takes on a "What! You here again?" expression. But then, his smile is open and friendly. More and more I am given to conjecture upon the secret life of this Juan de San Bernardo who has become my alter ego. Has he never, I wonder, felt the passionate desire to break out of the prison of himself? Even a saint must now and then cast aside the relentless conviction that he has been called. Under my breath I speak to him in the words of his namesake and countryman, Juan de la Cruz, who "one dark night / Fired with love's urgent longings / . . . felt . . . flowing in his breast" the desire for another, who would "wound his neck with a gentle hand."

It is my twenty-fourth visit. Each time I come, I see something that I had not seen before, the exact angle of his body to the table—it is a position unsuitable for writing, as the tablet is supported only by his left hand. And just today, I saw the exuberant Baroque sleeve that speaks volumes about the man who wears it. His is such an emphatic pose, perhaps not unselfconscious, as though he is aware of the stir he creates with his flair. In the early days, it seemed to me that he desired to express his emotions to the onlooker, but now the pose is clearly the result of his emotions.

This diabolical alcove—it is a space like no other in the world. I imagine an ancient grotto with its resident spirit, or a sunken vault. It is both here and nowhere. The only window in the cubicle is opposite the portrait. It faces west. I have discovered that, at noon, if I stand in front of the window and three paces to the left, my shadow falls upon him. Each time it seems to me that he gives a tiny involuntary start, as though a shadow has weight in his medium.

"Look, Juan!" Today I have brought a music box, although I understand that it is strictly against the rules of the Yale Art Gallery to play music here. "Listen! It is the 'Miserere' from Il Trovatore. I can see by the way you have ceased your writing and gaze off into the distance that you like this music. I can almost see you swaying to the rhythm." Oh dear! Wouldn't you know? The guard, Moises, has overheard and has admonished me with a wagging finger and a look of reproach. But he has heard it, I know! It is a beginning.

What in the world is he writing? I die to know. Is it a list of those condemned by the Inquisition, the accusations against them, and the justification for their being burned at the stake? Or is it a confession of his own sins? Perhaps it is nothing of the sort, but the act of atonement of one in the grip of a satanic compulsion. I have seen the same expression of nameless dread on the face of a man for whom each day's existence was a minefield through which he must pick his way, desperate to avoid speaking or even hearing the word that will trigger a painful attack of panic. Should the trigger word be overheard, nothing for it but he must write over and over again the phrase that is the magical antidote. Only then would he feel relief from the acute anxiety that is unbearable. But only until the next time. Now suppose, for the priest, the offending word was something he might be apt to hear frequently—*rosary,* say, or *sacrament* —then indeed, his suffering would be such as to resemble the pain of being eaten from within. But of course, this is mere conjecture.

As the weeks, and now months, have gone by, he has become more and more real to me. We have dispensed with the need for words. We have found a language of the soul, as he might put it, in which there is perfect understanding. In this language, his feelings are transmuted into my thoughts and vice versa. I have become receptacular to his thoughts. Now and then I seem to hear two voices conversing, mine and another's, softly, a sibilance, almost a whisper as from a great distance, yet very near. Of course! It is my voice that he strains to hear. Lately I have taken to visiting at twilight, when the last rays of the setting sun set him throbbing. If I didn't know better, I'd say that his face is not quite so pallid, but bears a faint tinge of pink—a fugitive glow, but no less limpid than before. A tiny vein has appeared on his temple, a branch of the superficial temporal vein, a twig of bluish blood. It is beginning! I feel the intoxication of leaving myself and becoming the other.

Beginning one month ago, I began to hear noises in my head. Along with the noises came a dull headache. At first it was the sound of drops of water falling into a pail. As time went by, the noises grew louder and louder. There was the sizzling of a thousand crickets, then the croaking of many frogs, then the thunk-thunk of an axe biting into a tree trunk. And along with the intensity of the noise, so has the pain increased. It is with me all the time now. Yes, the rhythm of the axe in my head is precisely that of the pulse at my wrist!

It is Thursday, the day when the Art Gallery is kept open until ten o'clock at night. At that hour, night seems to have absorbed the white of the walls. A giant wave of black falls from the painting into the alcove, and in the indeterminate gray of his eyes there is a dark voyaging. Madness flaps its wings beneath that skull. It is said that the writings of Juan de San Bernardo still exist, doubtless in the scriptorium or library of some ancient Spanish monastery. I would not dare to read them, nor even journey to the stone beneath which he was laid with his yearnings. I know what I know, and have no wish to know more. Listen! Faintly through the window comes the tolling of the bell in Harkness Tower, announcing the hour. Strange, that he seems more remote and unearthly at night than during the day, not painted, so much, as an emanation from the canvas. Still, I sense that a stage is being set. But as long as I can see him, I am not he. Seeing implies a distance between us. There is no doubt that he has taken hold of my gaze and brought it into contact with himself, absorbed it into the painting, which is at once flat and of unlimited depth.

Lately I have been thinking of myself as the Visitor for whom you have been waiting these three hundred and twenty years, ever since you were painted. Now all I ask of you is what God asks of you—your attention. I want you to notice me. Ah there! You have given me a sidelong glance! Bearing the suggestion of . . . I don't know what. My hat is off to you, Juan. It is not every portrait that can acquire a living lover, let alone a faithful friend. But I too have benefited. After months of dead air and a limp, flapping sail, there is a breeze, not yet a wind, but enough to stiffen the canvas and send my own pen scudding across a page. Because of you, I am writing again. Speaking of water, it is the reason for my tardiness this morning. I took a canoe out on the river. No, not the Quinnipiac, but the Mill River that runs through East Rock Park. Oh the happiness of a canoe! The paddle alone! The luscious splish-splash of it dipping in and out; the diaphragmatic thrust of the prow incising the living water. For some reason, I had put on my well worn beret, negligently, don't you know, at a jaunty tilt to one side *à la vie de boheme*. My sole nod in the direction of haberdashery is to the hat. I have a weakness for hats. This morning I wavered. Should I wear the beret or my red *tarboosh* with the blue silk tassel attached at the top? It was the fee I charged for repairing the incarcerated inguinal hernia of an Egyptian sailor brought to me from a freighter in New Haven harbor. In the end, I opted for the beret. Out of vanity, I suppose, I leaned over to see my reflection in the water. To my surprise, what with the ripples and spray, I had more than a little resemblance to you in your biretta. For a moment I had the notion that the canoe was drifting in someone else's dream. From beneath the waves you were looking at me with a faint riverine question in your eyes. What could it have been? Never mind. The things I saw! A line of turtles sunning on the bank, a pair of nesting swans, a host of white water lilies, weeping willows washing their long hair in the stream, while in their higher branches the black-crowned night heron roosted. And, oh yes, this: a mute and motionless white heron standing in the shallows on the watch for a flash of silver at its feet. Like your own mute and motionless hand, on the alert for words and images. Not much, I suppose, to one like you who paddles among the stars, but to me it had the richness of Paradise. I need no other. At different times of day the Mill River flows in opposite directions, as the moon would have it do. The water is now fresh, now salty. Near the point where the river flows into Long Island Sound, there is a low bridge, so low that you must lie back flat in the canoe to pass under. Here the water is black and thick as blood. And torpid; the paddle drags. No sooner had I emerged on the other side of this bridge than a dragonfly descended upon the canoe's prow, informing me that it was time to go, you were waiting. Out on the river, the noises in my head grow faint and distant. There is always the possibility that my noises are delusional, but if so, they are no less painful to me. Besides, I make short shrift of these psychiatric diagnoses. Which of us is not a little mad?

How long have I been coming here? The very repetition of the visits does away with time. I surrender to this absence of time in which the visits have taken on the ritualistic nature of a religious service, or the chanting of a mantra.

According to my journal though, it is three months and eight days since I have been visiting Fray Juan. Today will be the ninety-ninth time. Once again, I enter the Art Gallery, climb to the second floor, greet the security guard with a nod and a smile. Unaccountably, Moises does not return my greeting, but raises a hand as if he had something to say, then thought better of it. I turn the corner into the cubicle and . . . where only yesterday the priest, my priest, had been sitting at the writing table in his cell, pen poised in the air, there is only a blank wall with a portrait-sized discoloration where the painting had protected the wall from sunlight and dust. From the iridescent throat of the lone pigeon on the window ledge comes a terrible lamentation that is kin to my own sadness. A wave of dizziness sweeps over me. It is the last thing of which I am aware.

When I awoke, I was lying on a couch in the office of the curator beneath a cluster of concerned faces. It was the kind of concern that is much harder to bear than contempt.

"What . . . ?" I began.

"You fainted. The security guard carried you into my office."

"The painting," I whispered. "Where is it? What have you done with it?"

"It has gone into storage. We rotate the collection so as to give exposure to as much of it as we can. The Valdés Leal had been on display for six months. It was time to show something else in its place."

"No," I said. "That cannot be! That portrait is my life. It's me. I am he! Do you understand?" But of course it was no use. They did not understand. They exchanged nervous glances. Only Moises wore a look of compassion and ruefulness. Fray Juan is in storage, and will remain there for the foreseeable future. Nor is anyone permitted to go to the storage areas.

It is now a year since I have seen *Portrait of an Ecclesiastic* (its unfortunate title). But there is always the sharp and aching tooth of memory. Not a day has passed that I have not returned in my mind to that convent cell with its luminous priest. Over the course of three months and eight days, I had transformed myself into the priest and, in so doing, lost the self I had been. Nothing wrong with that; are we not all "such stuff as dreams are made on"? Day after day, I stood in that fated cubicle, tense with concentration of sight and sound, straining to penetrate into the painting, to slip into the figure on the wall. And it had happened! By that superhuman act of observation, I had caught hints of living expressiveness in his face, collected his half-heard utterances, and made them mine. Even his handwriting became indistinguishable from my own. But now, with so much time having elapsed, what had been made real has relented into paint on canvas; that transparent hand, the flesh long since having been burnt away by desire, that chiseled sepulchral head with its supraorbital ridges and deep eyesockets, no more than the pale fruit of Valdés Leal's brush. There are times when I think, Oh! Did I make it all up? The limpid glow, the sidelong glance, the peonies in a vase, the vein at his temple, the rumor of a pigeon's wings as it flew up from the ledge? Then it is that I search all through my mind for a metaphor to console me, but there are none left. I am on my own here, at last. But from this . . . transubstantiation, I have learned that passion and nonexistence have to be titrated drop by drop until the precise pH of art is achieved. One drop too much or too little, and it is lost.

I have learned, too, that only the imagination sustains us, the making of art. Put it in storage, and you may as well die. I am an old man. The hope of ever seeing Fray Juan again has vanished. I have only the memory of brightness that was his face, and that upraised hand. Once long ago, I saw a waterclock, an *horloge* . . . was it in Prague? Or Annecy? . . . in which a nymph was weeping away the minutes, tear by tear. I know how she felt.

EN RECONNAISSANCE

En Reconnaissance was painted by Édouard Detaille in 1875–76. The scene depicted takes place during the Franco-Prussian war in an Alsatian village not far from the city of Strasbourg. Although the artist did not name this village, I feel the strongest inclination to do so, to situate the event, to memorialize it, to have it not be anonymous. Let me call it, then, La Wantzenau, the name of the village outside of Strasbourg where my son has lived for some years. It is being entered by a troop of *chasseurs*. It is winter. Snow lies upon the ground here and there. The village is almost monochromatic, pale, ashen, bled out, a reflection of the breath-held atmosphere of the event. To look at any work of art is to take inventory

A Reconnaissance, by Jean Baptiste Edouard Detaille

of your imagination. In this talk, I shall try to give you access to your own as well as to mine. The painting is essentially French; it could be of no other national origin. I must be forgiven if on rare occasion I make use of the French language to achieve my purpose. It is dawn, I think, a cold dawn not yet tinged with red, if ever it will be. The light is pale, anemic, drained of energy. The army is made up of musketeers and horsemen drawn largely from peasants, who are accustomed to living without luxury and sustaining themselves in the most modest and frugal way. Still, I think these soldiers are exhausted from a long night's march, hungry and louse-ridden. They would like nothing better than to bivouac in this village. Minutes before, in the small street, a cavalry fight has taken place, scattering its terrible trophies on the ground. The fighting will have surged to and fro, as is indicated by the battle-scarred walls. There had been the neighing of horses, the clangor of metal upon metal, the stench of leather, hairy bloodshot men swaying in their saddles, hoarse voices raised to the breaking point, the groans of the wounded, drumbeats, a bugle stopped in mid-note, perhaps by a bullet through the throat of the bugler. Now a deadly hush has fallen over the village. The stones of the *petite rue* have absorbed the screams of the wounded, the groans of the dying. It is a time of arrested motion and silence brought on by the presence of Death in the form of the lifeless body of the Prussian officer and his horse. Within weeks, no one will remember precisely what happened here, no one but those two small boys pressed against the wall, who will live with the horror from that day on.

A single loud order is given: *"Sentinelles! Prenez-vous garde!"* (Sentries! Be on the alert!) A squad of sharpshooters precedes the main army, and advances cautiously along the crooked, bloodstained lane. They have paused and are scanning the lay of the land. Their leader checks them with a backward movement of the hand, while he listens to an urchin, a patriot of perhaps thirteen, pointing in the direction of the fleeing Prussian army. Note his thin blouse, cold red face, the hand in his pocket, his light small body, his scanty trousers. In one sense, he is the great artistic success of the painting—his gesture is vivid, true. The Prussian lancer and his horse had tumbled headfirst. Death has not separated them. They remain joined to one another, as though a single great heart had driven the blood of both parts of the Centaur. The spiked helmet lies at some distance from the head that wore it. You can almost see the arc of its flight through the air and hear the clatter as the helmet struck the stones, smell

the blue smoke that hangs in the air from the shots that felled them. They
are not yet cold, but pitifully, awkwardly dead. Whether mare or stallion
we don't know, only that the horse is still beautiful with its tawny hide
and dark tilted eyes. Later, the flesh of the horse will be used to make
broth for the wounded. The Prussian is of slim build, and with a pink
hard face. We see his saber, the spiked helmet with chinstrap, the boots,
and splendidly colored uniform of the *chevaux-leger*. We imagine the
moment of dying, the fall. "Between the stirrup and the ground / Him
terror sought, him terror found" (William Camden). One wants to quote
Byron:

> And there lay the steed with his nostril all wide,
> But through it there roll'd not the breath of his pride,
>
> And there lay the rider distorted and pale,
> With the dew on his brow, and the rust on his mail.

The faces of the sharpshooters, especially the stocky man with the
beard, announce their thoughts: "It served him right," "A bad business,"
"A la guerre, comme la guerre" (War is war). Their virility is never in question. They wield it the way Zeus wielded his thunderbolts. Virility took
them where they had to go and it sustains them. It would avenge them
too, if need be. Men sentenced to fight in wars have neither the strength
nor the desire for thought. When all is said and done, the foot soldier is
fighting for a life longer than the one he is destined to live. He who
engages in reconnaissance has a chance only if he summons up all of his
cunning and nerve. He must degrade himself to the level of an animal
whose instinct has not become atrophied from disuse as it has in civilized
men. What counts is only the instant of aiming and firing, the fending
off of the slashing blade, the thrust of the bayonet. Any thought further
than this would be fatal. But look more closely and something else
appears—the awareness of his own mortality. "There but for the grace
of God go I." There is almost a familial resemblance among these scouts,
like the buttons on a uniform. Taken all together the sharpshooters form
a group portrait of the brutality and hopelessness of war. One sees in the
faces of these men, some no larger than a fingernail, the blend of fury and
fear that is the lot of the soldier. These men glance sidewise at the dead
man and they tremble for themselves. In the faces of the sharpshooters,
the word *reconnaissance* realizes its highest potential. Here, both mean-
ings of the word—"to have a look around" and "to recognize"—are fully

expressed. We see in these faces the alert, nervous tension of the forward scout who, at the risk of his own life, is reconnoitering, searching out the immediate territory for danger; we see, too, the recognition of themselves in the dead lancer. *Chaque soldat se reconnais en l'homme mort.* They are strong men, mindful of their duties; that seems clear. Now, having beheld the body of the lancer, they are all, I imagine, moved by the same unfathomable feelings; but each of them is quite alone and dependent upon no one but himself and his weapon.

Édouard Detaille was a pupil of Meissonier, widely held to be the greatest of the French military painters who accompanied the army into battle. Meissonier, known for visiting the studios of his students, had taken considerable interest in the depiction of the dead lancer, even going so far as to position himself, sprawling, under the model of a horse on the floor of Detaille's studio. He invited Detaille to make a sketch, and offered to maintain the position as long as necessary. Another visitor was shocked to find the famous Meissonier so stretched out.

"En Reconnaissance" consists of a multiplicity of plots and subplots to compose the total effect. It is a narrative painting, a moment of truth distilled from the ongoing stream of events. Even as it was happening, time was moving on. But this painting is timeless. A past and a present are implied here in this village street scene that is caught forever in medias res. I really ought to have begun this talk by saying, "Once upon a time . . ." The eye takes in the story quickly, and it remains on the retina for a long time. All the shutters of the houses are closed, all the doors shut. Here and there above the walls of the gardens and courtyards appear the terrified heads of peasants, who had hidden themselves at the first appearance of the enemy, and now show themselves timidly, like birds after a storm. The gaze travels to the others in the painting. A wounded gendarme has collapsed against a garden wall, through the gate of which a man, peeping out, is trying to drag him. The soldier with an arm wound almost certainly faces amputation. Any wound of the extremities in which a fracture of a bone had taken place required amputation. If he is lucky, it will be done within the hour, before infection and gangrene set in. Another man opens a window to wave in welcome to the invaders. Two small boys press themselves against another bullet-pocked wall. You know that they will retain this scene in their nightmares for years to come. Each figure is fully engaged in his own activity, oblivious of the spectator. In the rear, through the gray snowy air, the rest of the army is coming up. It is a page torn out of history that requires the falsification of perspective, that monumental lie of art. One is struck both by the magnitude of the event and by its tiny-ness next to the hugeness of the war being waged all around the painting. If this had been painted during the Renaissance, there would be a Winged Warrior strolling among the white clouds above the village. He would carry a banner that said: "Mine is the punishing arm" or something of the kind. In that Renaissance painting, the sea of faces in the background would look for such signs in the sky, for circles of fire, blazing crosses. But here in La Wantzenau there is only History, whose other name is Annihilation.

All wars are regrettable, and most are stupid. But the Franco-Prussian War of 1870–71 was simply inexcusable. Napoleon III, the Emperor of the French, began the war because his advisers assured him that he could defeat the Prussians, and that such a victory would restore his declining popularity in France. Otto von Bismarck, the Prussian Chancellor, saw his chance to unify all the German states to form the Prussian Empire. On both sides there was a mounting clamor for war. In the end, Prussian efficiency overcame French dithering and Prussia won. This resulted in the loss of Alsace and Lorraine by France and the incurring of a huge debt to pay for the Prussian cost of the war.

Five years after the war, Henry James, writing his "Parisian Sketches" for the *New York Tribune,* reviewed the annual art competition known as the Salon:

> I have no doubt that the most popular will be the contribution of M. Detaille, the admirable military painter. It is indeed, already, of all the pictures, the most closely surrounded, and it has a good right to its honors. It is called "En Reconnaissance," and represents a battalion of chasseurs coming into a village street in which a cavalry fight has just taken place and scattered its trophies over the ground. A squad of sharpshooters is preceding the rest of the troop and advancing cautiously along the crooked, bloodstained lane. They have paused and are scanning the lay of the land in front of them— the leader checking them with a backward movement of his hand, while he listens to an urchin, a patriot of thirteen, in blouse and muffler, doing his boyish best to be useful, and giving damaging

information. The picture is remarkably perfect and complete—a
page torn straight from unpublished history. The variety and vivid-
ness of the types, the expressiveness of the scene, without a touch of
exaggeration or grimace, the dismal chill of the weather, the sense
of possible bullets in the air, the full man size of the little figures, the
clean consummate brilliancy of the painting, make it a work of art
of which nothing but good is to be said.

So wrote Henry James.

If a painting could be assigned a gender, this one is of the male persuasion. The brush of the artist was dipped in testosterone. Not least because
it lacks subtlety. There is no ambiguity in any of it. You don't have to
wonder about anything the way you do about that letter Vermeer's lady
is holding in Delft. There's no need to wonder what anyone is thinking.
The village, its inhabitants, and the soldiers are precisely what they seem.
There is only the blunt fact that for this moment the war has been
brought to a halt by the confrontation of the dead cavalryman and the
sharpshooters. Not that Detaille lacked restraint; notice how little blood
has been shed upon the stones. There is only the rare splotch, an accent,
and all the more powerful for that. Besides, the authorities discouraged
the portrayal before the public of gory wounds, great suffering, or the
spillage of French blood, on the grounds that it would have been damag-
ing to the public morale. Apparently Detaille got a good deal of adverse
criticism on account of his portrayal of the painful, humiliating, human
side of the war as against a glorification of the French army.

Édouard Detaille was born in 1848 into a well-to-do family. His father
was an architect. An elder brother was a marshal in the Imperial Guard.
His grandfather had been a *fournisseur* (supplier) to the army and had
recounted his military experiences to the young boy's enchantment. Early
on he was taken to watch maneuvers and reviews, all the while sketch-
ing. He was present at the arrival of the Queen of England in France,
and at the return of the troops from the Crimea. Detaille was one of those
people who know at age five exactly what they want to become. He
wanted to become a military painter. Perhaps he knew it while still in the
womb of his mother. While other boys played at soldiering, he composed
it on paper. Whether or not his parents worried that the boy sat all day
long drawing cavalry and cannon, they would have found it difficult to

break the mold once it had been set. Blessed with a rare visual memory and an innate facility for drawing, he was at last given the encouragement he needed.

At age seventeen, he entered the celebrated atelier of Meissonier, who urged him to "paint from nature, always nature, as I do." Meissonier was dazzled by the talent of Detaille and forced himself to subdue, without breaking, the young man's astonishing facility. Meissonier made him paint countless male nudes in the atelier. He remained a masculine painter all his life, feeling that the male was more beautiful than the female. "Tenderness of the paintbrush is neither my desire nor my fate. Behold the virility of Michelangelo," he remarked.

Rejected from military service because he was the son of a widow whose other son was in the army, Detaille was given a commission to travel with the army and carry out his paintings. He was always careful in his painting to support the cause of the army. He was forbidden to portray French defeat and often had to change the uniforms of the dead and wounded from French to Austrian.

"When I drew the Barricade, I was under the spell of the spectacle I had seen. These events enter your soul. One has been moved to the entrails and feels that it is essential that the memory of the event endure." His paintings were enormously popular with the public, to whom he catered and whom he did not wish to offend. Thus he was loath to portray disfigured corpses, the armless and legless wounded. In 1876 "En Reconnaissance" won all the votes in the Paris Salon Competition.

His schedule went something like this: He rose at dawn and painted until noon, interrupted only by meetings at the Institute. In the evening he went home to his mother or to the house of Valtesse de la Bigne, a famous courtesan of the Paris demimonde, whose numerous painter/ lovers were known as the Union of Artists and who became his longtime mistress. He himself was *tout Parisien jusqu'aubout des ongles* (A consummate Parisian down to his fingernails).

What did he look like? Rather a tall man, *soignée,* elegantly dressed, almost foppish, with a military posture, and the suggestion of the British gentleman/officer about him. With his chestnut brown hair and blond moustache, well-groomed, he seemed younger than his age. The effect of his strong nose was softened by pink cheeks and eyes that were gray to some, blue to others. He was of a cheery disposition, the only one of the students who did not have a falling-out with Meissonier. Imagine him then, standing before his easel, impeccable, military. He lifts a hand, brings the brush to the canvas, makes a small daubing movement, then leans backward to assess the effect. To his left, tacked on the wall, a sketch of "En Reconnaissance."

Detaille was never in financial need. He transformed his mansion into a military museum and lived long enough to enjoy electricity, telephone, and automobiles. His bed was an immense field of battle surmounted by a *baldaquin* of *velours*. In later years, he became quite the boulevardier, attending the brilliant salons of Valtesse, the circus, theatre, opera. He knew Jacques Offenbach, Fromental Halevy, Sarah Bernhardt, Emmanuel Chabrier, Charles Gounod, and the volcanic Rejane, who inspired in him a brief explosive passion. He had no familiarity with the Paris literary world. Politically, he was a nationalist, authoritarian, militaristic, anti-Marxist, and anti-Semitic. Would I have liked Édouard Detaille? I should have been as at home among the cannibals.

We wish strongly," he said, "for a war that will regenerate our poor country. It is a heroic remedy that will put an end to our downfall." This he said in 1907. His chief artistic interest was the simple soldier in his daily life. Thus he created with his brush what Stendhal and Mérimée expressed with the pen. He never really understood the Impressionists.

"We must part from the rubbish of Van Gogh and Cézanne—their vague impressions." As for the Cubists, he ignored them completely. He simply didn't get it at all. In short, Detaille was *un homme du passé,* entirely a prisoner of the nineteenth century. He took the comfortable path of the Salon, which heaped honors on him and at the same time put an iron collar about his neck and his unvarying style. Once the most celebrated artist of his time, he has become the fallen master of a dead art. Impressionism triumphed. Detaille is now listed among the second-raters of his time. Both his subject and his style became objectionable to the public. His value is said to be chiefly as the documentation of his times. But, like him or not, I must raise my voice in praise of Édouard Detaille. With the same primitive tools of art that have not changed in centuries—a stick with bristles at one end, a rectangular board, pigments, and oils—he has revealed to us the secrets of the human heart. More than a century later we gaze at this scene and we are moved at the bravery and vulnerability of the common man. Detaille was the last great military painter of the nineteenth century. He gave the simple soldier the mark of nobility. He proudly painted soup and drudgery, and in doing so, he plumbed the depth of each individual. This he did without neglecting the *mise-en-scène,* the setting that he presented in almost photographic detail. Perhaps it was that very photography that caused his downfall.

It has always seemed to me a kind of alchemy that from pigments dissolved in oil the whole world could be realized. Compared with painting or sculpture, language is inexact, either given to hyperbole or outright lying, while a statement in wood, ivory, marble, or paint insists upon a certain directness and simplicity.

This painting is an example of realism at its most undeviating. There are no symbols, not a speck of distortion for effect. It's as far from a Rothko or a Picasso as you can get. No need to put two and two together to make four. No need to accustom yourself to novelty in technique. What you see is what you get. Here is the world as you have always known it, and as you recognize it. There are those who would give a smile of indulgence at such a work, call it simplistic, unintellectual, deplore the fact that it makes no demands upon the viewer other than to see what has been included, and to imagine what has been left out.

Time was when realism was the reigning style of painting. As it was in poetry, drama and the novel, film. All of the *métiers* of art. What brought about the dissolution of art into its component parts, which the artist then felt free to jumble and put out of all order? I wonder if it wasn't concomitant with the breaking apart of the great colonial empires—Britain, France, Germany, Spain, Portugal. It seems to me that a parallel case may be made in the English theatre. Not so long ago, a successful play was "well-made." It had a beginning, middle, and an end. The audience left the theatre, not in a state of wonder as to what had taken place or what it all meant, but satiated by a good story, well acted and directed. Such were the plays of Terence Rattigan, say. Then, along came Harold Pinter, who dispensed with narrative, announced that no one could re-create history, and that everything was happening then and there. His characters don't speak to each other so much as around each other. There are long silences. What do they mean? And non sequiturs. Samuel Beckett's plays till corners of the same field. It's all quite mystifying. In poetry, one did away with rhyme, and substituted what is known as free verse. But half the fun of a poem used to be in the rhyming. Then along came Gerard Manley Hopkins with his "sprung" rhythm, Ezra Pound, T. S. Eliot, and, in this country, Hart Crane and John Ashbery. As for myself, I never have understood the appeal of Pinter or much of abstract, nonrepresentational art. Its soul is not visible to me. I have the heretical notion that one day a brilliant art historian will emerge who will announce to the rest of us: "The emperor isn't wearing any clothes." But I'd better quit this kind of murmuring against the current mode, or next thing you know I'll be led through the streets of New Haven in manacles and made to sit on the Stool of Penitence in the middle of the Green.

THE VETERAN AND ST. PETER

Could there be anything new to say about the works of Thomas Eakins and Jusepe de Ribera? If so, then let it be said by someone with credentials in the field of Art History. I have but gazed at these two portraits the way an old-time doctor (long before MRI and ultrasound and the rest of modern technology made the History and Physical Examination obsolete) gazed at his patients, trying to make a diagnosis. Just so have I invited both *St. Peter* and *The Veteran* to present their symptoms, then examined them, percussed and auscultated, as it were, each of the paintings, tapping out borders, sounding depths, listening for echoes, and all the while on the watch for the key dramatic detail that might give a clue to the creative act of painting the pictures.

I must say right out that when it comes to painting or sculpture, I should prefer anonymity to knowing the life story of the artist. Anonymity is purifying to a work of art. Anonymity doesn't clutter it up with the details of the artist's personal life—his illegitimate children, gonorrhea, bladder stones, hemorrhoids, his cuckoldry, his feuds, his madness. I *should*, that is, but I don't. I'm as nosy and prurient as the next gallery goer, and I thirst after the delicious details that show the man not as a genius garbed in immortality, but as another faltering, wounded human being who is just as apt as I am to disgrace himself and commit every sort of folly. Still, let me exercise a modicum of restraint.

Jusepe de Ribera was born in Valencia, Spain in 1591. At the age of sixteen, and already painting, he traveled to Naples, where he remained for the rest of his life. Small of stature and slight of build, he was called *il spagnuoletto* by his fellow artists. He is known as the foremost painter of the Neapolitan Baroque. Enormously successful during his lifetime, he

The Veteran, by Thomas Eakins

was a court painter to vice-
roys and received commis-
sions from Philip IV of Spain.
A great many of his paintings
are of saints and other religious figures. This *St. Peter*
was painted in the years between 1630 and 1640. The
artist died in the year 1652.
One can surmise that this is
an example of Ribera's mature
work.

For Thomas Eakins I feel
a special kinship in his having studied anatomy at Jeff-
erson Medical College with
the intention of becoming
a surgeon. The model for
The Veteran, George Reynolds,
had been an art student of
Eakins', one who the artist had used before as the diving boy in his
famous *The Swimming Hole.* Now here is Reynolds, some two decades
later, having returned from the Civil War, where he served as a civilian
conscript. The tragedy of the civilian conscript as opposed to the professional soldier lay not only in what was done to a man, but in what he had
to do to others and in what happened to him *inside.* The Veteran, as
depicted here, is a Whitmanesque figure, utterly beautiful, though
unaware of it, untraveled, unsophisticated, rural, the survivor who cannot speak of what happened in battle. His is a private, obscure greatness.
There is not the least hint of the glory of war, nothing of the heroic. He is
called "The Veteran" as if he were representative of all soldiery that has
come through a war. Of course, he is not. He is entirely unique, individ-
ualized. He is a veteran, all of whose growth and development are behind
him. The shine of youth has been burnished by a patina of suffering and
loss. He is the mature man who remembers. One enters the company of
these two superb specimens of masculine beauty at the risk of odious
comparison: One's own masculine beauty will be reduced to an absolute
minimum.

These are paintings that mean much more than they say. They can be "read" as well as looked at, and so are particularly appealing to both writer and doctor. Notice first the absence of any background or subsidiary figure that might suggest a context in which they exist. They are utterly alone on the canvas. No hills rolling away, no river winding, no trees, no animals, no sense of distance or landscape at all. We have only the faces and hands from which to diagnose their lives. In each there is revealed a strong spirituality; the soul of the man is visible. Much more than the photo-

Saint Peter, by Jusepe de Ribera

graphic instant is captured; a whole life is revealed. Just by virtue of having become a saint, Peter rivets our attention. Sainthood is as fascinating as pornography or evil. Saints are on a par with conquerors and notorious sirens—Napoleon and Delilah come to mind. Saints are usually a great pain in the neck while here on earth, pestering the rest of us to lead lives beyond reproach, submitting to no end of torment just to be a living rebuke to the unbeatifiable. We who love sin, scandal, the whole place caving in, become self-conscious, embarrassed under such scrutiny. It's entirely possible that the reason so many saints were martyred was that nobody could stand them. Here Peter is shown facing frontally, looking directly at the viewer, urgent to change our lives, driven by what he has witnessed. I imagine his voice to have the hoarseness of phlegmy old age and zeal. Even the beard swirling about his mouth is passionate. A charge has been laid upon him that he cannot ignore. After all, he was present on the mountaintop when Jesus was transfigured. He heard the voice from the cloud proclaiming, "This is my Son, my beloved, listen to Him." And after the tomb was discovered to be empty, Christ appeared to Peter. *Ophtheke* is the word used in the Greek Scriptures: *He was seen!* And for a moment Peter's eyes take on the glitter of the Ancient Mariner. They are red-rimmed, the lower lids rolled out and everted in an old man's ectropion (caused by a relaxation and a loss of turgor of the skin and of those fibers of the orbicularis oculi muscle that run across the lower eyelid). Partially encircling each pupil is the grayish-white arcus senilis of old age, the result of deposition there of fatty substances and proteins.

More than the zeal of evangelism, this portrait reveals a man consumed with remorse at having denied Christ out of cowardice. Here is the version written by Luke: "And apprehending him [Christ], they led him to the high priest's house. But Peter followed afar off. And when they had kindled a fire in the midst of the hall, and when they were sitting about it, Peter was in the midst of them. It so happened that a servant maid, sitting nearby in the firelight, earnestly beheld Peter and, when the time came, spoke up, saying, 'This man also was with him.' But Peter denied Jesus, saying, 'Woman, I know him not.' And after a little while, another seeing Peter, said, 'Thou also art one of them.' But Peter said, 'O man, I am not.' And an hour later, another man affirmed, saying, 'Of a truth, this man was also with him; for he too is a Galilean.' And Peter said, 'Man, I know not what thou sayest.' And just then, a cock crowed. And Jesus turned to look at Peter. And Peter remembered the word of his Lord: 'Before the cock crow twice, thou shalt deny me thrice.' And Peter left, weeping bitterly."

Just think of it! Peter's disloyalty was even deeper than that of Judas, who said, "The one I shall kiss is the man; seize him." What is a mean hypocritical kiss performed for thirty pieces of silver to a turning away from God? Nor did Peter even show up at the Crucifixion out of fear for his life. No, Peter's was a downfall that shook his whole existence. Anyone who has suffered the pangs of guilt knows well that it is more painful than unrequited love, than jealousy, certainly than physical agony. It seems to me that this Peter has not slept in days. Like Macbeth, full of remorse for having murdered his king, who prophesies that never again will he know peaceful sleep:

> Methought I heard a voice cry, "Sleep no more!
> Macbeth does murther Sleep, the innocent Sleep;
> Sleep that knits up the ravell'd sleave of care,
> The death of each day's life, sore labor's bath,
>
> Balm of hurt minds,"

Peter's will be a fitful sleep infested with nightmares.

> How can I live, that thus my life denied?
> What can I hope, that lost my hope in feare?
> *(from Robert Southwell's "St. Peter's Complaint")*

Were all the paint to fade or flake from this portrait, it seems to me that the remorse would still be there, etched imperishably into the bare canvas with a true Spanish vitality.

On the other hand, the Veteran's battle is long since over. In this crepuscular painting, whose landscape is darkness itself, he is seated facing downward and to the right, hands clasped, his gaze turned aside from us, veiled. The brightness of his eye is elsewhere. Only one side of the face is fully visible, the other is in deep shadow with only the outline of the cheek, beard, and hair to be seen. In that part of the face that is illuminated, we see clearly the texture of his skin, the lines and wrinkles of a man no longer young. Just above the eye, a strand of hair has fallen across his brow, and to the right there is a small round pink area, perhaps the scar of a wound that has healed over. He keeps himself to himself. We have no way to know, but I would guess that he is a man of sparse speech. When he speaks, it will be in a tired voice, subdued. Once, perhaps, as he is pictured (again by Eakins) diving into the swimming hole years before, he had been a merry, outgoing boy, but the War has quenched him. Of what, I wonder, could he be thinking? Is he remembering the smoke and clamor of battle? His fear? The rataplan of musketry and the neighing of horses? The screams of the wounded, and the ground red with blood? Or does he see again a flare of crimson in the sky that signals sunset and the end of the battle? Does he remember a certain peach tree cracked apart by a cannonball, a house burning, the torment of his own lice? Does he hear the far-off sound of a bugle? We do not know whether he himself had been wounded, suffered perhaps the amputation of one of his legs, as did so many others. Does all of this lie behind that stare? Is it the cold snowfall of memory that has transformed this face into—a countenance?

The Veteran wears a coat of rough herringbone, with a scarf of richer, soft fabric tucked under the collar. A vertical line beginning at the part in the hair runs down the nose, through the scarf and coat collar to the bottom of the canvas. This divides the painting into dark and light halves.

Both artists have used hair as an instrument of illumination. Saint

Peter's hair forms a subtle halo about his head. His beard is unkempt, an effect achieved by applying paint around the edges of the beard, then scumbling it, or rubbing it off with a finger, letting the canvas show through to give a woolly appearance. The whole suggests the naïve and morbid sadness of some miracle-working friar who believes that earthly life is but the anteroom to Heaven, that very Heaven to which he holds in his hand the key. For a good deal of my early life, I believed that Heaven was a walled place with a gate to which there was a key, and only lately have I come to regard that notion as symbolic. It is something of a comedown. Peter also is holding a book, presumably the Holy Scriptures. Never mind that the Bible hadn't been written yet and that he would not have been able to read it, as he was without doubt illiterate.

In the tiny crow's-feet around the eyes and the fugitive wisp of hair that crosses an ear, Eakins verifies the essential vulnerability of the Veteran. In his dark, plentiful hair there resides all that remains of his youthful vigor. It is a biblical irony that God placed all of Samson's strength in his hair, that most dispensable and transitory part of the body. Once shorn by the perfidious Delilah, in whose scented lap he had laid his heavy mane, Samson is weak, helpless. He would rue the day he lifted the flap of that woman's tent. Absalom, his long hair tangled in a tree, and slain, is another biblical victim.

Hair is the smoke of the mind, passing forth from the body lightly, carrying with it an air of vitality, mystery, and electricity. In this time of chemotherapy and the resulting loss of hair, baldness has come to be a mark of severe illness, or even approaching death. Such baldness touches the heart. Not long ago, one of a classroom of fifth-grade boys was diagnosed as having malignant lymphoma, for which he underwent chemotherapy, and became completely bald. Informed of this by their teacher, the entire class of some twenty-five boys opted to have their heads shaved so that when their classmate came back to school, he would not feel self-conscious. The teacher, too, shaved his head. In such a classroom, baldness becomes a mark of grace and nobility. In such a classroom, bald is beautiful. The cutting off of hair, under certain conditions, is an act of great significance. A nun, entering the sisterhood, goes hairless as the bride of Christ. An Orthodox Jewish woman covers her shaved head with a *sheitl,* a wig, so as not to stir lewd thoughts in men, and as a mark of devotion to her husband.

The hands of Saint Peter are those of the simple Galilean fisherman that he was, one who, day after day, cast his nets out over the water, then hauled them back in. His hands are big and broad, the fingers gnarled, and with the dirt of Galilee under each of his nails. They have the peasant's physical dignity. What is a hand but an arborization of veins, arteries, bones, nerves, and lymphatics, all covered with pliant skin, whose softness or lack of it reflects the use to which the hand has been put? No two hands share the same pattern of these parts, but each has responded to influences both local and distant. It seems incontrovertible that the arteries and their descendants, the arterioles and capillaries, grow from proximal to distal, greater to smaller. This outward growth depends upon local tissue conditions, the mechanical drag, that persuades the growing tip of the vessel to turn, evade, and deflect itself, so as to attain equilibrium with the other parts. Then, too, there is the lower pressure inside the veins, and the thirst of the fingers for blood and oxygen. All this to say nothing of the far-off propulsive thrust of the heart, and the slow simmer of hormone and enzyme. At last, after nine months of gestation, what is formed is an exquisitely sensate hand no part of which rebels against any other part. Such perfection should be incorruptible, you say. But incorruptibility is inhuman; it is for angels. Consider the deeds of the human hand, and you will know otherwise. It is in the dirt under Peter's nails wherein resides his divinity.

The Veteran's hands float apart from his face, as if adrift in a corner of the painting, a pair of gloves flung down. Their severance from the rest of the man creates an effect of unreality that is almost hideous, as though they do not belong to him. I cannot imagine him placing those hands on his knees. They are smooth and swollen; the knuckles cannot be made out. The fingers seem boiled, or fetal. What can Eakins have meant? Had he abandoned the hands, leaving them to the imagination of the viewer? The absence of any detail in the hands seems to me an evasion. In another painting by Eakins, *Girl Playing with a Cat,* there is a young girl in whose lap is a frolicsome cat. She is brandishing a fan in her play. But the hand holding it is not that of a thirteen-year-old girl. It is that of an arthritic old woman, crabbed and lumpy. In his depiction of Dr. Gross, the surgeon's hand is covered with blood. One might deem these hands of Eakins a deliberate mystery, something still imprisoned in the canvas, much as many of Rodin's figures have a hand or foot trapped in the marble. Isadora Duncan, the dancer, would have thought so. After visiting Rodin's studio, and declining his sexual advances (a

rejection she later regretted), Duncan wrote of the studio: "Life is everywhere but only rarely does it come to full expression, or the individual to
perfect freedom."

But what artist has not frowned down at his hands in resentment or
disappointment at their having let him down? All day long, they are what
he sees, the one holding up a brush or chisel or pen, the other at rest, waiting upon its dominant partner. Over the twelve years since my transition
from surgery to writing, my own hands have taken on a crafty, dishonest, crabbed look. Once, they had been lithe, gracile, ambidextrous. Now
the joints have thickened, the veins gone sclerotic, all except the salvatella,
the tiny vein that courses along the back of the little finger, and so named
because, in the Middle Ages, when bleeding was the universal therapy of
choice, blood let from this small vein gave the highest incidence of cures.
More than once, stumped for a diagnosis, and with the patient sinking, I
have drawn blood from the salvatella. Sent to the laboratory, such a specimen has never failed to yield up the correct answer. (Let the modern
radiologist cock up his nose and play the rhinoceros. About technology, I
do not agree with the prophet Daniel, who said that "many shall run to
and fro, and knowledge shall be increased.")

Once, my hands had been pink from frequent scrubbing, the nails
scrupulous; now they are blotched and hairless and stiff. As if they have
too much time on them. If there be any subject more threatening to a
painter or sculptor than the hand, I don't know what it is. To limn the
very part that is the limner would seem to be akin to the violation of the
taboo against taking the name of the Lord in vain. No good would come
to the blasphemer. The artist's hand is not to be depicted; it is to be wondered at. What has settled into the fingers must remain a mystery. Could
the unfinished rendering of the Veteran's hands be Eakins' way of not
taking up that particular gauntlet?

Once, Peter had been burly. Now there is pathos in the old man's
shoulders, grown thin, atrophic, the muscles wasted, burnt up in the fires
within that brighten his watery eyes; pathos, too, in the loose folds of skin
on his neck. The cloud-pale robe hangs loose upon his frame. He seems
bewildered, his wits led astray in a kind of Galilean turbulence, as if the
lake of his mind is dark, wild, storm-whipped. His thoughts come tumbling down the path of consciousness, too numerous and troubled to
catch. Here, then, none of your idealized saint; just a disheveled old man
with thinning hair, dewlaps, and wrinkles. And yet . . . he is the same

man who was granted a special appearance of Christ, who has received and accepted the charge to feed His sheep, and who has been given the power to make miracles. His shadow, even, heals the sick. All at once, he seems to become aware of our presence.

"Stop!" he cries. "I have something to tell you! *Ophtheke!* He has been seen!" But the words are caught and tangled in the tangle of his beard.

Two men, then, each in the decline of his body, but in the ascent of his spirit. Where they differ is that in Peter the tumult is visible, palpable; in the Veteran, it exists in memory, although no less compellingly. Peter confronts us directly, all but holds us by the sleeve; the Veteran is oblivious to our presence. He is a castaway, worn out; the Medal of Honor all but invisible on his breast—a "befitting emblem of adversity." His strength having dwindled, he sits in slippered reverie. He has known every kind of bestiality of which war is capable. Recollecting now in tranquility, he seems possessed of a terrible secret about mankind. There is a dreaminess that takes his mind over vast planetary distances. Should he suddenly turn and glance at us, the embarrassment would be all ours for having violated his privacy. Neither one of these men wears a mask, but each is laid open for us to examine, like Eliot's "patient etherized upon a table." Our own hearts soften with compassion as we gaze at them. Oh yes, I know there is no St. Peter here, no Veteran, just dabs of paint on a canvas. But still . . .

Which portrait do I like best? The Eakins, I suppose, although the choice is Solomonic, I assure you. It is like asking which of my children I love best. Perhaps it is a certain identification with Thomas Eakins that I do not have with Jusepe de Ribera. Eakins and I both spent our lives in North America, in the northeast part of the same country, not more than two hundred and fifty miles apart. We have both lived among Americans, and so were imprinted with similar art, science, and morality. Less than a century separates our birthdays. His was in 1844, mine in 1928— eighty-four years. I was born only twelve years after Eakins died. As Eakins was ahead of his time, I am behind mine. In some ways, we are co-eval. Then too, we have both studied anatomy, dissected cadavers. There is a deal of fellowship in that.

But more than all of that, it is the Veteran's ambiguity that I prefer. There is no such ambiguity in Peter. His zeal and remorse are all there to be seen. The temperature of the Veteran is warm, his fires banked; that of St. Peter is twenty degrees higher—he is aflame. The Veteran is entirely earthbound, entirely American, while Peter has become a citizen of this world, and even of the one hereafter. Unlike Galilee in first century Palestine, New Haven, Connecticut, is not the sort of place that encourages large spiritual adventures. Unlike Peter, who held the conviction that mortal life was a sad and painful affair, the sooner over the better, I myself am given to frequent attacks of cheerfulness and even, God knows why, optimism. St. Peter's ardor and anguish constitute a reproach. It makes a sinner like me feel inferior, guilty. Nobody likes that sort of thing. Not that I pooh-pooh, or otherwise sniff at the idea of miracles. I've been the "ocular witness" to a number of them in the course of three decades of surgery. But that's another story. Despite the opinion of the surgeons I know, most miracles are not performed by a doctor. They are performed by a saint. It's right there in the résumé. My favorite is St. Columba, who hand-copied his master's prayerbook in the dark, without candles: The five fingers of his left hand shone like so many candles while his right hand did the copying. Then there was St. Brigid, who would hang her cloak on a sunbeam. She must have been quite a trial to her family.

"Strangeness," wrote James Whistler, "is the condiment of beauty." This Veteran is mysterious, enigmatic. He is real enough but with a touch of the spectral, as if he were a shadow made incarnate. His is a phantom portrait that seems to want to withdraw back into the wall upon which it is hung. He sits within the frame of the picture, at the same distance behind the canvas as the painter stood in front of it. Even before Eakins began, this was the face of a handsome man. But now, it is something more, for it contains all that the painter thought into it. Whatever it was that Eakins may have felt for George Reynolds, there are few secrets that art cannot reveal. There is between subject and painter a feeling that cannot be faked. A portrait is what the artist sees. It is also what he thinks of what he sees. Eakins painted his Veteran with a tenderness that suggests a lover. I wonder what George Reynolds thought when he saw the finished portrait. Was it like looking into a mirror? Or was this someone he thought he knew but couldn't recognize?

It occurs to me that *The Veteran* is something of a self-portrait. "Only an aching heart conceives a changeless work of art." Or so said the poet Yeats. Eakins is not a passive artist. He does not remain hidden in his work. Here he enters the portrait in such a way that artist and model fuse, separate, and come together again. Both artist and model are in middle age; both have recently suffered the loss of their wives; both have suffered rejection as artists; both are battered by what they have endured. Moreover, the model for *The Veteran* uncannily suggests the face of Eakins himself, as we know it from photographs, which show a deeply unhappy man who had just been fired from the faculty of the Pennsylvania Academy of Fine Arts for using male and female nude models in his classes. George Reynolds was one of Eakins' most devoted students. It was he who, in revolt against the dismissal of his teacher, organized a student demonstration, and then resigned from the Academy in protest. Reynolds had served in the Ninth Regiment in the Civil War and had seen a good deal of fighting. He received the Medal of Honor for the capture of the enemy's flag in battle. If you look carefully, you can see this medal hazily painted on Reynolds' chest. Now distant from the battlefield, he has shed the shell that a soldier, like a surgeon, must grow, the one to do his killing, the other, his healing. Shortly after painting *The Veteran,* Eakins suffered an emotional and physical collapse. He left Philadelphia for New York, where he became a close friend of Walt Whitman. From there, he went out to the Dakotas, from which he returned with his vigor restored.

It is of interest that this painting, considered by Eakins himself to be one of his finest, was exhibited only once during his lifetime and remained in his studio unsold. People don't have their portraits painted anymore, although surely it is the preferred way to have your head taken off. A portrait is like a lighted candle by which the biography of the subject can be read. It is an arrogance to attempt to depict in mere words what Eakins and Ribera have so precisely and evocatively brought to fruition. In the domain of portraiture, the pen is a poor second best to the brush. While I have had to resort to such literary tricks as irony, metaphor, and suggestiveness, each of the painters had only to mount his brush, whisper a word, and ride wherever it took him. And where it took them both was to the Yale Art Gallery, and to me. For that, I must be forever grateful.

SEEING RED:
A CLINICAL LOOK AT ROTHKO'S #3

Marcus Rothkowitz was born in 1903 in the city of Dvinsk, in the part of Russia that is now Latvia. His father was a well-to-do pharmacist, who gave him and his two brothers a strict religious education. He studied Torah and Talmud and learned Hebrew. The language spoken at home was Yiddish. It was a time of widespread pogroms against the Jews in Russia. Many were beaten, robbed, and slaughtered. Between 1881 and 1914, two million Jews emigrated to the United States. This included my own grandparents.

Rothko was ten years old when he arrived with his mother, and they spent their first ten days in New Haven, Connecticut, with cousins. From there they went by train to Portland, Oregon. They wore tags to indicate that they spoke no English. During the next five years, Marcus became fluent in English, although he retained a heavy Russian accent all his life.

He would return to New Haven in 1921 to attend Yale. He lived then on Legion Avenue in the attic of a doctor's home. To earn money for food and bed, he waited on tables at the University. The clumsy, large immigrant with his accent must have been an object of curiosity, if not derision, for the Yalies in their white bucks and figured ties whom he served at table. (After six months Rothko's scholarship money was withdrawn and he borrowed money from Yale. Years later, Rothko offered Yale paintings instead of the money he owed. The offer was refused.) After two years Rothko dropped out of Yale, preferring to live and paint in New York City. Forty-six years later, Yale awarded Rothko an honorary degree.

In New York he enjoyed the excitement and sociability of the lower East Side tenement life. He loved the streets and walked them endlessly. He loved theater and acting and took part in many amateur productions. His only formal training in art took place at the Art Students League.

An early marriage failed quickly.

In 1938 he became an American citizen and dropped the "us" and the "witz," giving us the name by which we know him: Mark Rothko.

In 1945 he married Mell, a descendant of Abraham Lincoln. He was forty-one; she, twenty-three. They lived happily, but in abject poverty, for years. There are two children.

Rothko was a man of voracious appetite. He had a barrel chest, a large head, and huge hands. He was not handsome, but was a physically powerful presence, with his deep booming voice. He always wore glasses for his severe myopia.

In the 1950s he first experienced the mental depression that was to plague him until he died, and despite which he retained an enormous capacity for work and life. At home he grew moody, testy, and cynical. "Ivan the Terrible" he was called. But he was also a loving father and husband. There followed a descent into alcoholism, which heightened his melancholia and hypochondria. It didn't help that he had a deep distrust of doctors. A ruptured aortic aneurysm rendered him impotent. Not long after, the marriage to Mell failed. In 1970, Mark Rothko died by his own hand.

Until the last two years, my taste in art had been exclusively representational—anything, just so there be life stirring in it. Those arid abstractions—what did they have to do with the actual world in which men and women live, work, and die? I enjoyed the recognition of the objects, scenes, and creatures I knew, and the less distorted, the better. A Cézanne still life of apples, a Constable sky, a field of poppies—these were and still are the subjects that satisfied the art lover in me. The muddle of abstraction, I thought, was either jittery or inert. It didn't make you laugh or cry or wonder what was going to happen next. It was, at most, interesting. But along came Mark Rothko and his #3 [see back cover], which I shall call "Red" for purposes of this meditation upon it; and with this one painting I have become a convert. Sort of. Do not imagine that I have dismissed the entire genre of representational, figurative painting to dote on abstract art. It is only this one painting to which I have applied my senses, like a barnacle on a rock. As for all other paintings by Rothko, I do not "see" them. They are as opaque windows to me. Their shades are drawn. That is because I am not an art historian, do not see a painting in the context of an artist's *oeuvre,* nor any artist as part of a movement or era. Mine is the narrowest focus possible. One work at a time, and that one dwelt upon with the obsessive gaze of a doctor striving to make a diagnosis.

Rothko himself had little use for art history. He urged a new kind of art criticism, in which each viewer offers his personal response to a painting. "Only pure human reactions," he wrote, "in terms of human need.

Does the painting satisfy some human need?" asked Rothko. To which I would reply: Yes, Mark Rothko, this red painting does. And so I should like in this essay to do as the artist suggested and give my personal reaction to "Red." The fact that the painting is untitled (#3 is hardly a name) is a powerful commentary on its indefiniteness. It gives the viewer the right to project himself into the painting.

Make no mistake about it. This is a picture of Nothing in two shades of red. It is blank, unreadable, until the gaze of each viewer creates it anew for himself, causing it to undergo a kind of metamorphosis. Look at any blob of color or aggregation of marks, or even a blank wall, and before long the image is pregnant with shapes and figures, some recognizable, some not. Everything empty, like this canvas, will be filled by the gaze of the viewer. Nature abhors a vacuum. It is we who will create its forms out of undifferentiated red protoplasm. When we have finished, it will be pervaded by life. In the words of Brancusi, "Simplicity is, at bottom, complexity."

What we have here is a large, radiant, blood-drenched field, throbbing and corpuscular. "Radiance," said Rothko, "is the afterglow of explosion." The painting is hung so as to be seen at close quarters, the intention being that the first *experience* of the viewer shall be *within* the picture. It gives forth a charismatic warmth that bathes the spectator.

First, a few clinical impressions: By having in mid-career settled upon a format of monumental stacked rectangles for his life's work, Rothko no longer had to invent or compose. The scaffolding had been raised. He had only to lay his colors upon it. Having dismissed the tyranny of form, there is no teem of figures—animals, birds, fish, nudes, buildings, horses, sheep. Nor is there the narrative power of a face. Instead we have their absence, nothing but a red silence. Rothko must at one time have asked himself: Why bother to represent anything at all, when it already exists in real life? What is the point of painting an object or person precisely or in deliberate distortion? Say that we are sitting at a table in a café, drinking wine. Why paint it? Just *live* it. To paint such a scene would be to render it lifeless, inert, a mere imitation of life.

The canvas of "Red" is not divided up in the way that a Mondrian or a Picasso is divided up. There is an utter lack of figure, and therefore a lack of craftsmanship. In its place there is an urgency, a violence even, in the way that the colors are applied—with a brush such as that used by a

house painter, some five inches wide. He preferred used brushes, with
the pig bristles worn down and softer. The paint was slathered on, up
and down, up and down, the large bulk of the artist bending forward, all
of his body engaged in the coarse, crude, gross physical act of applying
the paint. He might have been painting a barn. But that is how an artist
should paint, with his whole body, the way a mockingbird sings—legs,
tail, breast, and wings all acting to pump the song from its throat. It is
about as far from easel painting as you can get. Notice that there is an
absence of perspective. The canvas is flat. So let it be flat. Perspective is a
ruse intended to deceive the viewer into thinking the canvas has depth.
Perspective is dishonest. Nor do the colors run right to the edge of the
canvas, but stop before the edge.

It seems to me that it would require the massive ego of a megaloma-
niac to pass this off as a work of art. And there was about Rothko something of the messianic, the "I Have Come" importance. One is told that
he was vain, quarrelsome, intolerant, autocratic, jealous, and slovenly of
habit. Not your notion of an ideal companion. In addition, he was as difficult to please as Jehovah. As for religion, he considered it one of those
illusions that conceal man's tragic solitude. Yet this "Red," so empty of
form, is suffused with light whose source is hidden within the painting.
It is nothing like the incomparable light that plays on the town of Delft,
but is an internal glow. Could this be an expression of the artist's spiritual
longing? I'm sure he'd have hated me for saying that. In Judaism,
Rothko's lapsed religious heritage, there is a taboo on depicting God or
even taking His name in vain. There are no statues or icons of the Jewish
God. Could it be that for some artists there are things that cannot or
ought not be shown in painting? From where else came this fascination
with the formless, the inconceivable? Or did Rothko sense an amorphous
presence on the canvas, which he then strove to depict? You get the feeling that, if you took the painting down from where it is hanging, there
would be a red and glowing stain on the wall; that, at the end of the day,
long after Rothko had put down his brush, the red had lingered in his
empty hand, the faithful fist keeping its flame alive.

So let us set out into the Great Elsewhere of Rothko's "Red." I shall
do my best to be your *cicerone,* although I don't pretend to know what
Rothko meant by his *#3.* He makes no effort to describe or explain. It is
so private as to verge on chaos. In this it is not unlike the visual hallucinations experienced by many people who have gone blind. Sudden flashes

of brilliant color appear to them. These are sharply focused, remain for seconds or even minutes, then vanish. The cause of these hallucinations is not known. Something happens within the eye itself, or in the old pathway of vision from the brain to the eye. But to conjecture about the origin of Rothko's act of artistic anarchy, his reduction of art to the bare minimum of meaning, would be fruitless. I am aware that, by giving this painting sense and words, I may be going against the senselessness and wordlessness that were the very intention of the painter. If in the end you do not see what I have seen, that is to be expected. As Rilke wrote, ". . . Ah, but what can we take along into that other realm? Not the art of looking, which is learned so slowly. . . ."

There are three ways of "seeing Red," and all are necessary for a full experience of the painting. You must look inside the rectangles; you must look back and forth between them; you must look at the whole painting. Notice how, at the border between the rectangles, migrant bits of color pass back and forth like electrons traversing a membrane. In Van Gogh, the forms themselves vibrate. Rothko, having dispensed with form, has only the vibration itself. What is the purpose of this red? Its purpose is to be painted, that's all. It is wholly, profoundly red. It is said that upon merely seeing the color red, one's metabolic rate increases by 13.4%. Scarlet, Jezebel red, crimson (as in Harvard), vermilion, cerise, blush, russet. Fiery; this canvas smolders. Will it burst into flames? Or burn itself out? No one knows. Here is the artist as Prometheus, who has stolen fire from the gods. Here is the red of strawberry, raspberry, cherry, currant. And the birds—cardinal, tanager, red-bellied woodpecker. The red of the garden—tomato, watermelon, apple. Salvia, poppy, carnation. American Beauty and rambling rose, a pomegranate halved. Ketchup, peppers, brick. Ruby, carnelian, garnet. It is the red of the roof tiles of France and Italy, where legend has it that people who live under red will prosper. Flowerpots, bricks. To the composer Scriabin, the key of C-major was red. Of the mountains in New Mexico called Sangre de Cristo, Willa Cather wrote that they are "not the color of living blood . . . but the dried blood of saints and martyrs preserved in old churches in Rome, which liquefies upon occasion." The red pigment for the paintings in the cave of Lascaux came from iron ore that was ground to powder, then mixed with animal blood. You can still see the shaggy red bison, horses, and deer painted there by Cro Magnon man twenty thousand years ago. Here is coral over Coccilana—that dark red cough syrup that was spooned down our throats in days of old. It is a streptococcal red, the red of measles (called rubella) inflammation, erythema, a hot red. Heat seems to emanate from the painting in radiant waves, the way heat will rise from pavement in August. It would, of course, be hot to the touch, with a heat that is almost animal.

In the matter of "Red," seeing is touching. To look is to palpate. For us to look at this tropical painting in December would be absurd. It is as far from winter as can be. It is more a painting of August. The obscurity tantalizes. But now, in spite of the artist, there *is* perspective. It is not the ordered recession based on geometry that creates an illusion of deep space so loved by the Renaissance painters. But it is perspective, nonetheless. All at once there is a way into the painting. You can step into the canvas. Raise your arms to part the thick red mist. The deeper into the crimson silence you go, the redder it gets. It is a Red Sea, parted, and you walk between its rolling crimson cliffs. Just as quickly the vision is drawn back into the canvas, losing its outline, flowing back into the sea of red. You step back out of the painting. From what land have you returned? All that is left is the memory of what had been glimpsed of the obscure and shifting territory below the surface of rational consciousness.

The more you look at this painting, the more you see. You see one thing filtered through another. There is the surface, and there is the undertow. Things are sensed rather than revealed. Some of this effect is produced by the edgings and aureoles that surround the rectangles. Notice the asymmetry of the two rectangles. They are a bit out of kilter. It is a deviance that animates them. There is a dark turbulence in the lower red, a flickering, an inflection that is absent from the upper rectangle. Quite say, and the painting is no longer opaque, but translucent, with light seeping into the red. Soon it becomes transparent, a window. Now you can see into and through it. What moments ago was nothing more than a couple of opaque stacked rectangles, soft at the edges, now floats on the canvas, free of its margins, striving to hold in color and light. It is said that Rothko achieved this unique inner luminosity by diluting the paint down almost to its disintegration, thinning it out until particles of pigment were barely clinging to the film of paint. Light strikes the painting, collides with the pigment particles, then rebounds to emanate from the depths to the surface, and from there to engulf the viewer in color.

Gaze on, and all at once the painting becomes a living organism. There is a controlled seething out of which the painting has emerged. Something like the primitive undifferentiated tissue called mesenchyme, which will develop into all the parts of a human being. It begins to inflate and deflate, like lungs, to throb and pulsate, as though driven by a distant heartbeat. Yes, that's it. The red of blood. Not a dry red, but saturated, drenched. Even your gaze is bloodshot. The upper rectangle is bright red, oxygenated arterial blood that has spurted here. The lower rectangle is venous blood, darker, returning to the lungs for a fresh draught of oxygen. It seeps. The two boxes, so nearly equal in volume—half arterial, half venous, at any given moment. This painting called "Red" is not the product of craft, or deliberate intention, but was driven by intuition and instinct, a "miraculous" object. As such, it can yield up the unexpected. Revelation. The red paint seems to surge up from the artist's unconscious. He is but the conduit.

Once, the canvas had been white, until that moment when Rothko dropped one drop of pure red into the water of the world, and it had spread to color everything. The wall around the painting is whiter now, as though having fainted. I remember the first time I set foot in an operating room as a medical student. The room was empty at the time, but the air seemed stunned, its walls white from the sights they had seen there. It had the same atmosphere as the courtyard of a medieval prison where, on axe-colored dawns, bloody executions had once taken place. One has the impulse to take a wet sponge and wipe away this red, as one would wipe away a bloodstain. But it would take all great Neptune's ocean to wash this blood away. More likely this red would "the multitudinous seas incarnadine." If this were a contest between the painting and the museum wall, the wall would be utterly defeated.

Rothko intended that his paintings be unframed. They are open, unenclosed, not sharply divided from their surroundings. Unlike the figures in a realistic painting, they are not trapped, immobilized. We stand before them at some risk.

The audacity of trying to translate paintings into words! Why else keep trying to do it if not out of dumb homage? "We should apologize," said Paul Valery, "that we dare to speak of painting." Words, my own medium, do not begin to achieve the color of paint on canvas. They offer, at most, a faint whiff of it, like the lingering scent of incense in an empty church. So many of my words are snowflakes, indistinguishable in their whiteness, and doomed even as they fall upon the page. But sometimes the blood finds refuge in them, too. What about the total absence of "story" in this painting? Don't you miss it? No, any narrative here would be intrusive. In "Red" we see as men saw before the invention of language. Freed from the encumbrances of civilization, we see with a pure untarnished vision, such as small children and animals must enjoy. In his notebooks, Edgar Degas wrote, "Nothing is as beautiful as two variations of the same color side by side." And now we see that it is true.

There are certain works of art that are prophetic. Rothko's *#3* is one of them. If, as is widely believed, Rothko committed suicide and was found on the floor of his studio in a pool of blood, then his *#3* was indeed premonitory. Had Rothko the least inkling in 1967 that the hands with which he was painting *#3* would one day be the accomplices of his self-murder, the "letters" of his blood? As for those hands, I should like more than anything to have felt them in mine. What does the hand of such a painter feel like? A hand that knows so voluptuous a red, that is patient and dreaming, that works from sunrise to sunset so that we may drink from his cupped palms the terrible carmine of his despair. What is a hand but eighteen bones gloved in skin, trussed with tendons and nerves, irrigated and drained by a tracery of blood vessels? It is in the act of painting or sculpting that one hand and then the other become more than two hands; they become the repository and dispenser of beauty and truth.

Here, then, is the death of Mark Rothko as abstraction, with the horror gone and only the penumbra of pain, and its quavering echo, left. Had he really slathered the canvas with a brush or had he slashed his forearms and bled onto it? Born a Jew—that fated race—but an announced disbeliever, Rothko's was a religion with only one sacrament—suicide. And here upon the wall of the Yale Art Gallery is its violent, annihilating premonition. With that, our eyes have come to the end of their task; there is no more to say.

Atrium: October 2001

It is a seven-block walk from the Yale Sterling Library to the Yale-New Haven Hospital. For thirty-five years, until my retirement from Surgery, I spent each working day and most nights at that hospital, albeit in buildings that have either been renovated so as to be unrecognizable, or razed. For the past sixteen years, I have spent every working day at the library where I read and write. Lately, I have taken to walking down to the hospital for lunch. In a courtyard set among the hospital buildings, there are a dozen tiny ethnic food stands—Thai, Chinese, Mexican, Indian, "Soul," Middle Eastern, and just plain American. In good weather, one can dine *al fresco* on one of the benches. Otherwise, one can take a container of food into the hospital. Which brings me to the Atrium, a vast open, high-ceilinged, bright space, at whose center is a large modernist fountain that, at first glance, seems to be a great ball of water in motion. In fact, it is fed by a stout erect metal pipe at the center and dozens of long narrow-gauge pipes that branch from it at angles. The openings at and near the ends of these secondary pipes are such that from each a circular screen of water issues. These circles of water abut and overlap each other, giving the illusion that the fountain is a gigantic ball of water. The water falls into a moat from which it is drained and recycled. A circle of lamps with copper reflectors illuminates the fountain from beneath the surface of the water in the moat. At any given time, numerous coins lie at the bottom of the moat, where they were tossed by the hopeful and the desperate. The flow of these waters produces a continuous soft, rushing noise.

Six quite tall ficus trees in pots rise well toward the glass cathedral ceiling, which is braced by steel girders. The bark of the ficus is smooth and atrophic, cadaverous. The branches and roots, complex and interwoven, form a mesh at the bottom of the trunk. "What are the roots that clutch, what branches grow. . . ." Large planters holding ugly tropical plants—pink bromeliads and white anthurium—serve as a boundary to mark off that portion of the Atrium used for eating from the rest, which is carpeted and made to simulate a hotel lobby, with faux-wooden benches and comfortable chairs and tables. Other large houseplants in tubs—sansevaria, cut-leaf philodendron, and giant dracaena—are placed here and there.

The immediate reason why I began to go there for lunch is that my vision has taken a turn for the worse. If only I could polish my lenses the way Spinoza polished his! I can read for only half an hour at a time without discomfort, and the world has become blurry. An interruption for an hour and a half at noon allows me to resume work later in the day. (Can one go blind from having seen too much?) But that is not the only reason. Perhaps I go to the Atrium to find characters for my stories. I admit that I peer out surreptitiously and eavesdrop, but that, too, is not all. For me, the Atrium is as much a bistro as it is a writer's observation post, a bistro where I go to sit among people I don't know, to enjoy their laughter, their earnestness, the pleasure they take in eating, and in each other. Perhaps I go there to be in the vicinity of the sick and their next of kin. It is with the sick that I feel a sense of belonging. The sick are my kind.

At noon, the Atrium pullulates with people—visitors; doctors in green scrub suits fresh from the Operating Theatre; medical students in short white coats, flaunting stethoscopes about the neck; nurses in white pantsuits, carrying trays of food; patients in pajamas or hospital gowns; pursy, clean-cut, well-groomed medical-equipment salesmen with briefcases, waiting to show their wares to these doctors; maids vacuuming the carpet or cleaning the tables; janitors; orderlies. Each wears the uniform of his calling. And here and there a patient brought there for diversion from the misery and boredom of illness.

At noon, as at any hour of the day or night, the Atrium is never without the distant sound of sirens. Every now and then the voice of the Page

announces a "Code 5"—the term for an emergency—and the ward where
it is taking place. This, to bring doctors and nurses scurrying to resusci-
tate. Once I was among those so summoned. And always the soft rushing
noise of the fountain.

And then, one day, this:

I have just finished eating lunch and am sitting on a bench in the Atrium,
a mere ten paces from the fountain with its murmur and glitter. In a
wheelchair, quite near, sits a thin pale boy. He is bald; his lips are crusted,
and with a sore at either corner of the mouth. Intravenous fluid drips into
his left arm. The bottle hangs from a metal pole attached to the wheelchair over his head. In his lap, a plastic bottle of water with a straw. Now
and then the scabbed lips flutter apart, and he takes a sip of air, then
another. He looks to be about ten years old and weighs perhaps eighty
pounds. His head is all eyes and ears. He seems to be studying me with
great interest and without any restraint, the expression on his face one of
glacial intelligence. It occurs to me that this boy hasn't the time for shame
or restraint, only for honesty. It is inevitable that we should talk

"What's that you're getting in the IV?" I ask. He glances for a moment
at the bottle on the pole.
    "It's my pet," he says. "Follows me wherever I go."
    "More like your guardian angel." He reacts not at all to this statement.
I try again. "Something like a Hospital God. You know, like the ancient
Gods of the hearth."
    "Lares and Penates," he mutters. "You a doctor?"
    "Used to be, long ago. Retired. I got old."
    "A condition I won't ever have to face." I am shocked at the tone in
which he says this. It is devoid of inflection or irony. I search all over my
mouth for something to say. For a long moment we are silent.
    "Who told you that?"
    "Don't," he says. "I'm way past that."
    "How old are you?"
    "Fourteen." Another surprise. "And you?"
    "Seventy-three. And a half. At my age, you count the halves."
    "I'm going to tell you my name," he says, "but first I have to ask if
it's OK."

"Of course it's OK."

"Don't be too sure. Now we are strangers, more or less anonymous. By giving you my name, I become somebody who can reach out to grab you, to capture. You could even want to grab me."

"I'll risk it."

"Thomas Fogarty." I see that the crusts on his lips hurt; he barely moves his mouth when he speaks.

"Richard. Richard Selzer," I reply.

"What would you like to talk about?" I ask. "Sports? Music?"

I feel scrutinized by the remorseless blue of his eyes.

"What will you do on your last day on earth?"

"My last day."

"The day when you are going to die."

"Can we talk about something else?" He gives a tiny shake of the head. The huge eyes insist; beneath them are smudges of violet. I'm caught and fluttering in that merciless gaze. He raises the water bottle to his lips and takes a tiny excruciating sip.

"Life hurts," he says. "I measure out the time by sips, see how few I can get along with."

Fourteen. I, who have taken to forgetting everything at an alarming rate, remember my fourteenth birthday when, whispering my own name, I wept. At that age I was already the man I would become in time, only more honest, braver than I am now. I too had not yet acquired irony. I was as intelligent then as now, as sensitive, as sorrowful. I see at once that this boy is rare, that I must not falsely console or cajole; he wouldn't stand for it. He has already passed through the flames, gone beyond despair and self-pity. He seems enveloped in a shroud of quiet resignation. I see, too, the man he would have become, all intellect and convibility. I know that his death is the only subject that interests him, this child that is father to the man. And why not? It is his work, his future. All at once I feel ashamed of the good health that has enabled me to live so long, the unfairness of it. Something else too: I feel the stirring of what I can only describe as love for this small skinful of marrowless bones with his mouth encrusted with sores and his gaze that penetrates. Why shouldn't I love him, I who want so much to love?

"You don't have to feel embarrassed for your age. It doesn't matter," he says. My God! He has read my mind! Either he is intuitive or I am transparent.

"What I would do on my last day?" He gives a tiny nod. Above our heads, the leaves of the ficus trees are motionless; there is no breeze to stir them. The swords of the sansevaria slash the motionless air. I have the sense—does he have it too?—that he is the older one, that along with such sickness comes the wisdom, poise, and integrity of years. This boy is ill in every way, but he is not ill at ease. That is my symptom. I hardly dare to speak. I begin.

"On the morning of the day I die, I'll betake myself to the edge of a forest, or be taken there by someone strong enough to carry me deep into the woods. Let it be a forest of great age with huge old oak, beech, and linden trees and a dense canopy above that permits rays of light to slant down to the forest floor. Put me there, I'll tell him, on that bed of shadow. Arrange me upon it. Now wet my lips with a little wine, and then goodbye, with my thanks. I'll go the rest of the way by myself." I see that the boy is listening intently, his eyes feasting on my face. The long gracile neck that lifts his small head toward me—it must take a thousand years to form a neck of such delicacy, and with the power to break one's heart.

"I'll hum or recite, a little of both, maybe, just to hear the sound of my voice. When it stops . . ." All at once, a tuning fork vibrates to a blow. "May I start over"?

The boy, Thomas, nods. I begin again. "It had all been arranged the night before. It is noon when the doorbell rings. Noon, that hour when both hands of the clock are raised up in supplication. From my bed, I can hear his deep voice rumbling. I recognize it as the voice of a former student of mine. Long ago I led him through his first appendectomy, his first herniorrhaphy. Now he is a great surgeon. It is a bond between us. He is big enough to fill the doorway of my room. He bends above the bed and scoops me up against his chest. I feel quite secure in his arms. 'Did you bring it? The wine?' I ask him. 'Oh yes I did. It's in the pickup truck.'

"We ride for a long time. When the truck stops, he gets out and comes around to where I am reclining. Once again he lifts me up against him. And he walks into the woods for a good way, to where great old trees are deeply rooted in the earth and their canopies sway overhead. Here the undergrowth is thicker. There are no paths. Not far away there is a small stream that splashes downward over rocks. A pair of mallards browses among the sad rushes. The iridescent green head of the male! I point down to a shadow on the ground. It is just my size. There, I tell him, put me there. And he does, deposits me gently upon a bed of moss, with fern fronds under my head for a pillow.

"'I'd rather stay with you,' he says.

"'No,' I tell him.

"'Do you mind if I wait in the truck?'

"'No I don't mind, only don't come back until morning. Promise.'

"'All right.'

"'In the morning, when you come, perhaps I'll be gone. Perhaps not. If I'm still here, cover me with earth and leaves so that I won't be cold. If I am gone, then you will know that I have become part of the forest. Don't try to know everything. Some mysteries are not meant to be solved; they are meant to be deepened.'

"Now I am alone in the depths of the pious forest. I feel light, buoyant, partly made of sky, as if an obscure transmutation is taking place, the sort of thing that is probably happening all the time, only we are unaware of it." I glance at the boy in the wheelchair wondering if he has understood me. He seems to be listening with more than his ears, but with his entire body, his flesh and his bones as well. And I know that he has understood fully.

"There is the fragrance of pine tar, mushrooms, and trees. It is so fresh that I cannot stop yawning. But different from the freshness of April. It is October, after all. In this fragrance it is easier to breathe. I inhale deeply and relish the expansion of my chest. How fine it is to fill my lungs with air, using my whole chest. I cannot inhale too much air. Oh yes, I breathe deeply and with a steady rhythm, raising up and lowering with each breath like a bark on a tranquil sea. I am all breathing now. The forest breathes with me. I take part in the breathing of the forest. It is as if I have not yet been born and am in the womb of my mother. I hear noises, the squeaking of a branch, a skittering as of tiny feet running through leaves. A chipmunk, perhaps. Or a fox. I send myself off in different directions. Strange, but I can see myself, the way one sees a mirage. From the truck, I look like a fawn. From the treetops, I am a smudge on the ground.

"I fall asleep and dream that the trees, the rocks, the little stream are peopled by spirits. I am aware of an unknown, unseen splendor. I am happy in the dream of it. To dream so is to be mighty. When I awaken, it is toward dusk. Hour by hour my mind separates itself from my body. I explore my imagination. Now I know that death is just a different kind of existence. Matter can neither be created nor destroyed. Call it whatever you will, it is only the form that changes in death. I become aware of the fluidity of things—not only memory and imagination, but the cells of the body too. There is an inner stream of life composed of blood, cytoplasm, nucleoprotein. It is all flowing." The boy's lips are parted; his breathing has speeded up, gone shallow; his eyes that never leave my face are shining. Only rarely does he blink or run the tip of his tongue over his crusted, ulcerated mouth. Once or twice I raise the cup to his lips until he takes a tiny wracking sip. All the while I speak in a low murmur that now and then disappears into a whisper so as to underline the privacy of what is passing between us, saying that it is meant only for him. One hand reaches toward me; I surrender a handful of my shirt to it.

"Night is falling and with it comes the feeling of imminence; something is about to happen. Darkness enters my body; I let it. The air around me shifts with the movement of actual angels. Solicitous spiders are weaving me a coverlet. I am the whispering of leaves, more guessed at than seen. Already I am only half flesh and blood, the rest moss, leaf, bark, and oiled fur. Soon I shall be a line of bubbles rising to the surface of life, then winking out. The odor is intoxicating—pine, mushroom, and something herbal. It makes me sleepy. I can hardly keep my eyes open. I yawn. Now I close my eyes, conscious of the world through my hearing alone. It is the deepest kind of repose. Crickets are stridulating, and something curious that chatters and comes and goes as it pleases. I feel the weight of the moonlight upon me like a soft comforter upon the body of a sleeper. I let the forest sprawl across my mind and, all at once, I feel myself inside the vista I have imagined. The night is a confusion of stars and fireflies. I cannot tell which is farther away, the one becoming the other, the here becoming there. It is a painless transition."

"So, Thomas," I say, in the voice of conclusion, "that is how it will be."

"Oh don't stop!" he says. "Tell me more. Please." The thin cotton hospital gown has come untied so that his left clavicle is outlined over its entire length. The slender graceful bone stands out below the fleshless neck, so much older and wiser than all the rest of his body. His expression is vague, yet insistent, as though he has already departed for somewhere else.

"But there isn't any more."

"Then tell it again." Do I imagine it, or has his face taken on a glitter, as with fever?

Suddenly there is a third person present. A nurse in a red pant-suit with a shower cap on her head, a mask hanging loosely at her neck, and white running shoes. Her manner is grimly cheerful, efficient.

"O.K., Tony," she says in a loud bluff voice. "Time to go back to bed. We'll be getting a blood transfusion this afternoon." I am appalled by her falsely hearty manner. I am distressed for the boy, who clearly knows that hers is a professional pose.

"It doesn't matter," he says. "I'm used to it. They mean well." Once again he has read my mind.

Tony! So it is not Thomas, after all. He did not give me his real name. Could he have thought that by taking another name, he could unload his illness upon that fictional alter ego? With what reluctance do those fingers release that handful of shirt! The wheelchair with its contents is already being propelled away. From across the Atrium, I follow with my eyes the radiance that accompanies it.

It is the next day, a quarter past twelve. All morning, my mind has been empty of thought other than of him. I am sitting in the Atrium on the same bench. Tony is not there. From across the Atrium, I see the same nurse in the red pant-suit, shower cap, mask, and white running shoes come toward me.

"Tony died this morning. All yesterday afternoon, he dictated this letter to you. I promised I would deliver it." And then she was gone.

Dear Richard,

It is just as you said it would be. Already I see myself lying upon a shadow in the forest where you have placed me, my head resting on a pillow of moss. I hear the sound of the waterfall. It is not unlike the sound of the fountain in the Atrium. From the brim of a cup scooped in bark, I drink an ample swallow of pale, icy air. It does not hurt to do so. Like you, I sing or hum *sotto voce* vague melodies, which I compose then and there. All around me there is a labyrinth of shadows. I, too, am "the whispering of leaves, more guessed at than seen." Already I, too, am made half of bark and oiled fur. Only a web of life still clings to my skin. I haven't the strength to shake it off, nor would I want to. Thanks to you, I have been made privy to the mystery of things. Your words move among the shadows, stirring the leaves. They make me think of "The Raven" by Edgar Allan Poe. "The silken sad uncertain rustling of each purple curtain." I wonder if you know that line, and love it as much as I do. My eyes are not entirely shut, like those of a cat sunning itself and drowsing. Between fluttering lids, my fuzzy vision is bordered by a gleam from far away. A moment ago, when the dawn came, it took me by surprise. As if it were the first dawn that ever was—rose yellow and . . .

At that point, the letter ends. I feel my body seated on the bench as the fated Atrium with its cadaverous ficus trees, its penumbra of death, whirls toward infinity. Then I listen to the sound of the fountain and I hear the blood coursing through the atria of my heart.

He was right in saying that by learning his name I could be captured. And so I am writing him down on these pages, not to dispense with him, but in the hope that, by doing so, I will save him, not as a human being, no, but as a character in a story, so that he will not be lost. He will have had conferred upon himself a continuing life. There are characters in the books I have read, and the paintings I have seen, who are more real to me than the people I meet in daily life, who yet wear the futility of flesh and blood. By writing him down in the pages of my notebook, I have given him that stronger reality, turned him into words and rescued him.

I had given him, as well, one of my dreams to play with. It was a ruse, a deception, I know. I, who believe in nothing supernatural, made use of it to prepare this boy for his death. It was as if after years of retirement, I had once again put on scrub suit, mask, and cap, and had taken up my scalpel.

But now I must begin a convalescence from an illness I never had. For no apparent reason, perhaps it is the memory of a leaf trembling, then falling, I will weep. Why do you weep? I am asked. I can only shake my head. There are times when I think that it is he who has entered a new life, and I who am dead. Oh, let the truth be known—I wanted to keep him for myself. He is unto me like a fountain in my mind, a place where it is always cool and fresh and where I can go to partake of its coolness.

Now and then a bit of spray will lay itself gently upon my face. In the days since, again and again Tony is brought back to me with stunning clarity by some errant gust or faint aroma. Then it is that the world trembles around me. The sky above the Atrium quivers, the plants and trees ripple, the whole Atrium founders, until I feel his gaze, clear and true, upon me, and I carry him in my arms, against my chest, and look into the lucid blue of his eyes.

"There," he says, pointing. "Place me there."

As for Tony, I am farther from him than he is from me. I have only to close my eyes to see him again sitting in the Atrium, his Johnny coat having come untied to expose one perfect clavicle. I think I have never seen anything more beautiful than that slender bone beneath his skin. It is for me a relic. I see too how, at the arrival of the nurse to take him away, the IV solution in the bottle trembled as if a train had passed a cottage at night, and a picture on the wall shook gently. I feel him in my arms, against my chest. I see him where I have placed him, in the shadow at the foot of the linden tree. I see his pale hand lying at his side as a leaf might come to rest there. Sometimes I speak to him, "With your eyes," I tell him, "lift this tree up, up, until it touches the sky so that you can climb it all the way to heaven." When I see a fugitive smile play upon his ruined mouth, I know why I was born.

AN EXPLICATION

The Atrium itself is immediately and intensely visual, rendered with a great deal of precise detail—the plants, the skylight, the furnishings, and above all the fountain. Despite the constant activity taking place within it, there is a sense of the inert, the lifeless, as well as a certain vulgarity. It is a product of pretension and interior decoration, as well as an attempt to disguise the true nature and purpose of the hospital. It is a denial of death in architectural terms. Such is the landscape, the theatre where the story takes place. It is the presence of the boy in the Atrium that lends it dignity and taste. Later on, there will be the equally precise portrayal of the forest, and the inevitable contrast between the two places. The forest is clean, pristine, mysterious, subtle. It is devoid of plastic, artificial wood, unnatural vegetation, paint and varnish. It is also devoid of pus, pain, lesions. It is what a hospice is, in contrast to a hospital—the ultimate refuge, a triumphant place where the imagination reigns and one is free of the agony and terror of mortality.

What are we to make of this short story, if we can even call it a short story? It is hardly more than an encounter between an old doctor and a dying boy, one of those fated moments when two trajectories intersect and there is a sudden moment of revelation. Is the story true? Did it happen? Yes, it is true. It happened. There was just such a coming together of the two in the Atrium of the hospital. But any reliance on narrative is problematical. We cannot be sure how much external reality has become annexed by the author's imagination and transformed by his fantasies. In fact, I suspect he has tinkered with the facts, left out a good deal, accented this, and not that. This is called artistry. In all likelihood, his love affair with the technical ended with his retirement from surgery. He is no longer a physician, a man of science; he has reverted to a more primitive form of being, one who is receptive to certain subtle influences and to intuition. The doctor in the story knows that he is performing a secret, sacred initiation upon the boy. He hurls himself into this primitive rite recklessly, forgetting himself until that very moment when he hesitates and says to the boy, "That's all there is. There isn't any more." "Then tell it again!" the boy pleads, clutching his sleeve. The doctor's loss of nerve is masked by the arrival of the nurse. The story "Atrium" flies in the face of science. It tries to keep the mysteries of life from being mowed down by the juggernaut of technology.

Is the story sentimental? Of course it is sentimental. Some of the greatest works of art are—all of Dickens, much of Verdi, the paintings of the Virgin and Child. But it is not the false sentimentality that consists of emotions one does not truly feel. It is further saved from sentimentality by the beauty of language. All right, it is a sad piece, one that has brought a lump in your throat. Perhaps you have shed tears. And that is good. I wouldn't want to live in a world where it never happens that one can weep precisely because another wept. Without sorrow, without compassion, the spirit shrivels.

Is it likely that a fourteen-year-old boy would or could write such a letter? No, it is unlikely, but it is possible. At fourteen, I was quite capable of writing such a letter. Let us not forget that, at age fifteen, Rimbaud was writing some of the great poems of rebellion. It is well known that mathematicians reach the peak of their genius in their teens, then quickly decline. Besides, it takes no great leap of the imagination to conclude that the doctor and the boy, Tony, are one and the same, that, in the act of preparing the boy for his death, the doctor has prepared for his own. By the end of the story, both doctor and Tony experience an epiphany when the continuum of mortality and immortality is sensed. Tony is no more and no less than the square root of the doctor. This story was not written with a dry pen, but with one dipped in my body's fluids. Nor was it written easily and quickly, but with a good deal of pain. As the author, I must always be grateful for the improbable gift of the instant when I glanced up to find the boy of the fountain looking at me.